THE YEAR OF THE TIGER

This novel is a work of fiction. The characters, names, dialogue, and plot are the product of the author's imagination, and are used fictitiously. Many actual events involving compact disk records and personal computer technology and products, which are a matter of public record, are used as background material. In addition, numerous events involving American and Chinese trade negotiations are included, as they form an important foundation for the plot.

Microsoft is a publicly traded company located in Redmond, WA.
Apple Computer is a publicly traded company located in Cupertino, CA.
Intel is a publicly traded company located in Santa Clara, CA.
IBM is a publicly traded company located in East Fishkill, NY.
Lotus Notes™ is a trademark of the Lotus division of the IBM Corporation.
Lisa™ is a trademark of the Apple Computer Corporation.
Macintosh™ is a trademark of the Apple Computer Corporation.
Mac™ is a trademark of the Apple Computer Corporation.
PowerBook™ is a trademark of the Apple Computer Corporation.
Power PC™ is a trademark of the Apple Computer Corporation.
Windows™ is a trademark of the Microsoft Corporation.
Windows 95™ is a trademark of the Microsoft Corporation.
Windows NT™ is a trademark of the Microsoft Corporation.
Pentium® is a trademark of Intel Corporation.
Pentium Pro® is a trademark of Intel Corporation.

THE YEAR OF THE TIGER

Elvet E. Moore

Pentland Press, Inc.
England • USA • Scotland

PUBLISHED BY PENTLAND PRESS, INC.
5124 Bur Oak Circle, Raleigh, North Carolina 27612
United States of America
919-782-0281

ISBN 1-57197-091-6
Library of Congress Catalog Card Number 97-075509

Copyright © 1998 Elvet E. Moore
All rights reserved, which includes the right to reproduce this book or portions
therof in any form whatsoever except as provided by the U.S. Copyright Law.

Printed in the United States of America

Acknowledgements

I wish to acknowledge my devoted and loving wife, Nancy, who encouraged me to write this novel, and who provided me with valuable feedback while I developed the story line. I also wish to acknowledge my mother, Mary Moore who recently passed away at the age of 92, for throughout her life she continually encouraged me to write. Before her death, she and my sister, Charlotte Norris, spent countless hours editing this manuscript. Finally, I want to acknowledge my friend, Sammy Lee, who provided me with numerous Chinese names, along with their cultural meanings, which proved to be a valuable resource.

Prologue

On 31 December 1997, China's newly appointed chairman, Keung Fu Huang, hosted a very elegant New Year's Eve banquet in the Beijing Imperial Palace. He spared no expense, since it was the first such affair to be held after China acquired Hong Kong from Great Britain. Twenty waiters in bright red uniforms busily served the guests fancy hors d'oeuvres and filled their glasses with the finest French wine and champagne. At 8:30 P.M. sharp a gong sounded, and the guests moved into the Royal Banquet Hall where they were served an exquisite twelve-course Chinese dinner, including pressed duck with plum sauce, Keung's favorite dish.

The guest list included Chee-hwa Tung, Hong Kong's new CEO, Keung's ten ministry chiefs, and fifty CEOs from Hong Kong's most successful electronics companies. In addition, each guest not accompanied by a spouse or significant other was provided a companion for the evening, compliments of Hung Sing, Hong Kong's world-famous escort service.

Keung had been planning this gala event since July, when China acquired Hong Kong. In spite of the complaints of his ministry chiefs, Keung scheduled the party for this particular evening, rather than waiting until 28 January, the eve of the traditional Chinese New Year, when Chinese people throughout the world would be celebrating the Year of the Tiger.

Keung had much to look forward to this year, for the acquisition of Hong Kong provided him with unprecedented access to the enormous personal computer, electronics, and software markets. Keung was concerned, however, because he heard persistent rumors that many of the leading Hong Kong electronics companies were seriously considering moving their operations to Singapore, where they were being promised the same freedoms they had grown accustomed to under British rule. Therefore, Keung invited the heads of these firms tonight to Beijing, hoping to put an end to such possibilities.

Keung's invitations stated that attendance at this party was mandatory, since the attendees were going to hear a very important announcement just before midnight. Keung planned to tell his guests that, because of their new relationship with mainland China, they would be able to participate in what was going to be the largest personal computer business opportunity the world had ever known. Keung reasoned that, when his guests fully understood the magnitude of the opportunity, they would surely think twice about leaving Hong Kong.

Keung also hoped they would look upon him afterward as a very shrewd businessman, for as president of the People's Republic of China, reporting to the late chairman, Deng Xiaoping, Keung had tried unsuccessfully to enter the lucrative CD record market. His abortive attempt had caused China to be branded corrupt record pirates, incapable of producing high technology products on their own. Tonight's presentation was clearly a vital one for Keung, for he badly needed this new venture to succeed.

In the rest of the world, New Year's Eve 1997 was no different than others had been for years. Most families were staying at home watching the television coverage of dance bands playing in major cities, while some more energetic couples were dressing up in their best party attire so they could attend gala affairs or private parties with close friends. Still other families were planning to go to bed at their regular time, as if nothing special were going on.

In New York City, Dick Clark was preparing his annual Times Square countdown, an American tradition for over thirty years, and in London, Ian Dickson, BBC's famous news commentator, was preparing to provide the world a blow-by-blow description of Big Ben chiming exactly twelve times.

Jim Shriver, a Brooklyn, New York, high-school senior, arrived home from a party shortly after midnight with his friend, Bill Casper. He wanted Bill to check out his new 3D game, "Sorcerer's Flight," which was simply awesome when played on the brand new 200-Mhz Pentium® Multimedia PC his family purchased for Christmas. To his chagrin, when he turned on the system and launched the game, it ran terribly slow. The 3D images seemed to take forever to be formed on the screen, and the good guys and the bad guys, riding in their glistening multicolored spaceships, seemed to crawl helplessly in front of his eyes. Even the background music and sound generated by the built-in CD player seemed to sputter and jerk. He knew something was terribly wrong, so he was forced to apologize to his friend. He told Bill he was sure it was just some unfortunate glitch. He privately hoped his father would be able to fix it in the morning, but he worried that it might be caused by something far more serious than merely a glitch.

Todd Burke, a Stanford University graduate student, was not able to party this year because he had a particle physics term paper due on Monday morning. He went to bed early, setting his alarm for 6:00 A.M. In the morning, after showering and gulping down a cup of strong black coffee, he drove across the Stanford campus to the computer center in his old 1966 VW bus, just as the sun was beginning to rise over the rolling California hills. He needed to log onto the Internet in order to gather some research material, so he switched on the main network computer, as well as the personal computer in his assigned cubicle. Todd often "surfed the net" for information, and he had become an outspoken critic of how long it took to receive information, especially during periods when many students were simultaneously using the service.

However, on this particular morning, the system response time was ridiculously slow, and Todd was becoming very upset! Here he was, up at the crack of dawn on New Year's Day, the only student using the Stanford computer system and probably the only person logged onto the Internet in all of California, and yet it was as though the system wasn't even turned on. Each request he made was taking an average of fifteen minutes to fulfill, and the data was being painted on the screen at an incredibly slow rate. He began to panic, for he was sure he was never going to be able to complete his term paper on time. He made a mental note to file a formal complaint on Monday morning with the university about the lousy service he was receiving.

Susan Malanowski, the MIS director of World Wide Transports in Chicago, asked her staff if they would mind working on New Year's Day, in order to switch the company over to a new computer system and have it ready to go by the following Monday morning. The installation of the new system was expected to be a very routine task, and she and her team believed if they started early in the morning they could be home in time to catch most of the afternoon football games.

They all arrived at 7:00 A.M. sharp, and by 10:30 they completed hooking up the last server node loaded with the new Windows NT™ network software. When they turned on the new system, however, they found the initialization checkout time (the time required to complete a series of test instructions) took more than five minutes to complete, rather than the normal few seconds. They repeated the test, this time using only the primary server node, but again they experienced an inordinately slow response time. They tried to send a brief e-mail message from one computer to another, and instead of what should have been a virtually instantaneous transmission, the message took more than one minute to complete its journey from the system administrator's computer to a computer in the next cubicle!

Susan and her staff met in the cafeteria and poured themselves large cups of coffee. They sat quietly and stared at one another in utter frustration and disbelief, for they had no idea what was wrong. Here they were, faced with having to stay and work on the system the rest of the day and all night, if necessary, because they obviously could not have the employees return on Monday morning to find such a crippled system.

"While I call the software vendor, will you guys try installing a new server? Also, try to replace the interface cards that connect each of the main trunks," Susan screamed, in utter frustration. To add to her frustration, when she attempted to get assistance from the computer vendor's twenty-four-hour technical support hot-line, she was continuously put on hold. It was as if all of the vendor's customers were simultaneously calling in for service on this particular New Year's Day! What in the world was going on? The system was behaving like the first network system she and her staff had installed over ten years ago.

On New Year's Day in Munich, Germany, Otto Daerr decided to go to work and try out the latest 3D computer-aided design (CAD) high-speed rendering software his company recently purchased for his engineering department. Otto, a very creative mechanical engineer, was a senior auto body designer at the Bavarian Motor Works plant, located in a small suburb outside of Munich.

With the new software running on his 300-Mhz Pentium II® computer, Otto expected to be able to complete new auto body designs in one-tenth the time it currently required. This was because the new software would let him visualize auto body designs from all angles, as he rotated 3D images of the body through 360° on all axes simultaneously, without noticeable flicker or redraw times. Otto spent the previous week attending a class at the software vendor's plant in Stuttgart. As a consequence, he felt he was ready to begin to use the program on his own computer this morning, even though the firm's computer support staff would not be present to help him through any difficulties he might experience.

Otto drove to the plant with great anticipation this morning. He signed in with the security guard and hastened down the hall to his office, where he switched on his computer, went into the lab to turn on the coffeepot, and prepared to have a really fun day, with no interruptions or distractions.

While making coffee, Otto did not notice that his computer took a long time to boot. By the time he returned to his office, the system was waiting for him to load the new 3D-software program, which he did. He opened up an existing auto body design file he prepared, using his much older, outdated software. However, he immediately realized something was dreadfully wrong. The picture of the auto body was being drawn on the monitor screen at a very slow rate!

Using the wall clock as a reference, Otto discovered the drawing took more than five minutes to complete! Each time he rotated the image of the car body on the screen to observe it from another angle, the image took another five minutes to be redrawn, not the fraction of a second guaranteed by the new software specification.

"This will never do," he said out loud. "The goddamn software vendor has sold me a piece of crap!"

Otto stormed out of his office and drove home on the autobahn at more than 260 km/hr. As a professional mechanical engineer, he never really fully trusted software engineers, nor did he trust companies that only designed and sold software products. What really made him angry was that during the training session the prior week in Stuttgart, the vendor had obviously done a very clever job of convincing him this new product was superior!

"How could such obvious sales tactics have taken me in?" he said to himself as he drove home at breakneck speed. "I'll show them on

Monday morning! Surely heads will roll when I make my report to my superiors! And to think I got up early this morning and wasted most of my holiday," he cursed out loud. Otto floored the accelerator on his new BMW and tried to think of more pleasant things to do with the rest of his day.

In Beijing at 11:00 P.M., the waiters began to remove dishes from the tables. As after-dinner drinks were poured, Keung, with the help of an interpreter, introduced and toasted each of his ministry chiefs and each of his guests, along with their spouses and companions. He then had everyone stand and toast the huge wall painting of Deng Xiaoping, while he said a few words in his memory.

Keung impressed everyone with his grasp of specific knowledge about each of the electronics companies that were represented at the banquet tables. When he finished, he turned the podium over to Kong Chau, his ministry chief in charge of business and foreign trade. He told the audience that Kong was going to give them a presentation they would never forget. He also told the audience that the business opportunity they were about to hear would make the aborted venture into CD records seem insignificant by comparison.

Kong stood up slowly, first tipping his glass of champagne toward president Keung Fu Huang, then toward Chee-hwa Tung, Hong Kong's new CEO, and finally toward his fellow ministry chiefs and the heads of the Hong Kong electronics companies. He began to speak, and with the help of the interpreter, he indeed made a presentation those in attendance would never ever forget. As it turned out, Kong would go down in history as giving a presentation the entire world would never forget!

Part 1

The Birth of the Chinese CD Record Industry

Chapter One

On 15 July 1994, Choi Tang, known affectionately by his friends as "CT," was promoted to the position of managing director of the Mao Zedong Laser Development and Manufacturing Works in Haikou, the provincial capital of China's southern Hainan Island. CT was born in 1960, during the Proletarian Cultural Revolution, to a poor Chinese family that was barely able to eke out a living on a small farm outside of Shanghai. As he grew up, he was singled out by the headmaster of his boarding school as a prime candidate to become a member of the popular Chinese Communist youth movement, which he joined in the early 1970s.

Besides having a very high IQ, CT possessed an extraordinary aptitude for mechanical design. As a consequence, he earned a government scholarship to attend Shanghai's prestigious Technical University. While attending school, he maintained a 3.9 grade point average, and he developed a keen interest in computer mass storage systems. In June of 1990, he earned associate degrees in both mechanical engineering and computer science, and graduated with honors.

His graduation thesis was well written and very timely. His thesis advisor circulated it widely among his closest peers and professors, gaining CT immediate respect. One copy found its way onto the desk of Shing Ling, the chief of China's ministry of technology and production. After reading the thesis, Shing informed the school he wanted CT to be assigned to his Haikou development section, since he had an immediate need for someone with CT's background. CT worked very hard and was very ambitious, so it was not surprising he became the youngest Technical University graduate to achieve the position of managing director of any major Chinese facility.

When CT first started working in Haikou, he was required to be on the job a minimum of ten hours per day. In addition, he and his fellow employees were required to attend Communist Party lectures on Friday evenings, which often ended up as philosophical discussions in some roadside bar, continuing on through the wee hours of Saturday morning.

At one of the Friday evening lectures, CT met Miu Chen, an attractive graduate of Beijing University. Miu worked as a computer technician in one of the adjacent compounds in Haikou. CT and Miu fell in love and were married in the summer of 1991. They were very much in love, and they fervently shared the same dreams for China's economic and political future in the new world order of things.

As a result of a joint technology and marketing venture established between China and Russia shortly after World War II, China became the principal supplier of long-playing records (LPs) to the Eastern Bloc countries in Europe. However, in 1985, when compact disk records (CDs) became available, demand for Chinese LPs dropped significantly. As a consequence, China's LP production plant in Haikou had to be shut down. Needless to say, this proved to be a major source of embarrassment for Shing Ling.

Hoping to save face, Shing signed another joint technology agreement with Russia in 1986. Under the terms of that agreement, Russia was responsible for developing the manufacturing methods and processes required to mass-produce CDs. However, after two frustrating years with no success, the ill-fated program was canceled—another major embarrassment for Shing Ling.

When Shing read CT's thesis, he decided he should hire CT and resurrect the project, but this time his own people would be in charge of the technical developments.

"I'll show the Russians," Shing said to his secretary, when she told him CT would soon be joining his development staff.

"Choi, your first assignment will be to head up a small team of engineers and technicians to establish a manufacturing process to produce CD records here in the Haikou plant," Shing told CT when he reported to work.

"It will be up to your team to develop the processes, acquire the equipment, refurbish the Haikou LP production facility, and have it all ready to go in less than one year. Any reasonable request for materials, equipment, and personnel will be granted to you, so long as you are able to convince me the plant will be able to begin producing CDs in high quantities by June 1991."

"I understand the scope and importance of the project," CT said.

"Do you think you can handle this program?" Shing asked, looking CT squarely in his eyes.

"Yes, sir. I accept this assignment with considerable enthusiasm. I've been anticipating this kind of project, and I'm confident I will be able to succeed. I wish to thank you for the opportunity to work for you." CT then bowed and went back to his own office, where he began in earnest to work on his exciting new assignment.

Chapter Two

Shing Ling was very proud of CT, because he and his team completed the difficult project one month early. It was only 1 May 1991, and Shing was preparing to preside over the opening of the completely refurbished Haikou factory. The Chinese president, Keung Fu Huang, planned to arrive in the early afternoon for the ceremony. Keung told Shing he wanted the plant to be known as the Mao Zedong Laser Development and Manufacturing Works, so Shing's facilities personnel installed a large sign outside the main lobby with the new name proudly displayed for the president to see when he arrived.

"CT, would you please come to my office?" Shing shouted over the plant intercom system. "I need to brief you on what will be happening this afternoon."

Although Shing's primary office was in the main government building in Beijing, he maintained a small well-appointed office in the same building as the Haikou development staff, so he could drop in on them from time to time to monitor their progress.

CT walked quickly down the hall to the ministry chief's office. "I hear our president is going to be here this afternoon," CT said. "I once saw him at a ceremony at the university, but I've never heard him speak. I look forward very much to this afternoon's meeting."

"CT, you and your team have performed a great service for China," Shing said as he patted CT on his shoulder. "Do you realize our Russian friends have yet to make their CD plant operational? And to think they were the ones we counted on when we tried to make CD records a few years ago!"

CT smiled at Shing as he was being praised. He was incredibly lucky, for he discovered many items of equipment could be purchased, so they did not have to be developed from scratch, as the Russians tried to do on the aborted joint development program.

"I want you and your team members to attend the ceremony this afternoon," Shing told CT. "Before you hear the president's speech, I feel I must tell you more about our plans for the manufacture and sale of CD records.

"When we started producing LPs jointly with the Russians, our market was strictly the Eastern Bloc countries. The people of those countries were denied substantially all recreational pleasures during the war. Once the fighting stopped, they clamored for radios and record players, and they didn't particularly care who the musical performers were.

"For example, I remember we recorded music using amateur singing groups from all over Europe, as well as from Asia, and we could still sell all the LP records we could make. In addition, our Communist trade practices made it difficult for LP records from the West to enter our market, so we operated under conditions the Americans would call a captive market. We literally minted money, but alas, those days are gone forever."

CT nodded his head in understanding. "I always wondered as a child why I couldn't find records in the music store by the Beatles, and now I begin to understand," he grinned. "But today our music stores in Beijing and Shanghai are full of CDs recorded by all of the popular Western artists, singing all of the latest songs. Are we going to be able to sell Chinese CDs using the same kind of amateur performers we used when we sold LPs ten years ago?"

Shing smiled and said, "CT, you are now beginning to see the problem we have. If we follow our old methods, we probably will not sell very many CD records, and all of your shiny new machinery may stand idle," he said, sadly shaking his head.

Shing watched as these last words sunk in, for he could see a frown beginning to cross CT's face. "CT, our problem is compounded by the fact that our president, as brilliant a man as he is, has no comprehension of our marketing dilemma. He just keeps telling me to go ahead and prepare for production, for he truly believes China will easily be able to sell millions of CDs."

Shing looked down and slowly shook his head. "Our great president, Keung Fu Huang, still believes that when China decides to make a product, the world will automatically want to buy it."

CT suddenly burst out laughing.

"What can possibly be so funny at a time like this?" Shing asked.

"Forgive me, Shing, but I thought of how funny it would be to go into a record store in New York or London and ask if they carried the latest Chinese CD record with the title, *Igor and the Muscovites play Gershwin*."

For a moment Shing looked sternly at CT, and then he, too, started to roar with laughter. "I get it. That's really funny."

"And what about the banjo act from Siberia that was rated number one on the Eastern Bloc top-ten charts in 1969? I think they called themselves, *Boris and the Slaves*, or something silly like that. Wouldn't they look funny on a CD label in Moscow today?" CT added as he burst out laughing again.

They both laughed so loudly that Shing's secretary knocked at the door to see if anything was wrong. "Forgive us. We were just remembering old times," Shing said.

Shing suddenly became very serious and took out an old bottle of Chinese rice wine, dated 1959, from his desk drawer. He poured two small glasses, one for himself and one for CT. He stood ceremoniously at attention, looking at the portrait of the president, which hung on the wall behind his desk, and asked CT to join him in a toast. Shing and CT toasted the president and vowed to find a way for China to succeed in this very important business venture.

CT was impressed with the loyalty Shing showed for the aging president, and he learned an important lesson. He learned how important it is for young technologists like him to maintain strict allegiance to their elders. He vowed it would be his lifelong job to provide the means to implement his elders' wishes, even if they were too old or too out of touch with technology to be able to fully grasp the implications of their requests.

"I need to get back to my lab and make sure things are straightened up and ready for the plant tour," CT said.

"Fine," said Shing. "By the way, I understand you and Miu Chen plan to marry next month. Is that right?"

"Yes. We decided we wanted to see more of each other than we do when we attend the Friday night lectures," he responded, grinning.

"Congratulations. Now, get out of here and let me get my office cleaned up. I don't want the president to think I'm a slob," he said, laughing.

President Keung Fu Huang and his entourage arrived by helicopter from the Chinese mainland, just in time for the presentation ceremony. Besides his usual complement of staff flunkies, he was accompanied by Business and Foreign Trade Ministry Chief Kong Chau, who was going to be ultimately responsible for implementing the sales plan for Chinese CD records.

The cafeteria in the development wing was set up for the meeting, but first Shing wanted to take Keung and Kong on a plant tour. CT would accompany them so he could describe each of the machines in the plant and show them how CD records are made. They all met in the lobby of the manufacturing wing, and Shing made his introductions, bowing formally. CT was very nervous, but managed to smile and bow when the president took his hand and thanked him and his team for all of the hard work that made this day possible. The plant tour took about an hour, and CT was no longer nervous when he found himself in his element. He discovered the president was quite knowledgeable about mechanical machinery, and he again vowed silently to do everything in his power to make this important venture for China become a success.

The ceremony in the cafeteria was a short one. All of Shing's staff were in attendance. As they arrived, they were served cookies and tea by young Chinese girls, who were introduced as children of various members of the staff. When Keung got up to speak, the children bowed, left the room, and stood quietly in the hall outside the cafeteria, where they tried not to giggle.

Shing was glad he briefed CT in advance, for Keung's speech revealed just how far out of touch he was with the reality of the CD record market in 1991. Keung took a drink of water, straightened his back, and began to speak in a quiet but firm voice.

"Gentlemen, it gives me great pleasure to come here to your beautifully refurbished plant to congratulate you on a job well done. My ministry chief of technology and production, Shing Ling, promised me this day would come by midsummer, and here we are one month early. Shing tells me it is because of the brilliance and hard work of Choi Tang and his staff that this achievement has happened. So, would

Choi Tang and his staff please stand so they can be properly recognized?"

CT felt embarrassed, for he believed he had not really achieved anything more than what he had been told to do. However, he decided at times like this it is proper protocol to beam all over, bow, and accept the accolades. CT took a moment to introduce each of his team members, and that made his entire staff feel very proud of their accomplishments and proud to be working for such a fine leader as CT. Keung took another drink of water and continued his speech.

"I would now like to present the coveted Chinese Medal of Honor to Mr. Shing Ling. It is particularly fitting that he receive this award, for without his planning and foresight in hiring a good staff and providing the necessary resources, this crowning achievement we are celebrating today would not have been possible."

Shing stood up and marched formally to the podium where Keung greeted him. The medal was affixed to a bright green scarf, which Keung placed around his neck. The two men shook hands and hugged each other. The audience applauded, and Keung continued with his remarks.

"Let me now tell you about some of our plans for this wonderful new CD record factory. Today I met many of the plant personnel who worked here a decade ago when we produced LP records. They reminded me we once manufactured fifty thousand per day, and we sold every one we made! In fact, it was the profits from those sales that helped us rebuild our military strength, and this has been instrumental in causing the Western world to take us more seriously in today's global political environment.

"I find it particularly exciting that we will again be able to sell volumes of records from this plant, and I'm especially excited about the fact that this time we will sell records into all of the world markets, not just to the poor Eastern Bloc countries!

"My business and foreign trade ministry chief, Kong Chau, who is here at my side, has told me the world consumption of CD records today is more than one-half million per week. In addition, the sales price of CD records is higher than the price we used to get for LPs. For that reason, I want to fill this plant with as much equipment as is required to capture the lion's share of the CD record market.

"Shing tells me that even with the initial complement of equipment I saw today, this plant would be able to produce more than one hundred thousand CD records per day. So I'm requesting a plan from Shing and Kong in thirty days that will outline how we can become the world's largest supplier of CD records in just two short years!

"Thank you all for indulging me. Sometimes I feel I'm just an old man who dreams of the future, but I want you all to know I am also interested in *your* future! I again want to congratulate each of you for the wonderful achievements you have made."

At the end of the speech, CT glanced at Shing. Shing had rolled his eyes up into his head, as he thought about the virtually impossible challenge China would have selling so many CD records. CT also glanced at Kong. Either Kong was a fool or an excellent politician, for he had no expression on his face whatsoever, except for a slight smile, as he clapped jubilantly with the crowd.

Chapter Three

Kong Chau was certainly no fool. He fully recognized the implications of what Keung Fu Huang meant when he stated that he wanted China to become the world's leading supplier of CD records in just two short years. He knew Keung would not rest until this difficult goal was achieved. If such a goal were not met, either he or Shing would certainly be held responsible for the failure.

Kong was determined he would not fail. His challenge would be to market and sell CD records in enormous quantities. With that in mind, he scheduled an emergency planning meeting with his staff members, to be held the day after his return to Beijing. He invited Shing Ling to attend, and asked him to come prepared to provide detailed production information, for he wanted his sales personnel to know what quantities they would have available to sell during the next couple of years.

Kong and his staff were already seated in the planning conference room next to Kong's office when Shing Ling arrived. Kong stood up and greeted Shing as if he were a long-lost friend. Shing was introduced to each of the staff members, and they were reminded Shing recently received the Chinese Medal of Honor. They all stood and clapped while he sat down. Kong asked his secretary to provide tea and cookies for all of the attendees, since the meeting would be a long one. He also asked his secretary to remain and take notes. Kong stood up and began speaking to the group.

"Gentlemen, our president and I returned yesterday from a visit to the newly refurbished Mao Zedong Laser Development and Manufacturing Works in Haikou. Shing Ling took us on a plant tour and told us his plant is now ready to produce CD records in high quantities," he said, smiling at Shing, who sat on his immediate right near the head of the long table.

"As a consequence, Shing and I have been asked by Keung to produce a plan in thirty days that outlines the quantities of CD records we believe China can produce and sell during the next several years. Shing has come prepared today to discuss the quantities he believes he can produce in his plant, but first I want to discuss the sales and marketing challenge we have in selling CD records in today's market.

"I want you to recall when we produced LPs right after the war. In those days, our market for LPs was limited to sales to the Eastern Bloc countries of Europe. However, we managed to sell many millions of records, partially because our customers had not been able to buy such items for so many years, and partially because trade barriers kept out Western competition.

"As a consequence, we sold records as fast as we could produce them, and we never once had to dicker on price," he added, grinning so widely you could see his gleaming white teeth mostly covered with bright gold caps.

Kong paused, took a long sip of tea, and continued. "Gentlemen, today is a much different story. The Eastern Bloc countries have access to records made from numerous suppliers around the world, and most established CD record suppliers have considerable manufacturing capacity, so they can meet almost any demand placed on them.

"My marketing director, Tak Chang, who is seated next to me, just returned from an international consumer electronics show held in Tokyo. He tells me there are now more than ten major suppliers of CD records, and the number is expected to increase this year. Isn't that right, Tak?"

Tak nodded in agreement. Kong paused, took another sip of tea, and continued.

"I don't want this next statement to leave this room, but based on the information I've received from my staff, I've come to the conclusion that if China were never to produce a single CD record, the world would not really care. There are already more than enough suppliers, including some major, well-known sources in Japan.

"This means we will have to be extremely aggressive in our pricing, if we wish to sell CD records in high volume in today's market.

In addition, we must have available nearly all of the popular recording artist labels currently being offered by our competitors! Otherwise we will fail, and we must not fail!

"Shing, when you took us on your tour, I don't remember hearing any information about the expected cost of CD records made in your new plant. You and I should talk further about this soon, for I believe we will need to sell CD records at between thirty-five percent and fifty percent below the prevailing world price, if we wish to meet the market penetration goals of our president!"

Shing gulped, as Kong continued. "In fact, I'm going to recommend a strategy where we announce Chinese CD records for sale at the same low prices LPs were sold for in the late 1950s. That will surely get the world's attention, and no doubt will kick off a price war, which we will need to be able to deal with by even further reducing our prices," he added, watching Shing, who was clearly upset.

Shing stood up, shaken by the challenge he had just been given. He knew there was no way he could meet his profit goals if the prices were reduced so drastically. And yet, he had to admit that Kong was probably correct in his assessment of the situation. The reality was that China was entering a market already adequately served by other suppliers. To gain market share in such a market would certainly require very aggressive pricing.

"Kong, we do need to meet on this matter. If you are serious about such low prices, it will be very difficult for me to achieve any reasonable profit from my operation."

Kong turned to his secretary and asked her to set up a meeting soon to discuss pricing, costs, and profits. He turned back to Shing and asked, "When can you be ready to meet on this important matter?"

Shing referred to his notebook, and said, "I would like to have a week to work with my staff to see what realistic cost goals can be. Is next Wednesday okay?"

Kong grumbled and said, "If that's the best you can do. Remember, we owe Keung our plan in thirty days, and time is slipping away."

Kong stood up and walked to the end of the table, where he continued. "We now need to discuss the matter of acquiring popular record labels. It is obvious to my staff and to me that we must have virtually all of the most popular labels, for if we don't, we won't be able to sell very many CD records, no matter what our prices are. Wouldn't you agree, Shing?"

"That makes sense," said Shing. "Do you know what royalty rate is currently being paid to top recording artists?"

Kong asked Tak Chang to comment on this matter. Tak told them it was common for top performers to receive royalties ranging from five percent to ten percent of the record's selling price, depending on the standing of the record on the charts. In addition, superstars were typically paid millions by the major record companies to prevent them from recording for a competitor.

Shing picked up on that comment immediately. "Kong, are you telling us that, in addition to selling CD records at very low prices, we will have to add additional royalties and other fees to our costs? If that is so, I can assure you it will be impossible to make any profit from this venture. It would be foolish for us to embark on this program if we know in advance there is no hope for profits. Don't you agree?"

"Who says we must pay such outrageous royalties?" screamed Kong. "Who says China must follow the commercial practices of the rest of the world? These musical performers are already being paid ridiculous salaries. Why should we pay them anything more? Perhaps after we become the dominant supplier of CD records we will need to pay them some small amount to encourage them to record new labels for us, but in no way should we have to pay them the ridiculous amounts paid by the West!"

Shing was now very concerned about what he was hearing. "Kong, are you telling us that you want to start a worldwide CD record price war, and in addition you want to thumb your nose at all of the world's top-notch musical performers? World opinion will almost certainly be against such an enterprise!"

Kong turned to Shing and said, "Shing, you should only concern yourself with producing CDs. Leave the marketing and sales strategy to me. I'm trying to do you a favor by suggesting a plan where we do not have to add ridiculous royalties to the cost of your products, and you wish to discuss world opinion!"

Kong's staff was enjoying this interchange, and all were watching Shing, whose face had turned ashen white. Shing did not say a word as he reflected on what he had just heard. Kong was recommending that China become a large scale international record pirate, and surely nothing good would come from that!

Shing wondered if Keung would go along with such a plan! Unfortunately, he believed he just might. Kong sat down, sipped some more tea, and began to speak in a more pleasant tone of voice.

"Gentlemen, I believe we should close this meeting and give Shing some more time to prepare for next Wednesday's meeting. At that same meeting, I expect Shing to provide me with production quantity information, as well as cost estimates.

"Meanwhile, I want all of the members of my staff to consider again what CD prices need to be for China to succeed in this enterprise. You must keep in mind that our president will not be pleased if we do not find a way to become the dominant world supplier of CD records in just two short years or less."

Shing continued to sit quietly in his chair. Clearly Kong was trying to set him up for a failure, for if he could not find a way to make enough CDs at a low enough cost, the failure of the plan would fall on his shoulders.

Kong's staff bowed and left the room. Kong turned to Shing and said, "I realize I put you on the spot today, but I firmly believe we have only one way to succeed. I believe our president's dream to become the dominant supplier of CD records will require China to enter the market in a very aggressive way, along the lines I've presented. Perhaps we will not need to drop our prices initially as much as I suggested, but if a price war ensues, we will surely need to do so eventually.

"Even if we could afford to pay the musicians their ridiculous royalties, don't you realize most of them already have firm contracts with other suppliers and cannot sign with us? You need to go back to your plant and find out just how cheaply you can make CD records, for you can be sure my plan will include the requirement for quite low prices!

"Also, Shing, when you took us on the tour, I didn't see any apparatus that would produce CD record masters from other supplier's records. I'm sure you can understand such a capability is required if we wish to implement a royalty-free strategy, for we will need to be able to copy all of the popular records as soon as they appear for sale by our competitors!"

Kong reached out and shook Shing's hand. He noticed a slight tremor, so he knew he was very much on top of the situation. He would continue to pressure his staff to make high-volume commitments based on very aggressive prices, for he wanted to be sure he would meet his part of the plan. If Shing could not achieve the necessary low cost or high production volumes, then that would be Shing's problem.

With regard to entering the market without paying royalties, Kong believed he could convince Keung that this was not only necessary, but it would be a way China could show the rest of the world just how fallacious the Western capitalistic practices had become.

Shing said good-bye and went down the hall to his own office, where he asked his secretary to call CT immediately. He sat down in his cushioned chair to reflect on the meeting. When CT came on the line, Shing asked him to arrange a conference room for an all-day planning meeting when he returned to Haikou the next day.

Shing wondered if he should tell Keung about his concerns, but he realized it would not be wise to do so yet. Maybe there could be some compromises possible between the demands of the sales and marketing department and the demands placed on his organization.

Shing did not care for the way Kong placed him on the hot seat in the meeting, but he couldn't help but believe Kong's plan probably made sense. If China's goal was to become a dominant factor in the CD Record market in such a short time, then drastic measures would definitely be required!

Chapter Four

Upon his return to Haikou, Shing called a planning meeting with CT and the other members of his manufacturing staff. He began the session by presenting a brief summary, outlining the difficult task before them.

"Gentlemen, when our president visited us last week, he asked Kong and I to present a business plan within thirty days. This plan must include both a sales plan and an operations plan. For my part, I need to show what is required to meet the quantity demand from the market, as well as to meet the very low costs required to make a profit from this enterprise.

"Because we are entering the market at such a late date, we will have to be prepared to sell our CD records at very low prices. As a consequence, we must begin immediately to work on a cost-reduction effort coincident with the manufacture of our first records. CT, I want you and your staff to review all the elements of cost and come up with an action plan for reducing those costs by one-half."

"Whew," CT said under his breath. "Ah, Shing, the production cost is almost totally dictated by the capitalized cost of the machinery we have just purchased," CT said. "There are very few laborers required to make the records, and the cost of raw materials is trivial."

"CT, I don't need to hear excuses," Shing shouted. "I repeat. I want you and your staff to come up with a plan to reduce the cost of the CD records by one-half, and I want that plan on my desk in two days. Do you understand me?"

"Yes, Shing. My staff and I welcome this challenge," CT said with a slight frown on his face.

This was not the way Shing usually operated, and CT was worried that something was very much wrong. However, he understood what he needed to do, and he told himself he would give it his best efforts. Shing turned to his production staff and asked them to develop various scenarios for producing CD records in quantities, so he could have a better feel for the maximum quantity that could be produced per day. He also asked them to tell him which items of production equipment represented bottlenecks, in the event greater quantity demands were placed on the plant in the future.

The meeting was adjourned by noon and everyone went away with their assignments. Shing asked them to return in two days with their reports. As they left, Shing reminded them again that no one was to think negative thoughts, for they needed to be able to achieve their president's wishes, period!

"CT, before you go, I would like to speak with you," Shing said, as the rest of the staff filed out of the conference room. "Do you remember our conversation about recording artists? Well, Kong and I have agreed that the only way we can sell CD records in high volume today is to be able to offer most of the popular labels from most of the popular artists. This means we will have to copy our competitor's records. So, CT, besides developing a plan for achieving very low costs, I want you to develop a means for copying CD records onto production masters that can be used in our production process." Changing the subject, Shing asked, "I understand your wife-to-be is a computer whiz. Is that right?"

"Yes, Miu is very versed in both computer hardware and software design principles," CT said proudly.

"Why don't you and she go away this weekend to discuss how to best implement a system for copying CD records? And while you're at it, maybe she can give you some ideas on how to reduce the cost of our records. I understand she minored in business accounting. In fact, I will personally excuse you both from this Friday night's indoctrination lecture so you can leave sooner.

"CT, I know I've given you a very difficult assignment. Please excuse my theatrics in the meeting. You must realize Kong is going to come up with a very aggressive sales plan, with extremely low prices compared with today's market prices."

"I guess there are already too many suppliers," CT noted, as he got up to leave Shing's conference room. "It sounds like we will have to muscle ourselves into the market, using price as our weapon. Isn't that about it?"

"As always, CT, you grasp the situation very well. Now go tell your lovely wife-to-be that you and she have to make plans for the weekend. I will now call the Friday night lecturer to excuse you both."

"Miu, you are a fantastic lover," CT purred in her ear after they finished making love on the bed in her tiny apartment. "Let's just stay here and relax for a couple of hours before we visit our favorite restaurant," he added, as he stroked her long black hair.

"That sounds fine," Miu whispered back.

"CT, you are also a most fantastic lover, but tonight you seemed to be very tense and preoccupied with something. Come now, you mustn't keep secrets from me," she teased. "In just one short month we will become man and wife, and it is important for us to share everything."

"I was afraid your roommate would walk in on us," he lied.

"That's silly," she said frowning at him. "You know my roommate left to visit her parents this weekend. I saw her say good-bye to you as you arrived! I must insist you tell me what is bothering you. I can see it in your eyes that you are very concerned about something. So, let me hear what it is, or I'll start tickling you from head to toe, and you know I can really get to you if I do that," she giggled.

She started to climb on top of him and began to rub her long fingernails along his thighs and under his arms, where he was especially ticklish.

"All right, all right," CT said. "Get off of me, please. You need to lie back and prepare yourself for a long discussion. A lot has happened in the past couple of days."

CT told Miu how Shing acted in the meeting and how he gave him and his staff a very difficult, if not impossible, task to accomplish. CT once again described the elements that made up the cost of each CD record, pointing out that more than eighty percent of the cost was the capital depreciation cost of the new equipment that had just been installed.

"There is another problem I've been asked to look into. Shing thought you could be of some assistance in helping me solve it."

"What's that?" Miu asked curiously.

"We need to find a practical way to copy our competitor's records, in order to make production masters for our plant to use to manufacture exact copies for sale. If we don't, we will have to rely on using unknown recording artists, and our record sales will be very low."

"Isn't that illegal?" she asked.

"Technically speaking, you're right. However, China has never signed an international trade agreement that prevents such copying from taking place. Based on that, I guess we are able to do whatever we want to do."

"I see why you were so preoccupied tonight," she said, as she snuggled up to him. "I don't see how you were able to even think of me with all of that on your mind. Why didn't you say something, so I could be sympathetic?" she asked, as she stroked his neck to relieve the tensions.

"Now you know why Shing let us skip the indoctrination meeting tonight," CT said. "He is hopeful we will be able to develop some ideas that will help him meet his part of the business plan so he can deal more effectively with Kong."

"Isn't Kong a pure politician?"

"Yes, and he will make sure it will be Shing's fault if the sales of CDs don't meet the forecast. I'm sure that's why Shing behaved so strangely today. He must be afraid of having to tell the president we can't make any money selling CD records at the prices needed to generate volume sales."

"Why don't we take a nap now? When we wake up we can shower and go to a late dinner. Over dinner we can discuss the two matters you have been given to work on. I'm sure we will find solutions after we rest up."

CT already had the same idea, and he was soon snoring softly on the pillow next to hers. Miu pulled up the covers, closed her eyes, and she too fell into a deep sleep.

When they awoke it was almost 9:00 P.M., so they hurried with their showers. They quickly dressed and hailed a cab outside of Miu's apartment, and were soon seated at their favorite table in the back of the Wing Fang Restaurant in downtown Haikou.

After ordering a six-course Chinese dinner, they began to continue their earlier discussions. Miu began by asking CT more questions about the factors making up the cost of CD records.

"You say the capitalized cost of the new equipment accounts for more than eighty percent of the cost of each record produced," she asked again.

"That's right," CT said for the third time.

"So what's the big deal, CT?" she asked with a twinkle in her eye. "Why not simply write off the equipment over a ten-year period, rather than over a five-year period? Wouldn't that result in each record costing about half as much?"

"But, Miu, we have always been told to use a five-year write-off," CT said, wondering if she was really serious.

"I know, CT, but Shing is facing a really difficult situation here. Didn't you tell me the new equipment will last considerably longer than five years? If that is so, why can't you use a ten-year write-off?"

"Shing will never accept that idea. He will tell me we have always used a five-year write-off!"

"CT, you can be so stubborn at times," she scolded. "You should tell Shing he is dealing with very modern automation equipment. Tell him it is time for the accounting rules to change!"

"Miu, what is the accepted accounting practice covering such a matter?" CT asked, as he began to warm up to her idea.

"According to one of my professors, the rules have to do with taking the entire purchase cost of the equipment and spreading it out over the expected life of the equipment. There never was any discussion about the write-off having to be any particular period of time, such as five years. The reason five years has been used in the past is because equipment used to manufacture electronic items typically either wears out or becomes obsolete in that time period.

"CT, you need to convince Shing the equipment you bought can reasonably be expected to have a life of ten years. Since he's the boss, he should be able to convince his accounting department to go along with him on this."

A light bulb went off in CT's head, as he listened to Miu. "If I can convince Shing the equipment can be expected to last for ten years, we have our cost reduction plan already implemented!" CT said, with a loud shout that caused the other patrons in the restaurant to turn their heads and look his way. "Miu, you are brilliant!" CT said, as he stood up and bent over the table. He landed a very long and passionate kiss on her lips to make the point.

"People are staring," Miu said quietly. "Why don't we eat our dinner now, and after we are finished, we can talk about the other matter."

They both ate quickly, for by now they had ravenous appetites. When they completed their last course, they told their waiter they would call him back when they were ready for dessert.

"CT, tell me something about the kinds of electrical signals recorded on the surface of each CD record," Miu asked.

CT described how the original analog sounds picked up by microphones in a recording studio are converted into digital impulses that are recorded on the surface of CD records.

"Because of that conversion, CD records do not exhibit scratchy sounds like the old LP records," he added.

"Is it true if the rate of conversion is high enough, the sound quality of a copied record is virtually identical to the quality of the original?" she asked.

"Yes, I believe that is correct. We need only to find an efficient way to copy the digital impulses from a competitor's record onto our production masters. However, to make numerous masters to use on our production floor, we don't want to have to wait until an entire two-hour CD record finishes playing. Instead, we need to speed up the conversion process."

"Why don't we copy the competitor's record in real time into a computer's memory bank, taking the necessary two hours or so to capture each and every digital impulse? Then, to make copies, we could dump out the data in parallel, which would be like recording each of the tracks simultaneously."

"I don't completely follow you, Miu," CT said, becoming quite interested in what she was saying.

"Well CT, what I'm suggesting is to play each record we plan to copy first into a computer in a serial fashion, whereas the production masters are produced by recording each track simultaneously in parallel. That would mean each production master recording could be produced from the computer memory in about ten seconds, if my calculations are correct. That should be fast enough, don't you think?"

"How long will it take for you to try this out?" CT asked, beaming all over.

"I think if you help me, I could have something working by tomorrow night. It might not be fully operational, but it should demonstrate the principle. With a little more work on my part, it should be ready to go in a couple of weeks."

This time CT stood up, bent over the table, picked Miu up in his arms, and lifted her out of her seat. He carried her off to a dark corner of the room, where they danced and kissed for several minutes.

"Miu, I love you so very much, but I love your ideas even more," he kidded, as she dug her finger nails into his neck to get back at him.

"Which do you love the most, my ideas or me?" she asked as her nails found their mark.

"You decide," CT said, kissing her again.

"CT, I'm beginning to notice you are no longer uptight or tense. Does that suggest anything?" she teased.

"Yes, it suggests we should sit down at our table and eat our dessert, for I just noticed the waiters are wondering where we went and what we are doing," CT teased back.

The two of them ate their burnt cream dessert in relative silence, each thinking of what they discussed that night. When they finished, they went into the bar and continued dancing and sipping after-dinner drinks until the wee hours of Saturday morning.

Chapter Five

Kong scheduled a follow-up meeting with his marketing and sales staffs. He asked each of his area sales managers to re-examine their individual markets and report to him how low the price needed to be for China to gain significant market share within two years.

Each staff member came to the meeting prepared to provide the information he requested, using a standard format for their presentations. Besides discussing prices, they were asked to describe the situation in each of their markets, including how many CD records were being sold currently, and whether the market was expected to increase or decrease during the next five years.

Kong listened quietly to the presentations, thanking each of his sales managers when they finished their talk. His secretary took notes and added up the figures, so Kong would have a composite picture of the market to examine.

When the last speaker finished, Kong stood up and walked to the head of the table. "Gentlemen, I wish to thank all of you for this update on the market," he said. "I can see you have all been very busy preparing for this meeting. The information appears to be quite complete and quite thorough. Again, I wish to thank each of you for a job well done!"

Kong scanned the notes his secretary provided him and began to summarize what he heard from the group.

"Are you guys telling me the unit sales of CD records are still growing at a ten percent rate this year?"

They all nodded yes.

"And are you telling me prices actually increased each year during the first couple of years in the most recent five-year history, but during the past three years, the prices at the wholesale level have been dropping an average of five percent per year?" Again they all nodded yes.

"Do you have any feel for how much excess production capacity there is and which suppliers have significant excess capacity?"

Kong's marketing director, Tak Chang, stood up to answer him. "Ah Kong, I believe the following is a correct assessment of that situation," Tak said, as he pulled out a memorandum from his folder.

The memo provided a rundown of each of the major suppliers of CD records, including one new Japanese supplier and one new European supplier who came on line recently.

"Obviously, these two new suppliers represent new capacity," Tak said. "From talking with many of the current suppliers at the recent Tokyo show, the existing CD record suppliers are about tapped out. I was unable to determine if they plan to add extra capacity this year or not."

"I guess it will depend on how well their sales build, don't you think?" Kong asked. They all agreed with him.

"Okay, gentlemen, here comes the most important question we have to answer today!" Kong got up from his seat and started pacing the floor.

"Considering what you have all told me about the size of the market, the rate it is growing, the capacity available, and the current market prices, what average price must we charge for our records, if we wish to own twenty-five percent of the market by the end of the first year of production? Please consider the same question if we wish to own more than seventy percent of the market by the end of the second year."

The room became very quiet, as no one wanted to be the first to try to answer such a difficult question. Kong knew such a question would separate the men from the boys, for if the prices were set too high, the resulting market share would be very small. Similarly, if the prices were set too low, the market share number might not be a problem to achieve, but the profitability of the enterprise would certainly suffer greatly.

"Come, come, gentlemen," Kong asked with a big grin on his face. "Isn't anyone going to volunteer to answer this question?"

Tak stood up and said, "Kong, I would like to try to logically arrive at such an answer. May I go to the blackboard and attempt to do so?"

"Great. I'll move to the back of the room and let you have the blackboard to work out your estimates," Kong said.

Tak started by presenting information he gathered on how CD record prices were established in the record industry. He had spoken with some of the major record company marketing personnel who attended the Tokyo show, and there seemed to be a fair amount of price fixing going on in this industry, just as OPEC sets the price of a barrel of crude oil.

"All of the current suppliers belong to an international organization whose stated purpose is to set industry standards of quality for the music they produce. However, I managed to sneak unnoticed into one of their sessions at the show. I overheard a rather serious pricing discussion in which the two new suppliers from Japan and Europe were in effect being told what their prices needed to be," Tak said.

"This is extremely important information," Kong pointed out. "Have any of you other gentlemen heard of such pricing practices?"

Several of the members of his staff said they suspected such practices, but Tak's direct input was the most specific example they had heard.

Tak continued with his discussion. "I believe when a market price is set by such an organization, it is probable each supplier to that market is making higher than normal profits. As a consequence, if China were to enter the market at a ten percent to twenty percent lower price, the current suppliers would probably be able to meet that number immediately, without causing themselves any undue economic hardship.

"Ah, Kong, I hate to say it, but I believe the fifty percent reduction in price you suggested at the last meeting may be required if we are to meet our market share goals. Perhaps we can increment our way down to such a low number. However, we need to start out with at least a twenty-five percent reduction, in order to force customers to take notice of our products and in order to force our competitors to make some kind of a move."

"What do you other clowns think?" Kong asked, taking on a serious demeanor. "You've all been sitting here not saying a word. Is

Tak's analysis correct, or is he full of it?" Kong asked, smiling so all could see his gold-capped teeth.

The noise level in the room suddenly increased, as many simultaneous conversations began to occur between the staff members. After about five minutes, Peng Hong, the head of North American sales, stood up and asked the group to be quiet, so he could present his own ideas.

"I believe we should first concentrate most of our sales efforts on some particular portion of the world market, such as South America, where the other suppliers have not yet become so well entrenched. To achieve sales in that market segment, we should be prepared to price our records very aggressively, so we capture literally all of that market by the end of the first year.

"As we employ a very aggressive pricing strategy in South America, we should price our records more conservatively in the rest of the world markets. For example, I recommend we enter those markets with only a ten percent reduction in price. In that way, we will force the other suppliers to sell their records at honest prices, and we can see how the world responds to having China as a new CD record supplier.

"After about six to nine months, depending on how we are doing in South America, we should start bringing down our prices in the rest of the world markets, and see if our sales volume picks up accordingly.

"In South America there will probably be almost no concern that we are offering most of the popular labels. Whereas if we were to focus all of our sales efforts initially in the North American market, dropping prices by large amounts, we probably would receive enormous flak from our competitors. They would no doubt immediately brand us all as record pirates.

"In summary, I agree with Tak. However, I do not believe we should attack all markets simultaneously with super-aggressive price drops. Rather, we should focus on South America as our price-leader market and participate in the other world markets with modest price drops to see how those markets respond."

"Do you agree with Peng?" Kong asked both Tak and his South American sales manager. They enthusiastically nodded their approval.

"Does everyone else agree?" Kong asked again.

Everyone in the room nodded, and you could tell from their faces there was considerable agreement and enthusiasm for the strategy.

"Okay, I want all of you to prepare your plans for the first year of sales, based on the strategy presented by Peng, and have those plans on my desk in one week. Please coordinate with Tak on the pricing you use in your plans. Remember, gentlemen, be aggressive. We must take the necessary steps to ensure China owns more than seventy percent of the world market by the end of our second year!"

Kong shook Peng's hand and thanked him for his very profound insight into the pricing challenge they were going to be facing. His staff received their marching orders, and the meeting was adjourned.

Kong stopped by his secretary's desk on the way back to his office to see if there was any mail requiring his action. On the top of the pile he saw a memo from Keung, which scheduled a meeting for the following Friday morning to discuss the CD record business plan.

"I thought we were being given thirty days," Kong fumed to himself. However, as he looked at his calendar, he reasoned that he would be able to meet this deadline. He wondered if Shing would have time to get ready, but he really didn't care much. In addition, with the new date, he and Shing would not be able to compare notes before the meeting with Keung, but again he didn't really care.

"I'll be ready, now that I have a very solid sales strategy," he said under his breath. "This meeting should be very interesting."

Once inside his office, Kong buzzed his secretary and told her to send in Tak, because there was a change in plans. Soon Tak knocked on his door, and Kong briefed him on the new timetable. Tak left to tell the guys to drop everything and pull their sales numbers together.

Kong sat down and reflected on the meeting. On the bright side, he believed his staff was turned on to the challenge ahead of them, which was to enter a mature market and buy market share like a bully would take candy away from children. In spite of their enthusiasm, however, Kong realized he and his staff were faced with an extremely difficult task.

Even if they concentrated their energies on South America, the record industry would come down hard on China in the press for using what they would no doubt refer to as blatant record piracy practices.

A more immediate problem, which Keung would no doubt uncover on Friday, was that China might not be able to make any profit from this enterprise, especially if the prices needed to be as low as fifty percent of the prevailing world prices. He wondered how Shing would deal with that issue in the meeting, since it would require him to reduce his costs considerably.

"Could you please call my cousin in Haikou?" Kong asked his secretary over the intercom. "Tell him it's urgent."

In a moment, the light on his phone started to blink and Kong picked it up. "How are you Mau?"

"I'm fine, Kong," his cousin answered.

Kong's cousin worked in the accounting department of the Mao Zedong Laser Development and Manufacturing Works Manufacturing Works in Haikou and was always willing to provide Kong with strategically sensitive data whenever he requested it.

"Mau, have you been able to find out what the cost of CD records made in the Haikou plant will be?"

"As a matter of fact, our accounting department ran its first cost estimates today for Shing's review. I made a copy of that information and just finished reviewing it when you called. The data suggests the cost will be about the same as the price you told me you would have to sell CD records for. Doesn't this mean we won't make any money?"

"Don't you worry about that," Kong said, trying to reassure his cousin. "I don't believe we will initially have to offer the product for such a low price," he said, telling a little white lie.

"Anyway, thanks for the information. I don't know if you've heard, but Keung has scheduled a meeting with Shing and me for this coming Friday. At the meeting, we will be reviewing the prices we must sell CD records for and will be comparing the prices with the costs."

"I'm sure you and Shing will be ready for the president," Mau said.

"Thanks again," Kong said, and hung up the phone.

Kong was fortunate to have his cousin working in the Haikou accounting department. His cousin's presence there afforded him the opportunity to be able to get his hands on critical cost information whenever he needed it, especially when preparing for meetings where he and Shing were expected to become confrontational in front of Keung.

Armed with that data, Kong began to plot how he would present the sales and marketing plan in the best light possible. He wondered what Keung would say when Shing was forced to admit there was no way he could make any profit!

"Not my problem," he said to himself.

Chapter Six

Miu and CT decided not to take the weekend trip Shing offered them. Instead, when they woke up on Saturday morning, they ate a light breakfast, jumped on their bicycles, and pedaled to Miu's laboratory, which was only a few blocks from her apartment.

"If you walk over to Lab Number Two, you will find a CD record player, which we will need today. Meanwhile, I'll set up a computer and some other test hardware on the workbench next to my office," Miu said.

"Fine. I'll be back in a few minutes."

By the time CT returned with the player and a selection of CD records, Miu was finished setting up the computer. "We might as well play our favorite songs while we work," he said cheerfully.

"I'm going to write a simple batch program that will take the output of the CD player and store it in a special directory location on my computer's hard drive. While I'm doing that, you should figure out how to connect the player to the computer's parallel port."

"No problem," CT said. "When I was in the lab, I saw just the cable we need. I'll be right back."

In half an hour, the two of them were ready to see if their setup would work. Miu opened up the special directory, clicked on the icon labeled STORE and pressed the play button on the CD record player. Music was heard from the speakers, but more importantly, on the monitor screen a bar graph was displayed showing the status of the data being fed to the hard drive. While the CD player continued to transfer its digital signals to the computer, CT and Miu went to the cafeteria to fix themselves some tea. "I don't believe we need to transfer all two hours of music to prove our point. What do you think CT?"

"I believe if we transfer half an hour's worth of data, that should suffice. After all, that will include more than fifty tracks worth of information."

When sufficient time passed, CT turned off the player and Miu clicked the close button on the bar graph dialog box. "Now, CT, tell me again your understanding of how a CD record data stream knows when a single track has finished playing. I think you said there is a burst of signals that are followed by a brief pause. Is that what's supposed to happen?"

"I believe so, according to all of the books I've read," CT answered. "Let's see if we can find those burst signals on the hard disk and see how they differ from the sound signals."

Miu scanned the directory's contents and announced she believed she found what they were looking for. "Look here!" she exclaimed. "Isn't that one, and look down here, isn't that the next one? I can now tell exactly where the data on each track ends, and where the next track's data begins."

"It looks okay to me," CT said enthusiastically.

They continued to scan the contents of the directory and discovered fifty-five individual tracks of sound data.

"Do you know how to make the computer produce a parallel output representing the information on those tracks?" CT asked.

"I believe so, but it will take me a few hours to write a program to enable the computer to do that automatically," Miu said.

"That's cool," CT answered. "I have some work I need to do in my office, so why don't I leave you alone for a while. I'll return later this afternoon. That way, I won't be a bother to you. I know how temperamental programmers can be," he added with a big grin.

"You're so understanding," she said, snuggling up to CT. "I'll see you later. Give me about four or five hours. I'm good, but I'm no genius," she laughed.

It was after 5:00 P.M. when CT returned to Miu's building. He found her staring at the screen of her computer. On the desk beside her was a huge bundle of paper full of program notes and code she had written. She looked up when CT approached her.

"How you doing, babe?"

"I thought this would be easy, but I wasted most of the afternoon chasing false data paths. However, I believe I'm finally on to something. If I just had a little more time, I believe I'll be able to crack it. Would you grant a poor little programmer just two more hours?" she asked, looking wistfully at CT.

"Do I have any choice?"

"Not if you want to look like a hero when Shing calls you on Monday morning to see how things are going!"

"I'll tell you what I'm going to do. I'll get on my bicycle and peddle down to the takeout restaurant at the corner and I'll bring us back several bags of our favorite nibbles. How does that sound?"

"Master, that would be just fine. Before you leave, though, would you go to the cafeteria and refill this cup of mine with very strong tea? I need to keep my brain engaged if I'm going to finish this program tonight."

CT left and decided to go back to his office to finish up some additional work. About 7:00 P.M. he peddled to the restaurant, ordered some food, and arrived back in Miu's office at half past seven.

He found Miu stretched out over her desk, sound asleep. On her table was a neat pile of papers, which appeared to be a completed program, with all of the listings. In the wastebasket were many crumpled bits of paper carrying the previous code, which did not work. On the computer monitor several parallel columns of data were flying by so fast they appeared to be all blurred together.

"It looks like she did it," CT thought to himself. "Wake up sleeping beauty," CT said, as he gently nudged her. "Our goodie treats are here, and I don't know about you, but I'm very hungry."

She opened her eyes, smiled, and let out a very loud shout. "It works! It works! Did you hear me? It works!" She jumped off her desk and grabbed CT, and the two of them spun around like two children dancing folk dances.

CT joked, "I never doubted you could do it, but I was beginning to wonder if you would get it done in my lifetime."

"Boy, what an optimist you turned out to be," she said, as she jabbed him quite firmly in the ribs. "And to think I was seriously planning to marry you. I just might reconsider that deal, unless you apologize," she teased.

"Okay, I'm sorry. Now please show me how this thing works, and we can take a break and eat, before these goodies get cold."

Miu showed CT what the data on the screen meant. She further showed him how the multiple channels of data were fed to the parallel port on the back of the computer. "These parallel signals can be used to record multiple sound tracks on a CD production master, which the plant requires to produce duplicate copies of CD records in high volume."

"This is nothing short of amazing," CT told her seriously. "I want you to show Shing how this works. I'll set up a meeting the first thing Monday morning, because I'm sure he will want to hear some good news."

The two of them cleared off her table and started eating the takeout food.

"How about taking in a movie tonight to clear the cobwebs from your brain?" CT asked.

"That would be great," she answered.

They left the lab at 8:30 on Saturday night, feeling really proud of what they had accomplished during the weekend. Not only had Miu been able to work out a method to copy CD records efficiently, but also she and CT had a very viable cost-reduction solution. They had every right to feel good about things, and they deserved some time off to clear their heads.

Chapter Seven

Shing arrived at his office early on Monday morning. He stopped by his secretary's desk and began to rummage through his mail to see if there was anything important requiring his attention. When he found the meeting notice from Keung, sheer panic set in. He could not see how he possibly could be adequately prepared for the meeting in just four short days. Why did Keung want to meet so soon? The more he thought about it, the more he began to sweat.

He immediately went into his office, closed the door, and phoned Kong. He thought if both he and Kong could not be ready in time, then maybe Keung could be persuaded to delay the meeting by at least one more week.

"Let me see if he can take your call," Kong's secretary said.

"Yes, Shing, what can I do for you?" Kong asked.

"Kong, have you seen the memo from Keung?"

"Yes. I saw it on Friday. It looks like the old man is either getting forgetful or is becoming anxious to approve our plan. Anyway, I yelled at my guys on Friday to hurry up and get me the data I need. I believe I'll be in good shape. The meeting is this coming Friday, isn't it?"

"I just saw the memo and I don't see how I can be ready in time. How are we going to be able to meet in advance, like we wanted to do? Do you think that there's a chance Keung's request can be delayed?"

"Do you want to be the one who asks him? I sure don't want to be the one. That's why I worked my staff this past weekend."

"Don't you feel we should meet and compare notes ahead of time, like we agreed to do? We could look like fools in front of Keung if our stories don't mesh," Shing said very soberly.

"Oh, I don't think it's that big a deal. You pretty much know what I'm going to recommend. All you have to do is show how we can make enough records profitably. What could be simpler?"

"I may ask for a delay," Shing said. "I need more time to get my numbers together, and Keung has to understand that."

"Good luck, Shing. Let me know what he says."

Shing jumped out of his chair and called his secretary into his office. He told her to cancel all of his other appointments, arrange an immediate flight to Haikou, and set up individual meetings with CT and the other manufacturing managers on Tuesday morning, for he and his staff had an enormous amount of work to do.

Kong, on the other hand, jumped out of his chair in great spirits. He had all the information he required to put together an outstanding sales and marketing presentation. Since he knew Shing had a major cost problem, he decided to inflate the volume opportunity numbers considerably higher than the data his people provided him. He saw no harm in doing so, since Keung would probably want to commit smaller quantities, once he understood how unprofitable this operation was likely to be.

"CT, I need to see you in my office immediately," Shing yelled over the plant intercom system. Shing's secretary had forewarned CT that Shing was going to be in Haikou this morning, and that he seemed very flustered.

"Good morning, Shing," CT said cheerfully, as he entered Shing's office.

"Why are you so happy?" Shing asked, looking very haggard and tired. "Oh, I get it. You and your sweet young thing must have had a real fine time this weekend. I hope it wasn't all fun and games, because we have some very serious work to complete today! For starters, how long will it take you and your staff to reduce the cost of the CD records by one-half, and how do you plan to do it?" Shing was not expecting a very positive answer, as he had just finished reading the accounting manager's report.

"Miu and I brainstormed this weekend, and she came up with what I believe to be a brilliant idea!"

"Oh, and pray tell what is your plan?" Shing asked sarcastically.

"It's quite simple. Do you recall when you signed the purchase orders for the new equipment? At that time I told you all of the major high cost items were highly automated, with a life expectancy in excess of ten years. Miu asked me why we don't simply apply a ten-year depreciation to the cost of capitalizing the equipment, for if we do, the cost of CDs is almost reduced in half," CT said, watching Shing's eyes very carefully.

"But, CT, we have always used a five-year capitalization period. Tell me again why you believe we can now use a ten-year life."

"I'm no accountant," CT said, "but don't we use five or ten years because we are supposed to use a figure that corresponds to the expected useful life of the equipment? I'm telling you this new equipment will not wear out, nor will it become obsolete in five years. There is no risk in using a ten-year depreciation for the major pieces of equipment."

Shing stood up and began pacing the floor of his office. He really did look very tired, but CT could tell he was considering this proposal carefully. CT did not know that Shing had already bought the concept one hundred percent, but was now trying to decide whether Keung would need to be convinced before he could apply the ten-year write-off formula. He also was wondering if his accounting staff would go along with the use of ten years. If so, would someone in the future raise the issue with Keung if he chose to say nothing? He concluded that he should tell Keung before the meeting. He was sure he could sell Keung on the idea without too much difficulty.

"CT, you should tell your girlfriend she is a genius," Shing finally said, with a big smile on his face.

Shing seemed to become more vibrant. In addition, he looked five years younger, as this was the best news he had heard in days.

"Were you and she able to develop a means for making production masters from our competitor's CD records?" asked Shing.

"Ah, Shing, Miu has a demonstration ready to show you in her laboratory. I will stop by and get you at lunch, and we can walk there and see it together. I can assure you that what she has put together will work. It will take a couple of weeks to complete the setup in a form that we can use on our production floor."

"Outstanding!" Shing said, rising out of his chair and patting CT on the shoulder. "I don't know what I would do without you and your lovely girlfriend. I'm certainly glad you two are planning to be married."

"Keung, I must speak with you immediately," Shing said into Keung's phone message system. With the good news he had received from CT, and having witnessed Miu's demonstration, he was now confident he could be ready for the meeting. However, he did need to inform Keung about his plan to use a different accounting method for capitalizing the new equipment.

Shing was in the midst of preparing his material for the meeting when the light on his phone started to blink.

"Ah, Keung, this is Shing. How are you today? I see you have requested we meet on Friday morning. This didn't give me much time to prepare, but I can be ready with my part. Do you think Kong can be ready in time?" he asked, with a slight smirk on his face.

"I just got off the phone with Kong," Keung said. "He actually thanked me for moving the meeting up so we can move forward more quickly into this exciting market."

When Shing heard this he thought to himself, "Am I ever glad I didn't ask for more time!" He realized Kong was up to his old tricks and was trying to get the upper hand even before the meeting started.

"So, Shing, what do you have on your mind?"

"I wanted to tell you when I present my cost numbers I will be recommending a more realistic accounting method to deal with the capitalization cost of my highly automated equipment. Should I run my ideas by your chief accounting man before the meeting, or should I plan to do that afterwards?"

"Shing, don't bother talking to my man. I sometimes think he lives in the dark ages. If you believe you have a better idea, include it in your plan. If it makes sense to me, I'll handle the accounting department. I trust your good judgment, so apply whatever methods you feel are justified. As you know, I want you and your operation to succeed this time. It has been far too many years since the Haikou plant has produced revenues, and our treasury needs more cash inflow."

"Ah, Keung, that is good news. I'll see you this Friday. I believe you will be very pleased with my presentation."

"Good-bye. I'm looking forward to your report."

It was midmorning on Wednesday when Shing finished putting his presentation together. He was rather pleased with himself, for his production staff had been able to show him exactly which pieces of equipment would need to be duplicated in order to increase production by sizable amounts. It was also evident from the numbers that the plant space was more than adequate to produce the entire world's requirement, if necessary. With this information and with lower cost estimates, Shing was going to be in a very strong position at the meeting. He would be able to show that profitability was not going to be a problem, and being able to produce enough quantity was not going to be a problem either. The only real issue would be whether Kong and his staff could sell enough to meet Keung's worldwide market share objectives.

Shing still had one concern, and that was how the world would view the fact that China was copying all of the popular labels and turning around and selling them at bargain-basement prices. That was bound to be a very sticky issue, and one that needed to be addressed at the meeting. However, try as he could, he could not figure out any other way for China to enter this market effectively in such a short time.

Shing summoned CT to his office in a much more soft-spoken voice than he had used yesterday.

"CT, won't you have a chair? Please close the door. We need to discuss another important matter."

Shing first flipped through his presentation to show CT what he planned to say at Keung's meeting. CT was impressed with the thoroughness and depth of information he included.

"It looks like you will be well prepared," CT said. "Do you know what Kong plans to say?"

"For his own sake, I hope he doesn't go too far out on a limb with unrealistic sales level promises," Shing said smiling, causing CT to burst out laughing.

"I'm sure he will, and that should keep him out of our hair," CT said.

"CT, I still wish we did not have to copy our competitor's records, but I don't believe we have any choice. I wish in addition that we had some other more legitimate products we could sell. You know what I mean, don't you?"

CT jumped up and said, "Shing, I think I know just the thing to satisfy our need to become more legitimate. Do you remember my master's thesis where I discussed the future use of CD records to store computer data?"

Shing said he did recall the content of the thesis.

"One legitimate product we could produce, at the same time we are producing CD records, is a blank, recordable CD record that can be sold to software vendors to record and distribute their software application programs. The industry calls such a product a CD-R, which stands for 'compact disk recordable memory.'

"According to the trade journals, this market is just now developing, and major software suppliers are going to need very high quantities of such CD-Rs. The beauty of this product is that we are selling blank CD records, so we have no copying issues to deal with. Also, there are only a handful of customers for CD-Rs, so the cost of distribution should be quite low."

"Do we know how to make CD-Rs?" asked Shing.

"Yes, we sure do. I started a small project last spring to try out some of the ideas described in my thesis, and I've been able to produce what I believe to be the most defect-free CD-Rs available anywhere in the world.

"You need to understand that there cannot be any discernible defects in the software computers run, so CD-Rs of extremely high quality are required. I believe I have developed a process for producing such high quality CD-Rs."

"What you are saying is that while we enter the record market with our pirated CD records, we can simultaneously announce to the world that China can produce defect-free CD-Rs. We can establish a world-class reputation for providing high quality CD-Rs."

"That's right," CT said.

"What price are people willing to pay for CD-Rs?"

"My understanding is that the current price is about the same as for CD records, but remember these are blank, so our factory cost will be somewhat lower than for our CD records. Also, any blank CD-Rs that don't pass our outgoing quality inspection can be easily diverted for use in our CD record production line. We will achieve virtually one hundred percent yield overall."

"Ah, CT, again you have made my day," Shing said, grasping CT's hand and shaking it vigorously. "By the way, I've been wanting to tell you something that I have in store for you in the future, if you continue to perform well. Once we are in volume production and are bringing in a tidy profit from this enterprise, I plan to promote you to managing director of this plant. When that happens, I can close my office here and return to Beijing on a full-time basis. That will allow me to spend more time on other matters demanding my attention. So, CT, what do you think of that?"

"Ah, Shing, I'm so glad you have such a trust in me. I will do everything I can to not let you down."

The two of them bowed and hugged each other. Shing gathered his papers and asked his secretary to arrange for his return trip to Beijing.

Chapter Eight

When Friday morning arrived, both Shing and Kong's secretaries were scurrying around their offices making copies of presentation material. There were the usual last-minute changes, accompanied by hasty phone calls to staff members to clarify data. The meeting was scheduled for 9:00 A.M. sharp, so at 8:45 both Shing and Kong left their offices loaded down with paper, notes, and Vue Foil transparencies. They were as ready as they were ever going to be for this all-important meeting with the president.

When Keung sent out his meeting notice, he failed to tell either of them whom he wanted to hear from first, so both men prepared scenarios of how they would behave and what they would say, depending on whether they were first or second on the podium. It seemed logical to Shing that Kong would be asked first to define the size of the market and to indicate how many he could sell. It was just as logical to Kong that Keung would want to first find out how many records could be made in the shiny new plant in Haikou and what each record was going to cost.

Shing and Kong arrived at Keung's mahogany-paneled conference room at about the same time, and they exchanged pleasantries as they took their seats on opposite sides of the magnificent forty-foot conference table. Already seated at the table were the usual cast of staff lieutenants who always attended such meetings. Some were merely note takers, while others were there to provide Keung with any information he might need. They looked up and nodded at Shing and Kong and continued to shuffle their papers to look important.

The Year of The Tiger

The conference room was at least sixty-feet long and forty-feet wide. Hanging on the walls were portraits of past Chinese emperors, chairmen, and other important dignitaries from timeless ages. In addition, prominent among the portraits was the portrait of the aging Deng Xiaoping, who had done so much for the Chinese Republic to turn it into a market economy. At the far end of the room, opposite the entrance, the wall was covered with beautiful silk curtains containing gold inlaid art forms depicting the various Chinese rulers, dating back to the days of the Crusades. Behind these curtains was an enormous projection screen, which would be used during the meeting to project the data Kong and Shing brought with them.

"Shing, it looks like you win. Your pile of papers is twice as thick as mine," Kong said loudly, so all in the room could hear him. He surveyed the room while he showed off his famous gold-plated toothy grin.

"Kong, I always need twice as much data in order to keep up with you," Shing responded. The others at the table chuckled, for they were well aware of the combative relationship between these two ministry chiefs.

At 9:00 A.M. sharp, the double doors at the back of the room opened, and the Chinese president, Keung Fu Huang, entered, along with his secretary, who was always at his side at important meetings. All parties in the room rose to their feet and bowed.

"Everyone, please sit down," he said. Keung remained standing at the end of the table, preparing to make some opening remarks, as was often his custom. He shuffled through his notes and began to speak.

"Before we start this important meeting, I wish to place this event into its proper historical context. Our plant in Haikou used to produce many millions of LP records, which were sold mostly to the Eastern Bloc countries after World War II. I don't have to remind you those sales generated quite a large profit for China. In fact, those profits made it possible for China to update its aging military technology. Now no one in the world can say China lacks the kind of weaponry necessary to deal swiftly and decisively with any country that threatens to make trouble for our peoples.

"Alas, technology has advanced and LP records are no longer salable, as a result of the development of the compact disk. When our sales of LPs dropped significantly, we started a joint development program with the Russians to develop the means for producing CD records in high quantities, but that effort ended as a failure two years ago. I blame the Russians mostly for such a fiasco. Unfortunately, we spent millions before we decided the program was never going to succeed.

"Fortunately, Shing Ling, my minister of technology and production, never gave up. He hired a bright young man from our technical school last year to develop the required production processes, so now we have one of the world's finest facilities ready to produce many millions of CD records. Soon, the plant in Haikou will once again generate enormous profits, which can be plowed back into our economy.

"I greatly appreciate all of the work Shing and Kong and their staffs have put into the presentations we are going to hear today. I can't remember the last time I saw so much paper brought to such a meeting. Because I was so anxious to hear more about this subject, I moved up the date for this meeting so we could approve the plan for entering the market within a few short weeks. I hope you gentlemen did not lose too much sleep getting ready for me. Now, who wants to go first? Shing and Kong stared straight ahead avoiding eye contact with Keung.

"Since neither of you raised your hand, I shall call on Kong first, for I recently visited the new plant in Haikou, and I'm sure we can make all the records we can sell. Kong, why don't you tell us how many that will be?"

Kong was surprised he was being asked to be the kickoff speaker this morning, but he was ready. He rose from his seat and carried a large folder with him to the podium. He gave a set of Vue Foil transparencies to the projectionist, who disappeared behind the translucent screen at the end of the room. When Kong arrived at the podium, he pressed a button and the curtains gave way, exposing a large screen. His first slide appeared, which was entitled, "CD Records Five Year Sales and Marketing Plan, 1991 to 1996."

Kong turned to his audience and thanked them for coming to the meeting. He then spent a few minutes acknowledging all the work his staff had done providing him with the information he was going to present to them.

He then turned to Shing, and said, "Before I present my numbers, I believe it is appropriate for Shing and I to comment regarding one of the basic assumptions we both have used in our presentations. We have assumed if we are to make the kind of impact we wish to make in this market, Chinese CD records must include most popular recording artists singing or playing most of the popular songs. Don't you agree, Shing?"

Shing nodded his agreement, so Kong continued.

"If you recall, Keung, when we sold LP records to the Eastern Bloc countries, we basically had a captive audience, and the consumers in those countries did not care who the recording artists were, since they had been starved for such entertainment for so many years.

"Ah, Keung, but things are far different now, for CD records containing songs by all of the popular recording artists can be purchased in most cities of the world. We have concluded that we too must be able to offer such records as well."

"Excuse me, Kong," Keung interrupted. "Won't that cost an inordinate amount of money to sign up all of the world's recording talent? Are you really serious?" he asked, with a growing frown on his face.

"Shing and I have discussed this matter at length, and I've held a number of meetings with my staff as well. Try as we may, we have not been able to come up with an alternative plan that makes any sense for us. Yes, we are quite serious on this matter. We need to be able to sell CD records containing virtually all of the popular recording stars singing or playing popular songs.

"Ah, Keung, please accept our assumptions for now. No doubt we will need to discuss this matter further. However, for the remainder of my presentation, please assume we have for sale virtually any CD record from any recording artist currently on the popularity charts."

"Okay, but I have a very uneasy feeling about such an assumption. We will definitely need to discuss this matter at length after you and Shing are finished," Keung said emphatically.

As Kong began his talk, the various staff persons at the table looked at each other and small frowns began to appear on their faces. They wanted the president to see that they too were concerned with the assumption, even though they probably didn't know it's full implications.

Kong was an eloquent speaker. He had a knack for presenting ideas and numbers in a way that made sense, even if the audience had no real appreciation for the subject being discussed. Shing had to admit to himself that Kong was head and shoulders better than himself when it came to making presentations. Shing rationalized that this was why Kong was in charge of marketing and sales, and why he was in charge of production and technology.

Kong spent the next hour defining the size of the CD record market, breaking it down geographically, and using data going back five years to show trends up to the current time. He then presented a forecast for what he believed the future five years would produce in the way of sales opportunities for China.

For the data covering the past five years, he used actual historical data provided by his staff. However, for the future forecast, he boosted his staff's data by twenty-five percent in order to get Keung's attention. He knew Keung wanted to believe the opportunity for Chinese CD record sales was enormous, so he reasoned, why not make it really big?

The next subject to be covered was pricing, which had to be presented very carefully. Kong was glad his staff had come up with the idea of using a particular market, like South America, to experiment with prices, for there was no way to prove empirically to Keung that a given price level would achieve a specific level of market penetration. About all he could say was that if you drop the price low enough, you will sell a lot of records, but he wanted to be able to show he had given more thought to the subject than that.

Kong spent fifteen minutes discussing what Tak discovered about how prices were established in this market, and he could see Keung was listening very attentively. Kong then introduced what he called a two-pronged marketing and sales plan. First, China would set up an aggressive sales channel in South America and would initially start taking business at prices thirty-five percent below the prevailing price in that market. Meanwhile, in the rest of the world markets, he recommended dropping prices to only ten percent below prevailing prices to flush out the price fixers. He believed that this strategy would work fine for the first six months of product delivery, but it would be necessary to ratchet the prices down again to continue to increase Chinese market share. For the second six months, he recommended dropping the prices in South America an additional ten percent and an additional ten percent in the rest of the world as well.

His strategy for the second year of production was to offer Chinese CD records to customers in all of the world markets at the same prices they used to pay for LPs. He argued that by doing so,

China would be able to take more than seventy percent of the market by the end of the second year.

"So, in conclusion, gentlemen," Kong said, "there is no sure way to be able to predict precisely how much of the market we can acquire by adopting the pricing strategy I've presented to you this morning. However, by using South America as an experimental market zone, we will be able to see how elastic the market is for our CDs. We can then apply the proper pricing strategy to the rest of the world markets to achieve our goals.

"I recognize the low prices I'm recommending will cause my friend, Shing, to spend many hours working on ways to reduce the cost of the product, but I'm sure he's up to the task, for after all, he recently received the Chinese Medal of Honor," Kong added sarcastically.

"Perhaps when he stands to give his presentation, it would be appropriate if we all recognized his important achievement by giving him a big hand," Kong said, with a big smile. Kong hoped this little bit of theatrics would embarrass Shing, especially since Kong believed Shing would have to admit in front of Keung and his staff that there was no way he could make much money if the prices had to be so low.

Keung interrupted Kong at this point. "Kong, I understand what you are recommending, but I'm not sure why you believe you have to sell Chinese CD records at such low prices. I haven't seen Shing's numbers, but I'm concerned we may not make much profit from this enterprise if we have to sell the records at such a low price level."

"Ah, Keung, you told me you wanted to own more than seventy percent of this market within a few short years. Isn't that right, sir?"

"Yes, that is correct."

"Then let me show you my commitment slide," Kong said.

Kong asked the projectionist to present his last slide, which showed various volume commitments he and his sales managers were willing to sign up to, as a function of various pricing approval levels.

"My staff and I believe in these levels, and we will not drop prices any lower than we find necessary to achieve them. However, we believe we need to have your authority to drop to very low prices if we find the sales levels do not materialize as we predict in the future."

All eyes were on Keung at this point, for they knew he wanted very badly to own the market for CD records. Keung turned to Shing and said, "Shing, we haven't heard from you yet, but can we make any money if Kong has to drop the prices to such low levels?"

Shing was trying hard to contain his excitement at this moment, for he realized Kong had over-committed himself well beyond what he really believed, hoping Keung would select a less aggressive market share goal, once he heard the cost of the records.

"Keung, as you will soon hear from me, my plant can make a very high profit, even if we have to sell our CD records at the low prices Kong has recommended. I want to congratulate Kong and his staff for preparing such an aggressive plan. We are proud to be a part of this team that will place China ahead of all other suppliers of CD records in the world."

The room became so quiet you could hear a pin drop. All eyes were on Kong, who was noticeably shaken by Shing's comment. Shing had called his bluff, and they all knew it. All Kong could think of was wringing the neck of his cousin who worked in the Haikou accounting department.

"Damn, I've committed myself to Keung for an impossible sales plan," he thought to himself. "My staff will think I'm a fool."

Keung seized the moment. "Shing, that is great news. We should now take a ten-minute break to allow you time to prepare your material."

Keung turned to Kong, who tried not to look directly at him. "Kong, assuming Shing's cost data is correct, I'm granting you the authority to proceed with your aggressive pricing plan. I like your initial two-pronged approach, and once China is established in the market, you have my blessing to proceed to price the product extremely low to gain market share."

The attendees stood up and headed for the restrooms. On the way out, Kong came up to Shing and put his arm on his shoulder as if they were big buddies.

"So, what rabbit did you pull out of your hat to get your costs so low? The last time we spoke, you seemed sure your costs would be about the same as my prices," Kong said, sounding skeptical.

"I told you we should have met prior to this meeting," Shing said, smiling as he walked toward his office to make a few last-minute phone calls. He had clearly won the first round.

When the meeting resumed, all participants were seated before Keung made his ceremonious entrance. All stood up and bowed and Keung once again told them to be seated. He smiled graciously at Shing and asked him to proceed with his presentation.

Shing started his talk by showing pictures of the Haikou plant when it first began to produce LP records. He next showed recent pictures of the plant equipped to make CD records. He presented a block diagram, depicting the various processes required to produce CDs, and for each block he showed a picture of an actual piece of production apparatus, so the audience could better grasp what was involved in the manufacture of CD records.

Shing was feeling very relaxed during this portion of his presentation, and he noted the audience was enjoying the background information, for they now had a better feel for the subject. After about half an hour of such material, Shing began showing slides containing production quantity projections. The data proved that Shing had both the space and the equipment necessary to exceed the first-year quantity plan Kong had committed himself to sell. He showed which equipment would limit the production volume in the second year and summarized the cost of adding additional apparatus.

Keung interrupted Shing at this point and said, "Shing, you have my authority to purchase any equipment you require in the second year of production, if such equipment is needed to keep up with the demand of the sales department. All you need to do is submit the necessary forms to me when the time comes."

Shing thanked him and continued with his talk, which now covered the cost projections for CD records made in Haikou. Before the meeting, Shing talked at length with his accounting manager to see if he would accept the concept of using a ten-year write-off for the equipment; the accounting manager found no flaw in the logic. So, as Shing outlined the various elements of cost, he used the longer time period, without drawing undue attention to it.

He watched Keung's eyes very carefully when he covered this material, and there was no hint of concern on Keung's part about any of his cost assumptions. In fact, he could tell Keung trusted him implicitly and was probably already thinking about becoming king of the mountain in the CD record business. He watched Kong's eyes, but apparently Kong was adequately snowed, for he did not even raise an eyebrow during this critical part of his presentation.

Shing's talk took about an hour and a half, including some relatively minor questions from the floor. When he concluded, Keung looked at his watch and said the group should break for lunch, which was set up for them in the main cafeteria. He said he would like to continue the meeting in one hour, for he wanted to return to the discussion regarding recording artists and popular record labels.

Kong said he had some important things to attend to, so he excused himself from the luncheon and hurried to his office. He immediately phoned his cousin.

"Mau, would you please tell me what is going on?"

"What do you mean, Kong?" Mau answered, sounding bewildered.

"Last week you gave me some cost figures, and today Shing has presented figures that are one-half of those. How can that be?"

"I don't know what you're talking about, Kong."

"Don't you work in the cost accounting department in the new Haikou plant?"

"Of course I do. You say he presented figures half of what I told you. That is impossible. He must be lying, or he must be very stupid."

"Well, the man is not stupid, and he would never discuss such low figures with Keung and his staff unless he knew how he planned to achieve them. Don't you agree?"

"That seems right. Let me see if I can find out something. I'm looking at the latest cost report from last week, and there is nothing to indicate the numbers have changed."

"You find out what happened. Do you understand me?" Kong screamed.

"Yes, Kong, but take it easy. You sound like things did not go well for you today."

"That is an understatement. I was counting on your figures being correct, and obviously they were not."

Kong slammed down the phone and closed his eyes. He had really screwed up, for now he was committed in front of Keung and his entire staff to sell enormous quantities of CD records. He wondered how he was going to broach this news to his sales and marketing staffs, who would no doubt think he was a total idiot for committing to such a difficult program.

After lunch, Keung began, "Gentlemen, tell me again about this business of having to copy all or at least most of the popular labels being offered by our competitors. Shing, why don't you tell me your understanding of the matter? We already have Kong's views."

"As I understand it, the current suppliers of CD records pay top performers or groups lots of money to get them to record songs for them. In addition, these performers receive a percentage of each record sold, which can be as high as ten percent if their record is on the top-ten list, and at least five percent as long as the record is selling reasonably well."

"Why don't we offer to pay the performers five percent of our sales price? Your cost figures would permit us that latitude and we would still make a good profit. Couldn't we?"

"That sounds logical, except for the fact that all of the current CD record companies have signed contracts that preclude the artists from recording for any other company. This means any new supplier is forced to find and negotiate deals with artists who are between contracts. That is very expensive and can take several months.

"As a consequence, when Kong and I discussed this matter, we both came to the same conclusion that the only way for China to enter the CD record market aggressively was to copy all of the popular records and to sell them considerably cheaper than the originals."

"Won't the sound quality of copies be poorer than the sound quality of the originals?"

"Not at all. These are digital records. My staff has come up with a means for rapidly copying records, storing the digital signals in a computer, and preparing high-quality production masters for use on the production floor. The system has been worked out, and I listened to a copy yesterday of extremely high quality."

Keung turned to one of his staff members sitting at the table and asked him what he thought the legal ramifications might be if China were to copy records on a wholesale basis, as was being suggested.

"Ah, Keung, I believe world opinion will be very negative, but on the other hand, customers for such records will be very happy! Such an action will no doubt set off a worldwide price war, as Kong has suggested.

"China's copyright law was put into effect in June of this year. Its purpose is to protect Chinese authors from having their manuscripts copied by other Chinese authors. However, it doesn't deal specifically with the issue of copying records or software.

"According to communiqués I have received from our Swiss ambassador, I understand China is currently being pressured to join the Berne Copyright Convention, which has been formed to address the issue of copyright protection of intellectual property between nations. No doubt some of the issues that will be dealt with by such a world body will be the copyright protection of records and computer software, as well as books."

"But we have not yet joined such an organization," said Keung. "Isn't that correct?"

"No, we haven't, and I see no legal reason we necessarily need to do so," his advisor said.

"So, does this mean we have no international legal problem here?"

"That's right, Keung. We have no international legal problem."

Kong interrupted the conversation. "My staff and I believe if we concentrate our initial low price thrust in South America, there will be less flak, because those people have almost no scruples and, if anything, the local press will probably cheer us on because of our low prices."

"But, Kong, the recording artists and the companies they have contracts with will be very unhappy with us, don't you think?" Keung insisted. With a growing concern in his voice, he said, "Gentlemen, I now understand the dilemma we have. If we take the position we are not going to pay any royalties or fees to the recording artists, and if we copy our competitor's records and undersell those same competitors in the market, there may be an enormous outcry from various world trade organizations, no matter what our legal position is. And yet, I'm not about to sit around and wait while we negotiate ridiculous fees with recording artists," Keung said, pounding his fist on the table for added effect.

"It's about time China showed the rest of the world enough is enough. The recording industry needs to be shaken up and we are just the ones to do it!" Keung shouted so loudly the room echoed his response.

Kong began to smile for the first time since Shing dropped his cost bomb on him just before lunch. It appeared Keung was going to let his sales staffs have their own way in the market. This was great news!

"However, gentlemen, I do wish we had some legitimate products for the Haikou plant to produce. Isn't there something we can make which we do not have to copy? It would make our case stronger with the world if we had a product or two that the world requires, but which we alone can provide. Do any of you have any ideas?"

"Ah, Keung, I know of one such product," Shing said. "What I'm about to propose has not been run by Kong yet, because we did not have time to meet this week, but I have a product that I believe will take the sting out of world opinion."

"Tell us what it is," Keung said, with a growing smile on his face.

"Besides the very large market for CD records, which Kong has so eloquently defined for us, there is another market for CDs that is just now starting to form. That market is the multimedia personal computer market, which will require large quantities of CDs containing software programs, rather than music. They are called CD-Rs."

"Oh, now you want us to copy Microsoft programs as well as record music," Kong blurted out. "How is that going to take the sting out of world opinion?"

"Please let Shing continue," Keung said, glaring at Kong.

"Thank you, Keung," Shing said, also glaring at Kong.

"My chief technologist, Choi Tang, whom you recently met, has been working on a product he calls a recordable CD-R. These could be sold in high quantities as blank CD-Rs to major software developers like Microsoft, Lotus, Corel, Oracle, and Borland."

"Why do these software companies need to buy blank CD-Rs?" asked Keung.

"They would use them to record the personal computer programs they develop; then they would sell them to personal computer owners who have CD players installed in their computers. By 1996, it is predicted that more than eighty percent of the personal computers being sold in the world will be equipped with CD players.

"And I want to underscore one thing," Shing added. "If we were to provide such products, we do not have to record anything on these records before they are sold. Rather, we sell blank CD-Rs. The software developers use the blank CD-Rs to record their own proprietary software."

"Are there many suppliers currently providing this form of CD?"

"Choi Tang tells me there are not very many suppliers who have the ability to make CD-Rs for this market. He believes he has the process for doing that. If that were so, China could openly enter this market, and in addition we could place ads in important trade journals telling the world we are in a unique technical position to offer high-quality CD-Rs for computer applications."

"In other words, we could take the high road with such a product line, while we pursue the low road with the CD records," Keung said excitedly. "I like the idea. What do you think of it, Kong?"

"Well, as Shing said, he and I have not discussed this before this moment. I would like my marketing staff to review the market size for CD-Rs. I suppose if the market is there, and if we know how to make them, then what the hell? We should be able to sell quite a few," he said, avoiding a full endorsement of the idea.

"Kong, when you review this market you should have your staff examine the incremental selling expenses required. Choi believes such expenses should be very low, for the list of customers for blank CD-Rs is probably less than ten major software developers," Shing added.

"What about our cost for such a form of CD?" asked Keung. "And does Choi Tang have an opinion about the prevailing prices today?"

"Our cost will be substantially the same as the CDs we make for records. This is because if we find a batch that does not pass our stringent defect-screening test, we can divert those to be used on the production line making records. As a consequence, we will achieve virtually one hundred percent yield. Choi believes the prices for CD-Rs of computer quality are about fifty percent higher than for CD records. No doubt as the volume builds and more vendors come on the scene, we should assume they will be sold for about the same price as the world now pays for CD records. However, there will be no reason to have this product fall into the same price war category as the records we make."

By this point Kong had calmed down, for he actually liked the idea of this product. After all, it was another product to sell, and he knew he would need all the sales he could get, and it really was a product that could take the high road, while he and his sales personnel figured out how to undercut the CD record market without stirring up world opinion too much.

"I want to thank my friend, Shing, for this wonderful new product idea," Kong said genuinely, as he stood up and shook Shing's hand.

"Would it be all right if I send Tak to your plant next week to discuss the product with Choi Tang? Does he have any units he can show Tak?"

"It would be great if you set up such a meeting," Shing said. "And, yes, Choi has some units he has produced. He will be glad to show Tak how they are used to load programs onto personal computers equipped with CD players."

Keung was pleased his two ministry chiefs seemed to be working in harmony again. He was glad the plan for CD production would include not only a legitimate product, but also quite possibly a product that not many other vendors knew how to make. This could be a definite feather in China's cap.

"Gentlemen, the meeting is adjourned. Please submit your final plans to me no later than one week from today. I want to again thank both Kong and Shing for their fine presentations. I feel we will succeed greatly in this market."

Keung turned to one of his staff and told him to authorize Kong the budget he needed to launch the product program for CD records and for the blank CD-Rs, as soon as Kong provided him with the financial details.

"Gentlemen, don't just stand there. Start selling CDs," he said, grinning from ear to ear. His staff clapped politely. China was about to become a major factor in the CD market.

Chapter Nine

Kong moved quickly once his sales and marketing budget received final approval from Keung's staff. He managed to convince his own staff he was not a fool, but rather a brilliant tactician, when he committed to such large sales numbers. His position was enhanced when Tak informed him the market size for recordable blank CD-Rs could be as large as fifty percent of the record market in a few years, especially since China had a high-quality product for sale, and there were few suppliers.

Kong sent an advance man to South America to visit all of the major CD record distributors. He returned with a list of seventy-five different labels, which would cover more than ninety percent of the current demand. Within a week, the Haikou plant received a box full of these records with instructions to proceed to make production masters and start the production wheels turning. The system Miu developed worked without a hitch, and soon CDs were moving down the line into the packing and shipping area. Employee morale in Haikou was now very high.

The brand name Kong suggested for the records was DragonFly, but China would not be mentioned on the label. The name of each record selection was embossed on the label in bright red letters surrounded by gold, while the name of the recording artist was less prominently printed in small green letters underneath the DragonFly brand name.

Kong set up a dummy corporation in Hong Kong, which he called K&S Industries (for "Kong and Shing"). K&S Industries was located in a large warehouse on the wharf, and it consisted of a small order-entry department, as well as a number of warehouse and shipping personnel. All DragonFly records would be sold from K&S Industries, thus hiding the actual source of the records from the public.

CT and Shing were impressed with the look of the final product as it arrived in the shipping area ready for delivery to the K&S warehouse. Kong and Shing agreed no one in the Haikou Plant would need to know the final destination of the records, so all shipments were always made directly to the K&S warehouse address in Hong Kong.

"How are initial sales?" Keung asked Kong over the phone. It was only three months since the product launch, and Keung was interested in finding out whether the South Americans were buying records from China yet.

"We are already ahead of our plan," Kong said proudly. "My man in South America managed to book initial orders from all of the major record distributors, and now that they fully appreciate our low prices, repeat orders have started to flow in. We were correct in our assessment that customers would not care if they were buying copies, so long as the quality is good and the price is right."

"Maybe we should have entered the market with a higher price," Keung jested.

"Ah, Keung, you wanted market share. Don't you remember?"

"I know," Keung laughed. "Have we received any flak yet from the recording artist community or from our competitors?"

"None whatsoever, which again tells me we did the right thing starting our program in a relatively obscure part of the world market. By the way, Keung, do you have a CD player at home? We want to send you some samples from our first production run."

"Yes, please send my wife and me one of each of the major labels. I'm sure we will enjoy them as we dine."

"Fine. I'll see to it immediately," Kong said.

"Keep me posted. When do you start to deliver into the other world markets? I think your plan stated you would start that program within three months of the South American product launch. Is that about right?"

"Yes, my North American man has already acquired a list of the most popular labels, and we are rounding up those records for our plant to copy. It looks like we will need to copy more than four hundred different labels to serve that market well. That should keep the boys in Haikou busy," he grinned.

"Load them up, if it's what you need," Keung said. "I spoke with Shing today, and he said plant morale is very high. They will welcome more business."

"Okay. I'll send off the box of records next week to have masters made. We'll enter the North American market as soon as we have sufficient inventory. After we start taking business there, we will enter the European market, which requires the same mix of labels, plus a few special labels for their market."

"Sounds like you have things under control. So long and have a good day," Keung said, feeling very exhilarated.

"Good-bye. I'll keep you posted," Kong added, feeling really good about how things were progressing.

"Let's sit down and finish our meeting," the moderator said, speaking to the ad hoc Committee on Copyright Infringement Policy, which was a subcommittee of the International Federation of the Phonographic Industry (IFPI) Organization, which was meeting in Los Angeles. "Does anyone have any new business to bring up at this time?" he asked.

"I do," said Laura Robinson, an attorney who represented many of the most famous country-western recording artists, including Dolly Parton, Kenny Rogers, Barbara Mandrel, and Crystal Gayle. "It's been brought to my attention that there is a flood of illegally copied CD records being sold into South America at low prices under the DragonFly label. Have any of you heard about that?"

"Which labels are included?" someone asked.

"My sources tell me the DragonFly records include almost all of the most popular labels currently being sold in the South American countries, and all of the major record distributors are starting to place orders.

"At what prices?"

"They are being offered at a thirty-five percent discount!" Laura said.

The moderator stood up when he heard that, and took over the meeting again.

"Don't the distributors have exclusive deals with their current legitimate suppliers?"

"Of course they do," Laura said. "However, in South America, such contracts are often ignored. Money there talks louder than contract obligations."

"We need to assign someone to look into this more thoroughly," the moderator said. "Is there anyone among you who has the time to investigate this situation?"

Laura stood up and told the group there was an investigative attorney in her office that she could assign to the task immediately. "I'll even foot the bill, for a number of my clients are being affected here," she added.

"Can I have a motion to the effect so Laura can proceed to investigate this matter?"

"I'll so move," said one member of the panel.

"And I'll second the motion," said another.

"It's been moved and seconded that you should acquire the services of your investigative attorney to find out more about this matter. You are authorized to proceed immediately. When do you think you can have a preliminary report for all of us to review?" the moderator asked.

"I think it will take about two weeks to contact all of the distributors and find out what's going on. When I'm ready with my findings, I'll ask you to call a special meeting of this group," Laura answered.

"Is there any other outstanding business?" asked the moderator. Seeing no hands, he adjourned the meeting.

It took the plant in Haikou about two weeks to prepare masters for all four hundred of the labels required to serve the North American market. Armed with a preliminary sales forecast provided by Kong, Shing ordered the plant to commence production of large quantities of records with the new labels, to be shipped to K&S Industries, where they would await new orders from the North American distributors.

Kong's North American sales team also contacted major software developers and provided them with samples of recordable CD-Rs for computer applications. With this product, Kong was taking the high road; the boxes that supplied CD-Rs were stamped "Made in China" in large, bold print, and were shipped directly from one of Kong's warehouses in Beijing, rather than via the K&S Industries warehouse in Hong Kong.

The response for CD-Rs from personal computer software developers was amazing. CT correctly anticipated his product would be freer from defects than similar products being provided from other suppliers. So, in addition to the increased production of records bound for North America, the Haikou plant found it necessary to add a second shift to produce CD-Rs, for the orders were flowing in at an increasing rate.

Since Kong was ahead of his sales commitments for CD records in South America, he shifted priorities and asked Shing to produce greater quantities of CD-Rs for immediate shipment to his Beijing warehouse. He then requested a slow-down of the production of records for shipment to the K&S Industries warehouse for the North American market, since he decided to delay the entry into that market by a couple of months.

Coincident with the delivery of CD-Rs, Keung authorized a number of ads that were placed in all of the appropriate world journals. These ads told how China's new high-quality CD production line in Haikou was "dedicated" to the manufacture of recordable CD-Rs for personal computer applications. Keung sincerely hoped such ads would help China gain credibility in the market before they entered the North American CD record market in a big way, selling DragonFly records at deeply discounted prices.

CT showed the ad to Miu and said, "Now the battle begins."

"What do you mean?" she asked.

"China wants the world to believe our primary mission is to provide very high-quality recordable CD-Rs to support the needs of the personal computer markets. We will of course not admit in such ads that we also plan to copy virtually every record label being sold by our many competitors."

"Have there been any complaints from anyone so far?" she asked.

"No, and that's rather puzzling," CT said. "We have already sold tens of thousands of records, and no one has said anything. Maybe our worst fears will not materialize."

"I still think we are doing something illegal," Miu stated with a worried look on her face.

"So do I, but I just do what I'm told," CT added jovially. "I can sleep better, though, because we are beginning now to sell many high-quality recordable CD-Rs."

"So can I," she said. "I would hate to think that I married a pirate. Aren't record pirates what you said the world would call us, if they find out what we are doing?"

"Ahoy, mate. I'll make you walk the plank if you ever accuse me again of being a pirate," he joked, as he pretended to have a saber in one hand, jabbing her with it.

"Enough of this business stuff. Let's pick up where we left off. Let's see, I was about to join you in bed after I turn off the lights. What happens next?" Miu asked.

Laura Robinson finished reading the report her associate had prepared for her. The situation was far more serious than she initially thought. More than seventy-five labels had been copied, the quality of the records was reported to be excellent, and the prices being quoted to the record distributors were in fact thirty-five percent lower than the prevailing market prices in South America, as quoted from other suppliers.

Laura asked her associate if the distributors had any loyalty to their current suppliers.

"Are you kidding? Loyalty in South America belongs to the lowest bidder."

"Aren't the other suppliers unhappy?"

"According to the distributors, the market size of South America is rather small in comparison with the rest of the world, so the complaints are currently only at the lower levels of their sales organizations."

"How many records have been sold under the DragonFly label so far?"

"More than twenty thousand, and the orders are increasing daily. The consumers are all delighted, for now they can buy CDs for only slightly more than they used to pay for LPs a few years ago.

"I think the distributors would be happy if DragonFly would take over all of the business. They all believe the volume sold would increase two-fold, and they would actually make more money."

Laura had enough information. She called the moderator of the IFPI subcommittee and asked him to set up an emergency meeting, which he did. At the meeting, she provided each attendee with a copy of her report. They were all aghast at the implications.

"Who produces the DragonFly records and where are they being shipped from?" someone asked.

"We aren't sure who the real producer is, but the company that ships them is a Hong Kong firm named K&S Industries. It's probably a front organization for the real record pirates," she added.

The moderator stood up and said, "Our obligation as the Subcommittee on Copyright Infringement Policy is to prepare our recommendations and submit them to our parent organization immediately. Laura, can you please do that in the next few days?"

"Of course, but don't we also want to let the U.S. Commerce Department know about this? It seems to me that it is only a matter of time before we will see DragonFly records for sale in record stores in every major mall in the U.S."

"Laura, we must follow procedures here," said the moderator. "First we have to make our report and let our parent organization discuss the matter further. The IFPI General Committee is the organization who would let the Commerce Department know, if they feel it is warranted."

"Well, I for one am really concerned," Laura said. "The K&S Industries outfit could really do a lot of damage to the record industry if they are not stopped soon."

"I understand your feelings," the moderator said. "However, we must follow the procedures handed down to us by our parent organization. So please get your report in shape and send it to me for my official submittal."

He then adjourned the meeting, leaving Laura very frustrated.

Chapter Ten

By January 1992, production at the Haikou Plant was in full swing. Chinese-made CD record sales continued to increase, as the pricing strategy was working in South America, and it hadn't been necessary to enter the North American or European markets to meet the 1991 startup plan.

However, the sales plan for 1992 called for dramatic increases in sales volume, so Kong decided it was time for his sales representatives to approach the major record distributors in North America and Europe for initial stocking orders.

"The distributors don't seem to want to do business with us, at least not for the ten percent discount we are offering them," Kong's sales team reported back.

"They don't want to piss off their current suppliers. We think we're going to have more difficulty entering this market than we thought. They are also asking us a lot of questions about how we have access to all of the popular labels."

"I was afraid of that," Kong replied. "Let's meet on this tomorrow morning and decide what we should do."

Kong's worst fears had come back to haunt him. His experience had taught him it is often quite difficult to enter an established market, no matter what price advantage you offer your customers. They were quite fortunate to have made immediate inroads into South America, but it appeared the North American market was going to be much more difficult to break into.

"Gentlemen, we have a serious problem," Kong said, when he met with his sales and marketing staffs. "We have met our 1991 sales plan, which was certainly aggressive, but now we face a much steeper ramp in 1992. Built into our 1992 assumptions are sizable sales from the North American and European markets. Without those, we will not accomplish our plan for growth.

"Peng, would you please brief us on what you discovered when you approached the North American distributors?" Kong asked his head of sales for North America.

"Of course," answered Peng. "We sent samples of our DragonFly product to all of the major distributors. We also sent them an introductory price offer, which amounted to a ten percent discount from the prices they currently pay their other suppliers.

"Personnel at K&S Industries followed up by telephone to see if they would place initial orders. To our amazement, not a single distributor showed any interest. Most said they had ample supply. Some said they had to honor their current agreements with other suppliers, and all asked who we were and how we had access to all of the popular labels."

"Have you personally followed up with any of these distributors?" Kong asked.

"Yes. I even went to Hong Kong to visit one of the biggest distributors who represents the Sony label. I know quite a few people there, so I invited some of my friends to lunch. I showed them some of our DragonFly product and again offered them the ten percent discount price. After listening politely to me, they said they were not interested in getting involved with what seemed to them to be a record piracy operation!"

"Did you ask your friends if a lower price would increase their interest?"

"Yes, I did. I even suggested that by 1993, DragonFly records would be selling for the same prices LP records used to sell for, which would be equivalent to a forty percent discount from today's prices."

"And what did they say to that?"

"They said I should come back in 1993 and invite them to lunch again."

"So what do you think they were really trying to tell you?" Kong asked.

"I think these guys are very loyal to their current suppliers. They don't want to do anything to cause them to lose their franchises."

"Do you think it would make any difference if we offered them an immediate fifty percent discount?" Kong asked.

"I don't believe it would, at least not initially. No doubt if we keep badgering them, we might get some of the distributors to buy some quantity from us to see if we are really serious, but we won't get anywhere near the quantity of sales we need to meet the 1992 plan."

"Does anyone in this room have any ideas?" Kong asked. "You can see this represents a very serious problem for us. There has to be some other way we can enter the North American market. We all know from our South American experience that customers like the product and they like the prices. The difference is the South American distributors are more loyal to money than to supplier relationships."

Tak, Kong's marketing director, held up his hand.

"Yes, Tak, what is it?" asked Kong.

"Why do we have to enter the market in North America through the established distributors? Can't we somehow reach over them and entice the major record sales chains to buy directly from us?"

"Tak, I've been looking into that possibility as well," Peng said. "It might work in selected markets, for example in some of the U.S. super malls, but I don't think it will work universally."

"I think you guys may be onto something," Kong said. "What if we tried to enter a narrow slice of the U.S. market through just a few super mall stores to get the ball rolling? It would seem to me that once we penetrated a few stores, the other distributors would see what was happening to their sales and would want to get on board."

"I have a cousin who is a high level purchasing manager for the Electro-Mart Record Chain in Los Angeles," Fu Ho, the sales manager for Asia, said. "The last time I spoke with him he said his company planned to establish their stores in each of the super malls throughout the U.S. and Canada. He told me that because of the size of these malls, they believe they can capture seventy percent of the U.S. and Canadian CD record market."

"Does he have a high enough level job to be able to convince his company to buy from K&S Industries, or do they also have a fierce loyalty to their current suppliers?"

"I can fax him tonight and give him some background information. He will call me back tomorrow morning."

"Please do that," Kong said. "Gentlemen, I think I'll close this meeting now. Please think about what you have heard. I urge you to provide me with any ideas you have to help us meet our plan."

Kong returned to his office and slumped down on his sofa and closed his eyes. His strategy to enter the North American market, offering only modest discounts, seemed to not be working at all. In addition, from what he heard at the meeting, dropping immediately to deep discounts might not work either.

"We can always sell CD-Rs," he said out loud, smiling wistfully. However, he knew the sales volume for computer software CDs would not even come close to making up for a lack of CD record sales in 1992.

"We really do need to enter the North American CD record market in a big way," he thought, as he dozed off on his sofa with his head spinning, trying to come up with a meaningful plan.

★ ★ ★

"I may have some good news for you," Fu Ho said to Kong over the phone the next morning. "My cousin answered my fax this morning. He tells me a very interesting story, which I need to share with you. Are you busy now? I can come right to your office."

"Yes, please come right away," Kong said, obviously interested in what he was going to hear. Ten minutes later, Fu Ho entered Kong's office. He bowed and closed the door, at Kong's suggestion.

"Ah, Kong, my cousin tells me the Electro-Mart Record Chain is aggressively trying to gain market share in the North American CD record market. As I discussed in yesterday's meeting, one of their strategies is to set up stores in twenty super malls across the U.S. and Canada."

"Fu, you already told me that," Kong said, anxious to hear something new.

"Okay, but he told me something else, which is very important," Fu Ho said excitedly. "He indicated they have made a corporate decision to deal directly with record suppliers, cutting the major record distributors out of the loop. This will allow them to sell their records at lower prices and still make the kind of profit margins they require."

"Has that policy been incorporated yet, and if so, who are their current suppliers?" Kong asked, his interest obviously aroused.

"Yes, it has been incorporated, and my cousin tells me the major distributors are really upset, but there is nothing they can do about it. Since they are breaking their distributor deals, they are now investigating which record suppliers they want to do business with. It seems to me that it is an ideal time for us to introduce ourselves to them."

Kong was way ahead of him. As Fu Ho was speaking, Kong buzzed his secretary to have Peng come to his office immediately. Peng was there in five minutes.

"Fu Ho, would you please tell Peng what you have told me just now."

Fu Ho spent the next ten minutes briefing Peng, who became very interested.

Peng stood up excitedly and said, "I think Fu Ho and I should arrange a meeting with the proper people from Electro-Mart immediately. Don't you agree?"

"Absolutely!"

"Do I have your approval to pay their way to Hong Kong for such a meeting, if necessary?"

"Do whatever it takes to get the right people together. If Electro-Mart represents as much as seventy percent of the North American market, and if we can get at least one-third of their business, we will exceed our plan for 1992," he said excitedly. "Now you two get out of here and make something happen!"

Laura Robinson finished her report and sent it on to the moderator of the IFPI subcommittee to submit to the general chairman of the organization. She hated bureaucracy in general, and in this specific case she really hated it, for as far as she was concerned her report should be causing sanctions of some kind to be happening right now, not at some future date after other people read her findings.

She assigned the investigative lawyer in her office to work on other tasks, and resigned herself that nothing much was going to be done about the DragonFly matter for a couple of months.

The phone on her desk rang, breaking her train of thought. "Hello, this is Laura Robinson. Can I help you?"

"Laura, I understand you are a member of the IFPI Subcommittee on Copyright Infringement Policy. Is that right?" the voice on the other end of the line asked.

"Yes, but who is this?"

"My name is John Bishop, and I'm the West Coast distribution manager for Columbia Records."

"I remember you, John. We once met at one of the new product release shows in Las Vegas. Do you remember meeting me there?"

"Yes, I do. I also receive copies of the meeting notes from the IFPI, and I spotted your name there as well."

"What can I do for you, John?"

"I think I should send you some material my marketing manager recently received. Some outfit in Hong Kong called K&S Industries sent him some sample CD records along with a price sheet indicating they have more than four hundred record titles for immediate delivery at prices that average about ten percent below what we currently pay our suppliers. We played their sample and the quality is excellent. This is obviously not your run-of-the-mill record pirate. This outfit knows how to make good records."

"John, I'm so glad you told me about this."

Laura told him DragonFly record sales were booming in South America, with price levels thirty-five and forty percent below the existing world prices.

"My God, Laura, how did they manage to get the distributors to buy their product?" John asked.

"I think your average South American distributor only has loyalty to the almighty buck. By the way, did you guys place an order with these clowns?"

"No way! We sure didn't," John answered sharply. "We have contracts with our current suppliers, and we don't want to mess around with record pirates. Life is too short for that!"

"Do you know if the K&S guys sent similar samples to all of the other major distributors?"

"I did a spot check, and everyone I spoke with received the same offer."

"Did any of them accept the K&S deal?"

"Not as far as I can tell, but remember these other guys are my competition, so it's possible some of them didn't level with me."

"John, if you could please send me the stuff you received, I'll get on top of this immediately. I have a list of all of the U.S. and Canadian distributors. I'll send them a fax immediately asking them to do likewise. As soon as I get the material, I'll call a special committee meeting to brief the other members. We definitely have a professional record pirate on our hands. We have to find a way to stamp him out before he totally ruins the industry."

"I always remembered you as a person who takes action. That's why I called you," John said. "My secretary will ship the stuff to you via this afternoon's Federal Express. You should have it first thing in the morning. Gotta run now. It's been nice talking with you," John said in closing.

"Thanks again," Laura said as she hung up her phone.

"Now maybe something will happen," she thought to herself as she reviewed her calendar. She decided to wait until she had more information before informing the subcommittee moderator. She called her investigative lawyer and told him to drop the other assignment and get ready to again investigate DragonFly.

Chapter Eleven

Peng Hong and Fu Ho arranged for a meeting to be held in Hong Kong between Electro-Mart and K&S Industries. Fu explained to his cousin that K&S Industries would gladly foot the entire bill for the visiting businessmen, so long as they were in a position to make decisions for their company.

Electro-Mart was founded in 1985 by a group of Taiwanese businessmen. Its chairman and CEO, Mao Chang (Manny) often visited Hong Kong on his way back to his native country. Manny was sympathetic to mainland China's need for increased commerce with the West, so he planned to personally attend this meeting, accompanied by his U.S. sales vice president, George Priest. He insisted, however, that they would pay their own way, for they did not want to be in a position of owing any favors to K&S Industries.

The meeting was scheduled for Saturday morning, 11 January 1992, in a rented suite of offices in downtown Hong Kong. Manny and George arrived the previous day and checked into the Hong Kong Hilton. Peng also checked in there, so they could easily meet for breakfast. Prior to the meeting, Manny was sent a packet of data about K&S Industries and the DragonFly brand of CD records, along with a letter indicating a willingness to negotiate very attractive prices. It was this latter statement that caught Manny's attention.

"Good morning, gentlemen. My name is Peng Hong, and I'm the sales representative for K&S Industries," Peng said, as he greeted Manny and George in the lobby. "As you can tell, I am quite versed in English, so there will be no need for an interpreter."

"Good morning," Manny answered, shaking Peng's hand. "This is George Priest, my VP of sales. He also is quite versed in Chinese, in the event you prefer we speak in your native tongue."

They went into the hotel restaurant and spent an hour exchanging pleasantries over a light breakfast. They took a cab to the meeting place, arriving just before 10:00 A.M. Manny started the meeting by indicating he would first like to provide Peng with background information about Electro-Mart. This took about fifteen minutes, and included a discussion about how Electro-Mart decided to cut out the traditional record distribution system in North America, since they demanded a twenty-five percent margin for their services.

"I despise leaches who claim they are helping me make sales," Manny said. "Those guys are nothing but glorified order takers." Manny then surprised Peng by saying, "Peng, before you give me a lot of crap about K&S Industries, let me tell you I know who you guys really are. I have lots of contacts both in Taiwan and in mainland China. I know that you report directly to Kong Chau, the ministry chief in charge of business and foreign trade. The only reason you guys sell CD records through K&S Industries is because you're afraid of being branded as record pirates. Isn't that right?" he asked, grinning from ear to ear.

Peng wasn't prepared for this turn of events, but he knew it would no longer be productive if he tried to convince Manny he was wrong. Peng had no choice but to smile and tell Manny he had him dead to rights.

"If what you say is true, are you still interested in doing business with us?" Peng asked.

"I wouldn't have sat on that damn plane for all of those hours if I wasn't interested," Manny answered. "Now, let's cut the crap and see if we can make a deal. First of all, your selection of records is okay, but you will need a lot more labels than four hundred if you want to make an impact on the North American market. I would guess the number is more like five or six hundred, don't you think, George?"

George nodded in agreement.

"Next, if my company acts as your sales arm in the U.S. and Canada, I must have an exclusive deal for at least three years. If I don't get such a deal, we might as well shake hands right now and go to Macao and start having some fun before we return to the States," he laughed.

"What volume can you guarantee us?" Peng asked. "It seems to me that we need some volume guarantees if we make you our exclusive sales outlet."

"Fair enough," Manny said. "I can guarantee you one-third of all of my sales. You shouldn't want any higher percentage than that, for you have to understand there will be an enormous flak level generated because these records are technically not legitimate goods, even though mainland China has not yet signed any international copyright agreements."

"How about one-third for the first two years, with a renegotiation clause allowing us to have up to one-half in the third year?" Peng asked.

"What do you think, George?"

"That should be okay," said George. "We both will be in a better position to see how business is then. Yes, I can accept that kind of a deal."

"Now, Peng, there is another important matter, and that is the brand name on these records. The name DragonFly has got to go. It doesn't take a rocket scientist to figure out those records are being produced in China, and we don't want any records with that brand name to appear on our shelves!"

"No problem. What do you want us to call them?"

"George and I have been discussing that on the flight over, and we decided we should have you brand them Electro-Mart. We will introduce them in our stores as a discount line of CDs. All of our stores are built on three floors, so we will feature the Electro-Mart line on our bargain basement floor."

"By the way, Manny, what do you think your other suppliers will think of this deal? Won't they be unhappy with you for signing with us?"

"By dealing directly with the suppliers, we can handle that easily," Manny said. "It's a dog-eat-dog world out there, and if those boys don't want our business, I can always crank you guys up in volume. You wouldn't mind that kind of a deal, now would you? So, Peng, what do you think?" Manny asked.

"Sounds like we should discuss prices," Peng said.

"George, that is your bailiwick," Manny said. "I'm going to take a stretch if you don't mind and walk around the block, while you guys decide how much all of this is going to cost me." Manny excused himself, while Peng and George began discussing prices.

"Peng, we know what your prices are in South America, and our contacts there indicate with such prices the market is growing nicely. Since we will sell ten times as many products, we must insist we always get your lowest world price. We hope you agree."

"What did you have in mind?"

"We would like a guaranteed fifty percent discount from prevailing world prices being paid to the other suppliers. The way that would work is for us to show you invoices paid to our other suppliers on a quarterly basis, and we would pay you fifty percent of that level."

Peng was taken back by such a bold proposal. After all, the other suppliers would no doubt drop their prices when the Electro-Mart line started to take market share. This could be a really down-and-dirty price war, and if he were always obligated to be one-half of their average price, who knows how low the prices would ultimately sink?

"I cannot recommend such an aggressive program to Kong," Peng said.

"Well, what can you sell him?"

"I think a thirty percent discount is more realistic. It seems to me that our presence in the market will cause the prices from the other suppliers to drop. So, if you are guaranteed a thirty percent discount from us, the prices you will pay us will continue to drop as well. I believe I can sell a thirty percent number, but not fifty percent. It is just too low!"

Manny reappeared from the hallway as if on cue. George asked Peng if he would mind stepping outside while he and Manny conferred.

"Manny, he bought the concept, and would you believe he is committing to thirty percent! I never thought in my wildest dreams we could achieve such a low price. Remember, on the plane we were willing to accept twenty percent below the average price we pay the others."

"Do you think he has the authority to make such a deal?" Manny asked, looking skeptical.

"He has indicated he has to get approval from Kong first."

"Let's pressure him to make his call and see if we can wrap up this deal. I want to spend a few hours gambling in Macao before we return home tomorrow."

When Peng returned, Manny and George said they would accept the thirty percent discount deal. "Do you think you can sell it to Kong?" Manny asked.

Peng said that while he was out of the room he placed a call to Kong and Kong told him he would accept such a discount deal.

"I guess we have a deal then," Manny said, shaking Peng's hand.

George opened his briefcase and pulled out a contract form. He told Peng he could read it when he had more time, but would he be willing to sign a letter of intent today? Peng indicated he would, so they both signed a one-page letter of intent and the deal was made.

"Now, let's all get some rest and meet in the hotel lobby at 5:00 P.M. I want to go to Macao and do some serious gambling this evening," Manny said. "Peng, I would like you to be our guest this evening, for I believe that this is the beginning of a very lucrative business arrangement for both of us."

Chapter Twelve

Laura Robinson hung up from talking with her investigative attorney. He had contacted all of the U.S. distributors, and to a man they informed him they had all received literature and samples from K&S Industries. This was clearly shaping up to be the beginning of a huge record pirate scam, and she couldn't wait until she met again with her other committee members.

"The meeting will now come to order," the moderator said. "Laura, you called this special meeting. The floor is yours."

Laura presented the latest information from South America, which showed DragonFly record shipments had increased considerably since their last meeting. The recording companies representing the other suppliers were now registering formal complaints with the South American Bureau of Free Trade, but to date no action had been taken against the record pirates.

She then handed out copies of a report that described the attempt K&S Industries recently made to penetrate the U.S. market. The only good news she had to report was that none of the U.S. distributors had signed up for any sales, but she reminded her committee members that the discount price of ten percent was not very much incentive.

"Laura, we all appreciate the diligence you have given to this matter. Your report on the South American situation has been sent to our chairman for his review. I will amend it to include your latest information. Will you please provide me a copy of this latest report for me to send to him as well?"

"Fine, but is anything happening yet?" Laura asked, obviously frustrated.

"Be patient. The wheels of bureaucratic progress turn slowly. I'm sure appropriate action will be taken soon. The chairman of our organization will call a meeting and a report will be lodged with the U.S. Commerce Department. They will then begin to address the potential damage K&S Industries may cause to the CD record industry in the U.S. If that is the only business we need to discuss, this special meeting is adjourned."

When Peng returned to Beijing, he immediately called a meeting with Kong to brief him on the deal he made with Electro-Mart. Kong was very pleased with his report and asked Peng just how many records they would sell. Peng referred to some of his notes and indicated that if Electro-Mart met its plan and released one-third of its requirement to K&S Industries, Kong's plan for 1992 would be exceeded. This news made Kong very happy, and he immediately sent a fax to Keung telling him the good news.

"What kind of a man is Manny?" Kong asked.

"He's a competitive gambler in everything he does. He obviously is gambling on using low prices and a discount product line to take over most of the North American market. He gambled fifty thousand Hong Kong dollars at the tables in Macao without batting an eyelash and won one hundred and fifty thousand in return. He is used to winning and no doubt will be a difficult man to deal with if we do not provide him with an adequate supply of records."

"Do you have a problem selling him records branded Electro-Mart, like he requested?"

"No, but it does expose us somewhat, for the plant personnel in Haikou will know the ultimate destination of such records. Maybe we should ship records for this market without labels and set up a low-cost warehouse operation in Mexico, where the labels can be added. Shipments to the U.S. and Canada could also be made from this same Mexican warehouse."

"Good idea, Peng. Why don't you call Shing and brief him? See if he has any other ideas for you to consider."

Keung was very pleased with the 1992 sales results. Volume exceeded the plan numbers, and the deal with Electro-Mart seemed to be a very good one. There was an additional benefit working with Manny, for he was taking on most of the flak from the recording industry and seemed to enjoy holding them off.

He was reported in the press as saying, "It's time you leaches in the record industry woke up and smelled the roses! Recording stars have long been receiving way too much money for their services." Reporters enjoyed his style and made him out to be some kind of a folk hero.

In October of 1992, China joined the Berne Convention, which was formed to address international copyright issues. Keung assigned one of China's leading elder statesmen, Tak Huang, to attend the meetings. He was given strict instructions to be sure China was not placed in a situation where it would not be able to copy CD records.

"You are to discuss our important CD-R production and develop legislation to prevent other countries from copying our advanced technology," Keung instructed. "But never ever let your fellow committee members find out that China is selling large quantities of CD records to the world markets," he emphatically added.

"This is John Toliver of the U.S. Commerce Department. How can I help you?"

"This is Matt Broderick, the chairman of the International Federation of the Phonographic Industry, known as IFPI. Have you heard of us?"

"Yes, I have. Weren't you the guys who sent us a report a year or so ago about some record piracy in South America?"

"That's us. What ever happened at your end?"

"Well, you know how things are here in Washington. We are quite busy chasing down larger issues. I believe we sent your report along to our counterparts in South America, who are presumably acting on it."

"I hope so, but we now seem to have an even more important situation to discuss with you. Have you heard of Electro-Mart, a major chain of record stores springing up all over North America in the super malls?"

"I don't recall the name, but I'm sure my daughter has probably spent most of her allowance at such a store," he laughed.

"They have been selling a line of discount CD records under their own brand name, but get this, they are offering discount records from most popular recording stars. As you can imagine, the record industry is up in arms. They have asked our organization to represent them and to get the Commerce Department to investigate where these records are being produced and put a stop to what seems to us to be a flagrant act of record piracy."

"It sounds like we should meet and discuss this," John stated. He decided if Commerce did nothing on this, he would get a lot of flak from the IFPI. He really did not need that sort of hassle.

"I have to be in Washington next week," the chairman said. "Can we meet on Tuesday afternoon?"

John checked his calendar. "That would be fine. Let's meet at 2:30 in my office, which is room 343 of the U.S. Commerce building."

"I'll see you there next Tuesday, John."

John Toliver was a career government employee who had worked for the U.S. Commerce Department for more than ten years. Because of his experience, he was insulated from having to worry about being displaced or reassigned each time there was a party change in the White House. He was one of the few men in Commerce who spent most of his career dealing with various aspects of Chinese-American trade.

Calls like the one from the IFPI chairman were commonplace, because it seemed every time anyone suspected anyone of copying any technology, whether it be records, VCRs, or even shovels, they always suspected the Chinese as being behind such deals. As a consequence, John learned not to jump to conclusions too quickly, for whenever he approached the Chinese with some unfair practice claim, he wanted to be absolutely sure he knew what he was talking about. In his business, if he cried wolf too often, he would lose his ability to negotiate in good faith the many legitimate trade deals the U.S. worked out each year with China.

Matthew Broderick, the IFPI chairman, arrived promptly and signed in with John's secretary. "Good afternoon, John. I'm Matt Broderick."

"Hi, I'm John Toliver. Won't you please have a seat."

Matt spent the next hour briefing John on the findings of his committee, including the reports Laura Robinson had prepared.

"Matt, why do you think it is the Chinese who are copying the records? For example, have your people found any connection between the DragonFly records and the Electro-Mart records?"

"As a matter of fact, we think we have. We sent samples of both to an independent testing laboratory, and they told us the composition of plastic material used to make both records is virtually identical."

"And what is the composition used to make records from one of the legitimate suppliers?"

"The testing laboratory tells us the composition is entirely different, and they tested ten different supplier's products," Matt added. "But here is the clincher. Are you aware of the CD-R manufacturing activity, which mainland China has been bragging about in the press?"

"Yes. I seem to recall a full page spread in the Wall Street Journal not so long ago that indicated China claims to have an advanced process for making CD-Rs. They also claimed they are now the world's largest supplier."

"Yes, and guess what we found when we had some of their CD-R records analyzed?"

"Let me guess. You found the exact composition used in the DragonFly and Electro-Mart records."

"You got that right. We believe that clinches the fact that China is behind this entire record piracy scam. How do we get the U.S. Commerce Department to act on such a matter?"

"You need to prepare a formal complaint, which should be filed to my attention, for I'm in charge of all Chinese-American trade matters. It sounds like you do in fact have a legitimate complaint here, assuming your data is correct," John said. "Of course we will want to perform our own tests to verify your results.

"By the way, Matt, are you aware China has not yet formally signed any agreement that precludes them in a strict legal sense from copying anyone's records?"

"No, I wasn't. I thought they were a member of the Berne Convention. Don't all members have to sign such a pact?"

"Technically, yes. But they have been able so far to avoid signing on the dotted line, even though at each meeting the other members are exerting enormous pressure on them. The Chinese representative at those meetings is a wise old man named Tak Huang. I actually attended one of their meetings, and this old guy was amazing to watch.

He danced around the subject for hours and wore everyone out. They keep letting China belong, even though they are technically in default."

"What recourse do we have, if in fact we can prove China is behind this whole record piracy scam?"

"We can slap them with trade sanctions, but there are a lot of constituents in the U.S. who do not want us to ever discuss such actions, no matter how justified we are in doing so. For example, we sell China lots of farm goods, machinery, and medicine supplies. The firms who enjoy those sales could care less about a record piracy matter.

"Matt, don't let me discourage you. It sounds like you've caught them red handed, and I can use that to my advantage as we prepare for the 1994 Most Favored Nation Trade Negotiations. Please file your complaint, and I'll start the wheels moving. Now, if you don't mind, I have to run to another meeting. You can rest assured I'll move on this matter very quickly. For starters, I'll send China a formal letter of inquiry within a few days after receiving your complaint."

"Thank you, John."

Immediately after Matthew left, John was on the phone with the commerce secretary. "Mr. Secretary, I believe I've discovered a way to keep the Chinese in their place during the upcoming negotiations," John said enthusiastically.

John briefed the secretary, who agreed with him that it sounded like the United States would be in a strong bargaining position. He suggested John start sending the Chinese a barrage of complaint letters, once he was convinced the data provided by the IFPI was accurate.

★ ★ ★

Keung asked his secretary to phone Kong. "Kong, this is Keung. The flak has started. Our ambassador received three formal letters of complaint this past week, and there is a gentleman from the U.S. Commerce Department who insists on meeting with him in Hong Kong next week."

"What should I do about all of this?" asked Kong.

"Nothing, just now. I just wanted you to be aware of it," Keung said. "You will probably get a call soon from the Electro-Mart people, for our ambassador indicated in his notes of complaint that Electro-

Mart was mentioned as being tied in with what they refer to as blatant record piracy."

"I'll tell Peng to be ready for such a call."

When Keung hung up, Kong immediately asked Peng to come to his office.

"Peng, the flak has started. You must tell all of the personnel who are in the chain of delivery that they are not to speak with anyone who seems to be asking them questions about our operations. Tell them also to report any such contacts immediately. Do you understand?"

"Yes, Kong, I fully understand."

During most of 1994, John Toliver found himself spending more and more of his time on the Chinese record piracy matter, which Commerce had given the code name Operation Plastic. He was clearly getting the runaround, for every time he set up a meeting, it seemed the person in China he needed to speak with would suddenly become ill or have to be out of town. He also requested a visit to the Haikou plant, which was mentioned in the CD-R advertisements as being the best source for high-quality CD-Rs for the software industry. However, each time he was promised a visit, there would be yet another excuse for the Chinese to not accommodate him. John knew for certain that he would be making many trips to Hong Kong before this matter would ultimately be resolved.

In Haikou, Shing decided it was time to promote CT to the position of managing director, as he had promised. Shing called his staff together one afternoon and made the announcement.

"CT, I know you will do well in this position," Shing said. "You are respected by all of your peers here in the plant. You gentlemen will probably not see as much of me now, for I have other urgent matters to deal with in Beijing," Shing added when he said good-bye to his staff. "I have enjoyed working closely with all of you."

The staff surrounded CT and congratulated him. They also bowed and shook Shing's hand as he departed. What Shing had not told them was that Keung was becoming extremely worried about the possibility the United States might impose trade sanctions against China if China did not stop the illegal manufacture of CD records. Keung told him to date they did not have proof, and to date China had not signed any formal agreement in Switzerland, but in spite of that, a lot of pressure was going to be exerted. So, he wanted Shing to drop all of his other duties, and help him deal with this problem.

Part 2

Apple Computer Vs. Microsoft

Chapter Thirteen

Shou Lee (Steven) was having one of his most severe migraine headaches. Two hours had passed since he took his usual dose of four Excedrin tablets, but he felt no relief, and his head felt like it would split in two at any moment. He lay on the sofa in the den of his small townhouse, which was located one block from DeAnza College, in the heart of California's Silicon Valley. His feet were propped up on two pillows, his eyes were closed, and he tightly held a cold wet towel to his forehead. Since the copyright infringement litigation began between his employer, Apple Computer, and the software giant, Microsoft, his migraines occurred more and more frequently. This one had all the earmarks of being his worst!

The cause of Steven's latest migraine was lying on the coffee table in front of the sofa in the midst of the afternoon mail. The latest edition of the *Apple Employees Monthly Newsletter*, dated Friday, 24 February 1995, was lying open on the table. Steven just finished reading it from cover to cover. The newsletter's headline blared out this message:

> The Apple Management Team is sorry to have to report to its employees that on the matter of the copyright infringement litigation between Apple and Microsoft, regarding whether Microsoft is permitted to continue to utilize a graphical user interface in its Windows™ Products, which is substantially identical to the Apple Macintosh™ graphical user interface, the 9th District Circuit Court has ruled in favor of Microsoft.

The rest of the newsletter contained a number of well-crafted articles written by members of Apple's management team, all of which were intended to boost the morale of the troops. However, Steven knew this legal event would prove to be a major turning point in the personal computer industry. Because of this ruling, the Apple Macintosh™ computer and future derivatives would never be able to seriously displace IBM-compatible PCs in business applications—the most important and fastest growing segment of the personal computer market. This legal ruling gave Microsoft a free hand to continue to pursue their strategy of further developing Windows™ operating systems for use in all IBM-compatible PCs, providing machines with the same efficiency of use that previously had only been available to users of Apple Macintosh™ computers.

Steven was one of several "technical experts" within Apple assigned to assist Apple's outside legal counsel, the firm of Bernstein, Fein, Clark, and Smithson of Palo Alto, California. During the several months Apple pursued the copyright litigation suit against Microsoft, Steven analyzed the various versions of Microsoft Windows™ software in detail in order to provide Miles Winthrop, the principal lawyer assigned to the Apple case, with technical ammunition to use against Microsoft in court. Consequently, Steven was able to observe the legal maneuvering of both sides firsthand, and he sensed for some time that Apple might lose this important landmark case.

Each time Steven thought about the impact of a court ruling against Apple, his blood would boil and his migraines would return. How could the arrogant fools who make up the American judicial system not see that it was Apple, not Microsoft, who sweated blood to develop and deliver in quantity the first personal computer with an outstanding user interface? It was also obvious to Steven that the interface would prove to be the most significant advancement in personal computer technology! Steven kept telling himself to continue to believe that somehow justice would be served in favor of Apple. However, as the headline indicated, it appeared that such was not going to be the case.

It all began in 1979, when a team of engineers from Apple were invited to witness a demonstration of a new computer system architecture being showcased by the Xerox Corporation at their Palo Alto Research Center. During the meeting, the Apple engineers were shown the difference between the ordinary interface required to operate personal computers and the newer, more "user-friendly graphical user interface," which would become known as a GUI-interface (pronounced "gooey").

To operate an ordinary personal computer, such as an early Apple computer, it was necessary for the user to type various commands on the keyboard in a language not familiar to most users, and which differed for every software application. However, with a GUI-based computer, the user needed only to use an electronic pointing device (mouse) to guide a pointer on the screen to a picture (icon) that contained the name of the program to be run. The user only needed to click a button on the mouse to start the application; once a program was running, other pictorial icons and menus could be incorporated to make the program easier to operate.

The demonstration so impressed Apple's CEO with the potential of personal computers built with GUI-interfaces that he shortly thereafter presented Apple's Board of Directors with plans for the development of a family of GUI-based Apple computers, which included the Apple Lisa™ and the Apple Macintosh™ machines.

A team of dedicated engineers was assembled and moved into a separate building, where they were given virtually unlimited resources to pursue these developments. Steven Lee, one of the persons hired to join the team, was given the task of developing the operating system software for the Macintosh™, which would turn out to become the primary software required to make the GUI design practical.

The Apple design team worked day and night, as if on some deep personal crusade, and the Mac™ (as it was affectionately called), was completed in time for its formal announcement on nationwide TV on Super Bowl Sunday, 22 January 1984. The Super Bowl event was followed by several multiple-page ads in all major magazines, which set new records for readership and advertisement recall scores. Clearly the Mac™ was Apple's crowning achievement, and the team that worked so long and hard on the project felt very proud, as did the Apple management, who referred to the Mac™ as "insanely great."

Steven was finally able to fall asleep on the sofa, but he woke up early on Sunday morning, still feeling tired and frustrated. He was unable to accept the legal outcome, so he decided not to report to work on Monday morning. Instead he would meet with Miles Winthrop, the attorney he had worked with during the past several months. He wanted Miles to brief him thoroughly on the entire matter. He hoped

Miles would be able to tell him it was still possible to have the verdict overturned.

As Steven dressed on Monday morning, he made a fundamental decision. He decided if Miles was unable to hold out any hope, he would immediately tender his resignation at Apple. He wasn't quite sure what he would do after he resigned, but he vowed he would somehow personally find a way to get back at the system for being so terribly unfair. The Mac™ was indeed insanely great, and it was dreadfully cruel what the United States judicial system had done. As Steven began to consider his options, he found his head cleared up considerably, and the last hint of his most recent migraine vanished.

Chapter Fourteen

Joshua Bernstein and Ira Fein founded the law firm of Bernstein and Fein in San Francisco in 1907. Having just graduated from Yale, these two young attorneys decided to move west where the air was cleaner and where the opportunities appeared to be more abundant for young, ambitious lawyers.

They were able to pass the California bar exam on their first attempt, and soon they began to practice law out of a small office on the top floor of the Wells Fargo Bank Building, located on California Boulevard in South San Francisco.

The move to California proved to be very lucrative for Joshua and Ira. The 1908 San Francisco earthquake provided an enormous amount of business for attorneys who were willing to get their hands dirty helping companies collect on policies that contained no formal language dealing with liability from earthquake damage. Their insurance claim business also grew as a consequence of the automobile becoming available in increasing numbers to inexperienced drivers—drivers who were causing bodily injury to pedestrians.

By 1914, Joshua and Ira were able to afford to move into a new suite of offices located in a renovated building on Market Street in downtown San Francisco. They felt really good about their decision to move to California, as California turned out to be truly the land of milk and honey for them.

Joshua and Ira weathered the great depression better than most. By 1931, the firm of Bernstein and Fein had grown to twenty employees, including twelve practicing attorneys and eight paralegals. By then they developed a reputation for being the most successful firm in the field of insurance claim litigation. Their client list included most of the more successful and prestigious companies in Northern California.

In 1919, both Joshua and Ira married daughters of prominent San Franciscan families; two years later, Joshua's wife gave birth to Isaac and Ira's wife gave birth to Jacob. The parents intended for their sons to become lawyers, so they were sent to the best private schools on the West Coast to prepare for the rigors of college. However, in 1942, both Isaac and Jacob were drafted into the Army, so they were forced to put off their college plans.

They both saw action in Europe and participated in the invasion of Normandy, managing to avoid becoming seriously wounded. Upon their honorable discharge in 1945, they returned to California and immediately enrolled in the Stanford University Law School, where they continued with their studies and received their law degrees in 1950.

Shortly after passing their bar exams, Isaac and Jacob joined their father's law firm as full partners and co-owners. In 1951, when their fathers retired from active practice, they took over the day-to-day operations, continuing to focus their energies primarily in the field of insurance litigation.

While at Stanford, Isaac and Jacob became close friends of Thomas Clark and Keith Smithson, who were attending the Stanford Law School on the GI Bill of Rights. The four of them often sat for hours in a local Palo Alto pub, discussing their future plans. It was a foregone conclusion that Isaac and Jacob would take over their father's practice, but the future was not nearly as well defined for Tom and Keith.

Tom and Keith became interested in the relatively new field of intellectual property protection, which had been introduced in 1948 as a new curriculum program of the Stanford Law School. The Stanford curriculum defined the term 'intellectual property' to include inventions, patents, copyrights, and trademarks. The curriculum was based on the following beliefs, which were enlarged upon in the university catalog.

If a company can legally demonstrate, and later defend in a court of law, that it first developed a product, conceived an idea, or produced an invention, before some other company develops an identical or very similar product, idea, or invention, then the originating company can legally prevent, or at least delay, a would-be competitor from entering the market with an identical or very similar product, idea, or invention.

Furthermore, a portfolio of inventions, patents, copyrights, and trademarks that can prove a specific company first developed a product, conceived an idea, or produced an invention, makes up what is known as the intellectual property of the company.

And lastly, it is very basic to the long-range financial health of a company that its intellectual property be legally protected at all times, because in many cases the intellectual property is the most valuable resource a company has while it is developing and growing its business.

The Stanford course curriculum included case histories carefully chosen to demonstrate how the protection of intellectual property was becoming a very important aspect of a company's business success. This was shown to be especially true for companies that primarily develop radically new high technology products. As the professors were quick to point out, the need for a company to legally protect its intellectual property represented a considerable business opportunity for legal firms to pursue, and that was the reason the Stanford Law School developed a dedicated intellectual property curriculum.

One evening, Tom and Keith invited Isaac and Jacob to attend a special lecture on the subject of intellectual property. The lecturing professor told them that, during the war, the United States Government pumped hundreds of millions of dollars into electronics research, so it was evident that during the 1950s there would be many new companies starting up their operations basing their business on the success of new and novel electronic products.

After the lecture, the four of them went to their favorite pub to further discuss what they had just heard. Isaac and Jacob certainly grasped the vast business potential afforded by intellectual property protection, as did Tom and Keith. However, they knew if they asked their fathers to consider making the necessary investment in the firm to pursue this new field, they would be told such a direction was "too far off the beaten path" and they should not try to pursue every new fad that comes along. They knew that since their fathers had been successful dealing with complex insurance claims, they would not want to spend any time trying to enter an unproven field.

In 1950, Isaac and Jacob joined their father's law firm and Tom and Keith hung out their own shingle in a small office in Palo Alto, where they were determined to make a go of it in the field of intellectual property protection. Business for Tom and Keith was not very good, but they never gave up their dream. In order to gain experience in the field, they helped a number of older established Bay Area companies review patent claims and prepare applications. This tedious work was not very glamorous and was not very financially rewarding, but it managed to help them keep their dream alive.

Tom and Keith were beginning to wonder when the big boom in new startup companies was going to occur, when one afternoon in 1955 they got a call from a man who was planning to start a new company in Mountain View. He told them his name was Bill Shockley and that he was the co-inventor of the transistor. He had heard about Tom and Keith's patent work from a friend at Lockheed, and he wanted to retain their services to help him protect the intellectual property of his new company, Shockley Semiconductor, which was going to design, manufacture, and sell transistors.

The meeting with Shockley was a surprisingly brief one. He spent very little time interviewing Tom and Keith, but rather said the reference he got from a friend was all he needed. He knew right off that they were just the kind of attorneys he wanted to be associated with. He outlined his plans and indicated there would be some very complex and very lengthy patent application and litigation work required, for the original patent for the transistor belonged to Bell Labs. However, he assured them that since his departure from the labs, he had developed many other ways to produce transistors, which were far superior to the original design. He was sure it would be possible to develop the kind of patent protection required to allow his new company to legally produce transistors without having to pay huge royalties to Ma Bell.

Tom and Keith sensed this could very well be the big case they had been waiting for. However, when they began to outline their fee structure, Shockley looked puzzled and started to frown.

"Don't you fellows understand the fundamental economics of new startup companies?" he asked. "My associates and I don't plan to draw any salary from this enterprise for the next two years. In fact, we are going to have to mortgage our homes in order to raise enough cash to purchase the equipment we required to produce our first devices."

What Shockley had in mind was for Tom and Keith to be retained with no fee, but with an option to purchase one hundred thousand shares of stock in the future at a low price. "When the company starts to sell its stock on the open market, we will all make millions," Shockley told them with a gleam in his eye. Shockley reasoned that Tom and Keith, as potential stockholders, would work night and day to help make the company successful.

"I have to go now and visit some potential investors. Why don't you boys think it over and give me a call in the morning. I sure would like to have you on my team," Shockley added.

Tom and Keith were now faced with a fundamental decision. If they accepted the deal, they would have to borrow money to maintain current activities, and in addition they would become very busy digging into all of the patent entanglements with Bell Labs. So they decided to call their friends, Isaac and Jacob, to seek their advice.

Isaac took their call, listening attentively, and said he and Jacob would call them back in the morning. He went into Jacob's office, closed the door, and began to brief him on the conversation. "Jacob, do you remember how we felt about intellectual property protection as a business to go into when we were in our last year at Stanford?" Isaac asked. "Well, our old classmates, Tom and Keith, have been trying to break into that field, and it sounds like they have just found a very hot prospect. However, they will need considerable financial help if they wish to pursue the opportunity that has been presented to them."

Isaac briefed Jacob on the whole deal and, after some discussion, the two of them arrived at the same conclusion. They decided to offer Tom and Keith a creative proposition that would require them to join their firm and form a satellite operation in the Bay Area that was dedicated to the field of intellectual property protection. They would be paid a modest salary to cover their expenses, and in return they would be given the freedom to take on as many deals as necessary to grow their business. They would be promised an opportunity to become full partners in the firm, once they achieved a prescribed level of business.

When Jacob placed the call to the fledgling firm of Clark and Smithson, Tom immediately answered. "Hi, Tom. How have you been? Boy do we have a deal for you!"

"Hi, Jacob. It's been a long time. Let me get Keith on the other line to hear what you have in mind." Jacob outlined the deal and both Tom and Keith, without a moment's hesitation, told Jacob to draw up an agreement. This plan would allow them to be retained by numerous startup firms, receiving most of their compensation in the form of the value of future stock; they would not have to charge conventional legal fees to fledgling companies such as Shockley's.

The papers arrived by courier the next morning. Once they signed, Tom and Keith called Bill Shockley back and accepted his deal. Within three years, the net worth of the Palo Alto satellite operation was more than twice that of the parent organization. Consequently, Tom and Keith were made full partners in what was now called the firm of Bernstein, Fein, Clark, and Smithson, with offices in both San Francisco and Palo Alto.

The business model Tom and Keith offered to startup firms became the preferred way for legal firms dealing with intellectual property to do business in the 1950s and 1960s. It was this model that appealed to Apple's board of directors when they retained the services of the Palo Alto firm of Bernstein, Fein, Clark, and Smithson in 1976 to handle all of their intellectual property protection activities.

Chapter Fifteen

On Monday morning, 27 February 1995, Steven Lee arrived at the Palo Alto law offices of Bernstein, Fein, Clark, and Smithson. He did not have an appointment, but he was sure Miles Winthrop would find some time to see him. Miles had been assigned to the Apple case since the very beginning and had been personally chosen for this assignment by Tom Clark because of Miles' specific knowledge of the United States Copyright Law. Miles always worked openly with Steven, so Steven was sure he would brief him on the latest series of events that led up to the recent ruling.

Steven signed in with Cindy, the attractive receptionist with blazing red hair, whom he knew on a first name basis. He asked her if he could meet with Miles this morning.

She looked at her master schedule and said, "Steven, I think it will be okay, but since he has not yet arrived, I can't be absolutely sure. Would you mind having a seat until he arrives? Would you like your usual cup of coffee while you wait?"

Steven nodded in the affirmative, so Cindy stepped into the alcove next to the waiting room and prepared his favorite brew, which was very black espresso with no sugar. Steven thanked her, and in two quick gulps, it was gone.

"Having a bad day?" Cindy mused.

Steven turned his head and said, "You know how Monday mornings can sometimes be!"

He slumped back in the soft leather chair and closed his eyes, for he really wasn't in the mood for small talk this morning. I'm really tired, he thought to himself. He had joined Apple at the age of twenty-seven, only one week after graduating from Berkeley with a master's degree in computer science, and he was immediately assigned the very challenging job of designing the operating system software for the Macintosh™ computer. This morning, Steven realized he had not taken any significant time off since. In fact, he was due to receive his fifteen-year pin this year, and he had only taken a few days of vacation since he began working at Apple.

Steven began reflecting on the fact that, here he was, a forty-two-year old confirmed bachelor, whose only hobby was his work. He lived and breathed computers. After the Mac™ design was completed, he volunteered to head up the activity within Apple to develop Mac™ user application software. In fact, during the past fifteen years, he had embroiled himself so deeply in the Mac™ world, he couldn't believe any other computer but a Mac™ was worthy of being placed on any serious user's desk!

Steven firmly believed that an IBM-compatible computer with Microsoft Windows™ installed was analogous to an old barn that had been painted with whitewash to make it look more respectable. Underneath it all was still the same old barn! God, how could the American judicial system be so terribly stupid? He stopped himself from proceeding with these thoughts, for he feared he might get another migraine headache.

Steven had always been a stubborn crusader when he believed in some worthy cause. He remembered when he was growing up in Hong Kong, the only son of a successful Chinese silk merchant, he couldn't understand why his grandparents were not allowed to leave mainland China to join the family. His father told him over and over again the Chinese Communist regime had harsh rules about certain things, and he should just be happy his grandparents were in good health and were able to write letters occasionally.

However, this did not set well with Steven. He spent endless days wandering around the Chinese embassy in Hong Kong, trying to find a way to free his grandparents. After almost a year of fruitless activity, he finally let go of the idea, but vowed some day he would renew his quest for their release.

As he daydreamed in his soft leather chair this morning, he wondered if they were still well, and if they still wanted to leave their native land. He did a mental calculation and realized they were now in their late eighties and he had never even seen them, let alone spoken with them! This situation just had to change before he and they got much older!

Just then, the telephone on Cindy's desk rang loudly and woke Steven from his deep thoughts.

"Good morning, Miles," Cindy said. "What time are you going to be in the office today? Oh, you don't plan to come in at all. okay, but Steven is here to see you. Would you like to talk to him? Steven, Miles is on the phone. You can pick it up on the table next to your chair. Good-bye, Miles. I'm now turning you over to Steven. Yes, Miles, I'll tell your secretary you won't be in today. Take care, and have a good day."

"Hi, Miles, this is Steven. Where are you? I took a chance you might be able to see me this morning. I guess you know why I'm here. I was hoping you could tell me why the judge finally ruled in favor of Microsoft. I also want your views on whether there is a chance the case will be appealed."

"Good morning, Steven. I would be glad to see you, but I have a bit of a problem myself," Miles said, with a chuckle. "Last night, Tom Clark called me at home and indicated he was not at all pleased with the outcome of the case. In fact, he was really pissed, for this is the first highly visible case the firm has ever lost. He told me there would be a board meeting this afternoon, and he was going to ask for my resignation!

"So, Steven, as you can see, I'm to become the fall guy. In fact, Tom asked me not to show up this morning. He said I could come by and pick up my things this evening, after everyone has gone home. So, Steven, what do you think of that?"

Steven was appalled, for Miles was the only attorney at the firm who knew anything about the United States Copyright Law. He had dedicated three years of his life working on this single case. Now he was being tossed out like so much wheat chaff.

"You've been given the shaft," was all Steven could think of saying. "Do you feel like meeting somewhere this afternoon, or would you rather get together some other time?"

"No, I think we should get together today," Miles said. "How about we meet after lunch in one of the small research rooms in the Stanford legal library? Incidentally, what are your plans now? I've sensed for some time you might bail out of Apple if this thing went the wrong way."

"I'll meet you at the library front desk at one o'clock. Regarding my plans, if Apple doesn't appeal this verdict, I'll resign immediately. I'll see you in a while."

"Sounds serious," Cindy said, as she could not help overhearing Steven's side of the conversation.

"You've got that right," Steven said, as he stormed out of the front lobby door.

After Steven left the law office, he went to a nearby pay phone and called his secretary.

"Hi, Sue," Steven said in a somber voice. "I don't expect to be at work today, for I don't feel well, if you know what I mean!"

"I understand, Steven," Sue replied. "Most of your staff has called in sick today. I guess it has to do with the Friday afternoon announcement. Isn't that so?"

"Yeah, I'm afraid so. What are the troops saying about the legal verdict?"

"The place is like a morgue," she said. "The engineering staff members who did not call in sick are just sitting quietly with their feet propped up on their desks, staring at their monitors. I believe a lot of them are updating their résumés. Is Apple going to make it?" she asked.

"Don't you worry," Steven reassured her. "One silly legal case isn't enough to bring down an entire company. I'll see you in the morning."

Miles Winthrop arrived a few minutes early and arranged with the Stanford library receptionist for the use of research room 201, which was in a far corner of the library. He and Steven could meet there without being interrupted. He was dressed casually and actually felt a sense of relief that this chapter of his life was over. After all, he had been working twelve-hour days for more than three years on just one case. He was really burned out. Of course he wished the firm had won, but he knew for some time that the chances for an Apple victory were quite small.

The fact he was now without a job did not bother him, for he had many connections in the Bay Area. He decided he would take a well-deserved rest for a month or so before seeking a new job with any one of a dozen legal firms.

Steven arrived shortly after one o'clock, and after shaking hands, the two walked down the hall toward room 201.

"How does it feel to be canned?" Steven asked.

"I should be bitter, but I guess if I were in Tom's shoes, I would have done the same thing. We all know that on major, high-visibility cases like this one there is always a great deal of risk, and of course a corresponding amount of reward if one succeeds. But, on this case, we failed to succeed. So that's about the long and short of it," Miles said, shrugging his shoulders. "Reality sucks, but life must go on," he added, with a grin.

"Is there any chance Apple will file an appeal, and if so, is there any chance Apple can win?" Steven asked seriously, after they sat down at the small conference table.

Miles stood up and went over to the window and stared for a long time at the Stanford campus below him. He turned slowly and returned to his seat at the table.

"Steven, I've known for some time Apple was not going to win. There is not going to be an appeal, and therefore there is no chance Apple can ever win," he added emphatically. "I know that sounds awfully harsh coming from me, especially since our firm's formal position for a long time has been that we believed Apple would ultimately win. Steven, please treat this next conversation in the strictest of confidence, for I feel I owe you the straight scoop, now that the verdict is in," Miles said with a very serious look on his face.

"When Apple first asked our firm to sue Microsoft, our people and the Apple management team held many long meetings, where we discussed how we should proceed in order to have the best chance of winning such a case.

"There was never a debate about the fact that the Macintosh™ was developed by Apple and was in production and selling in large quantities before Microsoft even seriously began their Windows™ software development effort. So, the main issue here was whether Microsoft stepped over the line and used some of Apple's intellectual property to help them reach their goals.

"Most members of our firm felt Apple should fight the case on the basis of Apple's extensive portfolio of circuit patents, since operating system software, such as what you developed for the Macintosh™, was considered to not be patentable.

"Specifically, Tom and Keith felt with the sizable number of patents Apple had been granted on various sections of the Macintosh™ hardware implementation, a case could be made that Apple could use to fend off the threat from Microsoft.

"I, on the other hand, argued Microsoft was not developing circuits, but was developing software. If a producer of an IBM-compatible personal computer needed to use Apple circuitry to be able to make use of Microsoft's Windows™ software, then fine, Apple would be able to collect patent royalties from each such producer.

"But, if Apple wished to have Microsoft cease its Windows™ software development projects entirely, we needed to find some way to win in the software arena. To do so would require us to break entirely new legal ground.

"Courts in the past have ruled in many high-visibility legal cases that computer software could not be patented. Hence, we had to find some other angle. Because of that, I recommended trying to find a way to apply the United States Copyright Law.

"Steven, that was when I got up on my soapbox and probably did my firm, and certainly myself, a great disservice," Miles said soberly. "I stuck my neck out a mile and said, with my expert knowledge of the U.S. Copyright Law, I could single-handedly create an argument that would not only win the case for Apple, but which would go down in the annals of the legal journals as the greatest contribution to the art of legal protection of computer software the industry had ever conceived!

"Tom Clark was initially concerned about using the copyright law to defend Apple's claims. He knew software could be copyrighted, but Apple also knew Microsoft had certainly not copied the Apple Macintosh™ software code line-for-line. Tom asked me what aspect of the U.S. Copyright Law would pertain to this matter, and I responded we might be able to develop our case around a radical new concept that I called the 'look and feel' concept.

"I told him when a person operated a computer with the Windows™ operating system, it would look and feel like the user was operating a Macintosh™ computer. Clearly, then, if we could develop a case around this concept, Microsoft should not be allowed to provide such a product as Windows™ under such conditions, for it would seriously hurt the future sale of Apple Macintosh™ computers.

"Tom reflected on my idea, for he wasn't sure we could afford to prepare such a complex legal case. He said his experience told him that for us to win a precedent-setting case, it would take three to four times the financial resources of a more ordinary case."

"How did you convince Tom the copyright law could be used as an adequate offensive weapon here?" Steven asked.

"Steven, I was on an enormous ego trip, and I lost my sense of perspective. All I could think of was the glory I would receive and the national attention such an achievement would produce if Apple were to win this case. Imagine, if Apple could prove Microsoft somehow violated the U.S. Copyright Law, and as a consequence was unable to sell Windows™ software! Now that is something that really would make headlines, and I guess my ambition ran away with itself," Miles added, calming down a bit.

"I guess I gave them the presentation of a lifetime, for when I sat down, everyone in the room stood quietly and watched Tom for his reaction. Tom stood up and started to clap, and the rest of the members of the firm stood up and cheered. At that moment, the "look and feel" concept was born, and I had the responsibility to breathe life into it. I guess Tom got caught up in the notion of being part of legal history in the computer industry. Anyway, I sure got the chance to prove my beliefs, and I must admit to you even with all of the cheering, I didn't have a clue how I was going to achieve the results I was promising.

"I was never so afraid in my life, but each time I thought about it, I kept thinking of what success would mean to me, personally. So, I proceeded to try and develop a strategy based on the untried concept of look and feel, using the U.S. Copyright Law as a basis.

"I won't bore you with all of the activities that went on after that momentous meeting. Needless to say, by the time Tom and the other members of our firm found out I was in well over my head, it was too late to pull back. After all, once you bury the opponent with paperwork claiming they have broken some particular law or set of laws, you can't suddenly decide you were wrong. No, you have to forge ahead and hope for the best, and that is what we did.

"We all finally agreed we were really in it up to our necks, so Tom started holding daily meetings with me to see if we could find some creative way to make the copyright law work to our advantage."

"Excuse me, Miles," Steven said. "I sat in on some of your presentations during the last couple of years, and what you presented made a lot of sense to me. Of course, I'm no legal expert, but it seemed to me you guys did a great job preparing and presenting Apple's side of the case."

"Thanks for the accolades, Steven, but what you didn't know was after each such presentation, we would retreat into our chambers and have very heated discussions among ourselves regarding what we should do next.

"We felt we couldn't level with the Apple management about how much in the hole we were, and yet the more we dug into the copyright issue, the more we found out how hard it was going to be to make our case stick.

"Steven, I must leave now to take care of some personal matters. However, I first want to close this meeting with one of my famous Miles Winthrop quickie discussions on U.S. Copyright law, as it pertains to computer software, now that I'm a battle-weary expert on the subject," he sighed. "What I'm about to tell you may seem almost trite in its simplicity, but such is often the case after you spend months embroiled in complex legal details, only to find out the judge goes back to basics and reads you the riot act when your case no longer makes any sense to him."

Miles proceeded to draw some analogies between copyrighting software and copyrighting books.

"If someone writes a book and gets it copyrighted, then if another person copies that book word for word, the originator can sue the second person for copyright infringement, and will most certainly win in a court of law. Similarly, if a software programmer, such as you, Steven, writes thousands of lines of code to implement software, which in this case produces a GUI-interface for an Apple computer, it is possible to copyright that software. Then if a second person copies each and every line of code, the originator of the software can easily win a copyright suit against the second person in a court of law. All he needs to do to win is have an expert witness compare the two software programs and testify that the copy is virtually identical to the original program.

"On the other hand, if an author writes a book on how to sail a boat and copyrights the book, the copyright law does not preclude a second author from writing a book on how to sail a boat, so long as the second author does not copy the text of the original author.

"Similarly, if a programmer at Apple develops and copyrights a software program and calls it software for a GUI-interface for a Macintosh™, that does not preclude another programmer at Microsoft from developing software code that creates images on a totally different computer system, such as an IBM-compatible computer, calling it software for a GUI-interface for an IBM-compatible computer.

"In this case, the second programmer is not violating the copyright of the first programmer, because it can be shown that it was absolutely impossible for the second programmer (at Microsoft) to use any of the lines of code used by the first programmer (at Apple), since the two computer systems were built using totally different hardware architectures."

"But Miles, what happened to Apple's contention that the 'look and feel' of the two systems were so similar?"

"Good point, Steven. We tried valiantly to appeal to the judge's aesthetic nature here. We used the argument that if a user used an IBM-compatible personal computer with Windows™ installed, he would experience the same look and feel a user would experience if he were to use a Macintosh™. We tried to copyright the notion of look and feel, but were unable to do so.

"The judge returned to basics and blew us away. Using the example of the book written on how to sail, the judge said that all books ever written have the same look and feel. He stated that all books have covers, they all have words on pages, they all are about the same size and weight, and most are read from left to right across the page. Our strategy backfired here. It's as simple as that. The judge really got impatient with us on this matter, for he was not at all impressed with our arguments that, since both computer systems looked alike and felt alike, Apple's intellectual property had been violated.

"In fact, the judge got on his soapbox and scolded us, saying he thought Microsoft had done a great service for mankind by making their Windows™ operating system look the same. It would now be easier for people to use computers, since they now would look and feel more or less alike.

"As the case wound down, Apple tried to include in its final arguments the additional notion of substantial similarity between the Apple product and the Microsoft product as used on IBM-compatible computers. However, because the interface was composed of elements not individually protected by copyright law, this position also proved fruitless.

"During closing, we were given a stern lecture by the judge, and as if that was not bad enough, the lecture was in front of the Microsoft attorneys, who I'm sure got a real big kick out of watching the proceedings," Miles added, with a sad look on his face.

"I felt like two cents. You should have seen the look on Tom's face when it was all over. I actually expected to be fired right there on the spot."

"Well, Miles, you at least gave it everything you had," Steven said. "I certainly wish you well. I'll call you when I decide what I'm going to do next."

"Okay, Steven, thanks for all the help you gave me. You probably are now the most knowledgeable person in the entire world on both the Macintosh™ operating system and the Windows™ operating system."

"That's for sure, Miles," Steven said, "but what do I do with all of that vast knowledge?"

"I'm sure you will think of something," Miles replied.

"Good luck," Steven said, as the two of them left the library.

Chapter Sixteen

Steven was feeling a bit sorry for himself, for he had just resigned from Apple, and his resignation had been accepted by his manager without a whole lot of discussion and without a counter offer. As was the usual practice in high tech firms in Silicon Valley, when a valued technical person resigns and the management of the company decides not to go out of their way to convince them to change their mind, they are summarily escorted out of the building with their personal belongings, without so much as a farewell from their peers.

Over the years, this practice was found to be necessary, as it prevents the departing soul from lingering around the office for a couple of weeks, causing others to be distracted from their work. Steven felt somewhat rejected, but he knew he would eventually get over it.

Before resigning on Tuesday morning, Steven went to his laboratory and downloaded some files he had personally developed, onto floppy disks from the IBM-compatible test computer he used to evaluate various revisions of Microsoft Windows™. These files contained what he called *Operating System Analysis Programs*. He rationalized that these files were his own personal property, for they had nothing to do with the ongoing development work he did for Apple; he thought they might come in handy sometime in the future, when he landed a job elsewhere.

As Miles Winthrop said when he and Steven met on Monday, Steven probably was the only individual in the world who knew the internal workings of both the Macintosh™ and Windows™ operating systems in intimate detail, and this knowledge had been gained in no small part through the use of these programs.

The Operating System Analysis Programs made it possible for Steven to slow down the execution of an IBM-compatible computer when operating in the Windows™ environment. Once the programs were loaded into the Windows™ directory, it became possible for the user of the computer to incrementally reduce the effective clock speed of the computer under software control. This enabled Steven to be able to literally step the computer along one line of code at a time, while watching on the monitor the impact each line of code had on the computer's behavior.

Without these programs, it would have been impossible for Steven to fully understand the internal details of the Windows™ operating system. By making use of these programs, he had been able to list for Miles all of the internal similarities and differences of the Windows™ operating system, compared with the operating system he developed for the Macintosh™.

Just before noon, Steven's phone rang. It was Sue, his secretary from Apple. "Steven, I was sorry to hear you resigned," Sue said. "I think it was awful you were escorted out of the building without any of us even being able to say good-bye to you. You've been a key Apple employee. Your group really respects your technical contribution to the development of the Macintosh™ operating system software."

"Don't worry," Steven said. "Escorting someone out of the building when they resign is company policy. I didn't take it personally. So, what are the troops saying about me?"

"That's why I'm calling. Your staff and many of your friends at Apple want to take you to dinner this Friday night and give you a proper send off. Can you make it?"

"Sure, I can make it, but you really don't have to do this," Steven added.

Deep down, however, Steven was glad they were making this gesture; after all, he had been at Apple for fifteen years and had made a lot of friends. He wanted to be able to shake their hands at least before he moved on with his life.

"Great! I'll spread the word here at the office," Sue exclaimed. "As soon as it's set up, I'll call you and tell you what time and where we will meet. Good-bye for now. I'll be seeing you on Friday."

"Good-bye."

Steven hung up and began feeling better about things. He knew he had done the right thing by resigning, for if he stayed on at Apple, he would have continued to feel bitter about the legal outcome and probably would have become nonproductive on the job. Also, he really did need to take some time off to think about a lot of things, and to sit back and get some rest.

With that thought in mind, Steven took off his shoes and sprawled out on his couch and clicked on the TV to watch the CNN World News Report. The announcer was talking about the latest trip representatives from the United States Commerce Department had made to mainland China. The announcer said there was a growing concern in the United Nations that normal trade between the United States and China might be curtailed if the Chinese did not put a stop to their illegal practices of copying CD records.

Steven smiled and said out loud, "My God, even the Chinese need a good copyright lawyer. I wonder if I should tell Miles to go interview for the job." When he realized how absurd that thought was, he laughed so hard his chest hurt. Steven closed his eyes and dozed off for the best sleep he had experienced in months.

On Friday evening at 5:30, Steven strolled into the bar at Johnny's Steak House on El Camino Real in Palo Alto. This restaurant was a popular hangout for Apple employees, and his secretary reserved one of the back rooms, where the group could be served drinks and food without being bothered by the other patrons. Happy hour was in full swing, so the bar was rapidly filling up with patrons who were able to purchase double-size drinks for only two dollars each. It certainly looked like the restaurant and bar were going to be very busy this evening.

A couple of Steven's friends were sitting at the bar waiting for his arrival. When they saw him, they came forward, shook his hand, and led him into the back room, where Sue had been for the past couple of hours decorating some of the tables. Steven was really impressed by all of this attention and, for a moment, wondered if he was doing the right thing leaving such a fine group of people.

"Hi, Steven," his secretary called out to him. "I was able to get about thirty guys and gals to come out tonight. As you can imagine, however, your boss won't be coming, which I guess is some kind of an unwritten company policy. Alan does plan to call you sometime and wish you well, however," Sue quickly added.

"I understand," said Steven. "I really appreciate this little bash. I hope I'm worth all the fuss."

"We had to eat somewhere anyway," she joked. "The group decided they might as well eat with you," she added, giggling.

By six o'clock everyone had arrived and, one by one, they crowded around Steven to discuss why he resigned and what he was going to be doing next with his career. As they crowded around him, Steven's friends kept handing him double-size drinks. Steven was not much of a drinker, but tonight he decided to let down his guard. By the time the group sat down to order food, Steven was feeling very tipsy, for he had consumed three double gin and tonics on an empty stomach!

When the meal was over and the dishes were being cleared away, Sue stood up and clanked her knife on one of the glasses to get the group's attention. "I've been appointed to be the master, or rather the mistress, of ceremonies."

This remark made everyone burst out laughing. Someone shouted, "Steven, I always thought you might have a mistress, and now your little secret is out!"

Again, everyone laughed, and Sue's face turned absolutely bright red, as did Steven's.

"Calm down, you animals! This is supposed to be a serious event. Our dear friend and comrade, Steven, has decided to depart from our midst, leaving us to fend for ourselves in the world of Macintosh™ computers and other related engineering and scientific endeavors. Steven has been our friend, our technical adviser, and a great contributor for the past fifteen years. Would all of you please stand and raise your glasses in a tribute to this great man."

As they stood, Steven felt very proud to have known these fine people for such a long time. He asked for another glass of wine, and raised it in tribute to all of his friends.

His secretary continued, "Steven, I hope you realize you absolutely must make a speech tonight. I know you don't like to make speeches, but we will not let you go without one," she laughed. "But before you stand before us and make a fool of yourself, we want to give you a token of our affection."

Sue retrieved a box wrapped in colorful paper from beneath the table and handed it to Steven. Everyone in the crowd started yelling,

"Speech! Speech! Speech!" while they clicked their glasses with their knives.

At this moment, Steven was feeling especially tipsy, for besides the three double gin and tonics before dinner, he drank several glasses of wine during the meal at the insistence of his secretary. He also just finished another glass of wine during the toast.

He slowly stood up and steadied himself by holding on to the back of his chair. "I guess you want me to open up this box first," he said with a noticeable slur.

"Yes, yes, yes," the crowd cheered. "We want to see if you can untie the ribbon. In your condition, we're not even sure you can stand up," they all shouted.

It was obvious that Steven, who rarely drank anything stronger than a single glass of wine, was going to need to be driven home after this event, for he was feeling no pain. Steven carefully steadied himself with one hand, while he opened the package with the other.

"There, you clowns, I did it, and I didn't even spill a drop."

After he said this, he realized it didn't make any sense. Again, the crowd laughed loudly as they were really enjoying this display of temporary helplessness from a man they greatly respected and loved. When Steven finally opened the box, he felt immediately humbled by the gift they had given him, for it was the latest Apple PowerBook™ laptop computer, which the group knew he wanted but had been too frugal to purchase for himself.

"I don't know what to say," said Steven, again with a considerable slur. "Did you guys rob the company store?" he asked with a big smile on his face. "I've wanted one of these beauties for a long time. If I knew I had to resign first to get one, I would have quit my job years ago!"

Again the crowd laughed loudly and stood up and clapped for several minutes. Sue stood and commented, "The guys always knew you were too tight to buy one for yourself, so they decided the least they could do was take up a collection and give it to you as a parting gesture of their respect for you. By the way, in case you haven't guessed, this is the latest version of the Apple PowerBook™ computer, which has the latest revision of the Mac™ operating software installed in it. Each time you boot up the system, a special screen saver will come on; it is a picture we took this week of your entire staff and friends at Apple. Wherever you go, you will have to stare at all of these ugly faces. We wanted to be sure you wouldn't forget any of us," she added, amidst much applause from the crowd. "And, don't you dare ever erase that picture," she laughed.

The crowd started chanting, "Turn it on, turn it on, turn it on." This Steven did, and when the system booted up, lo and behold, the screen displayed a high-resolution color picture of his friends, as well as some nice words at the top, thanking him for his many contributions.

Steven passed the computer around the room so each person could see the display. While this was happening, he drank a cup of black coffee Sue poured for him, in order to clear his head. He then started to make his speech.

"As you guys know, I'll never win a prize for giving the greatest speeches in the world. I'm sincerely touched by this display of affection for me, and again I wish to thank each and every one of you for this outstanding gift. I'll cherish it as long as I live and I'll never ever erase the screen saver. Each time I turn on the system, I'll take a moment to look at all of your smiling faces, even the ugly ones!"

This last remark brought down the house, and his friends again stood up and clicked their glasses and clapped and laughed heartily. Steven continued.

"Now, all of you have been asking me tonight why I quit. You all know how I've felt about the recent litigation matter. I got myself so caught up in it that when the ruling came down, I just felt I should step aside and look for employment elsewhere. I don't believe Apple will go down the tubes because of it, but rather I felt it was time I do something else with my life in the world of computing.

"No, I don't have another job lined up at this time, and I don't plan to even look for one for at least six months. You guys don't realize it, but I have hardly taken any vacation since I joined Apple. I intend to go back to Hong Kong to visit my parents and do some serious sightseeing.

"I also want to pursue my quest to see if I can find a way to get my grandparents out of mainland China, where they are being held under some form of political house-arrest. Maybe I can bribe some official by offering to give him this computer."

Again, the crowd was on their feet laughing and clapping. Steven began to feel very dizzy from all the drinks, and he began to let down his guard. With a glazed look in his eyes, he continued to speak, and the crowd noticed his slur was gone. His voice seemed to come from deep inside him, with a peculiar resonant quality. As Steven continued, the room was so quiet you could hear a pin drop.

"My name is Steven Lee, and I used to work for the Apple Computer Company. Before I take my leave tonight, I do want to say a bit more about the litigation matter, since all of you are my friends. I think it is terrible the United States judicial system has given Microsoft a free rein to continue to develop and sell their Windows™ operating system. Do you guys realize what that will mean? It will mean that every Tom, Dick, and Harry who owns an IBM-compatible computer can now have a system that behaves like the Macintosh™!

"Think of it. Microsoft is now free to sell its Windows™ operating system in a shrink-wrapped box for a hundred dollars, and this permits an owner of an IBM-compatible personal computer to experience a Mac™-like performance for very little cash outlay.

"If Microsoft had been stopped by our litigation action, every customer who wanted to have the ease of use of a Mac™ would have to buy a Mac™ from Apple instead, and those sales would add up to billions and billions of dollars for Apple! Instead, Microsoft receives millions of dollars that is almost all profit, and Apple receives nothing!

"Yes, in case you haven't noticed, I'm very bitter about this. And after my time off in Hong Kong, I plan to do something about it! I'll not rest until this travesty of justice has been corrected! When I return, I'll be contacting you to see if you want to help me in my cause! We must rise up and make our statement be heard by the legal community and the world! This matter must not be swept under the rug! We must find some way to fight this very unfair ruling!"

All eyes were on Steven as he completed his remarks, and no one was saying a word. Steven's eyes were totally glazed over now and sweat was pouring down his forehead. He was acting like someone possessed. His secretary looked at him in utter amazement, 'for she had never seen him behave like this before. Perhaps it was the liquor, but she feared it was much more than that.

To get things back under control, Sue stood up and started to clap. The group quickly joined in, and this seemed to calm Steven, who thanked them again for all of the fine times, and again thanked them for the wonderful gift.

"Steven, how about if I drive you home?" Sue asked. "I think you need a good night's sleep now."

"Great. I guess I did have too much to drink," Steven said with a definite slur. "Thanks again, everyone," he said, as the group started leaving the room.

In the car, Steven closed his eyes and was soon snoring loudly. Sue began to wonder how she was going to get him out of the car and into his townhouse. However, when they arrived at his parking lot, she saw his next-door neighbor taking out some trash to the dumpster, and she asked the neighbor to help her. The two of them were able to drag Steven out of the car and up the steps. She found a key in his pocket, so they dragged him into his living room and plopped him down on his sofa and took off his shoes.

"What a night," she thought. "I wonder if Steven really meant what he said?" The thought that he might be serious sent shivers down her spine.

Chapter Seventeen

Steven woke up on Saturday at noon with a terrible hangover. He found some tomato juice in the refrigerator and fixed himself a mixture of tomato juice, Worcestershire sauce, and Tabasco, which he heard would help get rid of hangovers. He tried to recall the events of the party, but could only remember receiving the nice gift and the beginning of his speech. He could not remember the remarks he made at the end, nor could he remember how he got home. He decided to call Sue and thank her for the party, and see if she could fill him in on the details of how the party ended.

"Hello, Steven," she replied, when he acknowledged who he was. "I was worried about you last night. You sorta flipped out, if you know what I mean. I guess you really had way too much to drink."

"How did I get home?"

"I drove you home, and luckily for me your next-door neighbor was outside when I arrived. He and I were able to drag you into your living room and put you on your couch. If he hadn't been there, I guess you and I would have spent the night in my car. That surely would have started some juicy gossip," she laughed.

"I want to thank you again for arranging the affair. I plan to send the gang a card thanking them for the really nice gift," Steven said. "Would you mind telling me what I said in the speech? I can't recall what I told the group, besides thanking them for the computer."

"You kinda scared us all, for you went off on some kind of tirade about how you were personally planning to take on the entire judicial system and show them how wrong they were in giving Microsoft the right to continue with their Windows™ development. I don't think the group took you very seriously. They felt you were tired and definitely needed a change of scenery, for you have been so wrapped up in this matter for so long it has gotten you down. Isn't that right?"

"Yes, I definitely do need a rest. I hope I didn't offend anyone with my comments."

"No, as I said, they all felt you were just in need of a well-deserved rest, and they all wished you well."

"Thanks again for driving me home. When I return from my vacation, I'll call into work and see how the old gang is behaving in my absence."

"So long, Steven, and please take it easy. And please don't drink too much in the future."

"Bye."

"So long."

"Steven, this is Alan Smith calling. Could you give me a call on Monday morning at my office? I would like to set up a meeting with you next week before you take off, because I need to be briefed on the status of your projects. Can you let me know if that will be okay with you?"

Steven returned home late Saturday night after going to the movies and listened to his answering machine. Alan had been his boss at Apple, and technically speaking, since he had been escorted out of the office the same day he resigned, Steven did not owe him the courtesy of having such a meeting. However, he understood Alan really did need to find out the status of his projects, and he didn't want to leave Apple totally high and dry, for they had been very good to him over the years.

On Monday morning, Steven returned the call. "Alan, this is Steven. When and where would you like to meet?"

"How about coming by the plant at noon today? I can reserve conference room A, right off the lobby. I'll send out for some sandwiches and sodas. I don't think we'll need to meet for more than a couple of hours."

"Okay, Alan, I'll see you then."

Steven felt uncomfortable when he arrived at Apple's lobby. He felt like everyone passing through the lobby was staring at him as if he were an alien from a distant planet. He reasoned that, with time, he would feel differently, but after all this was the first time he had ever resigned from a responsible job, and he wasn't quite sure how he should feel.

He signed in at the guest register and took a seat along the wall near the conference room. He didn't have to wait very long, for Alan soon appeared from the hallway leading to the engineering wing.

Alan was promoted to vice president of engineering a couple of years earlier. He had been responsible for the entire hardware design of the Macintosh™, and Steven and the other members of Apple's engineering staff respected him for his ability to manage complex engineering projects. Alan also respected Steven for his deep understanding of software operating systems for personal computers. In fact, he wanted to try to talk Steven into staying with Apple, but the Apple management thought better of it. They were concerned that Steven was probably burned out and would no longer be as productive as he had been in his earlier years.

"Hello, Steven," Alan said as he shook his hand. "I'm truly sorry I missed the little bash Sue organized for you," Alan said halfheartedly. "What are your plans now?"

"I need a rest," Steven said. "I plan to visit my parents in Hong Kong, and I'll take some time to do some serious sightseeing in the Orient."

"Then you have no plans to join Microsoft," Alan laughed, as he watched Steven's eyes carefully. Microsoft normally did not try to lure engineers away from the Apple staff, for the Apple software was so different from the kind of software Microsoft developed. However, Steven had intimate knowledge of both systems, and since he was quite visible during the litigation trial, Alan really did wonder if perhaps Microsoft had made him an offer he couldn't refuse.

Steven chuckled. "Alan, the odds Microsoft could ever lure me to work for them are about the same odds that I'll go out this afternoon and buy myself a new IBM-compatible personal computer. There is not enough money in the world that would cause me to do that!" Steven added, with a great big grin on his face. "But what do you think? Do you think they would hire me if I interviewed for a job with them? Just kidding, Alan."

The two of them went into the conference room where two other engineers, one from Steven's staff and one from the Quality Control Department, joined them.

"Steven, of course you know Tim, but do you know Joe from our Quality Control Department?"

"Hi, Tim. Glad you could make my party. Hi, Joe. I don't believe I've had the pleasure."

"Steven, as you know, this is a routine matter we always need to handle whenever anyone leaves Apple. I have a list of questions prepared on this piece of paper. We need to go through them one at a time to be sure we don't miss anything. Tim will be taking over some of your work, and I'll take over the rest until I decide how to reassign all of your projects."

Steven looked at the list that contained all of the projects he had been working on. One by one, he discussed each project, indicating the status and where the material associated with the project could be found. This part of the meeting took only a little more than an hour; about halfway through the meeting, sandwiches and sodas were delivered.

"Steven, you kinda shook us up a bit at your going-away party, when you took off on your tirade," Tim said, as they began to eat their lunch.

"As my secretary told me, I sure can't hold my liquor," Steven responded. "The next time I quit any job, I'll first pay a visit to Alcoholics Anonymous. I guess I was living and breathing this litigation thing for so long it kinda got under my skin. I plan to take a long vacation and clean the cobwebs out of my brain," Steven said, smiling sheepishly.

"Well, all of us at the party understood, and you didn't offend any of us."

Alan added, "Steven, the guys all said you drank too much. Shame on you, old buddy. You have to learn to know your limits."

"Why don't we continue discussing the items on this list," Steven said, changing the subject, which was beginning to make him uncomfortable.

The group continued to discuss the remaining projects, and Alan seemed satisfied that he had all the information he needed. Then Alan turned to Steven and began asking him questions about the Operating System Analysis Programs Steven developed to assist in preparing material for the copyright litigation trial.

"Steven, I asked Joe to attend this meeting because your analysis programs may be of some use to his department when they check out our new Apple systems. As you know, many of our new systems will be able to run in either a Macintosh™ mode or in a Windows™ mode.

"From what you told me several months ago, I understand you developed these programs to make it possible to slow down an IBM-compatible computer with Windows™ loaded in it. I think you told me that by doing so, you were able to analyze each and every software command at some arbitrarily low speed. Is that about right?"

"That's correct," Steven answered. He was now feeling a bit guilty about having taken a copy of these programs with him when he resigned. "I used those programs to slow down my test computer so I could observe each step of the Windows™ program and see if Microsoft used any of the kinds of commands I had written into the Macintosh™ software. As you know, we didn't find anything, which is probably one of the reasons we lost our case."

"Steven, is it possible to use these programs to slow down a Macintosh™ as well, and if so, would that be a useful thing to do when we check out a new system?" Joe asked.

"You would first have to re-compile the program on a Mac™ compiler, which would not be too difficult, and yes, I believe it would be a useful tool to have in your department's bag of tricks," Steven added.

"Steven, can you outline the structure of your program on the blackboard?"

"Sure, Alan," Steven said, as he stood up.

Steven drew a flow chart on the blackboard and showed the group that the beauty of the program was that it contained executable code with the same names as the executable codes found in the Windows™ operating system.

"If that be so, how can it be added to the Windows™ directory?" Alan asked.

"You merely have to place it into hidden files on the same directory as the primary files, and the code becomes invisible to the computer. However, when you enter certain keystrokes, the computer responds to my program files, and the speed of operation can be adjusted by clicking on the F2 function key. In my testing, I would often click the F2 function key one hundred times to really slow things down so I could visually observe the result of each and every command on the monitor."

"Doesn't the computer often hang up when you play around with its speed?" Joe asked.

"No, because I was careful to scale down all operations by the same precise amount. By clicking on the F2 key a number of times, you can in effect turn a fast Pentium® machine into a 486 machine. If you hit the F2 key even more times you can turn the computer into a 386 machine, or if you hit the F2 key a thousand times, I suppose you can make the computer behave like an old XT," Steven proudly stated.

"Well, Joe, I guess you got your answer," Alan said.

"Steven, please tell Joe where to find your programs on your computer. It sounds like the Quality Department should try to use them."

The meeting ended cordially. Steven and Alan strolled to the lobby and Steven signed out. As they walked outside together to say a few last pleasantries, Alan suddenly turned to Steven, with a big grin on his face.

"Steven, do you remember the time we sent some of our newest Apple machines to the PC Labs Testing Organization for an independent comparison with the latest Pentium® machines? If you recall, we got blown away and had to go back and install more memory and a faster processor."

"Yes, Alan, that was a bit of an embarrassment for us," Steven said. "But why are you remembering those events now?"

"Wouldn't it have been a blast if your Operating Systems Analysis Programs had somehow been installed in those Pentium® machines, with the F2 key punched a hundred times? We would have blown the performance socks off of such a comparison test, if that were the case. God, I would like to see the face of the manager of the test lab if that had happened. Don't you remember how biased he was in favor of the Pentium® boxes?"

"Alan, maybe you're the one who needs a long rest," Steven laughed.

They shook hands. Steven then headed back to his townhouse, with Alan's last comment planted indelibly in his mind.

Chapter Eighteen

Ming Lee was very excited. He called his wife from his office and told her that their son, Shou, was planning to visit them. He read her the short message contained in the fax he held in his hand:

Dear Father and Mother:

After fifteen years of dedicated work, I've resigned my position at Apple Computer. As you know, I've taken very little time off since I started working there, and frankly I'm burned out. I hope it will be all right if I stay with you in Hong Kong for several months, for I badly need to rest and catch up on things with you both. Father, I realized the other day that it has been almost two years since we last visited. That was when you came to California on business. Also, Mother, I hate to think of how long it has been since we last saw each other. I guess it was at the end of my junior year at Berkeley, when you convinced me I should take the summer off and return to Hong Kong for a visit.

I'll be able to join you in two weeks, after I make certain personal arrangements here. That would mean I'll arrive in Hong Kong around the first of April. If that is okay with you, please send me a fax indicating so. I'll fax you my exact travel arrangements, once I've made them.

Signed, Shou Lee (Steven)

While waiting for her husband to come home for dinner, Steven's mother began to worry. Why would anyone quit a job without any prospects for another? Could it be Steven had been fired, and if so, wouldn't that be a bad mark on his record? Or, could it be he is ill with some incurable disease? Anyway, she knew it was her job as his mother to worry about him until she was able to convince herself he was okay.

Ming arrived home at his usual time, a bit past 8:00 P.M. This evening he was filled with excitement over the fax he had received earlier that day. He brought his wife, Betty Lou, a dozen of her favorite roses, and he stopped at the local liquor store for a bottle of her favorite champagne, already chilled and ready to pour.

"Betty Lou, I'm home," he called out when he opened the door of their exclusive condominium located on the tenth floor of a high-rise building in downtown Hong Kong.

"I'm in the kitchen," Betty Lou replied, as she put the finishing touches on the meal she prepared for Ming. "We are having roast chicken and long Chinese noodles tonight, which is one of your favorites," she said.

"Great! This is a night we must celebrate, for our son is soon coming home. Here, put these flowers in the large blue vase and put this bottle of champagne in the silver holder with lots of crushed ice. This is a night to remember."

"Ming, you shouldn't spend your money so willy-nilly. After all, it will be two or three weeks before he arrives, and who knows, maybe he will change his mind. He's done that before, or have you forgotten?"

Ming frowned at her. "I'm sure he will come this time," Ming said sternly. "I believe he has just worked himself to a frenzy and needs a long rest. I look forward very much to his visit."

"You know me, Ming," she said. "I immediately started to worry after you read me the fax, for I don't know why he should just quit his job without any apparent reason."

"I'm sure he will tell us when he arrives," Ming added. "Now, stop your worrying and let's prepare to celebrate the occasion."

Ming turned on the stereo to some soft music. He then dimmed the lights in the dining room, placed the roses in a vase on the center of the table, and poured two tall glasses of champagne. Betty came from the kitchen and placed the food on the server. The two of them sat down and ate without discussing Steven anymore.

Betty Lou and Ming met in China in 1945. Ming was a soldier in the Chinese People's Army, and Betty Lou was an American missionary working as a nurse's aide, helping the sick and wounded as they were brought in from the battle fields to the main hospital in Shanghai. As a part of her training, Betty Lou learned to speak the local Chinese dialect fluently, so she was able to provide very effective comfort and support to the sick, wounded, and dying Chinese soldiers.

Before the war was over, Ming contracted scarlet fever from sleeping in damp fields full of dirty water and sewage. As a consequence, he was bedridden for several months and had to be slowly nursed back to health. In late 1945, Ming was released from the hospital and, shortly thereafter, was discharged from the Army. He returned to his old job at the Shanghai University, where he taught world history and political science.

While in the hospital, Betty Lou and Ming spent a lot of time together. He had some knowledge of the English language through the work he did at the university, so she volunteered her spare time to tutor him to the point where he could carry on a reasonable conversation with her in English. With her by his side, his long bout with the fever was easier to endure, and he looked forward to each of her visits.

After his release, Ming asked Betty Lou if it would be all right if he continued to call on her. She was flattered and immediately accepted. The two of them soon became inseparable, and in early 1947 they were married, first in a Buddhist ceremony, and later in a civil ceremony in the American Embassy.

Conditions in China were deplorable after the war, so Ming told Betty Lou he was going to contact some friends in Hong Kong to see if he could find work in their silk importing business. He told her it would be in their best interests to move as soon as possible, for he feared the Chinese government would establish an embargo on anyone leaving the country.

In 1950, Ming and Betty Lou crossed the border from mainland China into Hong Kong, each carrying a temporary travel visa, but neither having any intention of returning. They were fortunate to get such passes. Ming immediately took a job in his friend's silk importing business and Betty Lou took a job in a small hospital on the outskirts of Hong Kong.

When they embarked on their one-way journey, Ming told his parents he would send for them in a few months, once he and Betty Lou established themselves in their new home. However, this would never happen, for his parents were arrested shortly after Ming and

Betty Lou left, and were sent to Northern Manchuria to a detention farm for dissidents. A trial was held and they were accused and found guilty of being part of a group of liberal Chinese elitists who were trying to force the government to hold free elections, in order to elect General Chiang Kai-shek as the head of state.

At the parent's trial, the fact that Ming and Betty Lou had left the country illegally was revealed, so it was now impossible for them to ever return to China for any reason, for fear they too would be permanently detained.

The elder Lees were forced to remain in China, never to see their newborn grandson, Shou, who was born in 1952. Shou grew to be a very tall and handsome lad. While in grade school in Hong Kong, he took the English name Steven. Upon his graduation from high school, Ming and Betty Lou decided to send Steven to the University of California in Berkeley, for he had a profound interest in computers. He subsequently graduated from Berkley with honors.

Chapter Nineteen

The announcer at the San Francisco International Airport shouted, "Flight 101 for Hong Kong is now ready for boarding."

Steven was one of 175 passengers boarding the Northwest Orient Boeing 747 flight, which was a daily flight to Hong Kong. It was Friday, 31 March 1995, and the lady at the ticket check-in counter told him the flight would be full of both businessmen returning home and tourists who were taking early spring vacations. Since Steven had not taken a trip like this for a very long time, he decided to treat himself to a one-way, first-class ticket. As a consequence, he was one of the first passengers to be permitted to board the large aircraft.

Once Steven decided to visit Hong Kong, he had to sublet his townhouse, sell his car, and buy some sportier clothes. In addition, he had to place his savings in accounts that could be readily accessed in Hong Kong. Steven called several of his closest associates to wish them well and to thank them for all the support they had given him over the years. During these conversations, he was pleased that none of them brought up the unfortunate incident of his farewell speech, so he assumed they had simply dismissed the event. This suited him just fine.

Before leaving, Steven removed all of his software programs from his Macintosh™ classic computer, and loaded them onto his new Apple PowerBook™ laptop computer. He decided to bring with him the floppy disks containing his Operating System Analysis Programs, and he also purchased a new word processor program, in case he decided to write a résumé during the long flight to Hong Kong. In addition to the word processor, he bought some of the newest high resolution games, to which he soon became addicted. "Steven Lee," Steven answered when the stewardess in first-class checked his name on her roster.

"Would you like me to hang up your jacket so you can relax?"

"That would be nice," answered Steven. "By the way, just how many hours is this flight?"

"Normally this flight to Hong Kong takes fourteen hours, but today our captain has informed us we will have a strong tail wind. We should arrive one hour earlier than planned. Have you taken this flight before?"

"It's been more than fifteen years since I took a flight to Hong Kong," Steven answered. "I sat way in the back in the coach section. I think this will be much nicer today."

She smiled her approval and said, "Excuse me, Mr. Lee, but I need now to tend to some of the other passengers. If I can do anything for you, please don't hesitate to buzz me."

Steven settled back in his soft leather seat and depressed the seat button. He found he could recline almost horizontally, which would be great when he decided to take a snooze. He remembered the early days of Apple, when the sales guys were all told they could fly first class. "No wonder they were so loyal to Apple," he thought.

"Sit tight, mate," a tall man in a dark blue suit told Steven, as he slid in front of him to take the seat by the window. "Looks like we'll be flight buddies for the next fourteen hours or so. My name is John Toliver. What's yours?"

"Steven Lee," said Steven, as they shook hands. "Do you take this flight often?"

"I've been taking this flight a lot lately, and I'm afraid I'll be taking it many more times in the future," John answered. "What about you?"

Steven gave him a brief rundown on himself, indicating it had been many years since he had flown anywhere, let alone Hong Kong. He did not elaborate on recently leaving Apple, but rather indicated he was taking some time off to rest up and visit his parents.

"So, John, why do you fly so often to Hong Kong?"

"I work for the U.S. Government Commerce Department, and you probably have read in the papers that we and the Chinese are holding a lot of meetings lately because, let's just say, we don't agree with some of their trade practices."

"Are all of the meetings held in Hong Kong or in China?" Steven asked.

"Unfortunately, that's the way it is. The Chinese claim to be innocent of any wrongdoing, so they make us pursue them on their own turf. No offense, Steven, but if I never eat any Chinese food again, it will be too soon," he said, with a laugh.

Steven laughed as well. "John, you probably will not believe me, but I don't care much for Chinese food either. I was born in Hong Kong. but I've never visited mainland China. My favorite dishes are steak and French fries."

This brought a loud chuckle from John. The stewardess overheard Steven and said, "How did you know what we're serving for lunch?"

The stewardess announced everyone should fasten their seat belts and prepare for take off. John and Steven stopped their idle chatter and settled into their seats. The flight left on time, and once airborne, with the seat belt sign turned off, Steven stood up and walked to the galley to see if there were any good magazines to read. He found the latest issue of *Newsweek* and returned to his seat.

"Steven, you will find an interesting article on page forty-seven of that issue," John said, as he noticed the magazine on Steven's lap. Steven turned to that page and found an article entitled, "The Chinese are Being Accused of Record Piracy," written by Susan Hill, staff reporter. The article contained a number of color photos. One in particular caught Steven's eye, as it was a photo of three men who worked for the U.S. Commerce Department. The man in the center of the photo was John Toliver.

"So, John, does this article make you famous?"

"No, but it does a fairly good job explaining why I and my two associates, who are sitting across the aisle from you, are on our way to Hong Kong again for the umpteenth time this year."

"Are you their boss?"

"Not in the classical organizational sense," John said. "However, on this Chinese caper, they report to me."

The stewardess interrupted them and asked if they would like to have a cocktail before lunch. John obliged, but Steven declined, asking for a soft drink instead. The last thing he wanted was to become drunk on this flight and start discussing the Apple/Microsoft litigation case with this high-ranking government official!

While sipping his drink, Steven read the article. It was only four pages long, so it did not take him very long to finish it. "Are you now an expert on how the U.S. Copyright Law is supposed to protect the CD record industry?" John asked, with a twinkle in his eye.

Steven decided not to tell John about his recent experience with copyright law. Rather, he would try to find out more about the law as it applied to the CD record industry.

"I must admit I'm not very knowledgeable about such matters," Steven said. "By reading this short article, I still don't know much about the subject."

"Are you familiar with the term *chinese copy*, used often in the 60s and 70s?"

"Yes, I've heard that term used quite often," Steven said. "Isn't it usually used in the context of low technology items, such as toys, dolls, pencils, and the like?"

"That's right," said John. "However, we now believe the Chinese have gone too far with this copying craze of theirs. Take, for example, Elvis, when he was in his heyday. RCA records had to pay him millions of dollars just to get him to record his rock-and-roll music exclusively on their label. In addition, for each record sold, he would receive between five percent and ten percent of the retail sales price. If the Chinese decided to copy Elvis records, RCA would have a damn good reason to sue the holy crap out of them, for the Chinese would have an unfair business advantage, since they would not have to pay Elvis."

"How far has this record piracy practice gone?" Steven asked. "Are the Chinese actually copying most of the popular records and selling them without paying any royalties or fees?"

"Steven, I'm sorry, but I really can't reveal what we've found out so far in our investigations. Let me just say there are certain people in China who wish to profit greatly by not paying any artist fees or royalties. Since Uncle Sam is supposed to protect the interests of legitimate businesses, including the record companies, we are being asked to investigate this matter to the fullest extent possible."

"Thanks for the insight, John," Steven said. "I'll make sure I don't buy any black market records while I'm in Hong Kong," he laughed.

John cracked a smile as well. "Steven, do you want to know something funny?" John asked. "My twelve-year-old daughter keeps pestering me to buy records each time I take this trip. Somehow, she's gotten it into her head that I'll be able to get them at about half of what she pays for records at her local Electro-Mart Record Store. What she doesn't know is that the discount records being sold in the basement of Electro-Mart Stores are already being offered at half the price of the legitimate stuff."

"That's really funny, John. By the way, I assume you are talking about CD records here. I would assume if copies were made, the quality would be perfect, for the recording method for CDs is a digital process. I would think it would be impossible to tell the difference between a copy and an original."

"How do you know all of that, Steven?" John inquired.

"Well, after all, I'm a computer junky and they are now becoming an important medium to use in personal computers, since they hold vast amounts of digital data."

The stewardess started down the aisle and began to serve the first-class passengers the first course in their five-course meal. After finishing the salad course, Steven asked John one more question on the subject of Chinese CD record piracy.

"One more question, if I may. How does the United States stop China from selling copies of records, as long as the record stores keep buying them and customers like your daughter keep buying them, without caring where they come from?"

"Well, Steven, without going into the whole laundry list of things our government is prepared to do, our final trump card would be to stop the sale of foodstuffs, medicine, and the like, which the Chinese people really need in order to exist. It may sound harsh, but we're prepared to do just that. However, we hope we can settle this matter before such a harsh penalty needs to be invoked."

"Thanks, John, for the information. I'm always interested in how politics and technology intertwine. Anyway, I think I'll put on my headset now and listen to some pirated music."

Upon hearing that remark, John laughed so hard he almost choked on his lettuce, and the other two men seated across the aisle turned and stared at him, wondering what set him off.

The rest of the flight was uneventful. Two more meals were served, and two first-run movies were shown. Lots of drinks were served, but Steven declined them all. In between the food and the movies, Steven had time to prepare a résumé, using his new computer, and he also learned to play a couple of games. He was disappointed, however, when the battery gave out after only four hours of use. When he read his manual, it warned him such would be the case, unless he first enabled the power management system.

"Boy, what a klutz," he thought to himself. "Here I am, a computer whiz, and I forgot to read the manual before the flight. Oh well, the next time I'll bring an extra battery."

John opened his thick briefcase and spent most of the flight reading memoranda concerning the Chinese affair. After about four hours of such work, he became tired and dozed off for the remainder of the flight.

"Ladies and gentlemen, please straighten your seat backs, fold up your tables and trays, and fasten your seat belts," came the instructions over the intercom. "We will be landing at Hong Kong International Airport in exactly fifteen minutes. Your luggage can be picked up at baggage claim area number twenty-five. You will need to proceed from the baggage claim area to the customs area.

"Please fill out the white customs card in the seat in front of you and have it ready when you arrive at customs. I hope none of you have brought any fresh fruit or vegetables, for the customs officials will confiscate them. However, if you have such items, please give them to me so I can give them to our chef. The passengers on the return flight will appreciate eating your fresh fruit."

This last comment brought a loud chuckle from all of the passengers when they realized they were having their legs pulled by the stewardess. It had been a long flight and many of them were not in the mood for humor, but it was rather funny, nevertheless.

The plane landed smoothly and taxied to its appointed gate. Steven was one of the first passengers to disembark. He bounded up the gangway into the terminal. He immediately began to scan the many faces to see if he could recognize his father and mother. He saw them standing on the left side of the waiting room, and when they recognized him, they began to wave wildly.

"Father and Mother," Steven said, with tears in his eyes. "It's been such a very long time!"

Part 3

The Demise of the Chinese CD Record Industry

Chapter Twenty

John Toliver had the drill down pat. This was his sixth visit to Hong Kong since he became involved in the DragonFly and Electro-Mart record piracy matters. "The routine always seems to go something like this," he thought to himself, as he waited for his luggage. "We get off the plane, we check into our hotel, we call the Chinese Embassy to confirm our meetings, and then we get the runaround. I'm getting a little tired of their attitude. I wonder what dire circumstances they will think up this time to avoid holding the meetings we have requested?" John asked his two associates, as they walked out of the airport to hail a cab.

"No doubt they will come up with something very creative. Maybe this time we will wear them down by our sheer weight of numbers and our persistence." John firmly believed he had the Chinese dead to rights. Before the trip, he read several reports from a number of independent testing laboratories, which proved conclusively that records being sold under either the DragonFly or Electro-Mart labels, as well as blank CD-Rs, which were clearly branded "Made In China," all came from the same manufacturing process. All he needed now was to find out if the CDs were the product of some outlaw Chinese company that decided to enter the market, or if the Chinese president or one of his ministry chiefs formally sanctioned their production.

After John checked in, he phoned the Chinese Embassy and asked to speak with Wing Ma, the charge d'affaires.

"Wing, this is John Toliver."

"Yes, John. I've been expecting your call. Did you have a pleasant flight?"

"It was uneventful as usual. Can we now go over our itinerary?"

"Of course John. Let me first find my copy."

Wing returned to the phone in a few minutes. "Okay. I now have it in front of me. Go ahead."

"The most important thing we wish to do is visit your CD record factory in Haikou. Has that visit been arranged this time?"

"Don't you mean you want to visit our CD-R factory? We don't operate a CD record factory!"

"If you must insist on calling it that."

"Yes, John, I must. Let me see. I see by a memo I've received from the managing director of the Haikou facility that a visit has been arranged for you. I'm so sorry in the past we were unable to accommodate your wishes. If you and your associates will stop by my office tomorrow at 9:00 A.M., we will all travel together to the wharf, where a Chinese patrol boat will pick us up. Incidentally, the trip to Haikou will take a few hours, and the scenery from the boat is quite spectacular this time of year," he added.

"Wing, we did not fly halfway around the world to watch the scenery. We will be at your office at 8:30. We don't want your patrol boat to leave without us!"

"I'll be there and I will have tea brewing for you."

"What about the other meetings? I hope you sent my last memorandum to your ministry chief of technology and production. We must insist on meeting either with him or his next in command, as we have some very important issues to discuss."

"John, you must understand our ministry personnel are stretched very thin these days. I certainly did send your memorandum through channels, but I've not heard back yet. Perhaps we will get a reply by tomorrow morning."

"Okay, but you must understand this. My management have told me I'm not to leave Hong Kong this time without a face-to-face meeting with a responsible person from the ministry of technology and production. Do you understand me?"

"Of course. I'll do everything in my power to fulfill your wishes."

"Well, John, do we get to visit their plant this time?" asked one of John's associates.

John turned and said, "It looks as if we actually will be able to take that trip, unless something occurs tomorrow. If that is so, we need to decide what we want to accomplish. Let's discuss that further at dinner."

The three of them decided to take naps before dinner so the cobwebs from the long flight would have time to clear from their heads. Three hours later, dressed casually, they reconvened in the dining room. They asked for a table in the corner, where they would not be disturbed.

"Presumably, we will be taken to their plant, where we will see a nice clean facility. I'll bet a year's pay we only see boxes full of CD-Rs, and not a single box containing CD records. Does anyone want to take me up on that bet?" John asked.

Joe and Bruce both shook their heads. "Not us, boss."

"Here's what I want to accomplish tomorrow. Joe, you're knowledgeable about the various classes of machinery required to produce CD records. You need to take inventory of the number of major production items, so we can estimate their production capacity. You will need to be prepared to do it mentally, for I'm almost certain they will not allow us to take any notes during the tour.

"And you, Bruce, are knowledgeable about facilities. You need to size up the building from the inside and outside so you can estimate how much warehouse space they have to store CD records. They will no doubt show us a nice tidy warehouse which will only have CD-Rs in it, but you will need to estimate how much additional space they have for CD record storage.

"Now, Bruce, let's discuss the covert operation you initiated. What have you to report?"

"Before we left the States, I contracted for the services of the Chinese National Detective Agency here in Hong Kong, which has done work in the past for the CIA and the Commerce Department. They committed to having one of their most experienced field operatives take a job in Haikou in the warehouse and shipping department. We are planning to meet him tonight, so we can tell him exactly what we want him to do for us."

"Where will you meet him?" asked John.

"In a bar by the wharf. He's arranging for the night off, faking a need to come to pick up some of his personal belongings. No one will suspect he is anyone other than a warehouse laborer who is relaxing and having a couple of drinks."

"Fine, but I think I should not be seen with him. Do you agree?" John asked.

"Yes. I recommend Joe and I go alone."

"How do you plan to utilize him?"

"We will take the tour of the Haikou facility, as you have arranged it, and we probably will not find anything incriminating. Our man will watch the activity that occurs just prior to our visit and just after our visit. He will be looking particularly for the movement of large quantities of boxes full of CD records. He will also try to get into the production area to see the work in process. He will carry a miniature camera and will take pictures of anything resembling CD records. He will especially look for boxes labeled DragonFly or Electro-Mart."

"How long after we leave do you think it will take them to resume their normal plant operation?"

"Considering the quantity of records we believe they are producing, they can't afford to be shut down for more than a few hours. Our man should see some action right away. As soon as he has taken an adequate number of photos, he will quit his job, using the excuse of a family illness. If all goes well, in a couple of days we should have the pictures we need to nail these bastards."

"Okay, guys, let's order dinner now. You two must not be late meeting your man. By the way, how are you going to recognize him?"

"We're going to sit together in a corner table near the back window. We will order two bloody marys, which are almost never served in that kind of a bar. Our man will notice the drinks and will eventually walk up to us and ask if we are from England. If we say, 'Bloody yes, mate, we surely are,' he will know it is us and he will ask to join us. He will speak with a British accent, as he grew up in London until the age of twenty-one, even though he is a first generation Chinese national. He goes by the name of Chan."

"Sounds like everything is all set."

"I hope so. Now let's order our food. I'm starving."

It had been almost a year since Shing promoted CT to the position of managing director of the Haikou Plant, so he could return to Beijing and help Keung deal with the onslaught of communiqués and other complaints he was receiving as a result of China's record piracy practices. Even though China was technically not doing anything illegal, they were nevertheless stealing business away from legitimate record companies who played by the rules.

As far as DragonFly record sales were concerned, the South American distributors were a very happy bunch. Consequently, whenever recording artists complained with the South American counterpart of the U.S. Commerce Department, no action was taken. Customers were enjoying records at very low prices and the distributors' sales volume more than doubled. However, Keung was now receiving high-level complaints from the U.S. Commerce Department, as well as threats to invoke major trade sanctions against China if this activity did not cease immediately.

The situation surrounding the sale of Electro-Mart records was an entirely different matter. When the recording artists complained to the record companies who had contracted them, their complaints were lodged directly with Manny in Los Angeles, who actually enjoyed keeping them at bay. He usually just ignored their flak. To show them he couldn't be pushed around, he recently shifted the mix of discounted records he purchased from China up to fifty percent from the thirty percent he initially planned to order. This of course made Kong very happy, and Keung applauded him for exceeding his very difficult 1993 and 1994 sales objectives.

In addition, in 1993 Manny opened up a chain of stores in super malls in Canada and in Europe, and he gave the Electro-Mart label preference over the other labels. Sales of CD records through the Electro-Mart chain increased dramatically, and Manny soon met his goal of being the world's largest independent CD record distributor by dealing directly with the manufacturers of records, cutting out what he called the "greedy middle men."

"Please have Shing and Kong come to my office immediately," Keung told his secretary. "We need to make some very important decisions."

"Good morning, Keung," Shing and Kong said, as they entered Keung's office, bowing to their president. "We understand you need to speak with us."

"Yes, would you care for some tea?"

"Ah, Keung, that would be nice," they said, nodding to Keung's secretary, as she left the office to fetch it.

"Gentlemen, I believe we need to sacrifice the sale of DragonFly records in order to divert the pressures we are getting from the U.S.

Commerce Department. Did you see a copy of the recent memorandum we received? They now threaten to invoke major trade sanctions against China."

"I saw the memorandum," Shing said. "But what do you mean by sacrificing the sale of DragonFly records? Do you mean we should stop producing them?"

"Yes. We should stop producing them immediately. Shing, isn't it true the records being sold under the DragonFly label are first branded in your plant before they are sent to Hong Kong to K&S Industries for eventual sale to the South American distributors?"

"That is correct," said Shing.

"And Kong, isn't it true the volume of such records only accounts for about ten percent of your total sales plan, now that the Electro-Mart distributor has stores in Canada and Europe, as well as in the United States?"

"That is also correct," said Kong.

"All right. I want to stage an affair in Haikou to make it look like a renegade company operating without our approval has produced DragonFly records. Furthermore, we need the affair to make it seem that our government has discovered this flagrant act and is taking stern actions to stop such blatant record piracy. We must do this in full view of the U.S. Commerce Department men who plan to visit us soon."

"When are the men from the Commerce Department arriving?" asked Kong.

"They arrive next Friday, and they insist on visiting our Haikou Plant the following day. I believe this affords us an excellent opportunity to stage the affair, but we will need to plan it immediately."

"What do you have in mind?" they both asked.

"Shing, I want you to move all products branded DragonFly, which have not yet been shipped to K&S Industries, to another warehouse in Haikou, whose name is registered to a false company. We will claim this company is the renegade company we wish to put out of business. On the day the visitors get off of the boat in Haikou, they should witness boxes full of DragonFly records being crushed in the town square by Chinese government troops using heavy road equipment."

"The press should be there, including the Reuters News Service, so this event will become known throughout the world. The message we want the press to communicate is that the Chinese government does not sanction the infringement of copyrights, and that we have been trying to flush out the source of the DragonFly records for some time. We want the world to believe we now have finally put an end to such illegal production."

"Should I close down the K&S Industries operation?" Kong asked.

"Yes, most definitely, once you have made your last shipments from there."

"What do I tell my South American distributors?"

"You tell them the Chinese government has never sanctioned the manufacture of illegal pirate records. Tell them you appreciated their sales all of this time, but they will now have to purchase their product from other suppliers. Remind them the world price has dropped considerably, as a direct result of the DragonFly sales, so they should be thanking you."

"I'll begin immediately to arrange for the actions needed in Haikou," Shing said.

"And I'll prepare to take the proper actions with the South American distributors, once the word hits the press that the records are being smashed," Kong added. "I shall also close down K&S Industries. It will appear as if it was never open."

"Thank you, gentlemen. I hope we don't have to take further actions on this matter. How is Manny doing, Kong, with regard to holding back the pressure he gets from the record industry?"

"He is a marvel to watch," Kong said. "I believe he actually welcomes the flak he receives almost daily. We will continue to be able to do business for a long time in his markets, using him to buffer us."

"I hope so," Keung sighed. "China cannot afford to have an across-the-board trade war with the United States at this time. And we really do need the income we get from this enterprise!"

Joe and Bruce were dressed in jeans with pullover black sweaters and heavy work shoes. They appeared to be a couple of American seamen from a freighter docked in the Hong Kong Harbor. They arrived about fifteen minutes before their rendezvous with Chan. They took their place at the corner table near the back window.

"Two bloody marys, please," Joe told the waiter, who seemed puzzled by their choice of drinks. A half-hour passed and they began to wonder if something went wrong. Then a tall Chinese man in his early thirties entered from a side door. He saw them and came directly to their table.

"I see you are drinking bloody marys. Are you guys from England?"

"Bloody yes, mate, we surely are," Joe said, almost laughing when he thought of how absurd he sounded.

"Can I join you then?" Chan asked in almost perfect King's English. "My name is Chan, and I used to live in London."

"Sure thing Chan. What are you drinking?" Bruce asked, motioning to the waiter to take his order.

"I'll have a gin and tonic," Chan told the waiter. "So, what is this gig all about?"

Bruce spent the next fifteen minutes briefing Chan on the operation and what they hoped he could find out for them.

"You realize, Bruce, I only started working in the warehouse yesterday, so all I know to date is that they ship a lot of boxes each day marked 'Made in China.' As far as I can tell, the product placed in those boxes is little, flat, clear plastic boxes containing CDs with no labels on them. I assume, from what you just told me, that those are CD-Rs."

"That sounds right. Are you sure you haven't seen any boxes with CD records, labeled either DragonFly or Electro-Mart?"

"Not yet, but remember I've only been there one day."

"Will you have any excuse to wander through the production departments?"

"As a matter of fact, on Monday all new employees are supposed to receive a plant tour. That should work out in my favor. I should be able to see other products being produced, if in fact they are producing CD records."

"How are you able to take pictures without being seen?" Bruce asked.

"My camera is an extremely flat one, which I carry in my shirt pocket. It becomes actuated when I clench my fist, using a miniature pressure sensor. Don't worry, guys. I can take plenty of pictures, and no one will be the wiser."

"We will visit the plant tomorrow. We presumably will see little or no evidence of CD records. However, the minute we leave, there should be some kind of activity, which may be a signal that they have been holding out on us. That is when you need to find out as much as possible."

"I understand. I'd better get back now. I'll meet you again on Wednesday night, hopefully with some nice juicy pictures."

Joe and Bruce left the bar and hailed a cab to return to the hotel. "He seems like an able chap, don't you think?" Bruce asked.

"Yes. I hope he can find out something," Joe replied.

"I sure hope so too."

Chapter Twenty-One

Steven hugged both of his parents. "Neither of you have changed very much," he said, with tears streaking down his cheeks.

"Steven, you've grown up to be such a handsome man," his mother said, as she stepped back to get a better look at him. "Is that a little bit of gray hair I see mixed in with the rest?" she asked, smiling.

"Don't you embarrass the boy," Ming said. "Let's go to the baggage claim area and pick up his luggage. He must be very tired from the long flight."

"As a matter of fact, I could use a long nap," Steven admitted. "I've been sitting for over twelve hours, and I need badly to stretch out and relax."

During the drive home, Steven's mother talked nonstop about all sorts of things, and Steven found himself dozing off between subjects. He managed to be polite, however, and did answer his mother as best he could, even though he wished she would just let him close his eyes and rest.

When Steven asked about his grandparents, his father told him nothing had changed. They were still being held in a compound in Manchuria, and they were allowed to write once a month. His father told him he had saved several past letters for Steven to read.

"You'll have to translate them for me," Steven said. "Remember, you guys sent me to the United States and I never did learn how to read Chinese symbols."

"Here we are, Son," his father said as he pulled into the street where their townhouse was located. "We live on the tenth floor in that building over there. We use the parking garage across the street. I'm going to drop you and your mother off in front, and then I'll park the car. I can bring your suitcases with me, if you like."

"Fine, but let me carry my stuff. It's just a short walk into the building and up the elevator."

By the time his father returned, Steven was stretched out on the bed in the guest room and was sound asleep. His father looked in on him, and turned to Betty Lou and told her they should just let him sleep.

"He looks so pale and weary," Betty Lou said. "I hope he's not ill."

"He will feel a lot better by tomorrow morning. Don't you remember the last time you took such a long trip? It can tire out anyone."

"But we have so much to talk about."

"It can wait till morning. Remember that he will be with us for a long time. We will have plenty of time to catch up on things. Why don't you and I retire? In the morning, you can cook him his favorite breakfast, scrambled eggs with tomatoes and lox mixed in with it."

"Do you think that's still his favorite?"

"Believe me, Betty Lou, when he smells it cooking, he will be very pleased and he will surely remember it."

"Okay. Good night, dear."

"Good night."

Steven slept for almost twelve hours before he awoke to the smell of the fantastic breakfast. "Mother, are you fixing me my favorite breakfast?" Steven cried out from his bedroom.

"I certainly am, Son," Betty Lou answered. "Why don't you take a nice shower? When you're finished, your breakfast will be ready."

"Sounds good. I'll be out in a few minutes."

Ming returned from his morning walk about the time Steven emerged from the guest room. "How do you feel this morning, Son?"

"I feel really rested," Steven said. "I had a great sleep."

Steven and Ming helped Betty Lou serve the breakfast on trays, so they could eat on the patio. From their tenth floor townhouse, it was possible to see for miles, including the huge Hong Kong wharf area. Steven stood for several minutes, taking in the breathtaking view.

"You'd better eat your eggs before they get cold," Ming said.

"Sorry. I was fascinated with this view. I could sit here for hours taking it all in."

"So, Steven, would you mind telling us why you quit your job?" Betty Lou asked, not willing to wait any longer for his explanation.

"Let me first finish this wonderful breakfast. Then I'll tell you all about what happened," Steven said.

After the three of them cleared the dishes from the patio table, Betty Lou brought out a large pot of tea. While she served them, Steven filled them in on what his life was like the first ten years, before the Apple copyright litigation began, and how his life had changed since.

"Steven, how could one single legal suit cause your outlook to change so drastically?" Ming asked.

"I guess I became so wrapped up in the success of the Macintosh™, I just couldn't bear to think that some competing technology from a software company could encroach so significantly on our success, which we all worked so long and hard to achieve."

"I can understand how you might feel that way," Betty Lou said. "It's important that life have meaning. You have spent a third of your life working on a particular technology, and it must hurt dreadfully to see others exploit it so unmercifully!"

"I'm so glad you understand, Mother. Anyway, I decided it was time for me to try my hand doing something else. I'm sure there are many other exciting new challenges waiting for me to discover. After I've worn out my welcome with you two, I'll move on and try to find one," Steven added, laughing.

"Steven, you will never wear out your welcome here," Ming said quickly. "Maybe you should consider finding a job here in Hong Kong or in Taiwan. There are many electronics firms to choose from. The United States does not have a corner on all the world's creative jobs."

"Yes, Father, I know of many such companies. But what happens when China takes over ownership of Hong Kong, which is supposed to happen in the summer of 1997? Will these companies all thrive as well under direct rule from mainland China?"

Steven could not help but notice that the mention of that major world event caused his father and mother to look anxiously at each other. "Steven, as best we understand such things, the business outlook for Hong Kong will not be fundamentally different as a result of China taking over the country. No doubt there will be some changes in business practice. However, we believe the successful Hong Kong business practices and policies will remain essentially unchanged."

Steven again noticed his parents looking anxiously at each other. This time he decided to find out what was going on between them. "Something is wrong here, isn't it? When I mentioned the takeover of Hong Kong, you two became suddenly tense. Please tell me what is going on!"

Betty Lou looked at Ming, who nodded. They decided it was time they leveled with their son. "Steven, as you know, we have told you on numerous occasions the reasons your grandparents are being held in Manchuria. They were members of a movement aimed at overthrowing the Chinese regime right after the war, in order to replace it with a government headed by General Chiang Kai-shek."

"I remember that. Didn't he relocate to Taiwan and form an independent nation, which has prospered greatly?"

"That's right. Taiwan has prospered considerably more than mainland China, and that continues to be a source of embarrassment for today's Chinese leaders. Your father and I believe that is why your grandparents are still being held, along with hundreds of others, even though it has been more than forty years since they were first interned."

"So, what does this have to do with the acquisition of Hong Kong in 1997?" Steven asked.

Betty Lou again looked at Ming, who indicated she should continue. "We have never told you, but your father and I did not leave China with proper papers. We escaped the same regime that placed your grandparents into their internment camp. During their trial, it became known that we fled the country, so your father and I are on a "wanted for questioning" list. As recently as a year ago, your father received a communiqué from an old friend in Shanghai who insists he has seen such a list with our names on it. If we ever return to mainland China, we fear we will also be placed under arrest."

Steven was shocked when he heard this. How could such things happen in the modern world of 1995? This was barbaric! Now he could see why they were worried. Once Hong Kong is acquired, China could claim his father and mother have technically returned to the mainland. They could legally be placed under arrest! This was simply awful!

"Have you sought any legal advice?" Steven asked, with a very worried look on his face.

"Yes, on numerous occasions, and we continue to be told the same story."

"And what are you told?"

"If the Chinese authorities decide to come and get us, they will have the legal basis for doing so."

"Perhaps you and Mother should move to the United States. Have you considered doing that?"

"Your father is a successful Hong Kong businessman, and I'm very much involved in my hospital work here. We just haven't been able to convince ourselves that we should consider that possibility yet. However, as the year 1997 approaches, we realize we must give it more serious thought.

"Our lawyers tell us that perhaps the Chinese will pardon all such refugees in Hong Kong as a statement of good faith during the proceedings of 1997. The problem is we have no way of knowing if that will really happen. I've met a lot of my friends who are in the same status as we. None of us know what to expect."

"You've given me a lot to think about," Steven said. "I'm so glad you leveled with me. Perhaps the three of us talking about it will yield some alternatives you haven't considered."

"Perhaps so. We initially decided not to burden you with this information, but we are glad now we've shared our little secret with you," Betty Lou said sincerely.

"I think I need to go jogging and let this sink in," Steven said. "I noticed a nice trail in the park across the street. Are people allowed to jog on the trails around the lake?"

"Yes. We see joggers every day. Your mother and I will be here when you return. We thought that perhaps after lunch you would like to take a brief tour of the city."

Steven quickly donned his jogging outfit and running shoes and bid his parents farewell. As he headed for the elevator, he was very worried about what he had just heard. It was bad enough to have to go through life never being able to see or speak with his grandparents; but now his parents might be whisked away to some awful place to finish out their days.

"God, what is this world coming to?" he asked himself.

The park across the street from the townhouse was several acres in size and was situated next to a small lake full of swans. Steven thought how nice this would be for him to be able to jog in such a setting each day. As he began to run, his thoughts turned again to his parents. He decided he would spend the next several weeks brainstorming this subject, rather than worrying about what his next career move should be. After all, it would never do for him to return to the United States looking for a job, while his parents continued to live in fear of their future. They had done so much for him. Now it was time for him to find some way to help them in their time of need.

Chapter Twenty-Two

John Toliver and his associates arrived at the Chinese Embassy just before 8:30 A.M., where they were warmly greeted by Wing Ma, the Chinese charge d'affaires.

"Good morning, John. It is so good to see you again. It looks like the weather has cooperated. We can expect a very pleasant boat ride to the island of Hainan today," Wing said, showing a toothy smile.

"Yes, it will be a good morning, assuming we actually do get to tour the CD plant today, as promised," John answered. "I would like you to meet my two associates, Joe and Bruce."

"Glad to meet you both," Wing said, shaking their hands. "Please, won't you come inside for a few minutes and join me for some tea and biscuits?"

"Fine, but we must not be late," John replied.

The four of them spent the next fifteen minutes chatting about trivial things, including the weather, the NBA standings in the United States, and the status of the ongoing O. J. Simpson trial. "I'm amazed the U.S. Court System allows such a trial to be televised on a worldwide basis," Wing said. "I've even found myself watching sections of it, but only for my own amusement and entertainment, since I don't really care who wins the case. It does appear he may beat the rap, though, don't you think?"

"Only in the United States," John stated. "Let's leave now, so we don't miss the boat."

The boat ride from the Hong Kong harbor to the island of Hainan took just under three hours. Wing provided his three guests with special one day visas, since once they set foot on the island, they would be on Chinese soil. Once the boat was moored, it only took a few minutes to clear customs, as all of the necessary paperwork had already been prepared for their visit. A small tour bus was waiting to take them to the Haikou CD plant. The driver, who spoke only a few words of English, bowed many times as they climbed on board.

"We will be driving through downtown Haikou on our way to the plant," Wing said. "You will find it a very pleasant place. Perhaps some day you may want to vacation there."

John made no comment. He was deep in thought about what he wanted to accomplish today. He knew the Chinese would try to pull the wool over their eyes, so he wanted to avoid becoming complacent. His boss would not be happy if he were to return to the States with no more information than when he arrived.

As the bus turned into the center of town, there seemed to be some kind of a demonstration ahead that was blocking traffic. The driver and Wing began conversing rapidly, and then the bus proceeded toward the demonstration. Wing told his guests he believed it would only constitute a slight delay.

"What do you think it is?" Bruce asked.

"It's a bulldozer running back and forth over a pile of something in the middle of the street," Wing commented.

As the bus got closer, it was evident that the pile of something was an enormous pile of plastic boxes, the kind used to store CD records. Seeing this, John asked the bus driver to stop so he and his associates could proceed by foot to examine the scene more closely.

"John, look! It's a pile of DragonFly records, and the bulldozer is running back and forth breaking them into small pieces," Joe said excitedly. John and his associates walked around the pile, which they estimated to be at least twenty thousand records, all with the DragonFly label.

"Could it be the Chinese have staged this demonstration just for our benefit?"

"If so, this is an expensive demonstration. If they wanted to get rid of the records, they would only have needed to hide them for a while and sell them later on."

Just then, two Chinese police officers came out of the front door of a warehouse across the street, accompanied by two Chinese businessmen in handcuffs. They were taken to a car and driven away with sirens blaring.

"Wing, what is going on here?" John asked. "Can you ask one of the policemen if he knows?"

Wing went over to the policeman who appeared to be in charge and talked with him for a few minutes. He returned to where John and his associates were standing. "It appears the Chinese police have broken up a ring of CD record pirates. The two men who were taken away own the warehouse where these records were confiscated. They have confessed to having copied many thousands of records that they have been selling under the DragonFly label. The Chinese government is adamantly opposed to such copyright infringements. That is why their inventory is being destroyed."

"Does he know where the records were produced?"

"The policeman did not know. He believes the warehouse was acting as a shipping point for the records. No doubt the police will interrogate the owners and will soon find out the source. We should continue on our journey," Wing said. "The managing director of the Haikou plant expects us before noon."

"I suppose we should be on our way," John said. "But first let me collect a few samples of the records being destroyed. As you know, Wing, one of the matters on our agenda has to do with the origin of DragonFly records."

At that moment, a truck with the sign "Reuter's News Service" arrived, and two reporters jumped out. They first spoke with the police chief, then walked toward John and the others. To the left of John was a gray-haired, well-dressed Chinese man in his late fifties. The reporters began to interview him.

"Who is that?" John asked.

"I believe he is the mayor of this village," Wing responded.

The interview began in Chinese, but the mayor told them in fluent English that they could ask him questions in English if they wished to. "Can you give us your understanding of what happened here today?" the newscaster asked.

"I would be glad to. The Chinese government has suspected for some time the firm whose warehouse is located across the square has been engaged in the illegal copying of CD records for sale to South America. For the past several months, we have been watching this operation, and today we were able to catch them in the act of preparing a shipment of records."

"Where are the records being produced?"

"According to the government officials, the production plant for these records is somewhere near Shanghai. The government plans to raid that operation today as well."

"Do you know how the Chinese government feels about the copyright laws of other countries? It is our understanding you are a member of the Berne Convention, but we understand your country has yet to sign the accord."

"I don't know the exact facts regarding that," the mayor answered. "I'm sure our government does not condone such acts of piracy; otherwise, they would not have taken the action you saw here today. Now, I must go and attend to some important matters in my office."

"Thank you, sir. This is Joshua Clark of the Reuters News Service reporting from Haikou, China, where we have just witnessed the destruction of many thousands of illegal CD records produced in mainland China by some renegade company. The two men who operate the warehouse here in Haikou have been taken into custody, and we are told a second raid is taking place today with the intention of shutting down their production plant in Shanghai."

As the bus continued on its journey to the Haikou CD plant, John's mind was racing. He was sure the demonstration and interview he witnessed in the downtown square of Haikou were staged for his benefit, but there was no way to prove it. Or, could it actually be that there was some renegade company in Shanghai who was behind the whole DragonFly record scam? Anyway, he now knew with absolute certainty they would not find any DragonFly records in the CD plant during their tour today.

"Welcome to the Mao Zedong Laser Development and Manufacturing Works," CT said with the assistance of an interpreter. "It is my pleasure to be your tour guide today, for I'm always pleased to show you the advanced technology we have developed here in China that makes it possible for us to produce superior CD-Rs for the worldwide personal computer industry."

"We are pleased you have arranged this tour," John said, as he shook CT's hand.

"First, let us look at all of the exhibits here in the lobby. To facilitate tours such as this, I've found it necessary to acquaint visitors with what they will be seeing."

CT showed his guests a number of pictures and objects on display, which outlined the processes used to produce CD-Rs. When they were finished, CT said he would like to treat his guests to a Chinese luncheon in the cafeteria. "When we have completed eating, we will take the plant tour," he promised them.

John couldn't help but think that this was just another delay to give his people time to remove any evidence, but it was growing late and he was hungry, so he decided to not make any waves.

During lunch, CT told the group he and his team were hired for the specific purpose of developing CD-Rs for sale to the world. He even showed them an English version of his masters thesis, which he passed around to show the group he had been thinking of using CD-Rs in computers for many years. The luncheon was quite nice, and by two o'clock, the group was led out of the cafeteria and into the production area of the plant.

As John suspected, the tour yielded no new evidence for he and his associates to carry back with them. The plant was immaculate, and wherever product was stacked, only CD-Rs were seen. CT made it a point to show equipment and procedures that ensured the quality of the CDs was second to none. In the shipping area, boxes were piled to the ceiling, all labeled "Made in China." CT even pointed out several of the shipping labels that were made out to companies such as Lotus, Microsoft, and Borland, who were all leading software developers.

Joe and Bruce were allowed to carry note paper with them on the tour, so they were busy taking notes so that they could estimate the manufacturing capacity of the plant. By four o'clock, the tour was completed, and the group went back to the cafeteria. CT then made a summary speech and fielded a few questions from the group.

"I hope you are as impressed with this plant as my staff and I are. We have labored long and hard to become the world's leading supplier of CD-Rs, and we are pleased to be able to contribute to the growth of the personal computer industry. Are there any questions?"

Joe and Bruce had a few questions, mostly regarding some of the equipment they had seen. CT told them most of the equipment was developed by, and purchased from, other countries. There was very little equipment developed solely by China. He told them the way he configured the equipment was what made it possible to produce such a superior quality product.

"In addition, since we do not produce CD records, we do not need to reduce our quality standards to meet that low-cost market. We are most fortunate that we only make CD-Rs," CT added with pride.

John stood up and thanked CT for his time. He turned to Wing and told him they should be leaving now so they could get back to Hong Kong before dark. With that, the meeting was adjourned.

John called a meeting in his room shortly after their return to Hong Kong. "Do you think your man in the warehouse is ready yet to report anything to us?" John asked. "From what we saw today, I'll bet all of the DragonFly material was moved out before he started working there."

"He told us he would contact us by phone on Monday morning at the latest to give us an update. But, as you said, it doesn't look like he will be able to find very much evidence."

"If the DragonFly records are no longer produced in that plant, where in the world are Electro-Mart records being made, and where were they when we took the tour?" John asked, looking puzzled.

"They sure threw us a curve ball with all of that demonstration stuff," Joe said, "But what about that outfit here in Hong Kong that goes by the name of K&S Industries?"

"We'll check it out Monday morning. Presumably it is a shipping point for the DragonFly records into South America. If some renegade company in fact made the records, K&S should be able to provide us with evidence regarding their sources, if they are willing to talk with us," John said. "I'm having a search warrant prepared, to use if necessary."

"Do you think the Chinese government really has not been involved in the DragonFly record piracy?" Bruce asked.

"I'll bet a year's salary the government is behind this entire scam, and they sure are scurrying around trying to cover it up," John said.

CT called a meeting shortly after the tour bus left the parking lot. He thanked his staff for the support they gave him and told them such things were often necessary in the business world. He briefed them on the happenings that day in the town square, and told them that effective immediately they would no longer be producing DragonFly records.

"Now, please use your warehouse personnel to unpack all of the records in the boxes with the little "M" label on the bottom. As you know, those boxes do not contain CD-Rs, but rather contain unlabeled

Electro-Mart records bound for our Mexican labeling and distribution operation."

"Chan, can you give these guys a hand?" the warehouse foreman asked. "We have some repacking to do and we need to complete it by tonight, so we can meet our shipment plan."

"Sure, boss. What do I do?"

"You first set aside the boxes with the little "M" label stamped on them. You then open them up and take the CDs out and place them in the plain boxes on the other side of the room. Any questions?"

"No. It sounds straightforward to me," Chan said.

Chan and four others worked in relative silence, doing what the foreman requested. Chan wondered what the label meant, and he noted it for further examination when he could find the time. He secretly took several pictures of the operation, showing the boxes being opened, the CDs being placed in the unmarked boxes, and so forth.

"How come these boxes got packed wrong?" Chan asked one of his fellow workers.

"I don't know. This has never happened before, but I only do what I'm told."

"Are these new plain boxes scheduled for shipment tonight?" Chan asked.

"I think so. Didn't your boss tell you that was the situation?"

"Yes. Anyway, it looks like we'll be done by then."

When they completed the task, Chan and the others returned to their normal workstations to complete their shift. Just before shift change, however, Chan excused himself to go the bathroom. He purposely walked by the room where the switch took place, and discovered all of the boxes were gone. He walked to the back of the building to see if the trucks were still loading, and found one truck remaining, with a pile of boxes on a forklift ready to be loaded.

"Can I give you a hand?" Chan asked, knowing he wasn't supposed to be out on the loading platform.

"Sure, why not," the man said. "You can hold onto the boxes and steady them, while I lift them with the forklift."

As Chan did this, he saw a small label on one of the boxes that contained a Mexican address. "Now I know what the "M" label stands for," he thought to himself.

"Thanks for the help," the forklift operator said. "Where do you work in the plant?"

"I work in warehousing, but I was feeling kinda sick, so I came outside to get some fresh air. I feel a lot better now."

"Could you watch this forklift for me while I go take a piss?" the operator asked.

"Sure thing, but don't be too long. I need to return to my station."

Chan was elated. He was now able to take a very good picture of the label on the side of the box. He noted all of the boxes had the same address in Mexico. It was obvious these were not CD-Rs intended for software developers; rather they were unmarked CD records intended for the Electro-Mart stores, via Mexico, which was probably a labeling and distribution center for Electro-Mart!

★ ★ ★

"Chan called me this morning, and he has some very good information," Bruce said excitedly.

"Tell us about it," John said.

"Well, it seems the plant produces two kinds of CDs, besides the DragonFly records, which they presumably no longer make. One type is indeed CD-Rs, which do not contain labels and which are all packed in boxes labeled "Made in China." The other types are unlabeled "CD records," which are being sent to Mexico. Chan took a picture of the labels used on those boxes. He believes they are records being sent to Mexico for labeling and redistribution to Electro-Mart stores in North America and Europe."

"Then where were all the boxes with the Mexican labels when we toured the plant?" John asked.

"Chan said about half of the boxes we saw with the "Made in China" labels prominently on their side also had a very small "M" label stamped on the bottom. As soon as we left, the warehouse foreman had Chan and others unpack those boxes and put the CDs into plain boxes, which ultimately were shipped to the Mexican address. It was the old bait-and-switch scam."

"When will Chan return with the evidence?"

"He plans to quit on Monday morning after he has an opportunity to develop his pictures. He will then meet us on Monday night at his office in Hong Kong."

"Good work, Bruce. It looks like you hired a very resourceful agent. Now, let's go to K&S Industries and see what we can learn," John said.

The address of K&S Industries was a warehouse located near the Hong Kong wharf. When John and his associates arrived, they found it to be a totally empty warehouse that looked like it hadn't been used for years. A real estate sign was hanging on the door, with the name of a leasing firm. The windows were broken or dirty, and the door was scuffed and old.

"Do you think we have the right address?"

"Yes. This is definitely the address we got from the South American distributor who routinely receives records with the DragonFly label."

"They sure must have been busy clearing out of here. Our sources in South America told us that just one week ago they received another shipment of records from this very address."

"Maybe we can have Chan's detective firm investigate it. Someone in Hong Kong must be able to tell us whether this warehouse was in full operation as recently as a week or two ago."

"I guess we can't do much more here now. Let's go back and enjoy some R&R by the pool until Chan returns."

Chapter Twenty-Three

Steven and his parents were watching the CNN World News when it was interrupted by a special announcement. The newscaster broke in and showed pictures of the demonstration in downtown Haikou. The scene next shifted to the interview with the mayor, and Steven suddenly jumped up excitedly.

"I was sitting on the plane with that man standing in the background! His name is John Toliver. He works for the U.S. Commerce Department."

Steven listened intently to the interview. When it was over, he turned to his father and said, "John was written up in a *Newsweek* article I read on the plane. It seems the U.S. Commerce Department believes the Chinese are illegally manufacturing CD records for sale at discount prices, and he is trying to gather evidence to force them to back off. He even told me the United States is willing to place major trade sanctions against the Chinese to stop such activity."

"It looks like the person or company responsible has now been discovered, if what we saw on the news is correct," his father commented. "However, I find it interesting the demonstration occurred precisely at the same time John and his associates happened to be passing through Haikou. Don't you find that to be a strange coincidence?"

"That sure is rather interesting."

"Why don't the Chinese have a right to produce CD records, if they wish to do so?" Steven's mother asked.

"There's nothing wrong with the Chinese making them," Steven said. "However, they are being accused of copying records already on the market, without paying the performers any royalty payments. In addition, many of the most famous recording stars are signed up exclusively with other record companies. The Chinese are being accused of copying the records illegally and selling them for huge profits. Father, do you believe the Chinese government could actually be responsible, and the demonstration today is merely a staged effort to throw the U.S. Commerce Department off the trail?"

"I believe you've been reading too many spy novels. I read somewhere recently that China has become a member of the Berne Convention, which is an international group organized to set world standards for copyright protection. It doesn't seem likely the Chinese government would join that group, if they were engaged in illegal record piracy."

"I guess you're right. However, as you said, it sure seemed odd that the demonstrations occurred at exactly the time the men from the U.S. Commerce Department happened to be passing by."

Chan arrived at his office in Hong Kong at 8:00 P.M. on Monday. He went immediately to brief his boss, and soon after, he asked John, Bruce, and Joe to join them in his boss's office.

"Hi, I'm Adam Fitzsimmons, the head of this detective agency," Adam said, as he shook their hands. "And I guess you've already met Chan."

"I haven't yet," John said, as he shook Chan's hand. "I understand from Bruce and Joe that you had a successful mission."

"I think so," Chan said. "Let me start at the beginning."

Chan filled them in on all of his activities during the past week, including what he saw and what he did not see. He said he never saw any records with the DragonFly labels, nor did he see any boxes stamped with that name. However, he did see lots of boxes marked "Made in China," which were full of CDs without labels on them, all addressed for shipment to various software firms in the United States and Europe.

"Tell us about the assignment you had shortly after our visit, where you were asked to unpack and repack records," Bruce said.

"Yes, that was very interesting. Several of us were asked to repack more than one hundred boxes containing CDs with no labels on them. The original boxes they were packed in were marked "Made in China," and the boxes they were put into were not marked at all."

"And what else did you see on the original boxes?"

"A small "M" label stamped on the bottom. Here, I have a picture of it for you to see."

Chan pulled out a pack of several pictures, which clearly showed the "M" label on the original boxes, and other pictures showing boxes that contained no such markings. "Now, look at this picture," Chan proudly said.

"Oh, my, look at this, John," Bruce exclaimed. "It shows an address in Juarez, Mexico."

"Yes," said Chan, "and I took pictures of several boxes being loaded onto trucks, all containing labels with the same destination address."

"What do you make of this?" Adam asked Chan.

"From what Bruce and Joe told me, I'll bet those records are being shipped to Mexico, where Electro-Mart labels are being placed on them for sale and distribution throughout North America and Europe."

"Chan, did you hear what happened on Saturday in Haikou?" John asked.

"Yes, and it sure seems suspicious that the demonstration coincided precisely with your visit."

"Did anyone at the plant talk about it?"

"I overheard a couple of guys in the men's room discussing it. They seemed worried that the Haikou Plant might be shut down. They also specifically mentioned the name DragonFly, as if the Haikou Plant produced such records a short time ago. I tried to join them in the conversation, but they didn't seem to want to talk to me about it."

"Do you have any more pictures for us?"

"Yes. Here are a number of pictures of equipment and warehouse space Bruce and Joe requested. I hope it helps you estimate the plant capacity."

"Adam and Chan, you guys have sure earned your keep this week," John said.

"Any time you need any spy work done, give us a call," Adam replied, smiling.

"There is one more thing we want you fellows to do for us. Hopefully you can get on it right away."

"What's that?"

John briefed Adam and Chan about K&S Industries, which was presumed to be the shipping point for all DragonFly brand records into South America. "We assume that operation was shut down shortly before the Haikou demonstration, but we would like to get some proof that it was an ongoing concern prior to our arrival."

"Chan is already on another assignment starting tomorrow, but I have some time. How about if I poke around with some of my contacts and I'll see what I can dig up for you?"

"Fine, but when will we hear from you?"

"Give me a call on Wednesday afternoon."

"Okay. Now we had better head back to the hotel. Good day and thanks again for the prompt help."

John had just completed typing his report on his laptop computer when he heard a knock at the door of his hotel room. It was Joe and Bruce, who wanted to know if he wished to join them for an evening on the town.

"I don't think so, fellows," John said. "I think I'll eat a light meal in the coffee shop tonight and retire early. My jet lag has not worn off yet."

"Okay, chief. We'll try not to get into too much trouble," they laughed.

John read his report again to be sure he included all of the most important items. He saved it on a floppy disk, using a special encryption program that the Commerce Department developed for use by its field operatives. He then called the American Embassy courier to come and pick it up.

The courier arrived in thirty minutes and signed for the disk. Back at the American Embassy, the disk would be installed in a computer, and the encrypted report would be faxed to his superiors immediately, without anyone being able to read it who didn't have a similar encryption device on their computer.

"I expect a return fax tomorrow morning. Please deliver it to me whenever it arrives," John told the courier.

"CT, what is wrong with you this evening? You seem to be all tensed up and you've hardly eaten anything," Miu said.

"I've had one of the worst days of my life," CT said.

"Tell me about it," Miu said, as she began to rub his neck and shoulders to ease the tension.

CT briefed Miu about how he'd been told by Shing to remove all evidence of his plant ever making DragonFly records and how he had been told to have them delivered to the empty warehouse near the town square in Haikou. He also told her about how the records, destined for sale to Electro-Mart, were hidden in incorrectly marked boxes, so the U.S. Commerce Department people would not know such records existed in his plant.

"What does all this mean?" Miu asked. "Does this mean our plant is carrying out an illegal operation?"

"That's how I interpret it," CT said. "Let's turn on the television news and see if there is any further information we can learn from this situation."

In twenty minutes, the Chinese evening news broadcast was aired, and CT and Miu sat quietly watching it. After several world news events were discussed, the newscaster started talking about the DragonFly affair:

> The events of the past few days continue to unfold. The Chinese government troops have not only destroyed many thousands of illegally copied CD records found in a warehouse in downtown Haikou, but they have found the source of production, which is in this small plant outside of Shanghai. These next pictures show the destruction of the production equipment, thus stopping forever the illegal production of CD records bearing the DragonFly label. Officials of the Chinese ministry of technology and production have been quoted as saying that such piracy actions will not be tolerated. by the Chinese government.

CT stood up and started talking excitedly. "Miu, will you look at that picture of the old plant outside of Shanghai? The equipment being destroyed is the old equipment we used to produce LP records twenty years ago. When we renovated our plant, we shipped that junk to Shanghai to be scrapped. Now someone has placed that equipment in this old plant to make it look like it is being used to produce the DragonFly records."

"Does this mean we cannot trust what we hear from our government?" Miu asked, with a frown on her face.

"That surely is correct. Quiet now. Let's hear the rest of this."

A further development occurred today in Switzerland. Our representative at the Berne Convention, Tak Huang, today announced China has signed the official international copyright accord, which further emphasizes the Chinese government does not, and will not, condone the illegal copying of CD records or other materials covered by copyright laws in other countries.

"CT, what have we gotten ourselves into?"

"As I see it, our government launched the CD record program based on the false hope that China would be able to get away with copying records without paying the performers any royalties. Do you remember we discussed that when we first started production?"

"But now it seems there are pressures that are causing our government to be forced to cover up their plans," Miu added.

"I certainly believe that to be the case. Tomorrow, I'll call Shing and ask him to give me more assurance that we will not have to take further actions."

"Do you believe the Haikou plant will ultimately have to be shut down?" Miu asked, with a worried tone to her voice.

"I don't know. I hope not. I will need to speak with Shing."

Steven excused himself after breakfast and told his parents he wanted to take a long walk around the compound. "I just need some fresh air, and it looks like a really nice day," he said.

"Remember, we plan to take you on a tour of the wharf area after lunch," his mother reminded him.

"No problem. I'll be back in plenty of time."

When Steven left the building, he immediately hailed a cab and gave the driver the address of the Chinese Embassy. After a thirty-minute ride through the streets of Hong Kong, Steven arrived at his destination. The embassy was a palatial building with copious amounts of gold leaf paint on endless roof ornaments and garden statues. At the gate was a young Chinese soldier in a spotless uniform; he couldn't have been a day over eighteen years old.

"Shou Lee here to see the charge d'affaires," Steven said, when he was asked his name by the young guard. "I have an appointment to see him this morning."

"I'll need to search you first."

"Okay, but be quick about it. I don't want to be late."

"You may proceed to the front door where an escort will meet you who will take you to his office."

Steven walked briskly through the door, and a young Chinese girl met him, saying she would take him to the office, which was on the second floor in the back of the building.

"Good morning," Steven said, as he shook the hand of Wing Ma.

"Good morning," Wing answered. "What name do you go by?"

"Since I've lived in the U.S. for more than fifteen years, I've become accustomed to being called Steven."

"Then Steven it shall be. Now, what can I do for you today, Steven?"

Steven described in detail the situation surrounding his grandparents' arrest many years ago in China.

"Steven, do you realize this is the tenth time you have visited us to discuss this matter?" Wing asked, as he opened a file on his desk. "The first nine times were many years ago, of course, before I held this position and before you moved to the United States. Nevertheless, the circumstances surrounding their arrest and detainment have not changed. Their sentence was detainment without any chance for pardon, and that still is the situation."

"I guess I was hopeful their circumstances might change in view of the fact China will soon take possession of Hong Kong in the summer of 1997. I've heard some rumors that clemency may be granted to many political prisoners as a show of humanitarian good will."

"Steven, you don't understand the Chinese mind. At the time of the trial, what they and many others did was considered to be a very serious crime against the State. Just because we now are about to acquire a small plot of ground once owned by the British is no reason to assume that all sins of the past will be forgiven."

"Is there any way I can formally lodge a request for their release?" Steven asked, as he realized he was getting nowhere with Wing.

"You are doing so at this moment, my son. Believe me, I understand your position, but I'm powerless in such matters. If somehow you were to take your plea to higher authorities, you would probably make things much worse for your grandparents. Before our meeting today, I checked and found they are quite well. They are able to tend a small plot of ground and raise fresh vegetables. In fact, they are probably better off than many hundreds of poor peasants who try to make a living off the land. Conditions in China today are still quite difficult for most farmers and peasants. So, Steven, why don't you just accept the fact that what has been done is done. You can write them frequently. I'm sure they would like to hear from you."

"All right," Steven said. "Thank you for your time today."

"That's okay, Steven. I hope I never hear from you again on this matter. Is that understood?"

Steven left the embassy more determined than ever to find a way to get around the system and set his grandparents free. This was all the more important, for he now feared for his parents, who no doubt would be picked up like common criminals when Hong Kong was acquired by mainland China.

John Toliver awoke to a pounding on his door. He looked at the clock and it was 5:00 A.M., so he wondered who would want to see him at such an early hour. He slipped out of bed, put on his robe, and unlocked the door.

"Here's the response to your fax," the courier said. "You told me you wanted to receive it the moment it arrived, so I came over, even though it is quite early."

"That's fine," John said, rubbing his eyes. "You did the right thing."

After tipping the courier, John went into the bathroom and stepped into the shower to help wake up. He rang room service for a continental breakfast, which arrived shortly after his shower.

The floppy disk the courier delivered had to be decrypted using the software on his laptop computer, and this took only a few minutes. He printed out the return fax on his portable printer and began to read it carefully. It was from his boss at the U.S. Commerce Department, telling him what he and his associates should do next:

John, I agree with you. The demonstrations were for your own benefit as a ploy to take the pressure off of your investigation. You must, however, insist on still having a meeting with the ministry chief of technology and production, just as if nothing has happened. He must understand our position regarding possible trade sanctions, and you need to get directly from his mouth what he has to say regarding the incident you witnessed in Haikou.

With regard to the K&S Industries situation, you are doing the right thing investigating it. I have wire-transferred funds to the detective agency to cover the cost of this additional assignment.

I've also assigned a man this morning to look into the Juarez, Mexico matter. In your meeting with the ministry chief, you should definitely not let them know we believe they are using a Mexican labeling and distribution center to smuggle records under the Electro-Mart label.

After your meetings with the ministry chief, and after you have a report on the K&S Industries matter, you and your associates should return to the U.S. By that time, we should know more about the Juarez operation, and we can decide what to do next. Good luck.

Regards, Jackson Jones, Group Director, Foreign Operations.

After reading the message, John wadded it up into a ball and placed it in an ashtray and burned it. He still had his encrypted floppy disk if he needed to refer to it again. It was now 6:00 A.M., so John got dressed and went down to the lobby to get a cup of coffee and to read the morning news. On the front page of the business section, he saw the picture of the bulldozers destroying the records and he smiled as he looked at it. Below that picture, he saw the picture of a similar bulldozer destroying equipment in the plant in Shanghai.

He thought, "No way. That equipment looks like presses used to make old LP records." He kept the paper, for he wanted Bruce and Joe to see these pictures. He phoned their rooms, knowing they probably were sound asleep, having been out on the town last night.

"Wake up," he laughed. "We have lots of things to discuss."

"What a slave driver," Joe managed to say. "What time is it, anyway?"

Adam Fitzsimmons received the wire transfer shortly after arriving at his office the morning after the meeting with Chan and the Commerce Department people. He poured himself a cup of coffee and turned on his computer, which contained a detailed list of contacts he had developed over the years, as a result of being a Hong Kong detective.

"Hello, Cecil," Adam said to one of his contacts over the phone. "Have you ever heard of an outfit called K&S Industries, which is located on Riverfront Drive in the south section of the wharf near Captain Stark's fish processing plant?"

"It sounds familiar. Why do you ask?"

"I have reason to believe as recently as two weeks ago they were a thriving ongoing enterprise, and yet today they sort of vanished from the face of the earth. I need some kind of proof they ever existed and when they pulled the plug on their operation."

"I know several of the owners of businesses down there. One of them should be able to shed some light on this matter. When do you need to know something?"

"How about tomorrow afternoon?" Adam asked.

"I'll see what I can do."

"Great, and you will be paid the usual rate. You should bill me."

Shing's secretary opened the door of his office, and said CT had been trying all morning to reach him. "He seems quite anxious to speak with you."

"You may call him now. I have a few minutes before I need to go into a meeting with Keung."

"Ah, Shing, this is CT. I hope I'm not interrupting anything important, but I really needed to speak with you."

"Yes, CT. What can I do for you?"

"I followed your instructions this week and disposed of all of the DragonFly records as you requested. However, all of the events that transpired afterwards have me gravely concerned. It appears to me that Keung is having second thoughts about whether we can legally sell

Chinese-made CD records. Can you provide me with some insight? My staff is beginning to worry that the plant might be shut down."

"CT, when you took the job of managing director you became a member of our inner circle management team. I want to personally apologize for not briefing you on the entire strategy surrounding the DragonFly matter. There just wasn't enough time to do so. The U.S. Commerce men were on their way, and we had much to prepare before their arrival. By the way, I wish to congratulate you on how you handled their visit. The reports I've received indicate they saw nothing out of the ordinary. I'll probably meet with them in a day or so, now that the DragonFly matter has been resolved."

"I gather from all that has happened we will no longer produce DragonFly records. Is that correct?"

"Yes, we have decided to cancel that line of CDs. We are still able to meet or exceed our plan by producing only CD-Rs, as well as CD records bound for Electro-Mart stores."

"But why won't the Electro-Mart brand records be attacked by world opinion just as the DragonFly brand has been attacked?"

"Because we have a great ally in the United States, who is the head of the Electro-Mart record store chain. He takes all of the heat and enjoys doing so. Please don't worry. We have no plans to shut down your plant. If anything, you may have to expand your operation next year into the south wing, if our sales predictions continue to hold firm."

"I almost choked when I saw the pictures of our old equipment being crushed in the old Shanghai warehouse," CT said.

"I thought you would find that amusing. Now that you are an important member of our inner circle of managers, you will have to understand extreme measures are sometimes necessary to achieve our final goals. I hope this whole affair did not offend you."

"No, Shing, I understand why such things are required. My main concern is whether my plant will soon need to be shut down. What you have just told me makes me feel much better. I'll let you go now. Again, thanks for the information."

"Thank you, and again I apologize I did not have time to brief you on our plans. I'll try to avoid making that mistake in the future."

"Good-bye," CT said.

Shing hung up and went down the hall to Keung's office, where they discussed whether he personally should meet with John Toliver, or whether he should send some flunky. The two of them decided Shing should personally go to the meeting, which they assumed would be requested by John in the next few days.

Chapter Twenty-Four

Adam Fitzsimmons wasted no time contacting Cecil the following day to see if he had found out anything about K&S Industries. Since Cecil mentioned he knew a number of the proprietors of businesses along the wharf area in Hong Kong, Adam was certain he would be able to find out what he needed to know.

"Cecil, how's it going?" Adam asked over the phone.

"Adam, you won't believe what I've discovered. You sure have gotten yourself involved in a real nasty one this time."

"What do you mean?" asked Adam with considerable curiosity.

"My source tells me K&S Industries was a front organization for the Chinese government. As recently as last week, they were operating as a warehousing operation, storing illegal CD records made in China, and shipping them to South American record distributors."

"How does your source know all of this, and does he have proof?"

"He worked there until last week, when he was let go. He's very bitter about the whole thing. His wife just got pregnant and he really needs to have a steady job."

"Do you think he would be willing to testify in an affidavit for a fee, telling everything he knows about the operation?"

"He just might be, since he and his wife are really hurting for money. Do you want me to ask him?"

"Absolutely. Please do so right away."

"Who's your client on this one?" Cecil asked.

"The U.S. government, and I know from experience that they will pay big bucks for the right kind of information."

"Will they assure my man that his name will never come up in any report?"

"I'm sure that will be possible. As far as I know, they have no plans to go to court over this. They mainly want to nail the Chinese with the charge of record piracy. If they get sufficient evidence, they will be able to threaten China with trade sanctions, if they don't stop immediately."

"Wow, you really do get involved in some weird deals, don't you?"

"Yes, but I like the pay. Incidentally, if your man is for real, you can bill me double your usual rate."

"My wife will really appreciate that. I'll hang up now and see if I can locate my man. I'm sure he'll cooperate."

The man Cecil uncovered did not want his name known, and he insisted on being paid HK$15,000 up front, before he would open his mouth. John Toliver and Adam discussed this matter for an hour before John agreed to accept the deal. Adam told John that Cecil was very reliable and would not have provided the name of the person if he did not believe the man to be a reliable source of information.

"Come in, sir," John gestured to the man when he arrived at the suite of offices that John rented for the afternoon's meeting. He was a very thin and pale first-generation Chinese in his early thirties, with poor complexion and equally poor teeth. John decided to meet the man alone, rather than having Joe and Bruce present, since he did not want to intimidate him. However, the man brought along a friend to act as an interpreter, since he could scarcely speak English.

"My name is John Toliver and I work for the U.S. Commerce Department," John said, using the interpreter. He invited the man to sit down.

"Would you like to have some tea before we get started?" The man nodded that he would. After tea was poured, John handed the man an envelope containing a thick wad of one-hundred-dollar bills. The man counted them and seemed satisfied, so John began slowly asking questions regarding how long he had worked for K&S Industries, and what kind of work he did for them.

The man told John that when K&S Industries first commenced its operation, they placed an ad in the *Hong Kong Gazette*, to which he responded. After two interviews, he was hired to work in the warehouse. He further told John that K&S Industries only dealt with a single product, which arrived on a weekly basis in large containers mounted on palettes. Each container was filled with three thousand CD Records, all bearing the DragonFly label. A truck would pick up the containers every Wednesday morning at the Hong Kong airport and deliver them to the warehouse on the wharf. His job was to examine the open order report and repack the CDs into smaller boxes for shipment to an address in Buenos Aires.

"Was there an originating address on the containers or on the paperwork that came with the containers?" John asked. The man said there was a bar code of sorts, but no specific address that he could remember seeing.

"When was the last container received, before K&S Industries shut down its operation?" The man pulled out a piece of paper he removed from a container that day. The paper showed that the Chinese National Airlines flight 405 had been the carrier. That flight arrived in Hong Kong at 10:00 A.M. on the Wednesday before John visited Haikou.

"Was the shipping address in Buenos Aires always the same, no matter which records were ordered, and, if so, do you remember what it was?" The man said all shipments went to the same address. Again he reached inside his shirt pocket and pulled out a folded piece of paper that was a shipping label. He said he always placed this same label on all shipments, no matter what the contents were.

"When did K&S Industries start up its operation?" The man gave John a date, which was one month prior to the date the International Federation of the Phonographic Industry (IFPI) discovered that DragonFly records were being shipped into South America.

"What was the name of the man in charge at K&S Industries?" The man told John he never had any reason to visit the front office, since his job was to run the warehouse. He only knew his direct boss by the name of Chao, who was laid off the same day he was. Chao told him he planned to return to mainland China, where he lived prior to being employed by K&S Industries. He had no idea how to get in touch with him now.

"Is there anything else you would like to tell me?" John asked. The man summarized by saying he didn't want to be associated with any of the information he provided. He planned to leave and would no longer be available for further questioning. He said again that what he told John was all he knew about the operation.

John thanked him and let him go. He sat for a half an hour checking his notes, to be sure he had all of the facts straight before returning to his hotel to meet with Joe and Bruce.

"Jackson, you have an urgent call on your red phone," his secretary said.

"This is Jackson Jones, group director of foreign operations, U.S. Commerce Department. What can I do for you?"

"This is Gerald from your field operations unit. If you recall, I was assigned to see what I could find out about the Electro-Mart Juarez operation."

"Yes, Gerald. Have you been able to find out anything yet?"

"As a matter of fact, I've been really lucky on this one. I drove by the address given to me yesterday morning. At the very moment I got there, a fire broke out in the back of the building where some laborers were loitering and smoking. All employees left the building, and several hundred people from surrounding homes milled around watching the firemen do their thing. I was able to take advantage of the confusion and slip inside to have a look-see."

"So, what did you find out?" Jackson asked excitedly.

"I saw a number of long tables with CDs neatly stacked along one end and piles of record labels neatly stacked along the other end. Apparently, workers stick the labels on the records and put them into various shipping containers."

"What did the labels say?"

"They all had the Electro-Mart label, plus the name of the recording artist. I stole five or six of them to bring back with me. Each of the shipping containers had an Electro-Mart record store address on it. I was able to remove a couple of those stickers as well. I had my camera with me, so I took several pictures of the whole operation."

"Fantastic! Did anyone see you enter or leave the building?"

"When I left, one of the firemen came up to me and said something in Spanish. I merely said 'no comprehende' and kept walking back to my car."

"Gerald, I'm going to recommend you for a bonus this month! Where are you now?"

"I just arrived back in the States and am at home now. What should I do next?"

"I'm going to put you on the phone with my secretary. She will make arrangements for you to come to Washington for a high-level meeting, as soon as you can develop your pictures. Thank you very much for your good work. I'll see you in a few days."

"Good-bye, sir. It's been a pleasure talking with you. I look forward to meeting you soon."

Bruce and Joe knocked on John's hotel room door. "Come in, the door's not locked."

John spent the next half hour briefing them on what he found out from the man who used to work for K&S Industries. He phoned the airlines and found out the plane carrying the containers originated from Beijing.

"Sounds like we've got the bastards dead to rights," Bruce said.

"Not so fast, Bruce. We know the records were made in China, but we still don't know if the Chinese government had anything to do with it. We all saw the demonstration in Haikou. The Chinese will merely say DragonFly records were produced in Shanghai, as the TV newscaster claimed."

"I guess you're right. But how do we prove the Chinese government is responsible for all of this?"

"There probably will be no way, short of someone like the managing director of the Haikou plant turning against his government and testifying, and fat chance for that ever to happen!"

"So, boss, what do we do next?" Joe asked.

"My instructions are to demand to have a meeting with the ministry chief of technology and production. We will sit with him and accuse the Chinese government of being guilty of record piracy. We will threaten major trade sanctions and we will be generally nasty with him. No doubt he will puff on his opium pipe, and will tell us politely to go to hell."

John picked up the phone and called the Chinese Embassy. He was not at all surprised that the ministry chief would like very much to meet with John and his associates. Wing Ma recommended meeting in Haikou, at a hotel near the CD-R plant, where they could book a large conference room. He suggested meeting on Friday; John and his associates would meet again at the Chinese Embassy at 8:30 A.M., as before, to arrange for their boat ride to the island.

John remarked to Bruce and Joe, "It's amazing how easy it was for the charge d'affaires to arrange a meeting, once they believe they have the upper hand."

"Sir, it's a pleasure to meet you," Gerald said, shaking Jackson's hand.

"Likewise Gerald. I always like to meet top-notch field operatives like you. Gentlemen, we all seem to be here, so let's get started. My secretary will take notes, so I would prefer if you all stay alert and participate when called upon. We have some serious material to cover this morning."

Jackson stood up and talked for an hour using flip charts. He discussed the entire CD record piracy matter, including the original DragonFly findings by the IFPI, the Electro-Mart situation and the number of complaints lodged against that firm, the recent information he received from John Toliver, and the recent Juarez, Mexico discoveries.

"John Toliver has been instructed to meet with the appropriate ministry chief in China this week and threaten him with massive trade sanctions if they do not cease their CD record piracy practices. However, we fully expect him to claim innocence, in light of their recent demonstration. We strongly suspect the government is directly involved here, but we are not yet able to prove it."

Jackson sat down and continued. "Gentlemen, we need to find some way to call their bluff and shut them down. Do any of you have any ideas?"

The room suddenly filled with a number of different conversations going on simultaneously. Finally Jackson had to call an end to the chitchat and ask if anyone would like to stand up and present an idea.

Gerald stood up and went to the end of the table. "I recognize I'm only a field operative, but I believe I have an idea that will work. It should at least produce a major ripple in their plans."

"Go ahead, Gerald, tell us all about it, and don't be ashamed that you are a field operative. I used to be one myself!"

"Sir, it seems to me if you could find some way to get the Mexican government to close down the Juarez operation, even for a short time, perhaps only for a month, then the flow of records to Electro-Mart would dry up. In your earlier comments you indicated that Manny is a pure businessman. If he sees he will not receive any product for thirty days, he will be forced to buy quantities of legitimate records to keep his stores full.

"When Manny contacts his source, the Chinese may take a chance and try to ship directly to Electro-Mart stores so as not to lose the business. If such shipments are made, you should be able to trace them back to their source. If so, you would have the proof you need."

Gerald sat down, and those in the room started again talking simultaneously to each other. Jackson let this continue for a while and then stood up. "I think Gerald has a good idea here. What he's saying is that if we can't prove the Chinese government is behind this thing, we should at least be able to shut them down by pinching off their market. Then if they panic to avoid being shut down, we should be able to nail them. What do you guys think?"

"How do we get the Mexican government to shut down the Juarez operation?"

"I think I can convince the Mexican ambassador to trump up some reason, especially since we are about to hold trade agreement talks with Mexico regarding the NAFTA trade agreement extension."

"If the Chinese decide to risk their cover and ship directly to Electro-Mart stores, how will we be able to stop those shipments?" another attendee asked.

"That should be relatively easy," Jackson said. "We call in the head of the teamsters union and give him a big picture pitch. We threaten to make him a part of any litigation we may ultimately throw at Manny if his truckers accept any boxes marked for Electro-Mart. We do the same with the longshoremen, and with the air carrier unions that service the European and Canadian markets. We will effectively cut both the Chinese and Manny off at the knees."

"Can we get these union guys to hold the goods they do not ship until we can confiscate them?" Gerald asked. "If so, why don't we stage a demonstration at the port of entry, like the one the Chinese staged in Haikou?"

"Gentlemen, I believe we have a plan. By August, we should have the Chinese where we want them. If they somehow manage to wiggle out of our net, we can still play our trump card, which is major trade sanctions. However, a lot of U.S. companies don't want us to have to play that card, for obvious reasons."

Shing arrived on Thursday afternoon in Haikou and proceeded directly to the CD plant. He went straight to CT's office and closed the door. He spent about an hour explaining his strategy, including how he was going to send the U.S. Commerce personnel home empty-handed.

"CT, it is entirely possible the men from the Commerce Department will request a repeat visit of the plant tomorrow after the meeting. I know this is a burden on you and your staff, but please have your warehouse personnel repack the goods like you did before, so the only apparent inventory we have is CD-Rs."

"I can do even better than that," CT said. "We are scheduled to make our next shipment to Mexico today. I'll see to it that we ship all of our records, leaving only CD-Rs in the warehouse. In addition, I'll hold up CD-R shipments for a day or two, so the warehouse will be very full."

"Very good. If such a repeat tour is requested, I'll phone you, so you can be ready to see the gentlemen. Be cordial and answer any of their questions. CT, you should tell your staff they have nothing to worry about. Even without the sales of DragonFly records, we still are going to sell more CDs than our plan calls for."

"Shing, I want to thank you for briefing me today. My staff and I will beat our production plan. You can be assured of that."

After the meeting, Shing and his assistants checked into the Haikou Arms Hotel, where the meeting would be held the next day. They ordered a full course Chinese dinner and for a few hours were able to forget the problems of the world and just relax as friends. Shing excused himself and retired to his room, where he went over some notes he planned to use in the meeting.

On Friday morning, John Toliver and his associates arrived at the Chinese Embassy where Wing Ma, the charge d'affaires, greeted them. Wing told them he would not be accompanying them, but instead his beautiful assistant would escort them to the island. He said she would act as an interpreter at the meeting.

"Allow me to introduce Ting Lao, my able and quite beautiful assistant."

Ting was an extremely attractive Chinese woman, who bowed smartly as she held out her hand to John. "I'm pleased to be able to serve you," she said in perfect English. "Our ministry chief in charge of technology and production knows English fairly well, but I'll be at your side in the event he cannot understand some important statement you need to make during your presentation."

When John shook her hand, he couldn't help but notice the beautiful gold bracelet she was wearing. It contained ten different precious stones with Chinese figurines carved into the surface of each stone. He also noticed that she seemed to want to hold his hand a bit longer than was necessary for a simple handshake.

"I'm glad to meet you and am pleased you will be our escort. By the way, your bracelet is quite beautiful. Does it represent something special?"

"My great grandmother received it in the late 1800s as a gift from her lover. It has been handed down from generation to generation ever since. I'm pleased you like it."

"You'd better leave now," Wing said. "You're scheduled to arrive at the hotel in time for lunch with Shing Ling and his assistants. After lunch, the hotel conference room will be available for your meeting, which will start promptly at 1:30."

Shing and his associates were already seated at the table in the Haikou Arms Hotel main dining room when John Toliver and his entourage arrived. Shing stood up when Ting entered the room, and she walked up to him and bowed. Shing said in almost perfect English, "Ting, you grow more beautiful with each passing day, and alas I do nothing but grow older. I wish you would consider moving to mainland China so I could gaze upon you more frequently."

"Shing, I want you to meet the gentlemen from the U.S. Commerce Department," Ting said, seeming to be embarrassed by the show of affection from the elderly Chinese man.

After shaking hands and bowing, they all sat down at the magnificent table. Shing motioned to the waiter, and soon many large platters of Chinese delicacies were brought out and served to each person, according to their wishes.

"John Toliver, at last we meet. I have received many memoranda from you, and have looked forward to meeting you in person," Shing said, as he toasted the group.

"I, too, am glad we finally have met. As you know, I've taken many trips to Hong Kong hoping for such a meeting, but for some reason you or your designees have always been busy, tending to other more urgent matters, I suppose."

"As you can imagine, now that China has modernized itself, we are kept very busy establishing trade treaties with many countries in the world. Such matters seem to occupy all of my time, and the time of my able staff as well."

John couldn't help but take note of the fact that Shing was speaking perfect English, so he began to wonder why it was necessary for Ting Lao to be present. It was obvious that no interpreting would be required at the meeting. "She's either a spy or a hooker," John thought to himself.

When the luncheon was completed, the group left the dining room and went to a large conference room at the other end of the hotel. The room was set up for a meeting, with pads of paper at each place and copious pencils and pens. Also, at the end of the room was an easel carrying large pieces of stiff white cardboard to prepare summaries, if necessary.

Shing stood up and proceeded to make some introductory comments, which were intended to position China as a country that absolutely loathed anyone who would stoop so low as to make illegal copies of records.

"Gentlemen, my name is Shing Ling and I report directly to Keung Fu Huang, China's president. I am in charge of the ministry of technology and production. Members of my staff were responsible for establishing the facility you visited last week, where we make CD-Rs. You met Mr. Choi Tang, the managing director. He is a brilliant technologist, and is the one responsible for developing the processes that make it possible for us to produce the superior quality CD-Rs we supply to the world's major personal computer software developers.

"After the war, China and Russia developed the technology for producing LP records, which were sold only to the Eastern Bloc countries. My staff and I were responsible for establishing the manufacturing plant for that enterprise, and it was set up in the same buildings you visited here in Haikou. We strictly adhered to the world's copyright laws when we selected recording artists for our LPs, even though we had not yet officially joined any organization requiring us to do so. Most of the labels we sold used local recording artists, and we even encouraged the Eastern Bloc countries to provide us with the talent we required.

"When world tensions eased with the end of the cold war, LPs from other suppliers could be sold into Eastern Europe and, as you well know, the LP technology soon gave way to CD records. As a consequence, we had to shut down our LP production a number of years ago. A number of our technologists at that time tried to convince me we should develop the capability to make CD records. However, I firmly believed it would be folly for us to do so, for we would not be able to attract the kind of recording talent needed in order to offer the products consumers around the world would demand. I adamantly held my ground, saying China must not copy the property of others, even though we still had not signed any official agreement that would preclude us from doing so.

"Mr. Toliver, when I first received your memoranda accusing China of being responsible for the production of DragonFly CD records, I must say I was not happy you would believe that either I or the Chinese government would condone such piracy activities. However, I understand you have never met me before, and if I were in your shoes, I suppose I too would have suspected the worst.

"I did appreciate, however, that you called the matter to my attention. I immediately assigned some of my staff to investigate the matter to see if we could find out who in our land was responsible for this illegal act of piracy. I'm sure you noted the activity in the Haikou town square when you first arrived last week. Just a few days before your arrival, we discovered the source of this illegal operation, and we have now destroyed all of the illegal records.

"We were saddened to find those responsible for this illegal operation used to work in the Haikou facility during the days when LP production was at its peak. They were the most outspoken ones who tried to convince me the plant should be refitted to make CD records. When we disposed of the old LP production machinery, they purchased the apparatus and converted it for the production of CD records in the Shanghai facility, which we finally destroyed last week, along with their work in process.

"In any event, Mr. Toliver, we should both consider this meeting to be a celebration now that the pirates have been captured and their illegal works have been destroyed. You can report to your superiors that the DragonFly event is finished. I can sleep easier knowing our policy of not ever copying works of great value is being adhered to.

"So, is there anything else we can do for you this afternoon? If not, you should be aware that this hotel has a very fine oriental spa, where professional masseuses can melt all of the tensions of the body away. I almost always partake of the spa when my busy schedule permits. I heartily recommend it."

By this point, John was steaming inside. Shing tried to make the whole matter of record piracy simply go away by giving an eloquent speech. John knew Shing was lying through his teeth. As he considered what to say, John stood up and walked to the head of the table and turned to the group, with a very firm and stern look on his face. He collected his thoughts and, according to Joe and Bruce afterwards, gave one of the best speeches of his career.

"Mr. Ling, I must now state what the position of the U.S. Commerce Department is on this serious matter of record piracy. As my memoranda to you have indicated from the beginning, we in the Commerce Department absolutely believe the origin of the blatant Chinese CD record piracy is the Chinese government itself, not some renegade operation, as you are trying to suggest.

"I must commend you and your government, Mr. Ling, on your very creative theatrics for our benefit in the Haikou square last week, and for the related activities you displayed on national television as you trashed the Shanghai facility. You must think we are fools. We know there is no way that old LP record equipment can be converted to make CDs. We discovered another facility of yours in Hong Kong, which suddenly suspended operations just prior to our visit. We have proof that your front organization, known only as K&S Industries, was used to receive and distribute the DragonFly records. We interviewed a man who worked there, and he provided us with evidence regarding the origin of incoming shipments of DragonFly records. That origin, sir, was Beijing, China!

"You have not addressed any of our queries regarding the origin of records being sold in the U.S., Canada, and Europe under Electro-Mart labels. We have tested the compounds used to make Electro-Mart records, as well as the compounds used to make DragonFly records and as well the CD-Rs made in your Haikou plant. We find the materials are identical. These materials are considerably different from the materials used by legitimate suppliers of CDs around the world. So, we know with absolute certainty that these three classes of records are all being produced in China, and probably are being produced right here in your Haikou plant, even though you carefully removed any evidence for our benefit during our tour.

"Incidentally, as a show of good faith on your part, if you continue to state the only product being made in your facility is CD-Rs, I would like for my associates to repeat their tour right now, as we continue here."

Shing stood up, with a very unhappy expression on his face. "Mr. Toliver, we would welcome another visit by your associates, for we have nothing to hide. Ting, would you please take these two gentlemen to the lobby and call a cab. Please call CT and tell him he should expect two gentlemen from the U.S. Commerce Department to arrive in about ten minutes. Tell him to show them anything they wish to see. Would you please accompany them to the plant, as well, and see to it that their wishes are granted."

Ting nodded, and she, Bruce, and Joe stood up and left the room.

"Mr. Toliver, please go on, if you have a further statement to make."

John was clearly a bit shaken by this offer of another plant tour. He was sure Shing would have come up with some excuse, but he was now committed. He was hopeful Bruce and Joe would be able to discover something incriminating.

"Okay, Mr. Ling, thank you for letting my people again see the plant. Now, I want to return to the subject of the Electro-Mart records. These pirated records represent an even more important activity, since they are being sold in the United States, Canada, and Europe. All legitimate record companies are filing complaints with us daily, because their sales are seriously being impacted by the sale of these pirate records. We have lodged several formal complaints with Mao Chang, or Manny, who is the head of the Electro-Mart operation in the U.S., and he keeps giving us the runaround. He refuses to tell us where he gets his records. Believe me, Mr. Ling, we will soon subpoena him and he will be forced to tell us his sources. Again, based on our testing of the materials in these records, we know the source to be the same as the DragonFly records and CD-Rs you make in your Haikou Plant."

John paused to let his words sink in. He watched the others at the table, who were all staring at Shing for his reaction. Shing stood up and asked John if he would mind sitting down for a moment, so he could speak.

"Mr. Toliver, again I understand your frustration, because I too do not condone record piracy in any form. As I stated before, you and I have never met before, so you have no way of knowing I am a man of my word. Again, when I state the Chinese government is in no way involved in such piracy activities, you must take my word on it.

"Now, why is it we have not responded to your queries regarding the Electro-Mart records? That is because we too are investigating this matter. The Chinese way is to not make comments based on rumor or innuendo. Rather, we will make our comments known when we have absolute proof.

"We were hopeful the renegades we shut down last week would turn out to also be the source for the Electro-Mart records, but as far as we can determine, they were not. So, my investigative staff continues to sift through all of their leads. You can rest assured when we find the culprits, we will deal with them in the same manner as we did last week.

"I note the head of Electro-Mart is a Chinese-American, so perhaps we can investigate his ancestry and come up with a way to apply pressure on him, so he will reveal his source. In addition, if you find out who that source is, please inform me and we will take swift action."

Shing sat down and watched John carefully. John said nothing, but rather sifted through his notes for a memo he planned to read to Shing and his associates. He stood up and continued to speak.

"Mr. Ling, you have made your position clear. You have gone on record in this meeting that your government has nothing to do with the CD record piracy, whether it is DragonFly records or Electro-Mart records. You say you are investigating the Electro-Mart source, and you make us an offer to cooperate in that investigation.

"You should understand the Commerce Department's position. We are going to continue to investigate this matter with a considerable sense of urgency. As I commented before, we will soon subpoena Manny and see if we can force him to reveal his source of pirated records. We will also follow up on any leads we have from sources within your own country.

"With all due respect, sir, I do not believe your position that your government has nothing to do with this matter. As you know, our two governments will soon be meeting on the matter of trade, and we fully plan to suggest rather serious sanctions against China if we find any proof your government is behind this record piracy matter."

John pulled out several copies of a memorandum signed by Jackson Jones, indicating the official position of the U.S. Commerce

Department. He handed these to Shing and his associates, and they sat quietly reading it. When they finished, Shing stood up once more.

"Mr. Toliver, I regret we do not agree with each other, but I suppose that is impossible under these circumstances. I trust you will meet with your two associates after the tour, for you will see I am telling the truth. It is unfortunate that cultural and geographical differences make it difficult for us to see eye-to-eye on this matter, but I understand such things often take many years, with many meetings, before agreements can be reached. Perhaps some day you will find I am truly a man of my word."

Shing and his associates stood up, bowed, shook John's hand, and bid him farewell. Shing said rooms had been reserved for John and his two associates, and he again reminded him to take advantage of the spa. Shing left and headed back to the CD plant.

John checked into his room, took off his tie and jacket, and sprawled out on the bed. He had almost come to believe Shing in the meeting, but deep down inside he just couldn't let go of the idea that the Chinese government was somehow either directly or indirectly involved in the record piracy. As he went over in his mind the meeting with Shing, he fell asleep and found himself dreaming about piles of CD records all being crushed and eaten by a giant green dragon.

"Wake up, boss," Joe and Bruce said, as they pounded on his door. "We'll meet you down at the bar."

"Okay, guys, I'll see you there in a few minutes."

John looked at his watch and realized he had slept almost two hours. He got up and went into the bathroom to freshen up a bit. He then headed down to the bar to meet his associates.

"Did you find out anything unusual?"

"That place was chock full of CD-Rs, and we looked at all of the boxes in the warehouse and not a single one had an "M" label on the bottom, such as Chan found," Joe said.

"That's right. We were even shown the production lines this time. Every product on the line was a CD-R. For all intents and purposes, that plant has never produced any CD records, as far as we could tell," Bruce added.

"Boy, they are really good. I thought sure my offer for a tour would throw them for a loop, but either they anticipated it, or do you think they really don't make CD records?" John asked.

"I still smell a rat. That CT guy seemed to know we were coming. I've worked in similar operations, and guests arriving with a ten-minute notice usually have to cool their heels in the lobby while arrangements are being made. They seemed to be ready for us without even a moment's wait. I really do smell a rat here."

"How do you think I did at the meeting? Was I firm enough?"

"You did great. I could tell what you told him was really sinking in, even though when he made his comments he sure was smooth and was patronizing you big time," Bruce said.

"I agree," said Joe.

"After you fellows left, I gave Shing a copy of the ultimatum memorandum you have seen, which has Jackson's signature on it. He seemed to be worried as he read it."

"Well, we have nothing more to do here. What time does the van pick us up in the morning?"

"Ting said we should all meet in the lobby at 9:00 A.M. The van will take us back to the wharf where the patrol boat will be waiting to take us back to Hong Kong."

"Where is Ting staying tonight?" John asked.

"Hey, boss, you're a happily married man. You aren't thinking of having some company tonight, are you?" Joe laughed.

"Of course not, but I wonder why she came along. It was obvious she was not required to do any interpreting. And did you see how Shing acted with her? I wonder if he is the one who will be having company tonight? She didn't seem to care for him much, though.

"Why don't we all get something to eat and then meet in the famous spa later on, before we retire?"

"Sounds good. Let's go into the dining room before it gets too crowded."

Shing met briefly with CT after the meeting at the hotel and briefed him thoroughly. He again thanked CT for the help and again assured him the U.S. Commerce Department was being nicely kept at bay. He returned to the hotel and checked into the royal suite, which had a private door leading directly into the spa. He picked up the phone in his room and dialed a number he had often dialed before.

"Ting, this is Shing. I'm ready. I'll meet you in the usual room."

Shing opened the door leading to the spa, where he was greeted by a young Chinese orderly. He was handed a terry cloth bathrobe and a key. "Your usual room?" the man asked.

"Yes," Shing answered.

Shing entered the private spa room, and found it equipped as he had requested. In the center was a very large sunken hot tub with bubbling hot mineral water. Next to the wall was a heart-shaped bed with a heated water mattress. Along the other wall was a very expensive stereo system with pleasant music playing. A remote control device controlled the lights in the room. He slipped off his clothes and put on his robe. He went to a wet bar across from the bed and found a bottle of expensive champagne already chilling in a silver container. He lay on the bed and closed his eyes. He had looked forward to this liaison for some time, and was actually glad the U.S. Commerce agents insisted on meeting, since it gave him a perfect excuse to again rendezvous with Ting, his favorite Hong Kong call girl.

Shing dozed off and was awakened by Ting, who slipped out of her robe and lay down beside him on the bed. "I plan to serve your every need," she whispered in his ear, as she removed his robe.

John, Joe, and Bruce visited the spa, but they decided to forego the massage. Rather, they sat in a hot tub and let the hot mineral water relax them. They stayed only for an hour and went back to their rooms to retire for the evening. In his room, before John turned out the lights, he prepared a trip report on his laptop computer, and encrypted it onto a floppy disk, which he planned to send to Jackson as soon as he returned to Hong Kong.

The boat ride back to Hong Kong the next day was uneventful. "Ting, thank you for escorting us," John said as they left the patrol boat in the Hong Kong harbor.

"It was my pleasure. I hope you will have time to enjoy the sights in Hong Kong before returning to the U.S."

"We surely will. Again, good-bye."

When John checked into his room, he found a message waiting for him. He was told he should call the courier, for there was a floppy disk that he needed to see immediately. In ten minutes, the courier arrived and John gave him the floppy he had prepared, and sat down to read the message from Jackson. It told him they should return immediately to Washington. Without further ado, the three of them left for the airport to catch the late-night plane, which would arrive in Washington the following afternoon.

Chapter Twenty-Five

Jackson briefed John on his recent staff meeting, and told him his current ideas for flushing out the Electro-Mart record production source. "I also read your trip report. It sounds like the Chinese are working overtime to try to keep one step ahead of us. Incidentally, do you feel as strongly now as you did before the trip that the Chinese government is directly responsible for the record piracy?"

"I must admit I began to wonder about that during my stay there. However, upon further reflection, I certainly do believe that they are the ones responsible."

"Do you agree if we can find a way to stop the flow of records through the Juarez, Mexico facility, the Chinese will be forced to find a way to ship product directly to the Electro-Mart stores?"

"Yes, I do. Assuming the Haikou facility is the source, they have a large production capacity, and the Chinese cannot afford to have it become idle. The volume of CD-Rs is considerably lower than the volume of Electro-Mart records, so it would be an economic disaster if they could no longer produce product for Electro-Mart."

"I have a luncheon meeting with the Mexican ambassador today. I'll extract from him a commitment to shut down the Juarez facility as soon as possible, under some false pretense. I'll make it clear to him that if he does so, the U.S. will make absolutely sure the NAFTA agreement is extended in a way to favor the Mexican economy.

"John, I want you to contact the heads of the labor unions responsible for shipping goods from the Orient to either the U.S., Canada, or Europe. If China reacts as we believe they will, they will soon be applying for shipping permits to ship vast numbers of boxes.

I want to know the minute that happens. Tell the union bosses we will want to delay such shipments, as well as confiscate the material as evidence, once delivery takes place."

"I'll get on that right away," John said, as he rose and left Jackson's office.

The Mexican ambassador initially balked at the suggestion by the U.S. Commerce Department that the operation in Juarez be shut down. He said the owner of the facility was proud to be one of many small businesses that had been able to obtain a business license as a consequence of the free trade provisions of NAFTA. To shut it down for no reason would make no sense to the owner or to the employees. Jackson continued to apply pressure on the situation, until finally the ambassador came up with a proposal.

"If the U.S. government can provide the owner with the funds to upgrade his facility, so it becomes qualified to do electronic component and subsystem assembly work, then he could tell his people they were going to be furloughed for a couple of months, while the improvements are being made."

Jackson took the suggestion to the Congressional Budget Director, and subsequently the deal was approved. So, on 15 July 1995, the operation closed down, ostensibly for an upgrade, and Electro-Mart was informed no more product would be processed through the facility until further notice.

Meanwhile, John held several meetings with the union bosses, who actually looked forward to the possibility of engaging in a blockade of illegal CD records. He was able to get them to agree to inform the U.S. Commerce Department when and if CD records were found flowing through their operations. They also committed to help in any demonstrations, if the Commerce Department decided to hold such affairs.

"The lousy chinks have it coming to them," the outspoken head of the teamsters international union said at one such meeting. "It will serve them right for taking jobs away from loyal American workers."

"Peng, we have a serious problem," Fu Ho shouted over the phone. "My cousin at Electro-Mart called me last night and informed me the Juarez operation has shut down to be refurbished into an electronic assembly plant. The owner didn't even have the courtesy to inform us he was going to do this, nor did he give us any time to set up a similar operation elsewhere."

"How long will they be shut down?"

"My cousin tells me the plant conversion work will take at least two months to complete."

"My God, we do have a serious problem. Do you know if they made their month-end shipments?"

"My cousin says Electro-Mart has about four weeks worth of product on their various store shelves. However, Manny wants us to tell him within a couple of days what we plan to do, for he cannot stand to have empty shelves. He told me to tell you if you cannot supply him, he will immediately shift his requirement to his other suppliers."

"Thanks for telling me this," Peng said. "I'll call a meeting with the appropriate people here immediately."

When Peng informed Kong about the Juarez situation, Kong immediately called an emergency meeting with Shing and Keung to discuss alternatives. They met in Keung's private conference room.

Kong started the meeting by reminding Keung how China was currently selling records to Electro-Mart. He told him unlabeled product was first shipped to Juarez, where labels were attached. Then the shipments were broken down into deliveries to the various Electro-Mart stores.

"How long will it take us to set up a parallel operation?" Keung asked.

"Ordinarily such a matter could be accomplished in two or three weeks, but since we need to operate undercover, it will probably take a month or two."

"Do you think Manny will actually place orders with other suppliers?"

"Knowing him, he will probably say that in exchange for buying a larger proportion from them, he will need to get an even lower price. If he succeeds in doing that, and if he shuts us down to a trickle, we will have to really drop our prices before he will buy from us again."

"He doesn't have much vendor loyalty, does he?" Keung said, frowning.

"That's an understatement."

"Shing, what do you think we should do?" Keung asked.

"Ah, Keung, I think we have no choice but to begin immediately labeling our records in the Haikou plant. We could ship them to some neutral warehouse in Hong Kong and break the shipments down into smaller bundles for delivery direct to the Electro-Mart stores."

"Why didn't we do that initially?"

"We wanted to provide an additional shield against being discovered as the source of the records. However, I believe we can provide an adequate shield now, in the form of a Hong Kong warehouse, if we proceed carefully."

"Kong, what do you think?"

"Ah, Keung, I agree with Shing, for we have no other choice. We can be shipping in a couple of weeks, so Manny will not need to exercise his options."

"Okay, get going on this. But please set up the blind warehouse carefully in Hong Kong. It is a lot closer to home than the Mexican operation, and as you know, the U.S. Commerce Department is actively watching our every move."

When the meeting broke up, Shing and Kong went to their respective offices to make phone calls to set up the new operation. Kong told Peng and Fu Ho to contact Manny directly and calm him down.

"We must not let him have any excuse for cranking up his other suppliers. Do you both understand?" Kong said very sternly.

"We understand exactly what you mean."

John Toliver received a call on 7 August from the union head of the United Air Shipments Union in San Francisco. "Mr. Toliver, this is Clark Remington. I've just been informed a shipment of boxes bound for Electro-Mart stores in northern California has arrived. The shipment is currently being unloaded in one of our warehouses here at the San Francisco Airport. What do you want me to do with it?"

"Can you just sit on it for a couple of weeks, without anyone in your operation becoming concerned?"

"I sure can. We have plenty of other items here we need to ship, so I'll tell the boys to move those boxes into the far back area of our warehouse. I'll wait for your instructions before I do anything with them."

Within an hour, John received similar calls from all over the U.S. and Canada, and he provided the same instructions to each of the unions involved. He was told by each of his callers that the origin of the boxes was a warehouse in Hong Kong.

"Another K&S deal, I'll bet," he said to himself.

Likewise, in Europe, the head of the Euro-Air Shippers Union contacted the Commerce office in London with a similar message. He, too, was told to hold onto the shipment until further notice.

"Where is my damn product?" Manny shouted to the head of his purchasing group. "I was promised shipments last week, and when I phone the various shipping expediters, all I get is a lot of crap saying they are backlogged and can't get my boxes of records to my stores for at least a couple more weeks."

"My contact in Hong Kong said we should have received everything we ordered by now. They have put a tracer on it," his purchasing head said.

"Well, if I don't hear that records have arrived at my stores by Friday morning, I'll cancel the deal with the Chinese and start negotiating with the rest of my suppliers. I'll bet I can get a price almost as good, and I won't have to put up with all of the hassles from the feds anymore."

"What do you mean you haven't received the records yet?" Fu Ho screamed into the phone, as he spoke with his cousin in Los Angeles. "We delivered all of the items last week from our Hong Kong warehouse. I personally saw the paperwork, and I accompanied the shipments to the airport and saw them being placed in the cargo holds."

"Well, they sure didn't get here. Manny has given me just a couple of days to find the goods, or he will cancel all open orders with you. He really means it. He's tired of the entire hassle."

"We'll continue to try to find the goods from this end. Please tell Manny to cool it. We really did ship the goods. It seems that somehow they got lost in some warehouse somewhere. Tell Manny we'll find them."

On 15 August, Peng received a fax directly from Manny. It contained only two sentences: "Because of nondelivery, Electro-Mart exercises its right, per our contract agreement, to cancel all orders until further notice. If, in the future, you believe you are in a position to again deliver product to Electro-Mart, you should contact my purchasing manager."

"Kong, we are in real trouble now," Peng said over the phone. "We need to hold a meeting to decide what we do about this."

Shing, Kong, and Keung met in Keung's office. They all had solemn faces, and Keung was not his usual jubilant self. Prior to the meeting, Kong had sent Keung a copy of the fax with his comments attached, so Keung had time to reflect on the matter.

"Have you been able to trace the product?" Keung asked.

"Yes. It is being held up in various warehouses all across North America and Europe. The unions in charge of the workers in those warehouses all received instructions to not move the product until further notice. It seems our friends from the U.S. Commerce Department have decided to apply a squeeze on the supply. Unfortunately for us, their scheme is working."

"We obviously can't complain to them," Shing said. "Certainly not after we told them we were just as anxious as they to stop the flow of illegal records into North America and Europe."

"You're right," Keung said. "It seems they have outsmarted us. It also looks like Manny is taking advantage of the situation to distance himself from us, while he gets good prices from his other suppliers. I'm afraid we are the ones who have lost here. I see no other choice but to stop producing CD records and scale down the Haikou operation to only the production of CD-Rs."

At that moment, Keung's secretary burst into his office. "Ah, Keung, you must turn on the Chinese news channel and see what is happening in America."

Keung climbed out of his chair and turned on the TV. The announcer was showing pictures of bulldozers crushing hundreds of boxes of records. The scene was outside the San Francisco airport, and the announcer was indicating that the U.S. Commerce Department had intercepted a shipment of contraband records bound for Electro-Mart. The scene then shifted to the Chicago airport. The announcer said similar activities were taking place simultaneously in all major airports in the U.S., Canada, and Europe.

"We must have really pissed off John Toliver with our little charade in the townsquare of Haikou," Keung said, frowning.

"And he seemed like such a mild-mannered, gullible man," Shing sighed.

Keung addressed his secretary. "I need to prepare a statement for the press indicating that the Chinese government is very pleased the supply of Electro-Mart brand records has finally been stopped. Please call my press manager and have him come to my office immediately!"

"Well, gentlemen, it has been a fun ride, from nothing produced to large volume being produced and back to nothing again. Shing, I'm glad your man at least designed a CD-R product we can continue to sell on the open market without being hassled by the U.S. Commerce Department. That's all, gentlemen. I think I'll go home after my meeting with the press manager and listen to some of the nice soothing records we once produced."

Keung almost cracked a smile when he made this last remark, but inside he was feeling very upset with this outcome. After he collected his thoughts, he would spend hours with Shing discussing other products the Haikou facility could make for sale, because China sorely needed the income stream to help pay for their modernization programs.

Part 4

A Fiendishly Clever Plan is Born

Chapter Twenty-Six

It was noon when Steven returned from jogging in the park across the street from his father's townhouse. He went to his room, quickly showered and dressed, and joined his parents on the patio. August weather in Hong Kong is often unbearable, so even though he just showered, he began to perspire profusely. To cool off, he sat quietly in a reclining lounge chair, sipping a tall glass of ice tea that his mother had prepared for him.

"You should hear what they are saying in the news this morning," Ming said. "It seems the U.S. Commerce Department has discovered large shipments of illegally copied CD records, which they claim are being produced in China. This must be somehow connected with what you heard from the man you met on the plane, don't you think?"

"When is the next television newscast?" Steven asked.

"In about twenty minutes," his mother said, looking at her watch.

"If I doze off, please wake me so I can watch it." As Steven sipped his tea slowly, he closed his eyes and began to daydream. He was very concerned about the future safety of his parents. On several occasions, he tried to get them to face up to the reality of their situation, but they seemed to be convincing themselves that they will be pardoned for their past political crimes. He reminded them of what the Chinese charge d'affaires told him, but they were still unwilling to deal with the reality of their situation.

"Wake up, Steven. The CNN World News is about to begin."

The announcer started off with various news items of local interest, and then said CNN was now going to cover an important breaking news story.

"What you are seeing are many thousands of illegally copied CD records being crushed by bulldozers in the parking lot on the north side of the Chicago O'Hare Airport. All of these records bear the Electro-Mart label. According to authorities from the U.S. Commerce Department, these records are all illegal copies made somewhere in China and intended for sale in Electro-Mart stores in the greater Chicago area. We have been trying to get a statement from Manny Chang, the president and CEO of Electro-Mart, but we have been unable to reach him."

The scene shifted to Kennedy Airport in New York City, where a similar event was taking place. The local CNN announcer there was interviewing one of the bulldozer drivers.

"Who authorized you to drive your heavy equipment over these records and destroy them?" the announcer asked.

"The head of our union called us this morning and told us the U.S. Commerce Department requested that we do so. He said these records are being produced illegally in China, so we save jobs for hundreds of our fellow American workers by destroying them."

"Have there been any other shipments of these records in the past that you can remember? After all, they are addressed to various Electro-Mart locations in New York and New Jersey. Surely these are not the first such shipments of Electro-Mart records to pass through this airport?"

"I asked my shop foreman the same question this morning, and he told me that in the past, record shipments for Electro-Mart all came from Mexico, under one of the provisions of the NAFTA agreement. He couldn't remember any such shipments ever coming directly from Hong Kong or China."

The news shifted back to CNN headquarters in Atlanta, where the news anchors summarized what had just been shown. "It looks as if the U.S. government has been able to shut off the supply of illegal records from China, at least temporarily. A communiqué we received from the Commerce Department defined an illegal record as one being produced without the permission of the recording artist, and/or without paying any royalty or fee to the recording artist, or to the record company who has a contract with the recording artist."

"Didn't we hear a few weeks ago about some renegade firm in China being shut down because they were caught producing illegal records for sale in South America?"

"That's right."

The announcers moved on to sports and local weather, so Steven's father turned down the volume so he and Steven and Betty Lou could discuss what they had just heard.

"Father, this is incredible. Do you think the Chinese government is actually responsible for the production of these records? Has there been any official statement from them so far?"

"I haven't heard anything yet, Son."

The newscaster switched to a remote site, which was the office of the Chinese ambassador in Washington, D.C. Steven turned up the volume so they could hear.

"This is Giles Matheson, CNN reporter in Washington. I'm in the office of Chung Tseing, the Chinese ambassador to the U.S. He has a prepared statement to make regarding the illegal CD record matter."

"The Chinese Government wants to assure the American public that we are just as outraged over the production of illegally copied CD records as you are. For some months, we have been conducting an investigation of our own, for we have long suspected some renegade company in mainland China has been producing illegal records for sale through the Electro-Mart chain.

"Only a few short weeks ago, we shut down one such company, which was producing illegally copied records for sale into South America. However, the records that have been confiscated recently in airports across the U.S., Canada, and Europe seem to be the product of yet another firm, and we will not rest until we have also shut it down.

"You can be assured that the Chinese government will cooperate fully with the U.S., Canadian, and European authorities to track down the source of this illegal product and shut it down forever. We are a member of the Berne Convention in good standing, and we wish to uphold the rights of others through the international copyright laws, which all member nations have signed.

"Meanwhile, our CD-R plant in Haikou continues to produce very high quality recordable CDs for the world's personal computer software industry. We are proud of their accomplishments, for we understand the quality of the CD-Rs made in our plant is second to none, anywhere in the world."

As the ambassador spoke, pictures were shown of the Haikou Plant with all of its shiny new equipment. The ambassador clearly wanted the world to believe the entire investment made by the Chinese government was intended for the CD-R software market.

"Thank you for your comments, Mr. Ambassador. This is Giles Matheson, returning you back to CNN headquarters in Atlanta."

"Father, if the Chinese are behind this scheme, I'll bet they have been producing the records in the same plant where they produce the CD-R recordable disks for the software industry. I don't know the numbers, but I can't believe CD-Rs are being used in very high quantities yet. It would make no sense for the Chinese to set up a huge facility, like the one we just saw, just to make CD-Rs."

"You're probably right, Son. But now that the U.S. Commerce Department has stopped such records from entering the country, the Chinese will have to stop their production, at least until things cool down. That will be a terrible blow to their economy. I wonder how much revenue they were receiving from the sale of these records?"

"It must be millions of dollars," Betty Lou said. "The last time I purchased CDs in the Hong Kong Mall, I believe I paid HK$15, so it wouldn't take many records per month to add up to millions of dollars of lost revenue."

"By the way, Son, while you were jogging, the mail came. You have a letter from the American embassy here in Hong Kong. Were you expecting such a letter?" Betty Lou asked, with a puzzled look on her face.

Steven opened the letter and read it carefully. Unbeknownst to his parents, he had visited the American embassy to discuss his grandparents' situation. He hadn't been happy with the runaround the Chinese charge d'affaires had given him, so he was hopeful the American embassy would be able to provide him with some help.

"Damn," Steven said. "No one is willing to stick their necks out these days. They all seem to be afraid to make waves with the Chinese."

"What's this all about?" Betty Lou asked.

"I visited the American embassy last month," Steven said. "I know you keep telling me the situation with my grandparents is hopeless, but I wanted to see if there was another avenue to pursue."

"So, what did the letter say?" Betty Lou asked.

"All the stupid embassy head did was contact the same man I spoke with in the Chinese embassy. Guess what? He was told the same thing I was told. The letter merely states that the American government cannot interfere with Chinese political matters, especially those that occurred such a long time ago."

"Son, I'm sorry you keep running into a dead end on this thing, but remember, we both told you that you need to accept the situation as it is."

"But, Father, what I'm even more concerned with is what will happen to you and Mother in July of 1997."

"Son, don't you worry. Your mother and I are convinced the Chinese will not take away our freedom. Now why don't we all eat the hearty meal your mother has fixed for us?"

Chapter Twenty-Seven

Shing arrived at the Haikou CD plant the day after the meeting in Keung's office. He was given strict instructions to make sure all evidence was removed from the plant. He was told to brief CT and his key managers about the whole situation, and to obtain their oath of silence, in the event news reporters tried to interview them about any aspect of CD record production. Before he called the general meeting, Shing asked CT to join him in the conference room, where the two could be alone.

"CT, I presume you have heard the news."

"Of course, Shing. I have already taken steps to destroy all CD record production masters and any other material we have in the plant that would indicate that Electro-Mart records were ever produced here."

"I knew I could count on you," Shing said.

"Ah, Shing, what really happened? I thought we were technically not doing anything illegal."

"Technically speaking, you are correct. However, the U.S. Commerce Department must have concluded the only way they could shut down the operation was to stop shipments from getting into North America or Europe."

"What happened to our operation in Juarez?"

"According to our sources, the U.S. Commerce Department was also responsible for having it shut down."

"Is there any chance we will not be allowed to produce CD-Rs? As you know, we seem to have the best process in the world, and our order rate is increasing weekly."

"You have my personal word that there will be no more interventions on the part of the U.S. Commerce Department or any other similar agency. It was brilliant of you to develop the capability for CD-Rs, for without them, we would have to shut down the plant."

CT sat quietly for a moment in his chair and propped his feet up on the conference table. He stood up and walked over to the small window at the end of the room to view the courtyard outside. "I guess we will have to furlough some of our workers," CT said.

"That is one of the subjects I wanted to talk to you and your staff about today. If you or your staff can think of any similar product to produce in this plant, that might be unnecessary."

"Ah, Shing, that is what I want to talk to you about. I'm very unhappy with the outcome of this matter. I know we both recognized the risks of producing records without paying any royalties to the performers. Even so, I believe the U.S. Government is just trying to clamp down on our economy, so we fall further behind the rest of the world. You ask me if I think there is another product we can make. Yes, I know of one that would be of considerable importance to China and would help overcome the loss of revenue we now face."

"What product idea do you have?"

"Do you remember the apparatus Miu developed that we use to make production masters?"

"Yes, of course I do."

"Well, I believe we could use that apparatus to copy strategically important personal computer software for our own use in China. For example, isn't it true China currently is importing hundreds of thousands of software programs per month from Hong Kong, all of which originate in the U.S. from companies such as Microsoft, Lotus, and Borland?"

"That's true. In fact, I once heard we pay more than HK$200 per copy for most of those programs. Are you suggesting we stop buying software from the Hong Kong distributors and make our own by copying the programs?"

"That's right, but first I wonder if it is legal for China to copy such programs, so long as we do not try to sell them for a profit."

"Again, it is probably technically legal, but if we do this we certainly will not win any popularity contests with companies like Microsoft, will we?" Shing smiled.

"Miu and I have already copied a number of programs to prove the feasibility of the system. If you were to give us the approval, we could be in production within a couple of weeks. We would produce such software in three forms: as recordings on CD-Rs, as recordings on 5 1/4-inch floppy disks, and as recordings on 3-inch floppy disks."

"CT, I think it is a very good idea. Of course I'll need to discuss this with Kong and Keung. I have a meeting with them this Friday, so I'll certainly present your idea. Meanwhile, I'll try to find out just how much personal computer software China buys each month, so I can get an idea of what the economic benefit would be if we were to proceed with your idea.

"Now, will you call the rest of your staff? I wish to brief them on the entire CD record matter. Again, thank you for your help, and say hello to your charming wife for me."

"Manny, you can't avoid the press forever," Manny's purchasing manager told him during an emergency meeting held shortly after the first batch of records in the San Francisco Airport were destroyed.

"I know that, so let me read this press release to you and your staff. I want you guys to see if I've covered everything":

<u>Just released—Los Angeles, California, 15 August 1995</u>. Electro-Mart CEO Manny Chang announced today that he has fired his chief purchasing manager and two of his senior buyers when he discovered they had been purchasing illegally copied CD records from a firm in Hong Kong. Although Manny has long been a believer of buying records directly from the source of manufacture, he has always adhered to the principle that although he strives in all business deals to strike a hard bargain, he never knowingly buys any product that is produced illegally. Manny wants to assure his loyal customers that the temporary shortages, caused by many thousands of CD records being destroyed in various airports around the world, are now over and he has replaced those records with similar records from other legitimate suppliers. He wants to assure his customers that his stores will continue to offer the best prices and widest selection of CD records anywhere in the world.

The purchasing manager and his two buyers sat in stunned silence as Manny finished reading the press release. "Don't sit there with your tongues hanging out. What do you think of it? Will this get Electro-Mart off the hook?"

"Manny, that means the three of us are going to be your fall guys."

"Well, what else was I supposed to do? Hey, if you guys will pass by the personnel office on your way out of this meeting, you'll be pleased with the severance package I'm offering you. Don't take this personally, gentlemen. It's just business."

The three of them got up and somberly walked out of the conference room and down the hall to the personnel office. When they left, they were considerably happier, but they also were no longer employees of Electro-Mart.

At Keung's Friday staff meeting, he asked Kong and Shing to report on their activities as a result of the decision to stop making CD records. Kong reported he once again shut down the warehouse in Hong Kong, and Shing reported on activities in Haikou involving the destruction of all production masters and work in process.

"I presume you will have to reduce staff, as well," Keung stated.

"Yes, unless we can come up with another product to make there," Shing said.

"By the way, Keung and Shing, Fu Ho's cousin was fired yesterday by Manny. Apparently, Manny fired three guys to act as fall guys on this whole venture. In addition, he placed a large ad in several papers, apologizing for the whole deal. He assured his customers he would have never, ever bought the records if he had known they were illegal copies."

"He lies even better than we do!" Kong said loudly. He quickly shut up as he noted Keung was not pleased with what he had just said.

"Gentlemen, do you have any ideas for other products that we could make in our newly refurbished plant? Of course, we will continue making CD-Rs, but I understand the market for those has not yet fully developed."

"The managing director of the plant in Haikou has provided me with a recommendation for new products, which is contained in this report. Can we take a moment to read and discuss it?"

"Of course. Do you have copies for both Kong and me?"

"Yes. Here they are."

The recommendations were contained in a three page report. Included in the report was data that showed China was currently purchasing more than 100,000 sets of software per month, and the volume was increasing monthly. Obviously, if the plant in Haikou were to provide such software, enormous cost savings would accrue, because the cost of producing floppy disks was minuscule compared with paying on average HK$200 per copy.

After everyone completed reading the report, Keung turned to Kong. "What do you think?"

"Shing's boy, CT, seems to want to jump from the frying pan into the fire. We just got through having our hands slapped for copying CD records, and now he wants to copy computer software? Has he no shame?"

"Kong, stop the theatrics. I want your honest opinion regarding the assumptions in this report," Keung said sternly.

"I have no feel for the quantity of software China is buying currently, but I guess such figures could be checked easily enough. Shing, did you provide this data to CT?"

"Yes. I got it from our Central Accounting Office."

"If we don't mind taking a chance again copying stuff that belongs to others, what the hell? It would represent large savings in money outflow per month."

"Shing, did you speak with anyone from my staff regarding the legalities of this matter?" Keung asked.

"Yes. Your man tells me if we were planning to copy personal computer software for resale, we should definitely not launch such a program. However, if all we plan to do is copy software for our own use, we are in what he calls the gray zone."

"Did he have any recommendations for you?"

"Yes. He suggests we should not cut off our external purchases of computer software completely. Rather, we should gradually reduce our purchases, while making up the difference with internally manufactured software. In that way, it might be years before anyone gets suspicious, especially since our usage is increasing at such a high rate now."

Keung turned to Kong and Shing and said, "I believe we should launch such an enterprise immediately. I'll assign one of my staff to study the various kinds and quantities of software we buy. Shing, when do you think we could commence this operation?"

"CT tells me we could be ready in a couple of weeks, once he knows which software to copy."

"Kong, even though this does not represent a sale as such, since all of the product is being sold internally to Chinese companies and research establishments, I still want you to assign one of your inside sales persons to service this product line. Then, if we ever decide to sell such products outside China, we can be ready to do so at a moment's notice."

In Redmond, Washington, on a warm August 1995 afternoon, Jay Leno walked out on the stage of an outdoor theater set up on Microsoft's campus. The extravagant show was in honor of the product launch of Windows 95™, and the entire staff of Microsoft was on hand for the gala event. According to the press, the Windows 95™ product launch was the most expensive launch of any software product ever, and it was one way Microsoft had for showing the world that it alone was the "King of PC operating-system software."

Microsoft had been working on this product for a number of years, but once the copyright infringement case with Apple Computer was no longer a nagging issue, Bill Gates pushed his staff even harder to complete the product. There were several improvements included that would make its GUI-interface and Multimedia functionality even better than what the Apple Macintosh™ provided the personal computer marketplace.

Having the product available in August would ensure most personal computers shipped during the 1995 Christmas holiday season would contain Windows 95™, and the sale of IBM-compatible PCs during that period would gain significant market share over Apple products.

The enormous Microsoft product launch did not go unnoticed by Apple Computer executives, however. The head of Apple's Corporate Communications Department received approval to place several full-page ads in all of the important magazines and newspapers, in an attempt to counteract some of the Microsoft impact. These ads were written in such a way as to try to convince the buying public that Microsoft really did not have anything new to offer.

Steven's father noticed the Apple ad in the *Wall Street Journal*. He tore out the full center page and laid it on Steven's bed, so he would be sure to see it when he returned from attending a play with his mother.

"Goodnight, Mother. I'm glad we went to see the play."

Steven turned on the bedroom light and went to the bureau to empty his pockets. He noticed the torn-out center sheet of the *Wall Street Journal* on his bed. He picked it up and saw the Apple logo on the bottom. The few words in giant print simply said:

WE'VE BEEN THERE. WE'VE DONE THAT.
THERE'S NOTHING NEW. CHECK US OUT FIRST.
Signed, Charles Smoot
VP, Corporate Communications
Apple Computer

Steven thought to himself, "The bastards actually finished Windows 95™, and they did it in record time, too. I have to give them credit for that." Steven had obtained an early version of Windows 95™ from a friend who worked at Microsoft, so he was able to evaluate it as part of the work he did for the Apple legal team. He often marveled at the complexity of the product, but his evaluation showed that in no way had any of Apple's operating system code been used to produce the new operating system. Steven left his bedroom and found his father still sitting in the den reading a book.

"Thanks for cutting out the ad. It brings back memories."

"Sounds like a sour grapes ad to me," his father said. "It must have cost Apple plenty. I heard on the news tonight that they placed that ad in dozens of publications around the world. I guess they didn't want Microsoft to take over the entire world stage of personal computing."

"You know, Father, the sad thing is that the ad is essentially correct. I evaluated an early version of Windows 95™ thoroughly last year. Even though the design of it was elegant, the features it provides have been around for several years on the more advanced Macintosh™ computers. It's for that reason I finally decided to quit Apple and catch my breath. Well, I'm off to bed now."

Steven could not sleep. For one thing, he and his mother had eaten an eight-course, highly seasoned Chinese meal before attending the theater, and afterwards he insisted on taking his mother to a pub where fifties music was played each evening. They both drank a number of cups of strong coffee laced with brandy, and his mother began to slur her speech a bit before they finally left to catch a cab home.

Steven tossed and turned, and his mind kept going back to the trial and to his final meeting with Miles. Surely there must have been some way for Apple to defend their honor. They paid the law firm millions and what did they get? Nothing but a slap on the wrist from a judge, who probably didn't even know how to spell "computer." The judge's words, "I think Microsoft did the world a favor by making all computers operate the same way," kept ringing in his ears.

It was three in the morning and he still was not asleep. He got up to go to the bathroom. When he returned, he sat on the edge of the bed and put his head in his hands. Things were definitely not going well for him. He had been in Hong Kong for more than three months, and he was no further along obtaining freedom for his grandparents. In addition, he was now faced with the possibility that his parents would end up the same way. He had done nothing about finding a new job, and his mother was starting to bug him about this, for she was genuinely concerned he was going to turn into a professional bum.

He lay down on his bed, closed his eyes, and tried to find rest, but he noticed he was beginning to get a migraine headache, which would be his first in several months. His temples started throbbing and his mouth felt dry. He tried to think of other things to take his attention away from the headache, but the news of the recent weeks flashed by him.

"That guy John Toliver must have stuck it to the Chinese real well. I wish I could find a way to stick it to Microsoft," he thought to himself. Suddenly he sprang from his bed, sweat pouring from his brow. He remembered the final meeting with his boss at Apple, Alan Smith, who quipped about how his Operating System Analysis Programs could make IBM-compatible personal computers slow down, so Apple machines would appear to be far superior.

His mind began to race and his headache was gone. "I believe it can be done," he said out loud. "In fact, I know it will work, and, by God, I should be able to leverage my idea in such a way to get my grandparents and parents a full pardon!"

Although it was only four in the morning, he jumped out of bed and headed to the shower, where he turned the water on ice cold, jumped in, and began singing loudly.

"What in the world is he doing taking a shower at this ungodly hour?" Betty Lou asked Ming.

"I haven't the slightest idea. I wish he would stop that awful singing, though. I really need my rest."

After Steven's shower, he dressed in his jogging clothes and went into the dining room with his Apple Powerbook™ computer. He plugged it into the wall and brought up the word-processor program. He began to develop a plan that would turn out to be one of the most fiendishly clever schemes the world would ever encounter. As he typed, his head became clearer and he knew he had re-defined his mission in life. He knew his plan was going to work, and he knew he would succeed. He would have the last laugh, after all, and he would help the Chinese also have their last laugh.

"My God, Betty Lou, first he showers at 4:00 A.M. and now he sits in the dining room writing someone a letter, while he sings. When is he going to find a job and leave us in peace?"

"He's your son, and you wanted him to come visit us. Roll over and cover your ears and go back to sleep!"

Chapter Twenty-Eight

Wing Ma, the charge d'affaires of the Chinese embassy, arrived at his office early on Monday morning to organize his work. He scarcely began to sort through the pile of mail and other paperwork on his desk, when the guard phoned him from outside the compound.

"He tells me his name is Shou Lee and he says it is urgent that he speak with you immediately. I told him he needs first to make an appointment, but he seems to be irrational. He keeps telling me he must see you now, for he has very important news for the Chinese government. What should I tell him?"

"Tell him there is nothing more he and I have to talk about. The last time he visited me, we exhausted all avenues of discussion."

When the guard gave Steven that answer, Steven grabbed the phone from him, and shouted, "Wing, you don't understand. I have information of national importance to discuss with you. You absolutely must see me immediately."

"Steven, why won't you give up? I told you many times there is nothing that can be done to free your grandparents. Why won't you accept that?"

"Wing, what I have to discuss with you transcends that matter. For example, I have ideas that will make it possible for China to produce any quantities of CD records, without any interference from the U.S. Commerce Department. Surely you are interested in hearing about such ideas."

"Steven, I don't know what you're talking about. The Chinese government has never manufactured CD records. In fact, our government is cooperating with the United States in trying to find who is responsible for making the illegal records which were destroyed in various airports around the world. Now why don't you go home and stop bothering me?"

Wing hung up on Steven and returned to his desk full of papers to sort. Outside the compound, the guard yanked the phone away from Steven and told him to leave immediately, or he would call the Hong Kong police.

Steven finally left and went down the street to a bar on the corner. Even though it was early in the morning, and even though Steven rarely drank, he went in and ordered a tankard of beer.

"Having a bad day?" the bartender asked.

"What does it look like?" Steven grumbled. "I've been up since 3:00 A.M, and that's enough to drive anyone to drink."

Steven took out his Apple Powerbook™ computer, which had the detailed plan saved on the hard drive. He brought up the program and sat quietly at his table, sipping the beer and reading the plan over and over again.

"It's rock solid, and I know I can pull it off," he said under his breath. "But how do I get past that idiot at the embassy?"

By afternoon, Wing finished most of the important work he needed to accomplish, so he asked his secretary to prepare him his favorite brand of tea. As he sipped the tea, he thought again about the incident with Steven that morning.

"The poor lad needs to go back to the States and stop living in a dream world," he told his secretary.

"Maybe he needs to find a lover," she laughed.

"Yes, you are right. If he comes back, I'll suggest that to him," Wing said. "Do you want to volunteer for the job?"

The red phone on his desk began to ring. Wing pressed the special cryptographic button on the side of the phone, waited until the light stopped flashing, and then picked it up. "Hello. This is Wing Ma."

"Wing, this is Shing Ling calling. How are you today?"

"Ah, Shing, I'm fine. What can I do for you?"

"Wing, I need to come to Hong Kong to clean up some matters associated with the K&S Industries shut down and the subsequent shut down of the other warehouse on Main Street. My plans call for me to be there on Wednesday evening around 7:30. Can you arrange to have me picked up?"

"Of course, Shing. And do you wish to stay at your usual hotel?"

"Yes. I would also like you to acquire the services of Ting Lao for the evening. She should plan to be at the hotel after 9:00 P.M. as usual."

"It will be done. Is there anything else you need?"

"Yes. I'll want to meet with you for about an hour and brief you regarding the CD record matter. It is possible that some newscaster will approach you and try to get you to admit something. Why don't we meet first thing on Thursday morning in your office?"

"That would be fine," Wing said.

"By the way, Shing, there was a gentleman here today who claims to have ideas that will make it possible for China to produce CD records legally. Of course, I acted ignorant of the whole matter."

"Why would he be offering such information, even if he is sincere?"

"He has visited us many times seeking the freedom of his aging grandparents, who were locked away in Manchuria in the early 50s for political crimes."

"Perhaps we should hear him out. Would it be asking too much for you to speak with him before my visit?"

"Very well," sighed Wing. "I'll contact him and see what he has in mind for me this time," he said reluctantly.

"I'll see you on Thursday morning. Good night."

"Good night, Shing."

"It's the phone for you, Steven," his father called out. "Were you expecting a call?"

"No, I wasn't. I'll take it in the den. I have no idea who is calling me."

"Hello. This is Steven Lee. How can I help you?"

"Steven, this is Wing at the Chinese Embassy. I'll bet you're surprised to hear from me."

"Yes, I'm quite surprised. Are you feeling sorry for the way you treated me the other morning?"

"As a matter of fact, I did reflect on my actions and I believe I owe you at least the courtesy of one more visit. You must realize, however, I still do not know how to help you."

"When can you see me, and will you tell your guard I'm coming this time? I'm afraid he will pull a gun on me."

"How about coming by tomorrow morning at nine. My secretary will personally be at the guardhouse to pick you up."

"Fine. I'll see you then."

Steven hung up and went into the living room where his father was reading the paper. "Who was that?" his father asked.

"My friend from the Chinese embassy. He says he wants to talk with me again."

"Do you suppose he has news about your grandparents?" Betty Lou asked.

"I have no idea, but one can always hope."

"Shou Lee here to see the charge d'affaires," Steven said to the guard, who was watching him very carefully. "I have an appointment this time," he said, eager not to provoke him.

Wing's secretary appeared at the front gate to escort Steven. She was a very attractive Chinese girl with very long, dark black hair and a little impish look about her. When she held out her hand to greet him, she started laughing.

"What's so funny?" Steven asked.

"It's nothing. I just remembered something funny my boss told me yesterday."

"Steven, how are you?" Wing asked as he shook his hand.

"I'm fine, and I'm certainly glad you decided to meet with me."

The two went into the conference room at the back of the embassy. Wing's secretary followed them into the room and fixed them tea and biscuits. She then closed the door, so the two of them could talk privately.

"So, Steven, why did you seem so anxious to speak with me? Surely you must realize the situation with your grandparents has not changed since we last spoke. You said something about CD records. As I told you over the phone, our government is not involved in such production."

"Wing, I lied to you about the CD records, for I wanted to find some way to speak with you again. What I have to tell you has very little to do with records. I guess my little lie must have worked, for here I am."

"Then, what is it you wish to tell me?" he asked sternly.

"I'm a computer software expert, and I believe I have a software product that your country could sell to the entire world and make an enormous profit doing so. If my idea is of interest to your country, perhaps I can use it as a bargaining chip to help me obtain the release of my grandparents." Steven then pulled out of his pocket a three page outline of his plan.

"Here is a copy of my idea, prepared in outline form. I believe if someone in your country with software knowledge were to read this, he or she would immediately understand the importance and value of my product. Therefore, all I ask is for you to forward this outline to an appropriate person for review."

"What value do you place on this idea? Can you give me some feel for that, before I send it through channels?"

"How many personal computers do you think there are in the world today?" Steven asked.

"I really don't know, but let me guess. I would say there are probably more than a hundred million."

"That's not a bad guess, but the number is actually almost twice that figure."

"And your idea has to do with personal computers?"

"Yes. I have a product that all users of personal computers will want to buy, and it can be sold for a price of HK$100 each. In addition, the cost to produce this product will be less than HK$1."

Wing pulled out his pocket calculator and did the arithmetic. "Do you realize if my calculation is correct, the value of this product is more than HK$20 billion? And you would trade such a product idea for your grandparents' safety? You must really want to see them again."

"I have other personal reasons why I am offering your country this idea. If your country is interested, in due time, I will reveal my entire plan and my reasons for pursuing this matter with you."

"Steven, I most certainly will route your plan outline through the proper channels."

"How long will that take?"

"It turns out the first link in such channels will be visiting me tomorrow morning here in this very same conference room. If he is taken by the idea, I would say you should be hearing from me within a week."

"That sounds fine. Would you now please read the proposal and see if there is any part of it that is unclear to you?"

Wing skimmed the outline, not fully understanding what it contained. As he read it, he thought to himself that either Steven had cracked up, or he was just a brilliant fool willing to sell such a valued product for so little compensation.

"It seems to be quite clear," Wing said.

"I'll be looking forward to hearing from you soon," Steven said.

Shing Ling arrived on schedule at the Hong Kong International Airport, where a chauffeured limousine driver in a dark blue suit and matching cap met him. "Let me have your baggage claim check, sir," the chauffeur said.

"Thanks. I'll wait for you by the lounge."

The drive downtown was uneventful, and Shing relaxed in the back of the limousine, contemplating his next meeting with Ting Lao. It had been almost four years since he was first introduced to her, and tonight's liaison was probably the twentieth time he would be making use of her services. He gave his driver a generous tip, checked into his hotel room, and called her number.

"Hello, this is Ting Lao. Who am I speaking to?"

"Ting, my little flower, it is I, Shing, here to meet with you again. Have you had dinner yet this evening?"

"No. I waited for you, as usual. I always enjoy being with you and talking with you before we retire for the evening. I'll meet you in the private dining room in your hotel in about an hour. Is that all right?"

"That would be fine."

Shing had time for a shower and a change of clothes before meeting with Ting. As the hot spray of water hit his face, he thought how fortunate he was to be a ministry chief in China, especially since it would be less than two years before Hong Kong would be under Chinese rule. He wondered if he could work a deal then where he could be stationed in Hong Kong. If so, he could arrange for liaisons with Ting more often.

Shing spent the first hour of the meeting with Wing briefing him on the CD record fiasco. He wanted to be absolutely sure no one in the Chinese embassy would leak any information that might tend to incriminate the Chinese government, especially during the delicate trade negotiations between the United States and China.

"Our contacts believe someone employed by K&S Industries provided the U.S. Commerce Department personnel with certain information that could possibly be damaging to our government," Shing said. "I want you to hire an investigator to find out who that person is and silence him forever. Do you understand what I'm saying?"

"Your request is perfectly clear," Wing said.

"Now, tell me about the young fellow who wanted to urgently see you. Is he some kind of a nut, or does he have a credible idea to share with us?"

Wing told Shing about the many times that Steven had visited him in the past, going all the way back to when Steven was in college. He told him about the more recent visits, including the one yesterday morning.

"Can I see the product outline he gave you?"

"Of course. Here is a copy that I translated into Chinese after he left."

Shing spent fifteen minutes reading the document and then he read it again. He was obviously very interested in its contents.

"Wing, if this man is for real, and if his idea is sound, this could be worth billions to us. Where does he live?"

"He stays with his father and mother in a townhouse overlooking the wharf. As far as I can tell, he has no plans to return to the U.S. soon, but I could be wrong."

"Wing, I want you to encrypt this report and send it immediately to CT in Haikou. I want him to review it before I go there tomorrow. This could be very important. Please do not tell anyone else about this."

"My lips are sealed, as always."

"What is the status of his grandparents?"

Wing pulled out the file and let Shing read it for himself. When he was done, Shing asked for a copy of the file to take with him. He asked Wing if he had seriously attempted to seek their freedom, and Wing told him he felt it wasn't important enough to waste the time of the Chinese government. "No, I never really inquired into the matter. It's possible they could have been set free years ago if someone had applied enough pressure."

"I'm glad you didn't pursue the matter. If this fellow's ideas are worthy of being pursued, perhaps we can use his grandparents' freedom as a large trading chip. So, Wing, I'll take my leave now. Thanks for your continued support. When our nation takes over your little bit of land, I'll see to it that you are well taken care of."

"Thank you, Shing, and good-bye."

Wing's secretary escorted Shing out the front gate and into his waiting limousine. He had not planned to visit Haikou this time, but now he wanted to spend some time with CT, examining the product idea Steven had prepared for them.

"This is unbelievable," he whispered under his breath. "China can become absolutely wealthy, if what he says is true. I wonder what CT will say about this. I hope he agrees with my assessment."

Chapter Twenty-Nine

The fax from Shing arrived at CT's office an hour before CT planned to go home. He quickly read it and told his secretary to call Miu. "Tell her Shing wants to see me right away on an important matter, so I won't be able to come home for dinner tonight."

He went into his office and closed the door and read the fax again. His initial response was the same as Shing's. If Steven's product idea was valid, China could stand to make billions. It would make the CD record enterprise pale by comparison.

He got up from his chair and walked over to a filing cabinet, where he found a report he had received a year ago from a market research firm. The report contained an estimate of the number of personal computers in use by the end of 1994. He took out a piece of paper, copied the number down, and did an extrapolation into 1995. He sat down again to contemplate the potential size of the business opportunity.

"Whew," he whistled out loud. "I wonder if this guy Steven really knows what he's talking about. If he does, we could really clean up on the personal computer software market!"

"A table for two in the corner of the room where we won't be disturbed," CT told the head waiter in Haikou's most famous restaurant. Shing asked CT to meet him at the Haikou Palms Restaurant, which served an elegant cuisine. He said in the fax he would be arriving around 7:00 P.M., but it was 7:30 before Shing arrived.

They greeted each other, and CT motioned to the waiter to take their drink order.

"So, what do you think?" Shing asked. "Is his idea feasible?"

"I truly believe it is. If so, we absolutely must get our hands on his product. It could make China very rich, indeed."

"That was my reaction too," Shing said. "Just so I can better understand the whole thing, can you give me your impression of what the product is and how it would be distributed?"

"Okay, but his outline is somewhat sketchy." CT pulled out his copy of the fax and began to describe Steven's idea.

"First of all, he claims to have developed a computer software code sequence that. when introduced into an IBM-compatible PC using the Windows™ operating system, makes the computer run very slowly."

"Is this just some form of virus? I've heard of computer viruses, but aren't they usually just the work of pranksters?"

"That's correct, but only for ordinary viruses. He claims, however, that present day virus scanners cannot detect his code sequence. Once it is introduced into a computer, the computer will slow down by more than twenty times its normal rate, which would be very frustrating to the user of the computer."

"How does he plan to introduce his code sequence into all of the world's personal computers?"

"He says he has that figured out and would tell us how that can be done when he meets with us."

"So, what is the software product China would sell, assuming all of the computers in the world somehow slow down?"

"That is the beautiful part," CT said enthusiastically. "He claims he has developed an antidote code which, when loaded on the hard drive of an infected PC, will destroy the code sequence, thus causing the computer to again run at a higher speed. If we alone possess such an antidote, we could sell it to everyone who has an infected computer."

"In what form would the antidote be sold?"

"In either floppy disk form or CD-R form, depending on what the customer requires. That means the actual production cost would be extremely low, and most of the sales price would be profit for us."

"Why can't someone merely copy the antidote, just like we now copy software, such as Windows™ and other popular software packages?"

"That is one of the key questions we need to find out from him, for he claims he knows how to protect his antidote from being copied. He even claims he can make it self-destruct after a single use, so a large company with hundreds of PCs would have to buy a copy for each and every computer they own."

"Won't the world assume that if we are the only ones with the fix, we must have caused the computers to slow down in the first place?"

"That's certainly possible, but with the huge potential for business here, we should be able to work out a plan to prevent China from being blamed for this matter."

"CT, are you able to meet with this man on Monday in Hong Kong, if I make arrangements for such a meeting in our embassy?"

"Of course. I want very much to meet him to see just how far along he is with his idea."

"Very well, CT. I'll make arrangements for you to meet with him on Monday morning at nine o'clock. Would you like to bring your lovely bride with you and have a nice weekend holiday? She should be in the meeting anyway, because of her software knowledge."

"That sounds great. I'll have my secretary make all of the arrangements. I assume then that you will arrange for Steven to meet with Miu and me on Monday."

"I'll not attend this first meeting. If his ideas warrant further analysis, we will have to bring him to Beijing to make a final deal."

★ ★ ★

"Steven, it's the man from the embassy again," Ming announced when he answered the phone.

"Thanks, Father. I'll get it in the den."

"Hello Steven. This is Wing. I trust you've had a nice day."

"Yes, I have. I've been wondering when I would hear from you again."

"There will be a very knowledgeable man and his wife here in the embassy on Monday morning to discuss the matter with you. They are both quite technical in the subject matter of your product idea, so it should be quite a good meeting. Can you please come on Monday at 9:00 A.M. to speak with them?"

"Yes, I'll be there. Incidentally, Wing, does your embassy have any personal computers? If so, I would like to demonstrate my product idea for these people, so they can better understand its value."

"I'll have a PC set up in our conference room on Monday for you to use. Do you need any other special apparatus?"

"No, that will be fine. I'll see you on Monday."

"Good-bye, Steven."

★ ★ ★

"Shou Lee here to see the charge d'affaires," Steven announced to the guard, who by this time knew perfectly well who he was.

"I see you have an appointment, sir. I will ring for the secretary to escort you into our compound. I hope you have a good day, sir."

Steven was impressed the guard had been told to give him some respect, and he sensed that was a good sign. Maybe this meeting would be the beginning of the end of the long journey to free his grandparents and clear the name of his parents. He looked up and the sun was shining clearly and the air was fresh and not too humid. This certainly was going to be a glorious day!

"Good morning, Steven," Wing's secretary said, as she walked toward him.

"Good morning to you as well," Steven answered back. "Do I need any kind of special pass to carry this package into or out of the building? It contains some personal software files."

"Just show it to Wing when you meet with him. He will give you a personal belonging report to show to the guard when you leave the compound."

They walked toward the back of the building to the large conference room near Wing's office. Steven was served a cup of tea and asked to sit down, while Wing's secretary went to get the others. Steven walked over to the personal computer that was sitting on the end of the conference table. It was a 100-Mhz Pentium® machine, which would be just right for his demonstration.

"Good morning, Steven," Wing said as he entered the room with his hand extended. "I want you to meet Choi Tang and his lovely wife, Miu. His friends know Choi as CT, so you may call him CT. He speaks a little English, but Miu is quite fluent, so she will act as his interpreter. She also has a degree from one of our best technical schools, and is quite knowledgeable about computer software."

"I'm pleased to meet you, Miu."

"It is my pleasure to introduce you to CT. He is our young and energetic managing director of the CD-R plant in Haikou, which, as you may know, produces most of the world's CD-Rs for use in personal computers. He has written many papers on that subject, and he holds degrees in computer science and mechanical engineering."

"I'm very pleased to meet you, as well," Steven said as he shook CT's hand. I'm very glad both of you could meet with me today. I trust you have had an opportunity to read my outline."

"Yes, both CT and I have read it. We find it very interesting," Miu said. "Of course we have a number of questions we need to ask in order to help us understand all aspects."

They sat down and were served hot tea by Wing's secretary. After a few minutes of polite social chitchat, Steven stood up and walked to the head of the table.

"First, I should like to tell you a little more about myself." Steven spoke slowly and deliberately, so Miu could interpret for CT.

"I graduated from UC, Berkeley, fifteen years ago, with a degree in computer science. I took a job at Apple Computer, and was employed by them until five months ago. At Apple, I was responsible for the development of the Macintosh™ operating system software, as well as for the development of several of the Macintosh™ software application programs."

"Excuse me, Steven, but isn't your idea based on IBM PC-compatible software, rather than on Apple-based software?" Miu asked him, puzzled.

"That's correct," Steven answered.

Steven spent the next half hour briefing them on how Apple made the decision to design the Macintosh™ computer, and how Apple had attempted unsuccessfully to force Microsoft to cease work on its Windows™ software.

"As a consequence of the copyright litigation, I was assigned the task of critically evaluating the various Microsoft Windows™ products. Apple wanted to find out if Microsoft had somehow copied any of the Macintosh™ software, or if they had embodied any of Apple's ideas in their software. To help me do that, I developed a set of Operating System Analysis Programs. These programs made it possible to slow down the operation of an IBM-compatible PC to such an extent I could observe the operation of the operating system code virtually on a line-by-line basis."

"So, in your plan outline where you discuss being able to infect personal computers with a code that slows them down, I assume you are basing that notion on the application of those programs?" Miu asked.

"Yes," Steven said.

"Aren't those programs then the property of Apple Computer?" CT asked, using Miu to interpret for him.

"In their basic form they are. However, I have subsequently modified the programs so they can be used as outlined in my plan. In fact, I've brought the modified versions with me today to demonstrate what I mean on a personal computer right before your eyes."

"We would like very much to see your demonstration. Do you need any help setting it up?" Miu asked.

"No. Just give me a moment to load the programs," Steven said.

Steven turned on the computer and in a moment the familiar Windows™ icon showed on the screen. Steven examined the programs that were available, looking at all of the icons in the Explorer. He found the computer had Excel installed, so he clicked on the Excel icon to load that program.

"On this disk, I have a very compute-intensive spreadsheet," Steven said. "Are you familiar with spreadsheets and how they compute their answers?"

"Yes, we are."

"In this demonstration application, I have a spreadsheet where each cell contains very long formulas containing many transcendental functions. As a consequence, each time I change a cell value, the entire table must recalculate each neighboring cell. On a machine such as this, with a 100-Mhz clock, I estimate it will take on the order of thirty seconds to complete all of the calculations."

Steven loaded the application and asked CT to monitor his watch to measure the number of seconds it took for the machine to complete the calculations. He changed the value in one of the cells and pressed the enter key. On the screen, the values of each cell were changing in sequence as the machine whirred. According to CT's watch, it took approximately twenty-five seconds for all of the calculations to be completed.

"Now I'll install my special code sequence. The version I have on these two floppy disks contains programs that will attach themselves to certain of the Windows™ executable files. Once they are installed, I can adjust the amount of slow-down of the machine, simply by pressing the F2 function key a number of times."

"Will this ruin my machine?" Wing asked.

"Temporarily your machine will behave like an old 386-based computer, but I have here on another disk my antidote code, which will remove the contaminating files."

It took fifteen minutes for Steven to finish loading his files and to examine the hard drive directory to see if they were installed properly. "Okay, now watch closely. I'm going to press this function key five times, which will slow the machine down by a factor of five. That will mean the calculations we just witnessed will now take more than two minutes to complete."

Steven clicked the function key five times. He again retrieved the Excel spreadsheet program, and asked CT to measure the time required to finish the calculations. He changed a cell value and pressed enter. It was immediately obvious by watching the monitor that the operation was taking considerably longer to perform. The actual time required was just under two and a half minutes.

"That was only a nominal slow down," Steven said. "And yet, if you were the user of the computer you would be very unhappy you had to wait so long for the answer, don't you think?"

"I would be very unhappy," Miu said. "It's amazing how we get spoiled working with fast computers. And yet only a few short years ago none of us in China had access to any personal computers. We certainly have become spoiled as a nation."

"That is the essence of my plan," Steven said. "By causing most personal computers in the world to slow down, the users will clamor to buy the antidote disks, so they can again be spoiled by higher speed.

"Now, let me reduce the speed by a factor of twenty so you will really want to buy my antidote." Steven clicked the function key fifteen more times and asked CT to use his watch to measure the recalculation time. It took almost fifteen minutes to complete, which seemed like an eternity.

"Do you have any questions about what you have seen?"

"What about the impact on word processing programs?" CT asked.

"While typing reports using a word processor, the user will not find the reduced speed to be very consequential. However, when it comes time to print the report, the user will find it takes several minutes to print each page, and that will become quite annoying. It will also take several minutes for a user to open an existing document.

Let me turn off the machine now so we can continue the meeting. I'm sure you have many more questions for me."

"Aren't you going to remove your programs first?" Wing asked.

"How much are you willing to pay for my antidote disk?" Steven asked, which brought smiles from the group. "You have just seen the typical response from a user when he discovers his prize computer has suddenly slowed down to a snail's pace."

The group looked at each other and they realized the importance of what Steven was saying. If it were possible to infect most machines in the world, and if China alone had the antidote, it was obvious the market for antidote disks would be enormous.

"There, I've removed my programs from your machine." Steven patted the machine on its side affectionately. "You can now run swiftly and do your master's work." The whole group laughed as he performed these antics.

"Steven, would you mind taking a break, while we three talk about what we have just seen? My secretary can escort you down the street to a little donut shop, if you would like to refresh yourself."

"That would be fine, Wing. But if you don't mind, I'll take my software disks with me," he said, smiling. "I hope I'm not offending you. Will I need a pass to get them out of this building?"

"Yes. My secretary will take care of that for you. We understand why you wish to keep your property with you. You have not offended us."

"What do you think about this man and his software?" Wing asked.

"If he knows how to protect his software from being copied, there is no doubt we could sell hundreds of millions of copies of the antidote. I'm impressed by him, and I believe he is credible," CT said.

"I also agree," Miu said.

"How does such a code sequence get placed into the world's computers?"

"We need to quiz him thoroughly on that when he returns. In addition, we need to quiz him on how he protects his antidote from being copied. No doubt he will not tell us everything, but we need to be sure he is credible."

"Does he realize the economic value of his idea?"

"Probably not. Remember that he's still on a crusade to free his grandparents. If that is all he wants for his idea, we can easily accommodate his wishes," Wing indicated. "CT, are you set up to produce software in both floppy disk and CD form?"

"Yes. As a matter of fact, we have just completed implementing a plan for copying software for internal use in China. I'm sure Shing told you about that."

"Ah yes, I remember that. So what you are saying is you could easily produce the antidote code disks in high quantities."

"Yes, but do you realize the enormous quantity of disks we would reqire to serve the market? We would have to prepare ourselves well in advance to keep up with demand. I would love to have that challenge, though," CT said enthusiastically.

"Why don't we take a break now until he returns. I have some other matters I must attend to. When my secretary brings him back, you two can meet with him and continue your inquiries."

"Fine. I think Miu and I will take a brief walk outside now to enjoy the beautiful day."

"Steven, we have a few more questions for you," Miu said, as she held out her hand to gesture for Steven to join her and CT again in the conference room.

"Fine. I'll try to clarify any matters that concern you." The three of them spent the next hour discussing how his code sequence could be introduced.

"Keep in mind, I will build a timer into my code sequence, so the contamination files will cause computers to slow down at some specific date in the future. Between now and that date, it will be necessary for us to find ways to infect most of the world's computers. One way would be for you to install the code in hidden files on every CD-R you produce. More and more software is being provided in CD form, so if the timer were set to go off one year from now, all computers with CD players purchased during that time would become infected."

"What about the enormous number of computers already installed that do not have CD players included?"

"Most business computers today are tied into networks through network servers, and server software is being constantly upgraded. It appears Microsoft is winning the battle of network computing with their new Windows NT™ programs. Also, a number of businesses are tying their computers together using Lotus Notes™. If we can infect Windows NT™ and Lotus Notes™ software, all computers tied together using such networks will become infected."

"And how can we infect those software programs?"

"That is where I come in. I plan to return to the U.S. soon and seek new employment. With my skills and knowledge, I can easily get a job working for a firm in Fremont, California, which is responsible for evaluating all new software developed by Microsoft and other major software vendors. This firm performs what they call independent third-party software validation to make sure any new operating system software will run all of the old programs, as well as the new ones being developed. As a key employee there, I could easily introduce my code sequences into their validation suites of tests. From that moment on, every software package being evaluated would become infected."

"What about all of the millions of home computers?"

"That is where you guys come in. Aren't you planning some big event in 1997 when China takes over Hong Kong? Why don't you contract with all of the Internet search companies, such as Yahoo, Alta Vista, Excite, and Web Crawler, and have them include a Hong Kong web site, containing information about the events that will occur in Hong Kong prior to and during the acquisition. If you infect your web site with my code sequences, all of the popular Internet search programs will soon become infected. Then, whenever anyone at home uses them, the infection will immediately attach itself to their computers."

"Steven, it sounds like you have considered this matter very carefully," CT said through Miu's interpretation. "Now can you explain to Miu how you plan to develop an antidote code that cannot be copied readily? Also, please tell us why ordinary virus scan programs cannot detect your codes and remove them from infected computers."

"Of course. Let me go to the blackboard and give you some insight into the design of my programs. By the way, perhaps I should have left my disks with you when I took my break, for if you had tried to copy them using the traditional disk copy commands on the computer, the computer would have shut down and locked up. When I returned I could have easily discovered that you tried to copy them," he said. CT and Miu looked stunned, for they actually had planned to copy the disks, if he hadn't taken them with him.

Steven spent half an hour outlining on the blackboard how his programs were structured. Miu was impressed with his detailed knowledge. After another half an hour of questions, both she and CT were convinced he was very credible. They asked for Wing to join them for the summary of the meeting. They briefed him, speaking in Chinese, so Steven could not understand what they were saying.

"Steven, we want to thank you for your time this morning. Miu and CT must return to Haikou now. They will communicate what they have learned today to higher ups in China. You will hear from us soon. Again, thank you."

"Thank you all for your time. I look forward to hearing from you soon."

Chapter Thirty

Shing was excited when he spoke to CT about the meeting in the Hong Kong embassy. He told CT to arrange to come to Beijing the following week to brief Keung Fu Huang. He was sure Keung would be equally excited about the opportunity, once he understood it better. CT, with Miu's help, prepared a presentation to use at the meeting.

"This is your first formal meeting with Keung," Miu said. "You have to look and act very professional. I also want you to buy a new suit this weekend and get a hair cut."

"Nag, nag, nag," CT laughed.

CT never dreamed such a business opportunity would arise for China. For once, China could be a world leader in selling software to virtually all persons and companies in the world! In the back of his mind, however, he kept thinking of how pissed the world would be if they found out China was responsible for infecting the computers, but the thought of raking in billions on the deal kept him from worrying about such details.

"I must leave now to catch my plane," CT told Miu.

"You are so handsome, my wonderful husband. Good luck, and remember, Keung and his staff will certainly receive the information you have to present very well. How can they not be interested?" The sound of a cab outside blowing its horn interrupted their good-bye kiss.

"Keung, do you remember Choi Tang? He took you on the plant tour of the Haikou plant, when it had just been made ready to produce

CD Records. Since my return to Beijing, he has been the managing director there."

"Yes. Of course I remember him," Keung said, extending his hand. "I believe your friends call you CT. May I call you CT?"

"It would be a great honor if you would do so," CT said, taken aback by Keung's friendly manner.

"I understand you and your wife witnessed the software developed by the man who calls himself Steven. Shing has already briefed me on the possibilities it offers to China, but before making a decision, I wanted you to provide all of us with a more thorough briefing today. By the way, I'm very sorry I found it necessary to stop producing CD records in your plant, especially after you and your team worked so long and hard to establish the capability."

"I understand why you found it necessary to do so. However, I believe the product I saw demonstrated last week could well be the most important business opportunity China will ever be exposed to. May I now begin my presentation?"

"By all means."

CT spent the next hour explaining what he heard and saw in Hong Kong. He made sure Keung and his staff understood there was considerable risk in such a program, for China would be responsible for infecting personal computers on a worldwide basis in order to gain financially from the sale of a software antidote. On the other hand, the enormous sales opportunity such a venture would represent should offset the risk.

He closed his talk by describing the technology required to produce the antidote disks and explained his plant could be ready for such a venture in a very short time. As he closed, he reminded Keung that it would be necessary to produce an enormous inventory of disks, anticipating an enormous demand for antidotes, once the infection started to spread.

"Kong, you have been quiet during this presentation. What do you think?"

"From a pure salesman's perspective, this is an outstanding opportunity. I have just two concerns. First, how do we know the antidote disks cannot be copied, for if they can, we will not be able to sell nearly as many."

"And what is your second concern?"

"With all due respect, Keung, we just got our hands slapped trying to make a large business producing CD records. Now, with this product, we must first sneak around and infect all of the computers in the world with our secret software, in order to sell an antidote that only we can make. I'm quite concerned that somehow our nefarious act will be uncovered. If that were the case, I can imagine a considerable outcry from the world. It might be such a loud outcry that the world might actually threaten to declare war on us."

Keung turned to his staff members, who had been quietly listening to the conversation. "What do you gentlemen think? Do we have such a huge risk?"

They looked at each other, not wanting to be the first to speak. At the end of the table, a very old, gray-haired staff member stood up and made his way slowly to the podium.

"May I give you my opinions, Keung?"

"Yes, Ming, I always look forward to your wisdom. What do you think of the risk of being caught and of the consequences if we were?"

"I've been listening carefully to your every word," Ming said, as he turned toward CT. "I'm impressed with how well you were able to summarize this complex matter for all of us."

"Thank you, sir," CT said, as Ming continued.

"From what you tell us, this special code or virus can be designed so the computer receiving it can be slowed down just a small amount or it can be slowed down a considerable amount. Is that true?"

CT nodded yes.

"You also estimate a modern Pentium® computer, if slowed down by twenty times, will behave like an early version of a 386-based PC? Is that also true?"

"That is correct," CT said.

"One more question. Is it also true when a computer slows down because it is infected by the code you witnessed, the computer still works reliably, making no errors, but simply works more slowly?"

"That is also correct."

"Keung, if all of this is correct, we have very little exposure on this business proposition. We should proceed as quickly as possible and start raking in the billions from this deal."

"Hold it, Ming, why do you conclude we have no exposure? What if someone proves in the future it was we who infected all of the world's computers?"

"Do you remember in 1992 when the trade barriers were removed so computers could be sold to China?"

"Of course. I also remember we were sold old, outmoded technology, and our research and government laboratories had to throw out those machines in favor of newer ones only one year later."

"That's correct. And do you also remember the second machines we purchased did not run Windows™ programs very well, so we again had to throw out those machines and buy yet a third set of computers?"

"I certainly remember that," Shing chimed in.

"So, Keung, if for any reason we are found to be the ones who infected the world's computers, our official statement should be that we are merely getting back at the world for selling us junk in the past. We are leveling the playing field of world computing. We are making the rest of the world operate with computers of the same speed class we in China have been forced to use since personal computer technology became available on a wide scale."

"An eye for an eye," shouted Keung, who was suddenly very excited. "What do you think now, Kong?"

"That is an outstanding thought. I have no problem at all entering the market for antidote software, since if we ever face the wrath of the world, we can thumb our noses at them."

"And what do you think, Shing?"

"I agree totally with Kong. We don't want to admit we caused the infection, but if we are found out, we have a perfect explanation. I really like it!"

"Now, CT, what about the other concern Kong has? Are we absolutely sure the antidote software can't be copied?" Keung asked.

"I believe that before a business deal is worked out with Steven, he should be made to prove that to us in some fashion," said CT. "Miu and I discussed that issue at length on our way back to Haikou. She believes it should be possible for him to prove that to us, so we will not have any concern."

Keung stood up, obviously exhilarated. He walked back and forth in front of the conference table, as if in deep thought. "CT, how long do you think it will take for the infected code to be spread around the world?"

"We talked to Steven about that and it is his opinion it will take a year or so to be sure ninety percent or more of the world's computers have become infected. Obviously, if we try to sell the antidote prematurely, with only ten percent or so of the computers infected, we will lose the impact of this program."

"Gentlemen, I wish to propose the following," Keung said. "I would like to have the world's computers all slow down on New Year's Eve 1997, which will be just a few months after Hong Kong has been acquired by China. That will give us almost a year and a half to spread the infection, and we will be in a better position to market the antidote, using the sales and marketing organizations of the many computer companies who now reside in Hong Kong. Kong, your ability to sell such software would be greatly enhanced by making use of those channels of distribution, don't you agree?"

"I absolutely agree," Kong said excitedly.

"Okay, Shing, you should invite Steven to Beijing, where you and Kong can meet with him and see what kind of a deal you can strike. Before that, CT and his wife should invite Steven to Haikou and demand that he demonstrate how he can design an antidote that cannot be copied. Obviously, such a demonstration should be a requirement before we proceed with this deal. Are there any further questions or comments?"

"Keung, I believe you are making the right decision," Ming added.

"Ming, I must thank you for providing us with your considerable wisdom."

"Gentlemen, I have one more idea to suggest," Kong said. "I would like to call the antidote the Tiger Code, for it will be sold during the Year of the Tiger. What do you think?"

They all cheered and patted Kong on the back for his brilliant idea. They then left the room, looking forward to the enormous business opportunity the Tiger Code would afford China.

Chapter Thirty-One

Ming and Betty Lou were worried about Steven. He seemed to do nothing these days but sit in his room typing furiously on his Apple Powerbook™ computer.

"Are you preparing a résumé?" Betty Lou asked him earlier in the week.

"No. I'm working on a new product idea," Steven said, without even looking up from what he was doing.

The phone rang again, and Ming called out to Steven. "Steven, it's the people from the embassy again. Why do they keep calling you?"

"I'll take it in the den, Father."

"Steven, this is Wing at the embassy. You managed to impress CT and his wife last week. They have just faxed me a request. They want you to come to Haikou right away and provide them further information. Are you available to go on Monday morning?"

"Yes, but what kind of information do they request?"

"They have asked for you to come prepared to demonstrate to them that your antidote code cannot be copied. If you can convince them of that, they will want you to visit Beijing, where a deal may be negotiated. What do you think of that?"

"It will be easy for me to prove my point. Tell them I'll be there on Monday. How do I get there?"

"You should come to my office at 8:00 A.M. on Monday, and I'll arrange for my secretary to escort you to the island. It requires a boat ride, and the view is spectacular this time of year."

"Fine, I'll see you then."

Steven hung up the phone and went back to the patio where Ming and Betty Lou were lounging. He decided it was time he told them some of what was going on, so they would not worry about him so much.

"Father and Mother, I want to tell you what I've been discussing with the people at the Chinese embassy. I have a product idea that I believe they may have interest in; it ties in with their CD manufacturing plant in Haikou. My plan is to try and convince them my idea has merit. In exchange for selling them my idea, I'm going to insist they release my grandparents."

"What is the nature of the product?" Ming asked.

"It is a software product that they should be able to sell through the Hong Kong electronic firms they will inherit when Hong Kong is taken over by the Chinese in mid-1997."

"Do they seem interested?" Betty Lou asked.

"They must, for they have invited me to visit their CD plant in Haikou on Monday morning."

"Aren't you afraid they will steal the product and leave you with nothing?"

"I'll have to risk that."

"Be careful, Steven."

"I will."

When Steven approached the guard post outside of the Chinese embassy, he didn't need to state his name and purpose, for the guard saw him coming and immediately called for the secretary to come and meet him.

"We will need to leave now. A patrol boat waits in the harbor to take us to the island of Hainan. Here comes our cab."

"You know my name, but what is yours?" Steven asked, as they climbed into the cab.

"My name is May Chow, and I've been secretary to the charge d'affaires at the Chinese embassy for three years now."

"Have you been to the island of Hainan before?"

"No, this is my first trip. I hear it is quite beautiful."

The patrol boat was ready for them and the trip to the island was uneventful. Steven and May sat on the deck of the boat on two lounge chairs, basking in the sun. Halfway across the channel, a steward came out on the deck and offered them a rum-and-fruit drink, which was quite refreshing. Steven refused a refill, however, for he wanted to maintain a clear head at the meeting.

"Welcome to our CD-R plant," Miu said as Steven and May climbed out of the bus. "CT and I will first give you a tour of our plant, and then we will go to our conference room, where we want to discuss the matter of copying your software. To save both of us time, we have arranged for a lunch to be served during our meeting."

The tour was brief. Steven was impressed with the cleanliness of the facility. He could tell there was the capability for a very high rate of production in the plant.

"I understand every major software developer for PCs buys CD-Rs from you. Is that correct?"

"Yes," CT said, using Miu as his interpreter. "Our process produces the highest quality and lowest defect count of any producer. We began to develop this process a full two years before the rest of the industry. I believe we are the best because the rest of the industry is preoccupied making CD records, where the quality requirements are much less stringent."

"Let's go into the conference room," Miu said. "We want you to describe to us how it is you can design your antidote software so it will be impossible for someone to copy it."

Steven went to the blackboard, where he discussed the design of his antidote software. He showed CT and Miu that not only was it impossible to copy the files, but once the files had been loaded into a computer to remove the infection, the disk could no longer be used again. He then went to the PC located on the table and demonstrated what he meant to their satisfaction.

"That is a brilliant design," Miu said.

"But how do we manufacture disk copies in our plant, if it is impossible to copy the files?" CT asked.

"I think I know," Miu said. "Don't you have to write the files on the disk in parallel tracks, rather than in a serial fashion?"

"That's absolutely right," Steven said. "You are a very quick learner."

"We had one other concern about your code sequence. You said in your presentation the infection merely slowed down the computer, but in no way would it affect its reliability. In other words, if the computer were doing scientific calculations, the correct answer would eventually be produced, although it would take much longer for it to be computed."

"That's right. Let me show you why that is."

Steven returned to the blackboard and showed them how his design ensured all major operations of the computer worked in synchronism. "As you can see, all major arteries of the computer slow down by precisely the same proportional amount. This ensures that data integrity is not lost."

"I believe we have nothing more to discuss now," Miu said. "CT and I need to report the results of this meeting to our superiors. I believe you will be asked to visit some of our business people in Beijing to discuss the kind of a business deal you are looking for. You will need to get a temporary travel visa to go there. May Chow can prepare you one when you return to the embassy in Hong Kong. Are you able to make such a trip as early as this Friday?"

"Yes, I can. Should I plan to demonstrate my product while I'm there?"

"Yes, definitely. Have May Chow prepare paperwork so you can carry your software programs with you."

"Well, Steven, did the Chinese like your product idea?" Ming asked when Steven returned.

"Yes, Father, they did. In fact, they plan to have me visit Beijing on Friday, where I'll be meeting with some Chinese businessmen to discuss the matter further."

"Your product must be something they want very much."

"Yes, it seems to be."

"Can you tell us what it is?"

"I would rather not, just yet," said Steven. "I still haven't worked out all of the details, and you know how we engineers are. We hate to discuss things that aren't fully figured out."

"Won't you have to procure a travel visa to visit Beijing?"

"The Chinese embassy is already working on that. This Friday morning, I am to arrive at the embassy at seven sharp, and they will have all of the necessary paperwork completed, including a ticket for a flight, which leaves at eight in the morning. I'm scheduled to meet with the proper authorities in the afternoon, and will stay overnight. If all goes well, I should return on Saturday evening."

"What have you told them you want to receive for your ideas?" Ming asked.

"I would like to discuss that with you two. First of all, can you describe again for me the political climate at the time my grandparents were interned and you two left for Hong Kong? Were there many hundreds of people interned at that time, and was their only crime that they wanted General Chiang Kai-shek to return to power?"

Ming and Betty Lou discussed the climate in China just after the war and emphasized that there were numerous power struggles going on in China at that time. They estimated that there were probably several thousand good and loyal Chinese persons interned as political prisoners.

"What I plan to demand from the Chinese is the release of all such political prisoners, as well as the removal of any persons such as you from their black list. I want to make sure I include all those associated with that period of time in the world's history."

"Steven, I admire your courage, but my God, do you really think you can succeed with such a brash requirement? I would think the Chinese officials would laugh at you for being so brazen."

"Trust me, Father. I truly believe they will accept my terms, but again I want to be sure I include the proper list of people, which of course must include my grandparents, as well as you two, along with thousands of others just like you."

"Steven, why don't you just settle for the release of your grandparents?" Betty Lou asked. "You may succeed with that form of request, but you will surely fail if you ask too much of them."

"I understand what you're saying. I'll try to remain flexible in the discussions on Friday."

Chapter Thirty-Two

Steven boarded flight A223, which left Hong Kong at 8:00 each Friday morning, bound for Beijing. The passengers were a mixed group, mostly Chinese businessmen carrying thin leather briefcases. In order to board the flight, Steven had to show his papers several times. Each time the guards looked at the small package he carried containing his software, he was asked what purpose the software served. He repeatedly had to tell them it was for demonstrating a new product idea. They frowned, but let him pass.

The flight was terrible. Steven guessed that the aircraft was an old Soviet-made plane. Most seat belts were broken, pieces of the wall panels were peeling away from the fuselage, and there was no air conditioning. He was thankful that he did not have to visit the toilets, for he could only guess what condition they would be in.

However, once he was aloft, Steven closed his eyes and was able to doze off. A pretty stewardess came by and insisted he be served tea with some form of biscuit. He obliged and soon found this bit of food settled his stomach, for he was very uptight in anticipation of the meetings.

Because of the enormous business potential of his product idea, Steven decided to demand the release of many thousands of Chinese political prisoners and blacklisted escapees. In addition, he decided to demand a sizable financial nest egg for himself. After all, if the infection did in fact spread throughout the world's computers, as he knew it would, and if the origin of the infection were ever traced back to him, he would become a fugitive from justice. He planned, therefore, to insist on enough money to be able to disappear from the face of the earth to live out his life under an assumed name, if such extreme measures became necessary.

"Fasten your seat belts for a landing at Beijing International Airport," the stewardess announced over the loudspeaker system. She repeated the message first in Chinese, then in French, and then in English. Steven suddenly wished he had been taught the native Chinese dialect, for he was about to enter a world that was very strange, even though his father had lived more than half his life in China.

When Steven stepped off the plane, he saw a nicely dressed Chinese man standing at the back of a crowd with a placard with Steven's name on it. He walked up to the man and said, "Hello, I'm Shou Lee. I was told someone would meet me here this morning. I assume it is you."

The man answered in perfect English. "Yes. It is my honor to escort you to your meetings today and act as your interpreter. You may call me Tsi. I understand you prefer to be called Steven. Is that right?"

"Yes. Where do I pick up my luggage?"

"Luggage on flights from Hong Kong is always placed on the tarmac near the plane so that each garment bag can be thoroughly searched for drugs. That process will take quite a while, so I've arranged for one of my office associates to remain here and look after your belongings while you and I proceed downtown. Do you have your claim check with you? I see him coming now."

Steven gave the man his baggage claim check. He and Tsi then walked to the parking garage located next to the airport, where Tsi had parked a brown Mercedes sedan with government license plates. Tsi motioned for Steven to get in while he walked over to a booth to pay the parking attendant.

"Is this your first visit to Beijing?"

"Yes. I was born in Hong Kong and have never visited mainland China, unless you consider the island of Hainan to be part of the mainland."

"Technically it is, but I agree with you. It is a mere speck on the sea. You may not be aware, but mainland China covers more than twenty-five percent of the world landmass. Of course you will only be visiting one of our cities, at least on this trip," Tsi said.

Everywhere Steven looked he saw Chinese men and women on bicycles hurrying to and fro, dodging back and forth between old automobiles, which were mostly of European make. On each side of the street, groups of small children were walking along the sidewalks; presumably they were heading to school, since they were all dressed in neatly starched uniforms.

As they continued their drive through the city, they passed a pair of seven-foot goose statues outside one office building. Steven also noticed a McDonald's restaurant. "How long has that been here?" he asked.

"We have several hundred franchise businesses here now," Tsi commented. "We are not as backward as many in the west believe."

"How many people live in Beijing?" Steven asked.

"I'm not sure. I heard once there are more than ten million people here, who mostly live in the outskirts of the Beijing metropolitan area. There are also supposed to be one million privately owned cars and more than one hundred thousand taxi cabs. That makes for lots of pollution, for our vehicles are not yet required to have smog controls."

"Have you lived here all of your life?"

"Yes. My parents are still living and they tend a small farm on the outskirts of town. My wife and I usually visit them once a month. Steven, we are at our destination. That large building across the street from this parking lot is known as the Beijing Government Center. It contains offices for the many persons who work directly for the Chinese People's Government. My office is on the second floor. We will be going there first to check you in and review your meeting schedule."

Tsi parked the car in a spot designated for government vehicles. They crossed the busy street and entered the center. There were no elevators in this building, so they had to walk up the rather dingy stairs to the second floor. Tsi led the way to his office, which was about ten doors down the poorly lit hallway from the main stairs.

"Have a seat," Tsi told Steven. "Here's your meeting schedule," he said as he handed Steven a smudged piece of paper.

Tsi looked at his watch. "Your first meeting will be in about fifteen minutes on the fifth floor. We should leave so you won't be late."

"Okay, but I need to wash up first. Is there a rest room near your office?"

"Forgive me, but the only rest rooms are on the first floor. Let's go there now. We can then proceed to the fifth floor for your meeting."

★ ★ ★

"Gentlemen, I want you to meet Shou Lee, who calls himself Steven," Tsi said, speaking in Chinese.

"My name is Shing Ling, the chief of China's Ministry of Technology and Production, and this is Kong Chau, the chief of China's Business and Foreign Trade Ministry," Shing said in perfect English.

"I'm pleased to meet you both," Steven said.

"Tsi, as you can see from the meeting agenda, Kong and I will meet with Steven later today, after he has spoken with a number of our associates. Are you free to accompany him at those meetings? He will need an interpreter."

"Yes. I've arranged my day to be available as long as he needs me."

"Would you see to it that his personal belongings are checked into the hotel?"

"Yes, I will. Now, Steven, according to the schedule, you are to meet next door with members of Shing's staff, who wish to understand more about your product idea. They have a computer set up, so you will be able to demonstrate your product for them."

"Kong and I will meet with you later on, after we have heard from our associates. Until then, we hope you have a good series of meetings."

"Thank you. I'll see you later."

"How much does he want for his product idea?" Kong asked Shing, after Steven left the room.

"We're not sure. According to Wing in our Hong Kong embassy, all that Steven has discussed so far is his keen interest to find some way to free his grandparents from their confinement in Manchuria."

"Are they still alive?"

"Yes. I sent one of my men to check on them. They live on a small work farm in Northern Manchuria, where they have been held since their trial in the early 1950s. They have a small plot of ground they use to grow vegetables, and the state provides for their other needs. They live with several hundred other political prisoners, and they seem to be quite happy."

"What was their crime?"

"They were accused of plotting to overthrow the government when General Chiang Kai-shek wanted to return to power."

"Have they always been model prisoners, or have they tried to escape?"

"According to the records, they have accepted their plight and have not ever caused any trouble. They receive mail once a month from their son in Hong Kong, who is Steven's father. Incidentally, Steven's father and mother are on what we call 'the wanted-for-questioning list,' because they left China at the time of the grandparents' trial, and they did so under false pretenses."

"Shing, do you believe all Steven wants in exchange for his product idea is the safe return of his grandparents?"

"Certainly that is his primary interest. However, he probably will also want his parents' names cleared."

"That should not be very hard to arrange. I would assume Keung would grant him that without a moment's thought, don't you think?"

"I'm quite sure that he would."

"What if he wants money as well?"

"If he seeks money, we should see how much he has in mind and tell him such matters will require approval from our superiors."

"Does Keung want to speak with him?"

"Absolutely not. Keung wants to appear to have nothing to do with this matter, even though he will be very unhappy with us if we cannot find a way to strike a deal."

"Let's hope our associates find the product as exciting as we have found it to be, for China stands to make billions in revenue from this product."

★ ★ ★

Steven found the various meetings with both Shing's and Kong's staffs quite exhilarating. He was particularly impressed with the perception of his interrogators. It was 4:00 P.M. when they finished, and they had not even taken a break for lunch. Instead, they had tea and dainty sandwiches brought in so they could continue with their questions.

"Steven, would you mind staying here while we brief Shing and Kong?" Tsi said. "I don't think we'll be very long."

Shing's and Kong's staff members were very excited about the potential of Steven's product idea. They believed everything Steven told them was correct. They all said China would benefit greatly from Steven's product.

"Tsi, will you ask Steven to come join us now?"

Steven returned to the conference room and was asked to sit down at the end of the conference table. Shing stood up and summarized the results of the meetings so far.

"Steven, all of us believe what you tell us is quite feasible. If that is true, we are very interested in obtaining the rights to make and sell your product idea in the market place."

"I'm glad to hear that," Steven said, smiling.

"We would like to hear from you one more time how your product would be distributed around the world. Make the assumption we want the infection to take effect on New Year's Eve 1997. Given that requirement, how should we proceed?"

Steven went to the blackboard where he drew a time line, broken down in quarterly increments. He outlined the plan that he presented to CT about how the infection could be recorded immediately in a hidden file form on all CD-Rs produced in Haikou. He further described how someone in Hong Kong could develop an Internet web site intended as a Hong Kong informational site, in advance of the acquisition in June of 1997. All browsers of this web site would become infected. In addition, Steven planned to return to the U.S. to take a job at a software validation firm, where he would be able to infect the test and validation software. This would ensure that all new PC applications software would become infected, including the latest revisions of Microsoft Windows NT™ and Lotus Notes™ network software.

"Looking at the time line on the blackboard, do you believe there is enough time for over ninety percent of the world's computers to become infected by New Year's Eve, 31 December 1997?"

"I believe so, but we shouldn't waste any time."

Kong stood up and paced back and forth in front of the table. Finally, he sat down and turned to Steven. "Steven, how much do you want for your product idea?"

"I have three requirements," Steven said soberly.

"And what is the first one?"

"I want all Chinese political prisoners who were interned as a consequence of the government overthrow trials in the '50s to be freed immediately. This must, of course, include my grandparents."

"And what is your second requirement?" Kong asked, beginning to grow concerned.

"I want all persons who fled China in that same time period for the same political reasons to have their names removed immediately from any 'wanted-for-questioning' lists. And this must include my parents, if they are on such lists," he added.

"And what is your third requirement?" Kong asked.

"I want to have HK$1 million transferred to a Swiss bank account in my name on 1 January 1998, the moment the infection takes effect. Furthermore, I want to receive one percent of all future revenues China receives on sales of the antidote software."

Shing and Kong looked at each other in astonishment, and neither of them spoke. They were both obviously stunned, for Steven had not given them any clue he would be asking for so much money for his product. Shing was the first to speak.

"Steven, let's discuss your first and second requirements. We understand you want to seek the freedom of your grandparents, and you want your parent's names to be removed from any wanted-for-questioning list, if in fact they are on such a list. But why do you seek the freedom of so many hundreds of others, whom you do not even know or care about?"

"I realize I could have included only my family. However, when I began to think how the world would react if they find out China infected all of the computers for their own profit, I felt it would be in the best interest of China to hold out an olive branch to show that China cares for the welfare of other peoples."

"Do you realize many of those persons interned in Manchuria are better off now than if they were to try and make a living on their own?"

"Give them and their relatives a choice. If they decide to stay, that is their option, but if they wish to receive their freedom, they should be allowed to do so."

"Regarding your third requirement, I hope you realize the amount of money you suggest is preposterous!"

"Then make me a counteroffer. But remember, if I help you unleash this infection across the whole world, and if I'm found to be the person who not only caused the infection, but who developed the antidote, I'll become an international criminal. I'll need to have my identity changed and will need to hide out for the rest of my life. That will cost me a lot of money. In the meantime, China will be receiving billions from the sale of the antidote."

"Shing and I will need some time to confer on this matter. Tsi, would you please escort Steven to his hotel and accompany him to dinner? When is he scheduled to return?"

"He has a flight tomorrow evening."

"Steven, can you stay over a few more days? Kong and I may not be able to respond to your offer until Monday."

"That would be fine. I'm willing to stay as long as necessary to settle this matter."

"Okay, Tsi, please take Steven to the Shaoshan Maoija Restaurant tonight. I'm sure he will enjoy it thoroughly."

"Keung, we need to speak with you immediately," Kong shouted in the phone.

"Is it about the product idea from the one who calls himself Steven?"

"Yes, and he asks for millions in addition to the freedom of his family members."

"I was afraid of that. Why don't you and Shing come to my office in an hour? I'm sure we can find some common business ground that will satisfy his needs."

Kong and Shing briefed Keung at length. Keung asked them if they and their staffs believed the product idea was as Steven claimed it to be.

"Yes. We all believe the product is well thought out. We especially were concerned that some other person might be able to copy it, but we have been given assurances by our technical staffs that it cannot be copied."

"Does Steven really believe he should receive such a high amount of money for his product, in addition to setting free hundreds of Chinese political prisoners and traitors to the Chinese Republic?"

"It's hard to say. He has made a correct assessment, however, that some day he may need to go into hiding, and that can be very expensive."

"Let's discuss his first and second requirements. I've asked my assistant to give me a list of all such persons currently in Manchuria, as well as a list of persons on our various wanted-for-questioning lists. It turns out in Manchuria there are only a few hundred persons still alive, for most were in their late forties when they were sent there. As far as the lists go, we have very few persons on such lists, for over the years such lists have either been lost or destroyed."

"Are Steven's father and mother on such lists?"

"Yes, but only for questioning. They have never been accused of any political crimes."

"Then, can we accept his first and second requirements?"

"Steven has given me a good idea," Keung said. "It would improve my image and the image of the Chinese Republic if I were to grant freedom to these persons as a gesture of good will. I could indicate this act of mercy will be the first of several such actions we will take as we approach the date for the acquisition of Hong Kong. Yes, you can tell Steven I accept these requirements. Tell him within one week there will be a major press release in all of the world's major newspapers, which I shall prepare immediately. You can also tell him if he can wait for a few days, I'll make the necessary arrangements for his grandparents to accompany him back to Hong Kong. That should make him feel relieved and should soften him up, so he won't demand so much money."

"That should really help us in our negotiations," Kong said, marveling at how astute the president was.

"Now, regarding the money," Keung continued. "As a show of good faith, you may tell him I'll grant him HK$1 million up front. Then, when we have firm evidence the infection is working, which we should absolutely know by the end of January 1998, we will grant him a second HK$1 million."

"What about the ongoing percentage of sales?"

"If he insists on such an exorbitant amount of money beyond the two payments I've already stated, he will be signing his death warrant. You have my authority to accept a maximum level of half a percent of our revenues, if he absolutely insists on some form of commission. But I am telling you both that if he does so, once the infection has spread and we are selling antidotes, I'll put out a contract on his life."

"We understand, sir. Now, may we go and negotiate the deal? I assume there can be nothing in writing between any of us and him?"

"Absolutely not. The promise of a second payment of money should be all we need to ensure the project is completed on time with the expected results."

"Thank you, Keung," Shing said.

"Yes, thank you very much," Kong added.

"Go and get this program started. I have much to do today, so I hope you two don't need to talk to me any more on this matter."

"Tsi, will you tell Steven that Kong and I would like to meet with him in the morning in my office?" Shing said over the phone.

"Yes, I will. Do you have the authorizations you need to make a good deal?"

"We feel Steven will be very pleased. So please have him in my office at nine."

"Good morning, Steven. I hope you found your room at the hotel to be satisfactory," Shing said, as he greeted Steven.

"Yes, I was quite tired, for your staff worked me over pretty good," Steven answered, as he sat down.

Shing's secretary entered the room with a tray of tea and biscuits, and the next few minutes were taken up with idle talk as they ate their meager breakfast.

"Kong and I met with the president last night. You should be impressed that he wanted to hear all about your product plans and how they might fit in with China's plans for the twenty-first century. Of course, we discussed the three requirements you imposed on us to see if perhaps we could develop an appropriate counterproposal for you. That is why we are here."

"As I told you yesterday, if my requirements cannot be met precisely, I'll at least listen to reasonable counterproposals, but you must understand I believe I have a product idea that will make China very rich indeed."

"Okay, Steven, you will be glad to hear your first requirement will be met precisely as you defined it. All Chinese political prisoners interned as a result of the Chiang Kai-shek attempted government takeover will be pardoned immediately. This, of course, includes your grandparents."

"What about persons on the wanted-for-questioning lists?"

"They, too, will be immediately pardoned."

Kong and Shing watched Steven closely. He was stunned, for even though he believed the Chinese wanted to get their hands on his product, he wasn't expecting an immediate okay. He fought to avoid tears in his eyes, for this was what he had dreamed of for so many years.

"And if you can stay in China for a few more days, we can even arrange for your grandparents to return with you. Won't that be a nice surprise for your parents? They will certainly be very proud of what you have done for them."

Kong and Shing explained to Steven what had to happen to make all of this become official. Many papers needed to be drawn up, and the press release had to be prepared, which Keung would use as a means of softening the human rights issues that were constantly pressuring him.

Steven sat quietly drinking his tea, letting this sink in. He won the first battle. Now he needed to hang tough, because he knew he would need a lot of money if he were to be branded an international criminal some day.

"What about my third requirement?"

"Before you leave Beijing, we will provide you with a bankbook for a bank account in Switzerland with HK$1 million deposited in your name. We will need you to provide us with your social security number and have you sign the appropriate forms, of course."

Steven now was visibly shaking. His mouth became dry, and he had to ask for some more tea. Even though he had been working for fifteen years with a high-paying job, he had only managed to accumulate a nest egg of one hundred thousand dollars invested in various funds. Here he was, sitting in a dingy office in Beijing, China, being offered a cool million dollars. "And, tax-free, too," he thought to himself.

Steven composed himself, and asked, "What about my requirement for a commission stream, once China is selling antidote disks?"

Kong stood up and sternly faced Steven. "You must know your requirement to receive a further income stream based on one percent of the revenue from the sales of the antidote is absurd. Shing and I were almost embarrassed to present it to the president, for fear he would consider us to be fools to keep talking with you."

"Then, what is your counterproposal?" Steven asked, beginning to be a bit annoyed.

"After we have established that your infection is actually working, a second million will be placed in your bank account."

"That's it?" asked Steven. "Are you saying you will not pay me any commission for the juicy sales you will receive? Remember, you will be receiving billions, and all I want is my fair share. How about at least a half of a percent? Surely that will not break the Great Wall of China?"

Kong and Shing quickly conferred in the corner of the room, speaking quietly in Chinese. They returned and said, "Okay, Steven, you've got a deal. Let's shake on it."

Steven had no idea they would accept this deal, even at half the value he had originally presented. He did a quick mental calculation and figured he would pull in at least HK$20 million, and it could exceed even that amount. He began to tremble, for this was far more than he expected to receive. Here he was, about to return to Hong Kong a multi-millionaire, with his grandparents freed and his parents off the hook. Once his infection was proven to work, he would start receiving a huge income stream. He would never have to work again!

Steven held out his hand, which was by now very sweaty. "I'm glad to do business with you," Steven said. "I'll not let you down. You will make lots of money selling antidote disks."

"I know we will. You should return to your hotel and ask to extend your stay for a couple of days, while we make all of the necessary arrangements."

"Let's go, Steven," Tsi said. "You look like you need a long rest. How does it feel to be a millionaire?"

"I don't need a rest. Let's go celebrate," Steven shouted

Chapter Thirty-Three

Steven's grandparents were awakened from their afternoon naps when the government official called on them. They couldn't believe their ears when they were told they could pack their things, for they would soon be set free. Surely there must be some mistake, they thought, but the papers seemed to be in order. They were told to be at the train station in the morning. There would be a pair of tickets for them, along with an envelope containing money and travel passes. They immediately started packing their meager belongings and went to bed early, so they would not miss their train.

"Steven, everything has been arranged," Tsi said over the hotel phone from the lobby. "I'll meet you at the hotel cashier's desk. By the way, your bill has been paid, and the plane tickets for your grandparents have been purchased. I have them with me."

"Where will I meet my grandparents?" Steven asked.

"As soon as you and I complete the various forms and agreements, we will go to the government office, where they have just arrived. After you have had an opportunity to speak with them, we will leave for the airport, as your flight leaves in the early evening. You will be in Hong Kong in time for a late dinner."

Steven and Tsi sat down in a conference room off of the hotel lobby and Tsi explained to Steven the purpose of all of the papers he was to sign. The most important one was an official release of his grandparents into his custody. It included an official pardon signed by the president himself. Next, Steven was given a bankbook from the Credit Swiss Bank in his name showing a deposit of HK$1 million.

Tsi explained there would be no formal contract between Steven and the Republic of China; rather there would exist a "blood pact" between the two principals. His official contact in China was to be CT, and Steven was given a card indicating how he could reach CT day or night. Tsi said CT would like to meet with Steven one more time in Hong Kong before Steven returned to the United States. The purpose of that meeting was to develop a more detailed timetable for all events that had to transpire between now and the time the infection was triggered around the world.

"Let's go say hello to Grandmother and Grandfather Lee," Tsi said, smiling at Steven, who was again trembling with joy.

"My, you are such a handsome lad," Steven's grandmother said, as she hugged him. She was considerably shorter than Steven, with a slight stoop in her shoulder from all of the hard work she had no doubt been forced to do throughout her life. Steven's grandfather, on the other hand, resembled his father. He had a very thick head of hair that was silver gray. He pumped Steven's hand with a firm grip of someone who had worked with his hands all of his life.

"I wish I knew how to speak Chinese," Steven said, using Tsi to interpret for him. "Being able to see you both and hold on to you is like a dream come true."

"Steven, we had better go to the airport now," Tsi said. "You will have plenty of time to catch up on their lives when you reach Hong Kong."

The four of them left the government building and drove to the airport. Tsi stayed with them until their plane was called, and bowed and wished them well. Steven's grandparents had never been on an airplane before, so they were noticeably frightened.

"Mother, this is Steven. I've just landed at the Hong Kong Airport and I should be home in time for dinner," Steven said, calling from a pay booth, while his grandparents sat in the waiting room.

"How was your trip?"

"It was quite productive. As a matter of fact, you should set the table for two more guests tonight. What meal have you prepared?"

"We are having chicken and dumplings, but what do you mean set the table for two others? Who else is with you?"

"Mother, you won't believe it, but my grandparents are here with me. They have a full pardon, and they are very hungry for your chicken and dumplings!"

There was a long pause on the other end of the phone, and Steven could hear Betty Lou calling for Ming to come and speak with his son. She was saying that he wasn't making any sense.

"Steven, this is your father. What's going on?"

"Father, I have your parents with me. As soon as we get our luggage, we will catch a cab and will be there in time for dinner. They have a full pardon, and so do you and Mother."

"Son, you must have been drinking on the plane. How is it possible you could do all of this in such a short time?"

"I guess they liked the product idea I offered them. Anyway, I'll fill you in with more of the details when I get there. I see our luggage is coming up the ramp now. Tell Mother to set five place settings."

The three of them left the airport and hailed a cab. When they arrived at Ming's townhouse, Betty Lou had a beautiful table set for them. Ming and Betty Lou just couldn't believe their eyes when the grandparents walked in behind Steven. It seemed to Steven that the four of them embraced so long and hard they would suffocate each other.

"Son, I don't know what kind of strings you had to pull, but you have indeed performed a miracle," Ming said, embracing Steven.

"Yes, Steven, your father and I had given up any hope of ever seeing your grandparents again."

"And, here is a signed pardon for the two of you," Steven said, pulling out an official-looking document from his luggage. "In tomorrow's papers all over the world the Chinese president is going to officially pardon all persons associated with political crimes in the 1950s."

"I understand Steven insisted on receiving an outlandish commission as part of his deal." Keung asked.

"That's right," Kong answered.

"Well, you know the deal. You and Shing and I should be the only ones who know our plan. As soon as the infection spreads and we are firmly selling antidote disks, I will arrange for the untimely death of Steven. Was the bank account set up in such a way that if he were to die the funds remaining will automatically revert to the Chinese Treasury?"

"Yes. I saw to that myself," Shing said.

"Okay. You should proceed now to do everything necessary to spread the infection, per the plan Steven presented to us. I want you to put CT in charge of all technical matters. CT must not know of our ultimate plans, however. Do you understand?"

Both Shing and Kong nodded.

Steven received a phone call from CT, who arrived at the Chinese embassy with Miu a week after Steven returned from Beijing.

"Can we meet tomorrow? We need to put together a detailed schedule of events."

"Yes. I can be there at eight-thirty in the morning, if that is okay with you."

"Fine. I'll see you then."

"Son, was that the embassy calling?" Ming asked Steven.

"Yes, and they want to meet with me again to discuss my product idea."

When Steven returned from Beijing, he told his parents a little white lie about his product, for he did not want them to know the real situation. He told them his product was special advanced operating system software for personal computers, which would make PCs run faster. He explained the Chinese wanted to exploit this in order to gain a leadership role over Microsoft.

"It's so nice to have such a brilliant son," Shing said, patting Steven on the shoulder. "By the way, you mentioned at breakfast this morning that you sent your résumé to several firms in California. Have you any nibbles yet?"

"Yes, I have one so far. There is a firm I'm particularly interested in. It is called Advanced Software Validators, Inc., which is located in Fremont, California, near where I worked before. I'm arranging a formal interview with them. I received a note from one of their managers. He plans to visit Hong Kong next week and seems quite anxious to talk to me."

"You really do need to get a job now and get on with your life," Betty Lou said.

Steven and CT, with Miu as interpreter, spent all morning going over the many details of their plan. As requested by Keung, Steven was asked to build into the infection code a timer that would trigger at precisely midnight, 31 December 1997, in whatever local time zone the host computer containing the infection might be located.

"Are you certain such a timing trigger is reliable? It wouldn't do if computers were slowing down around the world at random. Our biggest sales opportunity will come about if all computers slow down at once."

"There will not be any problem making sure that the timer is accurate. Have you been able to get anyone to start to work on the development of a Hong Kong educational web site, which can be infected?" Steven asked.

"Yes, there is a small software development laboratory located only three blocks from here. They plan to complete the task in three months. After they are finished, I'll need you to infect their code and send it back to me in a composite form. I'll have the software company unknowingly sell the web site to all of the search-engine firms. In this way, any time anyone uses the services of a search engine on the Internet, the computer being used for the search will become infected."

"Great. That should work fine."

"And as soon as you get me the source code for the infection, I'll start embedding it into all of the CD-Rs we produce. How soon will I receive it?"

"I should have it ready in about a month," Steven said.

"How is your job search coming?"

"I have an interview next week. The firm's name is Advanced Software Validators, Inc. They have just been awarded a contract from Microsoft to validate all of their new Windows™ and Windows NT™ operating system software."

"What does validate mean, again?"

"Validation means to use an independent firm, such as this one, to take new software and test it thoroughly to be sure all existing application packages work correctly when loaded in a computer containing the new software operating system. There are literally thousands of applications on the market today, so firms like this one need to have expert employees in every software field in order to do their job properly."

"You shouldn't have much difficulty getting hired."

"I don't think so. I put on my résumé I had detailed knowledge of the Apple operating systems as well as all of the Microsoft operating systems. This knowledge makes me invaluable for a firm such as this. It will take me only a few weeks to infect all of their validation software, once I'm familiar with their engineering department and get to know the key people."

"I think that covers everything. One thing I did want to ask you: is there an easy way to sample computers around the world to see if they are infected, before the timer goes off?"

"Yes, I know how to do that. The easiest way is to design a test disk, which, when loaded in the computer, causes the computer to perform some silly function in the event the computer is infected."

"My management was curious about that. I guess they will want to receive assurances, as we proceed, that the infection is actually spreading. Could you make me such a disk?"

"No problem."

"I guess that covers everything. I have your phone number. As soon as I get situated in my new job, I'll contact you."

"Good luck to you, Steven."

"And likewise to you and your lovely wife," said Steven, as Miu blushed.

Part 5

A World Held Hostage

Chapter Thirty-Four

On 2 October 1995, Steven arrived at the Fremont, California offices of Advanced Software Validators, Inc. (ASV). While in Hong Kong, he was given an attractive job offer for the position of principle engineer in the newly formed Power PC™ validation department of ASV. Steven looked forward to working again, even though his primary purpose in taking this job was to enable him to infect new personal computer applications and operating system software. Steven was a shoe-in for this job, because of his extensive background in both Apple operating system software and Windows™ operating system software. Consequently, an offer was made on the spot in Hong Kong, which he readily accepted.

The receptionist smiled when he signed in. "I'm very glad you're going to join ASV, Steven. The management here has told everyone about your extensive background. I'm sure you will like working here as much as the rest of us do. It's really a neat company. Who are you supposed to report to this morning?"

"According to my job-offer letter, I'm supposed to report to Mary Cross, the head of personnel."

Steven had arrived in the States in mid-September and leased a townhouse only a few blocks away from where he previously lived. While in Hong Kong, he purchased a fax/modem PCI card for his Apple PowerBook™ computer. Shortly after he moved in, he sent a fax to CT, using the Hong Kong fax number assigned to him. In the fax, he told CT about his new job, his new address, and the fax number where he could be reached. He planned to leave his computer turned on at all times, so he would be able to receive messages at any time, day or night.

"Please have a seat, while I call Mary."

While he waited, Steven started reading a company brochure that was lying on the coffee table in the lobby. The brochure described how two ex-Microsoft software engineers formed ASV in 1990. He noted the current head count was just over a hundred employees, most of them software developers. Since the speed and complexity of personal computers doubled every two years, it was imperative that each new revision of applications software work properly, not only on the latest machines, but also on older machines. Recognizing that fact, ASV was established to provide the personal computer industry with an independent comprehensive software validation testing service.

Soon after being formed, ASV became recognized as a leader in their field. Hence, all newly developed personal computer software, prior to being released to the public, was sent to them for thorough testing and evaluation. An ASV seal of approval stamped on a package of software guaranteed that the software would work, period.

Steven was impressed by what he read in the brochure. He thought to himself that he was precisely in the right company and in the right position to proceed aggressively with his plan to infect major new releases of software.

"I assume you are Steven," Mary said, as she entered the lobby from the hallway.

"That's right," Steven answered. "I was told to report to you this morning. So, here I am."

"I need for you to fill out personal data forms before you report to the engineering section. Please have a seat in my office. I also want to explain our benefits package to you. You will need to read our policy manual and sign some confidential information forms as well."

An hour later, Mary led Steven to the back of the building, where he was taken to the office of his supervisor, Harold Atkins. It was Harold who had interviewed Steven in Hong Kong; he had been with ASV since its early days. Harold was employee number three.

"Steven, I'm so glad to see you again," Harold said, extending his hand. "I hope your return trip to the States was uneventful. Did you have any trouble finding a place to live?"

"No. I managed to find a nice townhouse in the same general area where I lived before. I understand housing is getting a bit harder to find these days, so I guess I was lucky. I did have to pay a lot more than I paid last year, but it's a nicer unit."

"That's certainly right. Business in the Bay Area is booming again, so things are tight all over. ASV was lucky to find this building a couple of years ago. As you will soon discover, we have considerable room for growth here on this site, so we should not have to think of moving again for at least five years."

Harold spent the next couple of hours showing Steven the engineering area, and introducing him to a number of employees who were assigned to the Power PC™ validation department. He then took Steven down the hall to the lab where the actual testing of new software was being performed.

"Josh, this is Steven Lee," Harold told the supervisor of the test facility.

"Steven, it's so good to meet you," Josh Logan said. "I understand you have detailed knowledge of both the Apple operating system and the Microsoft operating system. As you know, the new Power PC™ is capable of using both operating systems. This coexisting software system gives us fits when we try to validate new software for use on such a platform. So welcome aboard!"

Harold took a moment to explain to Steven how the elaborate plant security system worked at ASV. "Steven, one of the reasons we have become a leader in providing validation-testing service to all of the major software developers is because we established early on a highly sophisticated security system that protects our clients. We receive early versions of each new software release from all of the major software developers. It would be disastrous if any of our employees were to share information received in confidence from one vendor with a competing firm."

"I fully understand," Steven said. "How does your security system work?"

"On a strict need-to-know basis," Harold explained. "Each new software release we receive is assigned to a small team of individuals to evaluate. Other employees are not allowed to see any of the documentation or even witness the tests. We physically move the individuals assigned to a given project into a special testing area, which is assigned only to their specific project. We issue special passwords so the team members are the only ones who can gain access to their particular test facility."

"Isn't it necessary for some other ASV groups to check their work independently? There are so many variables, it seems to me that it is possible for human error or lack of knowledge to enter into the process."

"That is the responsibility of the Quality Assurance Department here at ASV. After the team is finished with their work, and after they have prepared a draft report for the client, we invite client representatives to spend several weeks here witnessing the testing first hand. Our QA department sets up this final acceptance testing for our clients and manages that process, which is independent of the work the team members performed."

"What keeps the team members from sharing what they learned when they are assigned to some other client in the future?"

"We dedicate them to a particular client. For example, twenty-five of our employees only work on Microsoft software validation, ten only work on Lotus software validation, etc. In that way, our clients also feel much more secure, and the chance for contamination of information is reduced considerably."

"Mary in personnel had me sign quite extensive confidentiality forms this morning. Have you ever had employees who breached such agreements, and if so, what kind of punishments did they receive?"

"We've only had one instance where one of our employees actually was on the payroll of one of the newer software firms who wished to gain early access to competitive information. He was discovered, and ASV prosecuted him to the letter of the law. In addition, the firm who employed him was fined such a high figure they had to declare bankruptcy and were forced out of business. As you can see, we really do take security seriously here."

"Am I going to be assigned to a specific client?" Steven asked.

"No. I want you to work on one of our important new R&D programs. You will be assigned to head up a small team of engineers to develop validation test suites required to thoroughly evaluate new software intended for use in Power PC™ computers. As we discussed in Hong Kong, such a development will probably take a couple of years to complete. During that time, you will not be assigned to any particular client, but we will want you to participate on several QA evaluation projects."

After they completed the tour of the facility, Harold and Steven returned to Harold's office, where the secretary fetched them coffee.

"I'm sure you will have plenty of other questions. For now, however, you should go to your office and read this draft project description. After you accepted the position with us, I wrote this draft as a justification for hiring you. Now that you are here, you and I need to expand on this write-up to formally receive approval for the project."

"Is it possible the project will not be approved?"

"Zero chance. This write-up is just a formality to receive final budget approval. If there was any chance the project was not going to be approved, I would not have been given the green light to hire you."

"I'll come by at noon with some of the fellows you met this morning and take you to lunch. Lunch for new employees is free the first day on the job, so bring your appetite."

"Okay, Harold. I'll see you then."

When Steven arrived home that evening, he was tired. It had been several months since he had put in a full day's work, and starting a new job always required him to concentrate more, since there were so many new things to learn. He decided to kick back and relax for an hour or two before grabbing a bite to eat. He took off his shoes, lay back on his bed, and closed his eyes.

"This is not going to be as easy as I thought," he said to himself. "I'll have to find some way to crack their security system if I want to infect all of the new software being evaluated. But first, I'll need to better understand the inner-workings of my department."

With that thought in mind, he fell fast asleep, but was soon awakened by a beeping sound coming from the other bedroom, which he was using as an office. He got up and went to discover the source of the beeping. The sound was coming from his Apple PowerBook™ computer. On the screen was a message telling him he had just received a fax.

When Steven retrieved the fax/modem program to read the fax, he saw nothing but gibberish on the screen, which meant the sender had encrypted the text. He plugged the special encryption disk CT had prepared for him into the A-drive slot on the computer. In a moment, the fax was readable. It was from CT.

> Good evening, Steven. I'm glad you are settled into your new job and home in California. Miu again acts as my translator for messages such as this, since she is able to write

According to the plan we developed together, you need to quickly complete the development of your computer infection software, so I can record the code on each and every CD-R I produce. These codes need to be in the form of hidden files that cannot be detected, and they must contain a timer that is set to be activated at precisely midnight on 31 December 1997.

Also, according to our plan, you need to have the antidote files completed in the next four months. This date is very important, since once we have the antidote files, we will need considerable time to prepare the vast number of disks required for sale to customers. Please acknowledge you received this fax, and provide me with your latest estimate on accomplishing the above tasks.

Regards, CT

Steven deleted the fax message from his hard disk and sat back and thought about what he read. It was obvious CT was going to be a hard taskmaster, and CT would continue to press him for results. He recognized, however, that he did need to meet his commitments in a timely manner for the plan to unfold on schedule.

"No time for socializing this weekend," Steven thought. "Work, work, and more work."

He reminded himself that he had a cool HK$1 million stashed away in Switzerland, so that took the sting out of having to work night and day on this project. He sat down at his desk and typed a return fax to CT, indicating things were on track. He also provided CT with the schedule information he requested.

Steven spent the better part of his first week at ASV refining the plan that Harold gave him. The plan details showed that it would take eighteen months to fully develop and debug the complex suite of validation tests required to check out applications destined to run on Power PC™ platforms. Steven included several intermediate checkpoints where he recommended client software be tested in order to provide technical feedback. He reasoned that such intermediate testing would also provide him access to client software, affording him the opportunity to carry out his personal mission of infecting new software.

"Nice job, Steven." Harold said. "I agree with you that we need to try the software out incrementally against real requirements, as you have suggested. I'll take this plan to the executive meeting Monday, and we should be off and running officially on your program. Incidentally, I would like for you to come to the meeting so you can meet the big wigs here at ASV."

"I'll be glad to," said Steven. "Just call me when you want me to stick my head in. Do I have to wear a suit, or can I show up in my normal work attire—blue jeans and a sweater?"

"Just be yourself," Harold laughed.

Chapter Thirty-Five

Shing arrived in Haikou to hold a meeting with CT. He wanted to understand in considerable detail all of the important milestones of the project. CT was prepared for him, now that he had received the fax from Steven.

The meeting commenced with CT presenting a number of Vue foils showing all of the critical milestones and how these milestones would ultimately lead to the world-shattering event on New Year's Eve, 31 December 1997.

"How will we know the infection has spread? Is there some way we can find out without tipping our hand?"

"Steven owes me a test disk, which is scheduled for January of 1997. By inserting it into computers, it is possible to see if they are contaminated."

"That's fine, but how do we insert such a test disk into sufficient numbers of machines to give us any confidence the infection has spread across the world?"

"Miu has come up with another brilliant idea here," CT said. "She says the test disk should be disguised as a free sample of exciting new software that can be sent to numerous companies and individuals around the world. If their machines are infected, certain results will occur, whereas if their machines are not yet infected, totally different results will occur. A follow-up call to the persons receiving the software would reveal the answer we seek."

"That sounds like it might work, but you need to firm up the details carefully. Remember, if we launch an advertisement that we have an antidote and the infection has only spread a slight amount, the

The Year of The Tiger

whole program crashes down on our heads. Does Steven have any ideas here?"

"I plan to discuss this matter with him at length."

"Now, what about the antidote disks? It seems to me that if we do manage to infect virtually all machines in the world, we will need more than two hundred million antidote disks ready for sale. Have you any idea how long it will take us to produce such vast numbers, place them in little boxes, and get them ready for distribution?"

"Yes, Shing, I've been giving that a lot of thought. For starters, we need to begin today to procure floppy disks from multiple suppliers at a high rate, but not so high that it would trigger too much curiosity in the world markets. Do we have good relations with the firms in Hong Kong and Taiwan that make such disks?"

"I've already sent a special envoy to Taiwan. He is prepared to make the proper deals. You need to provide me with details on exactly what kinds of disks we will require, and I'll take care of the rest."

"We will require only 3-1/2-inch floppy disks. Computers still having only the larger disk drives are probably very old machines, which we can ignore on a program such as this."

"It sounds like things are starting to happen. You must continue to apply pressure on Steven, since he is the key to this whole project. Do you think he will honor his commitments, or do you think he will try to sell his ideas to others?"

"I'm sure that up to the point where the infection is rapidly spreading, he will only deal with us. However, I am a bit concerned he might try to sell the antidote to some other firm once it becomes obvious that such an antidote has such great value."

"Keung and Kong and I hold the same concern. We may need to take appropriate action to watch him closely in the future."

Steven purchased a state-of-the-art Pentium® PC on Saturday morning and brought it home to set up in his office. He needed this machine to use as a development platform to complete the development of the infection software. The software programs he took with him when he left Apple were fine for use in an evaluation laboratory, but the infection software, which would be set loose on the industry, needed to have additional features added. For example, Steven and CT decided on a slow-down factor of 100:1 when the codes infected a high speed Pentium machine, whereas a slow-down factor of only 20:1 would be appropriate when the codes infected an older 486-based machine. Also, the details of the timer needed to be worked out to initiate the slow-down action at precisely the right moment.

By Sunday afternoon, Steven completed his task. He now had to test his software thoroughly. As he commenced to do that, another possible feature occurred to him, which he decided to incorporate. He decided he should modify the software so the infection would not impact the speed of Power PC™ or Power Mac™ computers. In this way, Apple would benefit, since the infection software would only affect IBM-compatible PCs. He was sure the Apple marketing department would exploit this windfall, once they understood what was happening.

Inspired by the notion that he could help Apple, as well as profit greatly from his enterprise, Steven worked long into the night on Sunday, finally completing his project at 2:00 A.M. He was starving, so he went to an all-night diner and bought a large steak with fries and a large tankard of beer. When he finally retired at 3:00 A.M., he fell asleep soundly and did not wake up till the alarm told him it was time to start his second week at ASV. Before leaving for work, he downloaded his software to CT via the fax/modem, using the encryption disk.

"CT is going to be impressed that I finished this task one week early," thought Steven, as he showered and dressed for work.

"How is the project progressing?" Keung asked Shing.

"CT informs me it is starting out well. In fact, he just received the first software code from Steven one week ahead of schedule."

"Does CT fully trust Steven?"

"CT believes Steven will be loyal to us up until the time the infection software is ready to trigger. However, he is concerned that when Steven senses the enormous sales potential for the antidote disks, he may try to sell his antidote software to other parties."

"Remember our deal. We will need to eliminate Steven for two reasons. The first is because he was too greedy during the negotiations, and the second is because he cannot be trusted to provide the antidote only to us."

"Ah, Keung, I agree."

"By the way, how did you like the ad placed in all the major world newspapers this past week? Did I sound believable?"

"I assume you mean the ad indicating China is releasing all of the political prisoners charged with crimes during the 1950s? I thought it was very believable. Have you any feedback from the United States yet?"

"Their ambassador paid me a very high compliment. He personally visited me with a letter signed by President Clinton, thanking me for easing human rights tensions. I'm glad Steven gave me such an idea, for it did not cost me much face with the hard liners in our government. After all, there are not many persons left in our detention areas."

★ ★ ★

In spite of the little sleep he got, Steven arrived at work full of energy and enthusiasm. He scheduled a meeting with Josh Logan, who had promised to show him how the test facility worked.

"Steven, here is a book I prepared for you, which details every piece of equipment in my laboratory. Why don't you bring it with you while you tour the lab, in case you want to take some notes?"

Josh spent the next two hours showing Steven exactly how ASV's validation testing was performed. A client's new, unreleased software is first loaded in a machine, and a bank of several PCs then performs literally tens of thousands of tests on the software, to see if any condition can be found where the new software produces an unexpected or undesired result.

"All in all, it takes about forty hours of testing to complete our entire suite of tests. When we test new operating systems, such as Windows NT™, we expect the testing to consume on the order of twice that much time, since an operating system is the hub of the computer. Everything needs to work just right, or the network of computers may hang up or fail to perform properly."

"How long did it take for ASV to develop the test suite for Windows NT™?"

"We've been working on that program for almost two years. We also found it necessary to spend a lot of time in Redmond with Microsoft, because they kept making last minute changes as they approached their release date."

"What do you know about Power PC™ software?"

"All I know is that a single computer hardware platform is called upon to run either the latest version of the Apple operating system software or the latest version of the Windows™ operating system software. It doesn't run them simultaneously, but I do believe there are certain commands that overlap and interact with each other. Isn't that right?"

"That's right," Steven said. "I've been reading the latest specifications to make sure I understand the exact degree of overlap. Do you think Microsoft cares if the Power PC™ becomes successful?"

"Are you kidding? Microsoft wishes Motorola and IBM would admit their Power PC™ chip was a big waste of money and resources. Each time they claim to have a faster solution, Intel just cranks up the speed on their Pentium® processor and scoops them. However, ASV must not play favorites. The sales volume on the Power PC™ is increasing, and our customers all want to be sure that their software will operate correctly on any platform, including the Power PC™."

"Can you tell me how you maintain client security, since the testing for all clients is done in your facility? I understand from Harold that separate teams of engineers are assigned to a specific client and they have their own lab, separate from the rest of the groups, so they will not inadvertently pass information to their client's competitors."

"That's right, but what they do in their own lab is analyze the code given them by the client. They then develop additional tests for me to add to my standard suite of tests. I just receive code patches to add in, and there is no way I can tell from those patches what goes on inside the client's software. No doubt, when your initial test suite is ready to be used, the engineers assigned to specific clients will do the same thing."

"I get it. You are the master caretaker for all validation software, and what the client engineers do is figure out additional tests required, to be absolutely sure their client's product is bulletproof."

"You got it," Josh said.

"Isn't it necessary for me to get from you quite a bit of documentation about your current test suite, so I can add the Power PC™ unique tests, rather than starting from scratch?"

"I'm glad you feel that way," Josh said. "I was concerned the Power PC™ department was going to try to reinvent the wheel. You should be aware, however, that Harold is not particularly a fan of just adding on more code to my current test suite. For some reason, he believes it's time to start all over again, and I have told him I totally disagree with him. Anything you can do to convince him you should build a Power PC™ shell over what I already have will make me real happy."

"Do you have any documents I can begin to study?"

"Yes, but you must realize that such documents are considered to be the crown jewels of ASV. We do not maintain a single document in hard copy form. Instead, we maintain separate module documentation on various hard drive disks, requiring special passwords before they can be examined. I think the only person allowed to look at all of our documentation all at once is the president, for he wrote most of the code himself."

"How am I going to be able to argue with Harold that I should build a shell on your stuff, if I don't know what your stuff consists of?"

"Let me think about that, Steven. It might be possible for me to assign a special password to you on a module-by-module basis. I'll get you a listing of all of the module types and what they do, at least, to help familiarize you. Give me a call in a couple of days and I'll let you know how I've progressed in getting you access to specific modules on a need-to-know basis."

Steven returned to his office with the documents Josh provided him. In order to introduce his infection software into the company's test suites, Steven would need to examine the test suite code structure in quite a bit of detail, for it was very important that his code attach itself to the existing code in such a way as to prevent it from being detected. It was fortunate that Josh and Harold disagreed on the future direction of the test suite, for Steven expected Josh to bend over backwards to help him gain access to the kind of specific information he would need to carry out his nefarious task.

"How is employee number 102 doing?" Harold asked, as he entered Steven's office. "Did Josh show you his domain? He sure is proud of it, don't you think?"

"Yes, he certainly is. How much of the test suite did he develop?"

"Josh was one of our early engineers, but he wasn't as savvy as he needed to be to develop all of the nitty gritty code. The management reassigned him a few years ago to run the test lab. He has been much happier and more productive since. Don't get me wrong, though. He does understand an awful lot about the intricacies of the test suite, and you can consider him to be a good sounding board for any new ideas you have."

"I presume I'll be provided access to detailed code listings and test flow structures used in all of the test suite modules, so I can use what he has as a reference when I develop my own test sequences?" Steven asked, deciding to see what Harold's reaction would be.

"You can have access to such information, but first I want to discuss with you the wisdom of doing that," Harold said. "The current suite of tests has been in use for several years. Literally hundreds of patches have been added to fix this or that programming error, or make this or that improvement. I, for one, believe it's time we developed a second-generation test suite, and I believe it would be wise if we did that coincident with the development of the Power PC™ test suite."

"Does the company have the resources to do that?"

"I believe so, but I must admit I've not sold the idea yet to the management. Their attitude will probably be *if it ain't broke, don't fix it*. They will no doubt worry that if we try to clean up our suites or modify them dramatically, we may lose our crown jewels."

"So, Harold, how am I to proceed with my project? If I wait on a new test suite platform to be developed, I'll surely spin my wheels for some time."

"I would like you to take two or three weeks to examine in fine detail the current suite of tests. I'll have one of the engineers who was on the original development team work with you to explain all of the patches and fixes that have been added over the years. After that review, if you believe your Power PC™ test suite can be added effectively to our current suite, then you should proceed in that direction. If, however, you believe, as I do, that the old suite is tired and worn, you and I should put together a presentation intended to convince our management it is time for an overhaul. Is that fair enough?"

"Sounds good to me," Steven said. "How do I gain access to the module documentation?"

"I'll take care of that in the morning," Harold said. "Meanwhile, you can read the documentation Josh gave you."

Steven returned to his office elated. He would be able to examine all of the code in each of the test modules. It should be a relatively simple matter for him to then add his infection software to the suite at strategic locations in the test sequence. He would be very busy, however. Two to three weeks was not much time to accomplish everything he had to do.

Josh saw Steven in the cafeteria the following day.

"Steven, I heard the good news. I understand Harold has provided you with a password that will allow you to examine all of the test modules."

"That's right. You must realize, though, that my assignment is primarily one to bolster his belief that the old test suite needs to be totally overhauled."

"Oh, dear. What happens if you convince him such an activity would be folly?"

"I don't know. I sure get the idea he's hoping I'll support his beliefs."

"What can I do to help you?"

"Can you set me up in one of the rooms adjoining your laboratory, with a computer system capable of running individual test suite modules?"

"I don't know if that is possible or not," Josh said. "Your password only grants you privileges to read the documentation on the hard disk files. It won't allow you to access the code for your own use. The company is paranoid about someone copying the files and selling them to one of our competitors."

"But how am I going to be able to pass judgment if I can't try out these codes?"

"I agree with you. I'll tell you what I can do. I'll arrange for you to come into my lab every afternoon at four o'clock to consult with me. While you're in the lab, I'll let you run one module at a time. I don't see how the management can complain about that."

Steven agreed with Josh that this plan would be okay. What concerned him was how he would be able to add his code sequences without Josh seeing him do it, but he would worry about that when the time came. Now that he had password approval, he would at least be able to scan the lengthy sequences of code to find the segments required to attach his infection software files.

Chapter Thirty-Six

Steven worked eighteen-hour days the following week. He arrived at work before seven in the morning and stayed until after eight in the evening. After eating a quick meal at a corner deli, he would continue working in his home office until the wee hours of the morning. While doing further work on his infection codes, he discovered a bug in the software he previously downloaded to CT, so he had to make changes and send CT an updated copy. In addition, he discovered that he needed to break his infection software code into smaller segments that which could more easily be attached to the ASV test suite module files.

As Steven examined the validation suite test modules in more detail, he began to agree with Harold. The ASV test suite was really patched together and probably would not work very well as a platform for the Power PC™ test suite. Before he would reveal this finding to anyone, he had to attach all of his code sequences onto the existing suite, so new software being validated by ASV would pick up the infection.

While in deep thought one evening, Steven received a fax from CT that had an annoyed tone to it. CT had already implemented Steven's first software release in his CD-R production line. By the time the new code was received, more than fifty thousand CD-Rs had been produced carrying the original code in hidden files. CT wanted assurance that the most recent code was final, for he did not want to have to repeat this situation. CT also wanted to know if the earlier release would be detectable, or just wouldn't work.

Steven sent a return fax indicating he was sorry. "Yes, you are correct. The code I sent you will not work at all, but it will not be detectable," he assured CT. He vowed he would do a more thorough testing job to avoid such a fiasco in the future.

After two weeks of sleepless nights, Steven completed his task of breaking down his infection software into twenty segments, with each segment designed to be attached to each of the twenty ASV test suite modules. His challenge now was to find a way to attach them without Josh suspecting anything peculiar.

While eating breakfast one morning, the solution to his dilemma came to him. He would simply tell Josh that each of the code segments represented typical code patches needed to check out portions of his yet-to-be-developed Power PC™ test suite. Surely Josh would not suspect anything if his work was presented in that way. He would have to proceed with caution, however, for if Josh were to become too inquisitive, he might ask Harold what Steven was doing.

"Josh, can I spend more time in your lab this week? I want to try out a number of Power PC™ code patches I've developed, to see how well they work with each of the test modules."

"Steven, I'm really not supposed to let anyone have access to the test suite code, as you know. Why do you feel it's necessary for you to be able to run such an exhaustive evaluation? Can't you determine all you need to know from the documentation and from the examples of testing I've allowed you to witness so far?"

"I suppose I can, but if I want to prove to Harold the current test suite is a suitable platform for the Power PC™ suite, I really would like to run small examples on each module. If your system doesn't crash, that should prove my point, don't you think?"

"I agree with you. I'm simply concerned that my management will absolutely go into orbit if they knew what we are doing. I would feel better if you had Harold's okay first. Why don't you speak with him about this?"

Steven returned to his office and sat down with his feet on the desk. He was worried that if he brought this matter up with Harold, he would want to know many details. At the least, he would wonder how Steven managed to develop these code patches so quickly, and his curiosity would no doubt cause Harold to ask for an explanation of how each patch worked, and how it would prove whether the current test platform was sound or not. Steven concluded it would be a disaster if Harold were to become involved.

After lunch, Steven returned to Josh's office. "Josh, Harold has been tied up in meetings since you and I last spoke. I have another idea, however, that I would like for you to consider. Why don't I simply release my code sequences to you, as if they were client tests. You can run the entire sequence of modules with these codes added, and see if the test sequence crashes or not. I'll provide you with a list of 'go/no-go' criteria to use, and you can provide me with the results. In that way, I'm not able to witness the crown jewels in action, and you will be an objective observer of the process. I'm sure Harold would prefer that approach, anyway."

Josh quietly considered the matter. He got up and paced the floor for a moment and turned to Steven. "Steven, I'm willing to do this just once, as I want very much to be able to prove my test suite is an adequate platform for the Power PC™ codes to be built upon. Are you sure the code patches you are giving me will be able to prove that?"

"Absolutely. Obviously, they are a far cry from the final test sequences I'm going to develop, but they contain enough of the code to prove the point."

"When can you have them ready for me?"

"I can be ready by tomorrow morning."

"Fine, but until then only you and I should know about this experiment. Do you agree?"

"Agreed."

Josh arrived at Steven's desk just before noon, having completed the sequence of tests Steven requested. He was grinning from ear to ear, for he had not seen any problem running the code patches that Steven provided.

"It seems to be a solid go," Josh said. "Here are the test results, and I don't see any failures. You should look over these printouts, however, and examine the documentation, so you can draw your own conclusions. Does this mean we have enough evidence to show Harold he should get off his soapbox?"

"I certainly believe so," Steven lied.

"When can you and I meet with Harold to present your findings?"

"Give me a couple of days to boil down this data along with my other observations about the test suite."

"Fine, but I want to be in the meeting so I can watch Harold's face when he realizes I've been right all along."

Steven returned to his office. By using Josh, he had been able to infect ASV's test suite. From this point forward, all client software being tested by ASV would become infected, and the infection would spread throughout the software industry quickly and quietly. There was no turning back now, for the timing codes he included would kick into effect at midnight, 31 December 1997.

Now Steven had to decide whether he wanted to continue to work at ASV on the Power PC™ program, or whether it would be better for him to find some reason for leaving, so he could do the work necessary to support CT. As it turned out, that decision would be taken out of his hands.

"Steven, could you come to my office, please," Harold spoke into his intercom.

When Steven arrived, he found Harold with a frown on his face, sitting behind his desk, along with Josh and one of Harold's principle engineers.

"Let's all move into my conference room," Harold said, as Steven entered.

After they sat down, Harold closed the door of the conference room. He stood up, started pacing the floor, and began to speak. "Steven, Josh came to me this morning and told me something that bothers me a great deal. He tells me you provided him with a set of code patches that you developed to see if the current test suite platform would support Power PC™ code. Is that correct?"

"Yes, I did. I felt it was important to try out small chunks of code to help determine if the current test suite was an adequate platform for me to use."

"He told me you initially wanted to perform the tests yourself, using each of the code modules on some computer in an adjacent office. Is that correct?"

"Yes, that made more sense to me. If the current suite is an adequate platform, I should try to find out as much as possible about its characteristics."

"When did you have the time to develop these code patches?"

"I'm a bachelor, so I do a lot of work in my apartment. I developed them at home in parallel with studying the documentation Josh gave me."

"Are you telling us these code patches are snippets of Power PC™ code?"

"That's correct."

Harold turned to his principle engineer, who had been listening to this discussion with great interest. "Bill, would you tell Steven what you told me this morning?"

"Yes. I analyzed the code sequence for module one, and found it contained pure gibberish. There is not a single line of code that has anything to do with Power PC™ code."

"Steven, what do you have to say about that?"

Steven began to sweat. He knew he had been found out. He knew they did not know the nature of his code, nor did they know that once it infected their test sequence, there was nothing they could do to remove it. However, they were right in their assessment. It had nothing to do with Power PC™ testing.

"Harold, perhaps I've been burning the midnight oil too much, for if Bill here found the code to be gibberish, perhaps I should have been more careful when I designed it."

"Steven, don't shit me. Bill has looked at all of your codes and found each code patch to be pure gibberish. What are you up to? We at ASV pride ourselves on our ability to hire reputable people. Our procedures here are in place to avoid competitors from ripping off our secrets. You've already gotten Josh in a whole lot of hot water, but don't make things worse for yourself by feeding us more bull this morning. I believe you intended to rip off our test suite. If Josh had given you your own lab, I'm sure you would have succeeded. Thank God he didn't do that. We guess that once you couldn't have access, you had to follow through with your bullshit and give him some gobbledygook to test, hoping it wouldn't be discovered. Isn't that what happened?"

"I prefer to make no comment," Steven said, with sweat forming on his forehead.

"Okay, gentlemen, you can leave now. Josh, when I'm through with Steven, I would like to see you again. Steven, I'm very disappointed. Your knowledge is exactly what ASV needed to make inroads in the Power PC™ marketplace. I don't know who you're working for, but I would advise you to get out of here and never show your face in the Bay Area again. High tech companies like ours have ways to blackball the likes of you."

Mary Cross entered the room. Harold excused himself and the two of them spoke out of Steven's earshot. "Mary will escort you to the front lobby. I hope I never see you again."

Mary did not speak as she walked Steven to the door. She turned and walked back to Harold's office, where he and Josh were having a heated discussion. "Do you think he actually was able to steal any of our code or documentation?" Mary asked.

"What I gave him to read is not the problem," Josh said. "He had access to all of our hard disk files to examine. However, it would not have been possible for him to make copies, so other than what his brain retains, he has not done much damage."

"I think we have all learned a lesson here," Harold said, looking sternly at Josh.

"I sure have," Josh said.

Chapter Thirty-Seven

In Haikou, CT and Miu completed the conversion of the code received from Steven into the format required to record the infection code files on each CD-R.

"Did you have a chance to examine the differences between his first release and this one?" CT asked.

"Yes, and I understand why he needed to release this version. He forgot to include certain file command codes that trigger the timer section. I believe it was an honest mistake. Remember, he has everything to lose at this point if the infection does not spread."

"Okay, but I worry that our whole program hinges on his ability and his loyalty to our cause. I'll continue to provide you with all of the code he sends me, so you can analyze it. I'll sleep better when you tell me you know how he is able to slow down computers."

"I understand, dear. I'm just as worried as you are."

"Mother, this is Steven. I decided I should phone you to see how you and Father are and to find out how my grandparents are adjusting to their new freedom."

"Steven, it's so good to hear from you. How do you like your new job?"

"I find it very challenging," Steven said. He had decided not to tell his parents he had just been fired. "I'm working long days and nights again."

"Your father has gone to town to do some shopping with your grandparents. You should see how happy they are together. He still

The Year of The Tiger

can't quite believe what you did for us. Did you see the ads placed in all the major papers recently by the Chinese president? He announced to the world that he has released all such political prisoners. And to think you caused that to happen! It's too bad we have no way to announce to the world that it was really your doing."

"I'm just happy I could help," Steven said.

The two of them talked for more than an hour before hanging up. Steven lay down on his sofa and turned on the CNN News, to see what was happening in the world. The announcer was discussing the current round of trade negotiations between China and the United States, and the gist of the story was that Congress was going to offer China a most-favored-nation status, due in part to the recent humanitarian act of the president. Such a status was going to pave the way for mutual trade of most commodities, including electronic components, computers, and many other items that had not been allowed in the past. Steven dozed off at the end of the newscast and slept for several hours before being awakened by a beeping sound coming from his computer.

He got up, went into the bathroom, and splashed water on his face. He then went into his office and inserted the encryption disk in the Apple PowerBook™ computer and retrieved the fax. It was from CT, and read as follows.

> Good afternoon, Steven. Miu and I have set things up here to record your latest release on all CD-Rs being produced. In about one week, these devices will be received by Microsoft, who recently placed a large order with us. No doubt they will be used by Microsoft to supply their new Windows95™ Office Suite to buyers of new computers. Do you have any ideas how we can determine if your code is working? Please send me your thoughts.
>
> In the broader sense, what do you think of the idea that we distribute free software with some hidden code that will detect whether a given computer is contaminated? We both agreed we want to make sure a large percentage of the world's computers are contaminated before we start selling the antidote. How can we find out if that is actually the case? Please think about this and send me your ideas.
>
> Regards, CT

Shing's envoy to Taiwan returned and was called into Shing's office to report his findings. "Ah, Shing, all of the floppy disk vendors were very glad to receive me. When I told them how many we planned to buy, they really became interested."

"What requirement did you discuss with them?"

"I discussed various quantities, ranging from one hundred thousand per month to one million per month, starting immediately."

"And did you speak with the two Hong Kong suppliers?"

"Yes, but I determined they were not equipped for our volume. I feel we should place orders with the three Taiwan firms instead."

"Did they ask why we needed so many disks?"

"They were very curious. I told them we were placing renewed emphasis on developing our own software for use by the People's Republic of China, and we anticipated the need for large quantities."

"Good. Now, please contact my business administrator. He will prepare purchase orders, totaling one million per month, split three ways. Accompanying the purchase orders will be a forecast that increases to a total of five million per month by the end of 1997!"

Shing then asked his secretary to contact CT in Haikou. "CT, soon you will begin receiving large quantities of floppy disks. They will be shipped directly to your facility for storage. You can expect to receive on the order of one million per month, starting early next year. When can you begin to record the antidote program on these disks?"

CT explained to Shing that the infection software he received from Steven had to be revised, due to an oversight on Steven's part.

"Ah, Shing, Miu and I want to do some thorough testing before recording millions of antidote disks. I believe I should not start making those disks until March of 1996; and only then if we are totally satisfied the code works."

"That's fine, but remember, you must allow enough time to create a huge stockpile of more than one hundred million antidote disks when we announce to the world we have such a solution."

"I know. I'll plan carefully."

Steven completed a fax and sent it to CT, using the encrypted disk. He provided a status report on his activities at ASV. He told CT he successfully infected their test suite and then resigned his position. With regard to the matter of how they could determine if computers around the world were becoming infected, he provided several ideas for CT to consider. He said he was now going to start work on the antidote software and would have it ready in about one month, which would fit the schedule they developed.

The following day, Steven received a reply from CT, which stated:

> Good morning, Steven. Now that you have completed your task at ASV, Miu and I believe you should return to Haikou and work here with us until you finish the antidote code. If you are here, we will also be able to discuss the matter of confirmation. Would you have any difficulty coming here for a month?
>
> Regards, CT

Steven arrived in Hong Kong on 15 November 1995. He decided he would not let his parents know about this visit. Before he left California, he phoned them again and said ASV was sending him on a business trip to Europe to visit major personal computer firms, so he would not be reachable in California. They thought it was really nice ASV thought so much of their son that they would send him on an important business trip so soon after joining them.

"Hello, Steven. Do you remember me. My name is May Chow. I'm the secretary to the charge d'affaires."

"Of course, May, I remember you. We took a boat ride together once. Will you be accompanying me again?"

"Yes, if you don't mind. We will get on the boat as soon as we arrive at the wharf. I know you must be tired, but we have arranged a nice room for you in Haikou, as well as a delicious Chinese dinner. CT and Miu will join us as well for dinner."

"That would be fine. Let's get my luggage and be on our way."

Steven slept for about four hours and was awakened by a gentle knock on his door. It was May, who asked him if he would like to come down to the dining room now and join them. Steven said he would be right down, so he jumped out of bed, showered, and soon arrived at the dining room.

"CT and Miu, it's so nice to see you both again."

"Hello, Steven. You are looking well."

The four of them were served a twelve-course Chinese dinner, and Steven ate every bite, as his trip to Hong Kong had made him very hungry. During the meal, they did not discuss the project, but rather discussed the trade negotiations going on between China and the United States, and other news events going on in the world.

"I'll arrange a cab to pick you up in the morning and bring you to our plant." CT said. "Also, May, I'll arrange a cab in the morning to take you back to the wharf for your return trip to Hong Kong."

"Thank you, CT. I'll see you tomorrow. Good night, Miu."

"Till tomorrow."

Steven and May walked together through the lobby. May turned to Steven and said, "Why don't we meet in the spa? They provide bathing suits, and I'm told the hot spring water really relaxes your muscles, especially after a long trip such as you have just completed."

"That sounds like a great idea. I'll see you there in a few minutes."

Steven was the first to arrive. He signed in at the desk and went into the dressing room to put on the bathing suit provided by the attendant. He entered the hot tub area and was surprised to find no one was using the spa. He jumped in and laid his head back on the edge and closed his eyes. The hot, bubbly water really did relax him, and he soon dozed off.

"Wake up, sleepyhead," May said, as she slid into the tub next to him. "You really are tired from your long trip, aren't you?"

Steven opened his eyes and for the first time took a good look at her face. "She really is beautiful," he thought to himself. "You're right. I'm very tired," he said.

May snuggled up close to him and began to run her big toe up and down his leg, in a teasing motion. "Why don't we request one of the private massage rooms?" she said. "I understand they contain a large hot tub and a nice, soft water bed full of very hot water. Let me make the necessary arrangements."

May led Steven through the door at the end of the spa and opened a door marked "Private: Do Not Disturb." When inside, she asked Steven to lie down on the bed and relax.

"Steven, you are so tense. Please lie down on your back and allow me to loosen all of your muscles."

Steven began feeling things he had never felt before. Her caresses made him tingle all over, and soon he found himself pulling her down on top of him.

"May, I've never been with a woman before. You will have to teach me what I'm supposed to do."

"You are doing just fine. Why don't we slip out of these bathing suits so we can be more comfortable?"

The two of them fell asleep on the warm waterbed. The next thing they knew, it was 6:00 A.M., and a gentle knock on their door awakened them. They dressed quickly, so they could return to their individual rooms and collect their things. Outside May's room, Steven pulled her to him and gave her a long, passionate good-bye kiss.

"Good-bye, Steven. When you return to Hong Kong, please give me a call. I would love to see you again."

Chapter Thirty-Eight

Miu put the finishing touches on Steven's office, which he would use while in Haikou. It was next to hers, so it would be easy for them to discuss the project, if necessary. She then left the building and pedaled her bike home.

"Miu, is the office ready now for Steven?" CT asked.

"Yes, and as you requested, I've installed an auxiliary personal computer in the closet behind the office. Each line of code he writes will be instantly recorded on the hard drive of the auxiliary computer, and he will have no knowledge of this happening. When he has completed his work, we will have copies of both the source code and object code for the antidote software."

"Good. Now I'll be able to sleep better."

"I'll be able to sleep better if we make love first," Miu said. "I'm sure by now May has seduced Steven, and just thinking about that has turned me on."

"And just hearing you talk about that has turned me on," CT said, as he pulled her onto the bed beside him. "Some time you and I should spend a night in the infamous Haikou Arms Spa, don't you think?"

"Shut up, you animal. Let's get down to business."

"Steven, here is an office you can use while you are here to develop your antidote software. Will you require anything else to do your work?"

"It looks like I have everything here I need. Let me get started and I'll meet you and CT for lunch in the cafeteria."

Steven asked CT and Miu to leave him alone for the next couple of weeks while he concentrated on writing the code. On the eighth day after his arrival, he emerged from the office and told them he was ready to try out the antidote. Miu led him to her testing laboratory, where a Pentium® system was set up. Steven repeated the demonstration he used before, and again showed them the spreadsheet calculations took a very long time to complete. He installed his antidote disk, pressed the "run" command, and in about fifteen seconds, re-booted the computer. This time, the spreadsheet behaved just as one would expect from a fast Pentium® computer.

"It looks like it works," Steven said.

"It does on this machine. But how do we know it will work on a machine that becomes contaminated in the field?"

"I know what you mean. We certainly do want to be sure the antidote is foolproof."

"Can I use the antidote again on this second machine?" CT asked.

"You won't be able to, but let me demonstrate."

Steven installed the infection software, and again demonstrated how the computer slowed way down. He installed the antidote, but when he rebooted, the machine was still slow. The antidote disk had only been able to be used once, as Steven promised.

"Let's go out for lunch today," Miu said. "We should begin to talk about how we can confirm the infection is spreading around the world."

"Good idea," CT said.

"Let me shut down the equipment in my office," Steven said. "I'll meet you two at the front door." Steven returned to his office and carefully removed all the files he developed. He carefully copied them onto floppy disks, using an encryption code he developed that made it possible for him to copy files, even though users of the antidote disk could not do so. He shut off the computer and turned off the lights. In the closet, however, the auxiliary computer contained all of the files he developed, unbeknownst to Steven.

After ordering platters of assorted Chinese delicacies for lunch, CT turned to Steven and began to ask questions.

"Steven, in my latest fax, I said we are currently supplying large quantities of CD-Rs to Microsoft. All of the disks we sell them now contain your infection software, in the form of hidden files. How do you suggest we determine if new CD software sold by Microsoft will cause computers to become infected?"

"My understanding of the PC industry is that each time Microsoft announces a new software application or suite of applications, they allocate their products to all of the major manufacturers of personal computers, on a worldwide basis. I would assume, therefore, that the Hong Kong manufacturers of PCs will soon be getting copies from Microsoft to install on their new machines. If someone loyal to mainland China works for such companies, we could provide such a person a floppy disk containing a detection code. When the detection code is loaded in a machine, some benign message could be made to appear on the screen that would tell us the contamination was present. Then, when the antidote is loaded, the message could be made to change."

"And you think if Hong Kong computers show they are contaminated, all new computers made using the infected Microsoft disks will probably behave in a similar way?"

"It would seem logical to me. We could also do some spot checking at the various computer shows, where all of the world's PC manufacturers bring their latest systems loaded with the latest Microsoft software."

"When is the next show?"

"The Hanover Fair in Germany is the next big European event, and the Comdex Spring Show in Atlanta is the next big U.S. event. I believe Japan will also be the host for such a show in June, if I remember correctly."

"How long will it take you to develop such a detection disk?"

"I can have one ready in a couple of weeks," Steven said.

When the meal was served, the three of them sat quietly eating from the tray full of delicacies. Steven was beginning to tire of Chinese food, but it was obvious CT and Miu showed no such tendency, for they kept heaping more food on their plates.

"Steven, how do we confirm the infection software is being spread by our new Hong Kong web site?"

"Where do you stand on that development?"

"I want you to visit the firm when you return to Hong Kong. If you recall, it is located one block from the Chinese embassy. The purpose of your visit is to return their beta version of the software and tell them it is working correctly. Miu has a copy in her lab, and she wants to help you load your infection software on it, so we can be sure we are doing it right."

"Good. Once the web site is installed, you should provide some free giveaway on the Internet, which is accessible when the viewer clicks on a single button. Pressing that button will introduce a coded pattern that can be made to enter the customer's computer. The response generated can be made to differ, depending on whether the infection is present or not. You will need someone to statistically examine the responses from such queries.

"And how long will it take me to have such a code?" Steven said laughing, anticipating CT's question. "I know the answer. It will be ready in two weeks." They all laughed. "It should be installed on the web site beta software before it is given back to the developers."

The waiter showed up with tea and biscuits. Again, CT and Miu piled their plates high with the goodies. "Don't you two ever eat at home?" Steven asked sarcastically.

"We overslept this morning," CT said, as he blushed slightly. "By the way, did you have any difficulty sleeping your first night after you got off the plane?"

Steven found himself blushing, and could only answer that it had been a long time since he slept so soundly. Miu winked at CT.

"Okay, Steven, one last avenue we need to pursue. The infection you spread at the ASV company is supposed to become attached to any new software that is brought in for validation. Isn't that right?"

"Yes, and as we speak they are evaluating the latest version of the new network software from Microsoft, which is known as Windows NT™. Since that software is not sold currently in CD-R form, it will be sold as a stack of floppy disks in a compressed file format. Large corporations typically use such network software, and Microsoft is proud to announce its customer list to show their competitors that they have landed big accounts. I can provide you with a list of those customers. If you have some way to use the detection disks we discussed earlier at selected computer sites, that is one way to sample whether the infection has appeared."

"I assume some of the major users are located in Hong Kong," Miu said.

"Yes, and what you may want to do is have someone work for the janitorial service in those firms, so he or she can slip a disk into selected computers while cleaning the office at night. A simple message on the screen will verify whether the contamination is present. After loading the antidote disk, the message will change, if all is well."

"Steven, if you can develop these detection disks for us in the next couple of weeks and add the special button to the web site, we should be in a good position to verify how well the infection is spreading. Why don't we go back to the plant now and get busy. I also want to show you something in our warehouse. It will impress you."

On their return, CT took Steven into his warehouse; in the far corner was a large palette full of floppy-disk boxes. "This is our first shipment of fifty thousand disks," CT said. "Each week, we will receive an even larger shipment, until this warehouse is full. Our intention is to have more than one hundred million disks ready to go with the antidote code installed before the infection is triggered. Now I think you can see why it is of supreme importance that your code not have any glitches in it, as it will take us an enormous amount of time and effort to produce such a large quantity of antidote disks. We don't want to have to record them more than once."

"I get the message loud and clear," Steven said.

Steven had to stay an additional three weeks in Haikou to complete the tasks CT defined for him to do. Quietly and efficiently, the auxiliary computer copied his files, so Miu could have her own personal record. She, too, worked long hours. From her office, she had modem access to the auxiliary computer, so she could examine the code Steven was generating.

"Steven is a very clever programmer," Miu said one night over dinner in their apartment. "I have no doubt the infection will spread as he predicts and that his antidote will work just fine. Has Shing commented on what he plans to do to prevent him from selling the antidote to others?"

"No, and I really don't want to know," CT said, insinuating something dire might happen to Steven ultimately. "With the billions of income involved here, Keung will do almost anything to prevent the antidote from being made available to others."

"Why don't they just give him a lot of money and have him live on some desert island, like in a Hollywood movie?"

"He already has been given a lot of money. However, I understand from Shing that he wants too much money. They have to draw the line somewhere, I suppose."

CT and Miu accompanied Steven to the wharf, where he boarded the Chinese patrol boat for his ride back to Hong Kong. He had one more stop to make, which was to deliver the web site code to the developer. Unbeknownst to them, he had also arranged a liaison with May before returning to the States. He decided that as much as he would like to do so, he would not contact his parents, as it would seem odd to them if he were to show up suddenly without preparing them for his visit. After all, they thought he was touring Europe on the expense account of the ASV Corporation.

"Good-bye, CT," Steven said. "Good-bye, Miu."

"Good-bye, Steven."

Chapter Thirty-Nine

Steven returned to California in early December 1995. He was glad he lived in California, for even though the nights were chilly, the days were usually nice, even when it rained. Before he left for Hong Kong, he arranged for a housekeeper to clean his townhouse and place his mail on the kitchen table.

"I didn't know I knew this many people," Steven said, eyeing the huge pile of mail. He sorted it into two piles—junk mail and important mail—and sat down to begin the arduous task of plowing through it. Several letters were invites to parties from some of his Apple buddies; he carefully placed them in a special pile so he could decide later which party or parties he should attend. When he came across an official-looking letter from the ASV Corporation, he immediately opened it. It was from Mary Cross, head of personnel.

Dear Steven:

This is to inform you that the ASV Corporation plans to investigate your background thoroughly, as we believe you accepted a job with us under false pretenses. You will be contacted soon by the Farwell Detective Agency, who we have under contract to work on this case. We hope you will fully cooperate with them.

Yours truly, Mary Cross, director of personnel

"Great," Steven said out loud. "Just what I need in my life now. I wonder how thoroughly they look into things? I wonder if they will find out about my Swiss bank account? I wonder if they will find out about my recent trip to Hong Kong? I wonder if they will contact my parents? Oh, shit, why doesn't ASV just leave me alone?"

He clicked on his answering machine. Besides lots of messages from friends wanting to get together with him, he came across a message from Lamont Dickinson of the Farwell Detective Agency. Lamont wanted to set up an appointment to talk with him. He said it was in reference to the letter he just received.

"I suppose I should talk with him and tell him as little as I can get away with. After all, he's not a cop, so I should be able to tell him anything that occurs to me without hurting myself," Steven thought to himself.

Lamont Dickinson was a sleazy-looking guy who wore an old suit that looked like it hadn't been pressed in years. Steven met him in a diner near his townhouse. Lamont said he would exchange a free lunch for some information. The meeting lasted for about two hours, and it was obvious Lamont was trying to feel Steven out to see if he had some devious motive for accepting the job at ASV. Steven kept his cool throughout the meeting and was relieved Lamont did not probe into his recent whereabouts or any other sensitive subjects. When they left, Lamont said he would appreciate it if Steven would keep him informed of his whereabouts.

"Is this kind of treatment standard in the Bay Area these days?" Steven asked as they walked toward their cars.

"No, but ASV is super sensitive about their crown jewels. I've been used several times by them, performing this same function. If they thought the janitor on the night shift was spending too much time standing near the copy machine, they would do a slam-dunk on him without even thinking twice."

CT placed a phone call to Shing so he could give him a complete briefing of the project, including the work Steven did while in Haikou. "I'll be glad when you can report to me the infection has actually spread," Shing said.

"Me too," CT replied. "I am pleased to report that Miu now has a complete copy of both the source code and object code for the antidote software. She is actively analyzing it and should soon know exactly how it works. We want to try it on some computers infected in the field, to ensure it works, before we start making millions of copies for sale."

"Keep me posted. By the way, are the floppy disks arriving according to plan?"

"Yes. We may have to clear out the old warehouse on the edge of our property in order to find room to hold all of them."

"Fine. Just remember to keep the environment dry. I'm told floppy disks do not like to be stored in damp places."

"I'll personally check on that. Is there anything more I can tell you?"

"No. Just keep me informed as soon as you have information on the spread of the infection."

Three months passed since Lamont met with Steven, so Steven spent an enjoyable holiday season with several of his old friends. He told them things did not work out for him at ASV, so he was enjoying his free time, and would probably continue to do so for some time.

In April of 1996, Steven made plans to attend the Spring Comdex show in Atlanta to try out his detection disk. He packed his bag and prepared to enjoy the drive across the country. He called his parents once a month now, each time discussing his wonderful job, so they would not suspect he was doing anything other than working hard like he had always done at Apple. Before driving to Atlanta, he called them again, but this time his mother started the conversation with a barrage of questions.

"Your father and I received a phone call this week from a Mr. Dickinson. He told us you were fired from ASV, and they were investigating your background. What's going on, Son? Are you in some kind of trouble?"

Steven gulped. The moment of truth was upon him. He always knew sooner or later he would have to inform his parents he was working on a special project for the Chinese government, and the job with ASV was just a part of an overall plan to infect all of the world's computers.

"Mother, I've not leveled with you or Father since I returned to the States. I'll write you a letter soon explaining the entire situation. Please don't worry about me. I have plenty of money and I'm quite busy. The job at ASV just did not work out for me. I'm leaving in a few moments to drive to Atlanta to attend a computer conference. When I return, I'll talk with you again. Please don't worry about Mr. Dickinson. It is a policy of ASV to investigate any employee who leaves them so soon after being hired. Believe me, Mother, I'm not in any trouble. I've done nothing wrong."

"Steven, please take care of yourself. You must understand we are both very worried about you. I wish you could tell us more now, but if you can't, please do so when you return."

"Thank you, Mother."

Steven hung up and hopped in his car for the trip to Atlanta. He had a lot of planning to do, for it would be a year and a half before the infection would trigger. What should he do with himself in the meantime, and where should he live? He could not take his mind off of May Chow. Since he returned to the States, he phoned her almost every day. She also seemed to be very interested in what he was doing, and looked forward to his calls.

The Atlanta Convention Center had hosted the Comdex South Computer Show for the past ten years, and more than one million people were expected to arrive this year from all over the world to see what new products the personal computer manufacturers and their software vendors had to offer.

After Steven checked in to his hotel, he immediately caught a cab and told the driver to take him directly to the convention center. The floor of the center was laid out to accommodate several hundred booths and floor displays. He received a floor plan when he registered, so he sat in a snack booth and drank a cup of tea while he planned which booths he should visit.

Steven registered as a freelance writer, claiming he planned to write articles about the latest in computer technology. He even printed some fake business cards before he arrived. His detection disk was designed to produce a display of the internal performance of any computer it was loaded into. However, if the bar graph displayed in red, it would mean the computer was infected, whereas if the bar graph displayed in green, it would mean the computer was not yet infected.

Steven planned to go from booth to booth and introduce himself and see if he could place his disk in the vendor's latest machine, in order to log its performance. He would claim he was writing an article comparing products, and would send the vendor a copy before it was published.

His first stop was the Acer booth. Acer was showing off their new line of multimedia products, which sported fancy-colored cabinets and monitors. Included in each system was the latest version of the Microsoft Office Suite™ and Windows 95™. The young lady he spoke to was quite interested in seeing how her products would perform, so she gladly let him load his detection disk. Steven was elated, for the performance bar graph on the screen displayed bright red, indicating the computer had the infection. The other members of the Acer team crowded around him and asked what the bar graph meant. Steven told them it displayed the effective MIP performance of their machine, averaged over multiple applications.

"Your MIP rating is quite high," Steven said. "You will receive a favorable rating in my article."

"How about checking our economy model?" the girl asked.

"Sure," Steven said. "What software is installed in it?"

"It's a 100-Mhz Pentium® machine with Microsoft Works installed, rather than the Microsoft Office Suite. It also has Windows95™ installed."

Steven inserted his disk, and the bar graph on the screen appeared in green, as he suspected it would, since the version of Microsoft Works installed was an earlier revision.

"What does it mean if the bar graph is green?"

"It means the performance is less. However, your MIP rating is still quite good, even in this economy machine. Thank you for your time. I'll be sure to send you a copy of my article for your comments before I publish it."

Steven continued down the hall until he arrived at the Compaq booth. He singled out one of the sales persons and went through the same ritual with her. The bar graph showed up bright red, and the MIP performance on the screen was comparable with the Acer machine. The Compaq economy model contained the latest version of Microsoft Works, so it too displayed the bar graph in a bright red color.

By 5:00 P.M., Steven had visited more than fifty booths, and every computer that contained the latest Microsoft Works or Office Suite for Windows 95™ was infected. He sat down at a restaurant booth and relaxed for a while, thinking about what he had seen. He was elated over the results, and he knew his plan was working. The next day, he would visit the booths where network computers were being demonstrated. He knew ASV was working around the clock to validate the Windows NT™ software and the latest version of Lotus Notes™, so they could be shown off at Comdex. If machines containing these products were contaminated, he would know for sure that the contamination had been a direct result of the ASV testing!

"Hello, I'm Steven Lee."

"Hi. What can I do for you?" the IBM floor person asked.

Steven gave him the same spiel he used on the other vendors, but this time said he was planning to write an article on the next generation of network servers. He was shown several models on display and was given a brief pitch on their features.

"This is our most recent network server product with the latest beta version of Lotus Notes™ installed."

"Has this version of Lotus Notes™ been validated?"

"As a matter of fact, we have a report we can show you written by the ASV Corporation that gives us a clean bill of health. Are you familiar with what an ASV seal of approval means?"

"Yes I am. Now may I insert my disk? I'm interested in seeing how your performance stacks up."

The bar graph on the server displayed a considerably higher MIP rating, for the machine contained four separate 200-Mhz Pentium® devices working in parallel. But, more important to Steven, the graphs were bright red!

"I have another disk I would like to run now, which will modify the graphics driver. I want to see if the MIP rating remains just as high. May I install it?"

"Of course."

Steven installed his antidote disk, for he wanted to see if the antidote would work on this very fast machine with multiple processors. He previously tried other antidote disks during his walk around the floor yesterday, and in each case the antidote worked, turning the bar graphs green.

"She works just fine," he said. "Notice the graph turned green, but the MIP rating stays the same. You will receive a very high score in my article."

He continued his testing all day, and found machines containing the latest beta version of Windows NT™ or Lotus Notes™ were all infected. This meant he had successfully infected the ASV validation test suite!

The next morning, Steven checked out of his hotel and began his return trip to California. His plan was working and he now had to decide what he should do next, while he waited for the infection to be triggered around the world on 1 January 1998.

In Hong Kong, the design firm CT used to develop the Hong Kong web site was busy taking orders for the free data packet they offered viewers. The web site had only been introduced a few weeks ago, but already there were more than one hundred thousand requests. More important to CT was the fact that each request contained a short code sequence at the bottom of the order form. Each of these requests was therefore coming from an infected computer! When CT received an update from the manager of the firm, he was very pleased.

The night shift foreman at Ocean Electronics needed to hire extra employees to test and ship a large order of new personal computers. As was typical, once a new product line was demonstrated at Comdex, customers placed volume orders. One of the extra employees brought with him a detection disk provided by CT.

"Your job tonight is to turn on each computer, press the sequence of keys shown on this chart, and record the results. If any machine fails to work in the way prescribed on the sheet, place it on the palette next to you, so it can be sent back for re-work."

CT's man followed the instructions, but he also installed the detection disk and noted the response on the monitor. The word "okay" would quickly flash in red on the machine if the machine was infected, whereas it would flash in green if the machine were not infected. Tonight, each machine he checked out flashed in red!

The janitorial firm sent its team after hours to the headquarters of the Prudential Life Insurance Company in Hong Kong. Prudential recently announced it upgraded its internal computer systems to use fast network servers built by Network, Inc. in Hong Kong. Each computer was tied together using Windows NT™. In addition, Prudential was one of the first firms to connect its corporate data system to the Internet, for fast access to worldwide mortgage and other pertinent financial information.

CT arranged for one of his men to work for the janitorial firm. During the evening's cleanup work, his man was able to try out his detection disk, and each time "okay" flashed in red. When the man inserted an antidote disk, the "okay" flashed in green. Trying to use the antidote disk in a second machine would not work, proving each antidote was only good for curing a single machine, rather than curing a whole group of machines on the network.

When Steven returned to his townhouse, he found his Apple PowerBook™ computer beeping incessantly. He inserted his encryption disk and found four faxes from CT. Each contained congratulatory messages indicating the infection was spreading as planned. The last fax asked for him to provide a status report from his Comdex trip.

Steven typed a quick report and sent it off to CT. He lay down on his sofa and began to think what his next move should be. As he dozed off, the phone awakened him. When he picked it up, it was Lamont, who wanted to see him again.

"Lamont, why did you have to bother my parents? I didn't want them to know ASV fired me. You had no right to interfere with my personal life."

"Steven, my job is to know more about your personal life than you know yourself. If you don't like it, get a lawyer and try to constrain me. You will find out, however, what I'm doing is perfectly legal, for ASV believes you are some form of an industrial spy. Now, will you tell me who you are really working for?"

"I'm currently unemployed," Steven shouted back.

"How are you able to support yourself?"

"I managed to put aside some money when I worked for Apple."

"Apple must have paid you very well, for our man in Switzerland tells us you recently set up a bank account in Zurich. How much money do you have there?"

"None of your business!"

"Steven, I'm going to make it my business. We have ways to find out things. If you don't cooperate, we'll eventually find out what makes you tick. Now why don't you tell us who hired you and what you were supposed to do at ASV? The boys there tell me you spent more time trying to find out about their test suite than you did working on your new project."

"I had to know what they already had so I would not reinvent the wheel. Man, they sure are paranoid!"

"Being paranoid is what makes them successful. That's why they sic us on anyone who works such a short time for them."

"They fired me, remember. I didn't quit. I liked my job there, but they kicked me out."

"Okay, Steven, so you don't want to cooperate. Fine, but I have one more question for you. Why is it you visited Hong Kong recently and stayed for more than a month and never even visited your parents? Incidentally, we didn't tell your parents about that little trip of yours. We thought we would wait until we had your answer first."

"I have a girlfriend there and we took a trip around the Orient together," Steven responded, trying to think up something plausible to say.

"Our records show you have never had a girlfriend before. In fact, we were beginning to wonder if you were gay."

"I refuse to sit here and listen to your insults. Good-bye."

Steven stormed out of the restaurant, leaving Lamont to pick up the check.

"Harold, this is Lamont. I just finished chatting with Steven, and he definitely is hiding something. He claims he is unemployed, but he recently opened a Swiss bank account. He recently visited Hong Kong and spent more than a month there, shortly after you guys canned him. Are you sure he wasn't able to take any critical ASV documentation with him?"

"As far as we can tell, he was only exposed to very preliminary technical data contained on our hard disk files. We were not about to let him see the actual code sequences until he had been with us for several months. Do you think he's employed by someone in the Orient?"

"It sure looks that way. I'm in touch with a detective agency in Hong Kong who will pick up his trail there. I'll contact you when I have more information."

★ ★ ★

"CT, thank you for coming to Beijing for our status meeting. Would you present your status to Keung, Kong, and me?"

"Ah, Shing, yes. I'm happy to report everything is on schedule. We have absolute verification that the infection is spreading on a worldwide basis, and we have proved each antidote disk can only be used once. If a user tries to copy the disk, the antidote no longer works. In addition, my warehouse now has more than two hundred thousand floppy disks with the code loaded and ready to go. My plan is to have more than one hundred million by the time the infection triggers."

"What about the work your wife is doing? Does she know yet how the infection code works, and does she understand the antidote code as well?"

"Miu fully understands both codes now. She tells me Steven is a brilliant software developer. She sees things in his code structure she has never understood until now. Yes, she is totally knowledgeable. If Steven were no longer available for whatever reason to modify or support the product, Miu would be able to provide such support. Steven is no longer required to make our project successful."

"We have several months before the trigger date. What will Steven be doing between now and that date?" Keung asked.

"That is certainly a concern to us," Shing answered. "He may get the idea he should sell the antidote to others, for greed is a very strong motivator."

"Where will he go, and how will we know where to reach him? After all, he has a million dollars to spend, and he just might decide to see the world and enjoy its pleasures," Keung said.

"We have assigned one of our most specialized agents to ensure we know his whereabouts at all times," Shing answered.

"Who is that?" Kong asked.

"Her name is May Chow, and she works as the secretary to the charge d'affaires in the Hong Kong Embassy. We discovered Steven was a virgin, so we arranged for May to become close to him when he last visited Haikou. May told us that Steven is quite smitten by her, so the two of them are in constant contact. I don't think it will be too hard to know how to reach him whenever we need to."

"Thanks, CT, for your status report. Continue to build antidote disks and prepare for the greatest business opportunity the world has ever known," Keung said, as he shook CT's hand. "Shing, I want you and Kong to remain. I have another subject to discuss with both of you.

"Gentlemen, is it time now for us to terminate Steven?" Keung asked, after CT left the room.

"I think so," Kong said. "According to CT, Miu understands the product, so why should we wait?"

"There is one concern I have," Shing said. "If we show our hand and somehow fail in our first attempt, Steven would no doubt retaliate and would no doubt provide his antidote to other firms such as Microsoft, who would distribute them at no charge to all of their customers. I believe we are better off if we wait until we announce the antidote. I'm sure May Chow will be able to keep track of him until then."

Keung stood up and paced the floor. Finally he sat down and said, "Shing, I bow to your wisdom on this. Even though we possess the knowledge, there is certainly the possibility Steven might turn on us before we can profit from this enterprise."

"Ah, Keung, I have a great idea," Kong said. "Isn't his account set up so whenever anything happens to him, the money is automatically returned to our treasury?"

"That is correct," Keung said.

"Then why don't we pay him a bonus right now, as a result of the success so far? Why don't we tell him we have placed an additional half million in his account as an advance against future commissions? That should buy some loyalty from him, don't you think?"

"That is an outstanding idea," Keung said. "What do you think, Shing?"

"Sounds good to me. How should we proceed?"

"You should have CT contact him and congratulate him for a job well done so far. CT can tell him effective immediately he has HK$1.5 million in the bank. Is there anything else we need to discuss?"

The meeting ended and Shing told CT what to do. When CT returned to Haikou, he sent a fax to Steven giving him the good news.

Chapter Forty

Steven decided to leave California and return to Hong Kong. The idea of detective Lamont digging into his personal situation made him feel extremely uncomfortable. In addition, he really missed May and wanted to be closer to her. And he wanted to visit his parents and grandparents more frequently. It was evident now that the infection was spreading, so he had nothing to do but wait till the timer triggered the infection on a worldwide basis.

His Apple PowerBook™ computer started beeping again, so he went into his office and retrieved the fax. It read as follows:

> Hello, Steven. I have some good news for you. Because the infection is spreading as you predicted it would, my boss, Shing, has recommended you for a cash bonus. If you check your account in Switzerland, you will find an additional half million dollars, which was deposited yesterday. Congratulations. You deserve it.
>
> What are your plans now? It seems all you have to do is wait until the day when all computers slow down. Do you plan to travel, or are you going to seek other employment to occupy your time? In any event, it is important we continue to communicate frequently.
>
> Regards, CT

Steven was jubilant. The Chinese were really happy with his work. They obviously did not need to provide him with any bonus, since it was not part of their deal. He was now assured that he would have no financial problems, and he could freely travel and enjoy himself. He thought ahead to when the trigger would occur, and he decided he would need to find some permanent hideout; if it was discovered he was the source of the infection, the whole world would be on the lookout for him.

Steven decided that when he returned to Hong Kong, he would introduce May Chow to his parents and grandparents. Steven's mother had long given up hope of having any grandchildren, for Steven had shown no interest in girls. She would surely be happy when he introduced her to such a lovely person as May.

"Hello, Mother. Hello, Father. It's good to see you again," Steven said, as he met them in the baggage-claim area of the Hong Kong International Airport.

"Steven, I've never seen you look better," Betty Lou said, fully expecting him to look haggard and tired. "I do hope you will tell us what you are doing these days."

"Let's go home first, Mother."

"Fair enough."

Steven spent the ride home talking about his grandparents and how they were getting along in Hong Kong. Steven's father told him he found them a small apartment unit in their building, so it was just a short elevator ride down five floors to see them. He also arranged with the management of the townhouse for the elder Lees to have a small garden plot to putter around in where they could raise vegetables and flowers.

"Do they miss the old country?"

"I don't believe so. Most of their closest friends passed away during the past five years."

"Do they speak any English yet?"

"They have been attending English training lectures weekly in their building, along with several other elderly couples, but still do not use many phrases."

Steven closed his eyes and was fast asleep by the time the car pulled into the parking garage. When the engine turned off, he woke up with a start.

"I guess I never will get used to jet lag," Steven said as he rubbed his eyes.

"Let me take your luggage," his father told him.

After taking a shower and shaving, Steven emerged from his bedroom feeling a lot better. His mother fixed him some Chinese soup and biscuits, which helped him wake up. After finishing the meal, Steven asked his mother and father to join him in the den. He wanted to brief them on what was going on.

"Hello, Lamont. This is Jules in Hong Kong."

"Hi, Jules. How's business there?"

"It keeps me hopping. Anyway, you wanted me to report to you the minute Steven arrived."

"That's right. Our sources here tell us he sold his townhouse, his car, and all of his personal effects, and boarded TWA flight 101 for Hong Kong last night."

"Yes. He arrived here an hour ago and met his parents. I presume he's with them now."

"Are you able to maintain a twenty-four-hour surveillance on him?"

"That's the plan. I'm going to stick to him like super glue."

"Keep me posted every couple of days."

"Will do. Have a good day."

Steven told his parents he was working for the Chinese government on the software product he sold them. He did not tell them what the product was, however, but only referred to it as a product that would make the Chinese become instantly the number one software supplier in the world to the personal computer market.

"Why did you bother going back to the States and take the job with ASV, if you had this other deal cooking?" his father asked.

"When I left here, the Chinese were definitely impressed, and they released my grandparents and many hundreds of other persons as a down payment for my idea. However, they needed more time to evaluate its performance before they could actually employ me to work further with them on it."

"Tell me again why ASV hired a detective agency to check up on you."

"Because over the years they have developed a super-secret suite of tests that are required to validate the performance of new software applications. They suspected me of having ulterior motives in seeking employment with them. According to the detective himself, they run close to paranoia all the time."

"Well, Son, what are your plans now? Where will you be living as you work for the Chinese? Will you be able to stay here with us, or will you need to find some place to stay that is closer to your work?"

"I'll find out when I meet with the Chinese this week. Don't worry about me. Everything is fine."

Steven met May Chow at her apartment on the west side of Hong Kong. He had been there once before, just prior to returning to the States. May greeted him warmly and kissed him long and hard after she closed the door.

"Steven, I'm so very glad you returned to Hong Kong. I hope we will never have to be apart again."

"May, I've not been able to sleep at night, because I missed you so much."

"Are you hungry?"

"For what?"

"For lunch, silly," she said, jabbing him in the ribs.

"What are we having?"

"Your favorite, shrimp soup with won ton noodles."

Outside the apartment, Jules was sitting in his small English sports car. He had seen Steven enter the apartment a half-hour prior and called in the address to one of his friends on the Hong Kong police force. His cellular phone beeped, and he picked it up. "Yea, this is Jules."

"Are you sure you gave me the correct apartment number?"

"Yes I am. I can see the address from where I'm sitting."

"Well, hang on to your seat, for the lady who rents that apartment is one of China's most notorious spies. We have never been able to prove that, for every time we get the goods on her, she somehow manages to disappear or wiggle out of our grasp. Anyway, her name is May Chow, and she fronts as a secretary, working for the charge d'affaires at the Chinese embassy."

"Thank you very much," Jules said, hanging up his phone.

"My, oh my. The plot thickens," he thought to himself.

Inside the apartment, Steven and May finished their light lunch and moved out onto the veranda, where May served cups of hot spiced tea. Steven spent an hour updating May on everything that had happened to him since they last were together. He even included the activities of Lamont and why the detective agency was on the lookout for him.

"Is the project you are working on for CT going well?"

"Yes. In fact I've received additional money as a bonus. I guess they believe I've done a good job for them."

"That's wonderful. And now that you have become a man of the world, what are your plans?"

"I need to remain in close communication with CT, in the event he wants me to do further work on the project. Other than that, I'm free to travel the world, slay other dragons, or just sit here at your feet worshipping you."

"Why don't you make Hong Kong your permanent residence? In that way, you and I can see each other frequently. You can visit your parents and grandparents any time you wish, and you can hop on the boat and visit CT whenever such a visit is required. Also, if you want to travel, you can hop a jet plane to anywhere in the world. Doesn't that make sense?"

"It certainly does. I've had my eye on the new high-rise apartments that look out over Hong Kong Harbor. Do you know the ones I'm referring to?"

"Yes, that would be a very nice location. I believe they will be ready next month. I'll tell you what. Why don't you and I go there now and take a look at the model unit? It would be fun."

Jules followed the cab that picked up Steven and May. It was a relatively short ride to the wharf area. The cab stopped in front of the new high-rise building and Steven and May got out and went inside. They came out shortly thereafter, laughing and carrying on like two teenagers.

"May, I can't believe it. I actually am able to afford to live in such a plush place! And it is already furnished. All I have to do is move in my stuff next week, and I'll be the first resident."

"Steven, you deserve such a fine place to live. After all, from what I know of the project you are working on, China owes you an enormous debt of gratitude."

"May, will you move in with me?" Steven asked, not sure how she would respond.

"Steven let's not move quite so fast," she said. "We can see each other frequently, and I think we need to know each other better before we make such a commitment."

"That's fine," Steven said. He realized there would be plenty of time for a more permanent commitment later.

"Lamont, wait till you hear what I've got to tell you." Jules spent the next several minutes telling Lamont about May Chow and what he observed.

"And you say he's cozy with a Chinese spy?"

"That's what I'm telling you. What do you think it means?"

"I haven't a clue. Why don't you keep an eye on him for another week or so? Then we'll decide what to do next. I really don't want to get involved in some international spy situation. My practice only deals with industrial espionage."

"Mine too," said Jules.

"Shing, May Chow is on your line," Shing's secretary said over the office intercom.

"Hello, May. How are things with you?"

"Things are fine. I wanted to let you know about Steven and what his current plans are." May told Shing she believed that Steven was still very loyal to China.

"He is also very pleased he received such a large bonus. He plans to live in a new high-rise apartment building near the wharf in Hong Kong. He wants very much to keep seeing me frequently, and I don't doubt he will, from time to time, want to take extended sightseeing trips. What should I do if he asks me to accompany him?"

"You should go with him. The closer you two become, the surer we are he will not decide to sell the antidote files to other parties."

"I understand. I'll be his constant companion," May said obediently.

May then told Shing about the detective agency that was digging into Steven's personal life.

"That worries me, May."

"It worries me too. Hopefully they will stop prying, now that he has moved to Hong Kong permanently."

In Beijing, in February of 1997, Deng Xiaoping, the man some called "the last emperor of China," succumbed to Parkinson's disease, respiratory illness, and old age. This meant that President Keung Fu Huang would become chairman of the Chinese People's Republic, after a brief period of public and political mourning. Keung was quick to call a meeting of his ministry chiefs to assure them that the policies he had been carrying out would not change materially.

"As all of you should realize, Deng had turned over the day-to-day reigns of the government to me some years ago, when he first became ill. During the past five years, I have scarcely even talked with him about any matters of policy," Keung said.

"There will be a state funeral, a period of national mourning, and then back to business as usual. However, I will need to meet with dignitaries from all around the world to allay any fears they might have about China's economic reforms. Shing, I want you to take over some of my other duties for the next few weeks. As I understand things, the program for contaminating the computers is well on track, so this should free you up sufficiently to give me a hand. Is that correct?"

"Ah, Keung, that is correct," Shing said. "You can count on my support during these next several weeks."

During the first half of 1997, Steven enjoyed his newfound wealth. He took frequent trips throughout the Orient, and even spent an extended vacation in Europe. May accompanied him on most of his trips, and the two became inseparable. Steven took May frequently to visit his parents and grandparents, and Betty Lou was very happy they were together as a couple. Betty Lou no longer asked Steven what he did for the Chinese government, for she sensed he didn't want to talk about it.

After six months of surveillance by Jules in Hong Kong, Lamont told ASV he could no longer find out anything of value about Steven. All he could say was he was really thick with this Chinese chick who was purported to be a spy.

In July of 1997, Hong Kong was officially taken over by the People's Republic of China, and Chee-hwa Tung, Hong Kong's new CEO, formally took office. The city was visited by thousands of dignitaries from all over the world, and there were many lavish parties given in celebration of the event. Because of his connections with the Chinese embassy, Steven was invited to many such affairs, and he was always accompanied by May. They were considered by many to be representative of what a modern Chinese couple should be like. In August of 1997, Steven received a fax from CT requesting him to come to Haikou to discuss important details of the project. Steven arrived the next day to meet with CT.

"Steven, as you know, the infection is set to be triggered at midnight, 31 December 1997, which is only five months from now. My warehouses are stuffed full of antidote disks, but there is still a lot of marketing work required before we can release the antidote for sale. Therefore, I'm asking you to go to Beijing and help Tak prepare the required documentation and associated literature. Can you please go and help him?"

"Of course," Steven said. "When should I leave?"

"Here are some tickets and a travel visa. The flight leaves on Monday morning. Good luck and have a safe journey. When you arrive, please contact me in the event I have other information for you."

"May, I have to go to Beijing on Monday morning to work with Tak. It looks like I'll be gone for several months. I'm going to miss you."

"Steven, why are you going?" she asked, genuinely curious, for she had not been told by Shing that this request would be made.

"They want me to help launch the product. I guess the Marketing Department needs a lot of help. After all, this is going to be a giant splash and they have to do it right."

"I'll miss you too," she said. The two then made love for what would be the last time for several months.

"Shing, why did you invite Steven to spend time in Beijing?" May asked over the international telephone in the embassy.

"I should have told you. We decided it would be better if we had him here in our midst, where we could watch him closely as we proceed toward the day when the infection software triggers around the world. Do you see anything wrong with that strategy?"

"No. I just was curious why we didn't discuss it first. That's all."

"My oversight," Shing said. "Anyway, you won't have to baby-sit him for several months. I would think you would be happy about that."

"Yes, I am," she said, not fully meaning it. "I'm sorry I bothered you."

"Any time. You know I always like to talk with you."

May hung up the phone and sat staring at the ceiling for a few minutes. She should be happy she did not have to keep Steven company for a long while, but actually she rather liked his company. In fact, she had to admit to herself she was falling in love with him. He was a very caring and tender person who was a far cry from the Chinese bureaucrats she had learned to despise. The kind of men she met at the embassy always wanted special favors from her.

"Oh, well," she thought to herself. "Perhaps it's best we be apart for a while to see what our true feelings are for each other."

Chapter Forty-One

Steven was kept very busy helping Tak and the marketing department get ready for the product announcement of the antidote disks. Data sheets had to be prepared, brochures describing how to use the product had to be written, price sheets had to be approved, and advertising copy had to be designed for all of the world's major newspapers and magazines. Steven was invited to Kong's planning meeting so he could provide input to the marketing plan. Tsi was again assigned as his interpreter.

"Tak, would you please describe for my staff what your total marketing plan is for the sale and distribution of the antidote disks?" Kong asked.

Tak went to the blackboard, where he outlined all the elements of the plan. He said the product would be called the Tiger Antidote Disk, because it would first be sold during the Year of the Tiger.

"First of all, advertisements that are scheduled for Monday, 5 January 1998, will be sent to all major newspapers and magazines. These ads will explain that the Chinese software industry discovered a very peculiar infection several months ago that caused computers to slow down. The ads will further explain China immediately assigned software personnel to develop an antidote, which can be purchased from a worldwide network of distributors as well as directly from numerous electronics firms based in Hong Kong. Finally, the ad will say customers can expect to receive a disk within a week after receipt of order, since China has built a large inventory of Tiger Antidote Disks, anticipating a huge demand."

The Year of The Tiger

Tak continued by describing the sales channels he was going to use, the discounts he recommended for each sale, the pricing plan, and the literature that would accompany each disk. He recommended a very inexpensive folded plastic enclosure for each disk, with a single piece of paper included inside that explained how to install the program. He added laughingly that the literature would say it was illegal to copy the disk without the approval of the People's Republic of China. Everyone in the room laughed, for they knew if anyone tried to copy the disk, they would destroy its contents and have to purchase another one, anyway.

Kong thanked Tak for his presentation and asked for questions or comments from his staff. Several issues were raised and discussed. Kong then turned to Steven and asked him if he saw any holes in the plan.

"Just one, Kong," Steven said. "You have the sales channels well covered for the major accounts, but in the U.S. you will need to provide mail-order catalog coverage for the individual home computer users. I would recommend you select one of the well-known catalog firms and give them the franchise to sell the disks, just like they sell other types of after-market products to the individual computer user."

"Tak, what do you think?"

"It sounds like a good idea. I'll speak with Steven after this meeting to get further information."

"If there are no more questions, the meeting is adjourned," Kong said.

On 1 October 1997, Keung held a high level meeting with a number of his staff members, in order to prepare himself for his first summit meeting with President Clinton that was to take place on the 28th of October in Washington, D.C. As is always the case with such meetings, each side has their own agendas and priorities. Keung's objective was simple; he wanted to receive assurances from the United States that China would continue to be given most favored nation status and be permitted to join the World Trade Organization, whereas President Clinton's objective was to receive assurances from the Chinese leader that China would make sweeping reforms in all areas of human rights.

"Ah, Keung, it is in the United States' best interest that China be admitted into the World Trade Organization, so you should stand firm in your demands for such membership. By no means should you have to give Mr. Clinton any concessions," one of his advisors said.

"But Chang, you have heard all of the rumors about how the United States absolutely will insist that I free all political prisoners who were intent on overthrowing our government shortly after the Tiananmen Square incident. They also believe we were inhumane in our dealings with the re-unification of Tibet with China. I am told they will be like bull dogs on these matters. I am afraid they won't let go of such incidents, even though I did pardon all of the persons charged with the overthrow of the Chinese government in the 1950s," Keung answered.

"Keung, you should inform Mr. Clinton very firmly that these matters are internal Chinese matters, which simply cannot be discussed, period!"

"Of course I will take such a position, but nevertheless I am concerned that the Americans will not let go of this subject."

"Ah, Keung, I have what I believe to be a brilliant idea for you to consider," Kong said.

"Yes, Kong, what is it?"

"We need to do something highly visible to make Mr. Clinton realize that a refusal of Chinese membership in the World Trade Organization could result in grave economic consequences throughout the world markets."

"And what do you suggest?"

"I suggest that we leak various stories in the press a week or so before your meeting. These stories need to state emphatically that China takes very seriously the matter of being admitted into the World Trade Organization; furthermore the stories should infer that if China is not permitted to become a member, then China will be forced to change many of its current trading policies which allow much-sought-after- goods and services to be sold to most of the major industrial nations of the world. We should even threaten huge tariffs on critical items. The stories in the press should also tell the world that China is quite concerned that a number of conservative right wing groups in the United States, such as the Christian coalition, are vowing to keep China out of the World Trade Organization, and that such groups are heavily influencing President Clinton, who claims to be a devout Baptist."

"That sounds nice, Kong, but how will such stories in the press influence the course of the summit meeting?"

"Ah, Keung, you do not yet realize the enormous economic influence you have on the world, as a consequence of the recent acquisition of Hong Kong. I believe such stories, when properly placed in various business magazines and periodicals, will cause the Hong Kong stock market to go into what some will call a 'meltdown' for a few days or weeks, which in turn will trigger similar huge drops in the value of stocks across the world. Believe me, if that were to happen, President Clinton will get the message loud and clear."

"What do the rest of you think?" Keung asked, as all of his advisors began to discuss the matter.

"Let's do it," they all shouted. "Such a happening just before your summit meeting should have a profound effect on the outcome of the meeting."

"Then, Kong, since it was your idea, would you please draft a press release and have it on my desk Monday morning. I will call in my press manager to work with you so it can be placed strategically in the correct business periodicals."

"Now, gentlemen, are there any other matters we need to attend to?"

They all shook their heads no, so the meeting was adjourned.

The visit to the United States by a Chinese head of state was the first such visit since Jimmy Carter was president. Keung and his entourage were given the red carpet treatment, including a tour of Williamsburg, Virginia, before finally arriving at the White House to begin serious talks. After two days of meeting, Keung and President Clinton held a joint news conference, which included a barrage of questions aimed directly at various Chinese human rights issues. Keung side-stepped these questions quite skillfully, leaving the members of the press quite frustrated. President Clinton's comments regarding these issues were that the two of them had "agreed to disagree," and then he went on to discuss various matters of commerce. He did not however commit that he was going to recommend China for membership in the World Trade Organization. In fact, he made a point of not commenting on that matter at all.

★ ★ ★

"Ah, Keung, it is good to see you again. Could you brief me on how your meetings went with Mr. Clinton and his congressional leaders?" Kong asked, as he sat down in Keung's office shortly after his return. "According to the papers we have read, your assessment of the American's pre-occupation with so-called human rights issues was clearly evident. Also, I am curious how Mr. Clinton reacted to the wild excursions in the world's stock market, which our press release cleverly caused," he said smiling, wanting to receive full credit for that idea.

"Kong, I have been so humiliated in my life," Keung said in an outraged tone. "Mr. Clinton almost totally ignored the economic matters associated with the world markets, and instead he continued to demand that I set free all of our political prisoners, no matter what their crimes to the state. He is a complete ass, and I wanted to call him that many times during our conversations. To top it off, he had me talk with a number of congressional leaders, including the wily Newt Gingrich, Speaker of the House. The purpose of such talks was obvious; they all talked about nothing but goddamn human rights issues!

"Then President Clinton talked for hours about the freedom of religion in the United States, telling me that under such a system all persons have equal rights. Yet, I kept asking him, what about freedom of cultures, and why is it that the United States does not accept the reality that the Chinese culture is not the same as the culture of the United States. I reminded him that I had set free a number of political prisoners from the 50s and he did thank me for doing that; but then he got back on his soap box and insisted that China free all political prisoners, no matter what their crimes were.

"I continued to tell him that, similar to the liberation of the black slaves in American history, my reforms represented a great social change and advance. I also reminded him that further progress in China-U.S. relations hinges on correctly understanding our common interest and as well properly handling our differences. I tried to show him that our course is to choose socialism as a way of life, but with Chinese characteristics, where state enterprises will often control private corporations that compete in the free market."

"Were you able to discuss the issue of membership in the World Trade Organization?"

"Yes briefly, but he would make no commitments. I do believe the gyrations of the stock market did have some influence on him, however, and perhaps he will not give in to the right wing groups, which, by the way are in fact holding considerable influence over his head, as your clever press release indicated."

"What is the next step?"

"I'll tell you how I feel right now," Keung said in a loud voice. "I wish we could trigger the Tiger Code virus immediately, and not have to wait until New Year's Eve. I can hardly wait to see how Mr. Clinton and his 'human rights' advocates will deal with such a calamity. Is there any way we can move the timetable up on this event? I understand from Shing that the virus is spreading around the world, as we believed it would."

"I'm afraid not, Keung. As you may recall, the code has a timer built in for New Year's Eve. So, you will just have to wait patiently with the rest of us a few more weeks for this profound event to occur."

"So be it, I suppose. Now, if you will excuse me, I have several day's worth of mail to read. Thank you for stopping by to see me today."

★ ★ ★

On 1 December 1997, Keung called a high-level meeting with Shing, Kong, and some of his staff confidants. "Have all of the electronic firms been contacted to attend our gala New Year's Eve Banquet?" Keung asked one of his staff members.

"Yes, and they all accepted. Those without spouses have agreed to make use of the escort service we offered them. We want to make sure their every need is taken care of."

"Fine. Now, Kong, will you tell us what you plan to say at the banquet when I introduce you? Remember that this could well be the most important speech you have ever made."

Kong stood up and walked to the podium. He took out some notes he prepared and gave a speech to the group, which he said would be the essence of the speech he would give on New Year's Eve.

Kong began by showing the audience samples of the ad that would run the following Monday. He then turned to Shing and praised him for being able to develop such a sophisticated antidote in time to save the world's computers from becoming obsolete. He also praised Shing for developing an antidote that was incapable of being copied, thus assuring a high sales volume for the disks. He next discussed the size of the market for the Tiger Antidote Disks and said he would show each of the CEO's how much money they would make in the first year alone. Kong added at the end that he was honored to be the person on Keung's staff to introduce this program.

"It's not every day a salesman has the opportunity to tell his distributors they stand to make several billion dollars from a single product," he added with a big smile.

"Any comments?" asked Keung. "I think it's a very good pitch."

Keung's staff all agreed.

"I would like Shing and Kong to remain for another subject," Keung said, excusing his staff members. As the staff members filed out of the room, Keung's secretary came in and poured three cups of tea for the next meeting.

"Shing, what is Steven's status now?"

"He is living in the government-housing complex, where he is under twenty-four-hour surveillance. We don't believe he suspects anything, for he's been kept very busy working with Tak on the literature for the marketing plan."

"You two gentlemen should recall that once we are assured the infection has spread, and once there is a substantial demand for Tiger Antidote Disks, I've arranged for Steven to have an unfortunate accident. It will be swift and painless, and the world will be a better place to live in; after all, he has done a very dastardly act. Imagine, infecting all of the world's computers."

"It should take no longer than two or three weeks after the advertisements appear in the press before we have a good feel for the sales potential. Major computer firms will no doubt wish to see demonstrations before they buy disks, and that will take some time. Perhaps we should allow a month," Shing added.

"How do we manage to keep Steven in Beijing for a month after the infection takes place?" Kong asked.

"Why don't we tell him he will receive a Medal of Honor from the chairman—and that the chairman wishes to make sure sales are at a high volume before he gives such a coveted award?" Shing asked.

"That should work," Keung said. "Anyway, Shing, you make sure he is where we can find him at all times. When I place the contract, you will be advised."

In Hong Kong, May Chow sat quietly reading the papers in her apartment. She had to admit to herself that she really did miss Steven, and when he returned, she would tell him that. She was initially assigned only to keep tabs on him, but now she wanted to be with him for very personal reasons. She hoped he would understand, and she hoped he felt the same way about her.

Chapter Forty-Two

In Beijing, the clock struck 11:00 P.M. on New Year's Eve, 31 December 1997. Dishes were being removed from the banquet tables, and the waiters were pouring after-dinner drinks. With the help of an interpreter, Keung Fu Huang, newly appointed chairman of China, introduced and toasted each of his ministry chiefs, their spouses, and their companions. Then he introduced and toasted each of his Hong Kong guests along with their spouses and companions. It had been a gala affair, and Keung was about to have Chou Kong, his ministry chief in charge of business and foreign trade, make an important announcement.

Keung impressed everyone with his grasp of specific knowledge about each of the electronic firms represented at the banquet tables. When he finished, he turned the podium over to Kong.

Kong stood up slowly, first tipping his glass of champagne toward his fellow ministry chiefs and then toward the heads of the Hong Kong electronics firms. He began to speak, and with the help of the interpreter, he made a presentation those in attendance would never ever forget. As it turned out, Kong's presentation would go down in history as a presentation the entire world would never forget!

"Ladies and Gentlemen, it is my pleasure to speak to you this evening. I'm Chou Kong, the ministry chief in charge of business and foreign trade. I'm particularly happy to be able to meet all of the heads of the Hong Kong electronic firms, for you will play an important role in the future of China.

"Tonight I'm pleased to be able to announce a personal computer software product that we in China recently developed and that each of your firms will be permitted to market. The total sales value we expect from this product in the first year of sales alone should exceed HK$20 billion!"

Kong paused and took a drink, while he let the impact of this huge sales number sink in. The guests immediately began chatting with each other, for they could not believe there was such a product opportunity of such large magnitude. Kong continued.

"My good friend, Shing Ling, and his research staff discovered that on this very night at the stroke of midnight, an insidious infection or virus will significantly modify the performance of most of the world's personal computers. This infection has been lying dormant for several months, but it will spring to life at midnight, causing personal computers containing it to slow down markedly. Imagine, all of the users finding their shiny new and fast machines are now slower than the machines they once used five years ago!

"Because Shing's researchers discovered this infection some time ago, they have had time to develop what they call a 'software antidote' that will destroy the infection. It is this antidote that we will offer for sale to every personal computer user in the world, and your firms will be authorized distributors for this antidote disk. I have one such disk in my hand now, and we refer to it as the *Tiger Antidote Disk*. You will no doubt recognize it as being an ordinary 3-1/2-inch floppy disk, but it has a sales value of at least HK$100."

Kong paused again and took another drink. One person in the audience stood up and asked if Kong would take a question from the floor. "Yes, you may ask your question," Kong said.

"If the product is merely a software code on a floppy disk, what keeps users from copying it, thus reducing our sales potential considerably?"

"I'll address that in the remainder of my comments." Kong continued.

"We had the same concern, so our researchers surrounded the antidote code with a protective software shield. If anyone tries to copy the code, the code becomes disabled, and the purchaser will have to purchase yet another disk. Also, once the antidote is used, the disk becomes worthless. As a consequence, it will not be possible for the disk to be passed from user to user in a large corporation. Instead each and every personal computer in the world will need to have a new antidote disk installed, in order to remove the infection.

"We believe the fair market price for each antidote disk is HK$100. So, with more than two hundred million personal computers in the world, that is how we came up with our HK$20 billion sales opportunity. There will be other opportunities for those of you who make personal computers, for you will be the only suppliers, starting tomorrow morning, who will be able to guarantee the delivery of personal computers that are not infected."

Kong had the audience eating out of his hands. The room was so quiet, you could hear a pin drop. He moved to the side of the podium and reached for one of the ad copies. He continued.

"On Monday morning, this ad will appear in periodicals across the world. It announces that China discovered the infection, and it will tell the world how they may purchase one of the antidote disks. We have included the names of all of your firms on our list of authorized distributors."

"When can we take delivery of these disks? It sounds to me like we will be swamped and won't be able to make shipments. How many of the antidote disks will you have in stock ready to go when the ads appear?"

"We anticipated we would need to have more than one hundred million ready for immediate shipment, so during the past several months, we have been stockpiling them. Within an hour after this banquet is over, we can start to ship boxes to your receiving stations.

Ladies and gentlemen, my assistant is going to hand each of you a brochure describing the program in more detail. Included in the brochure is a list summarizing what it means if a computer slows down significantly. You should have no difficulty selling all of the disks you can get, and we do not believe the price of one hundred dollars is exorbitant. Are there any questions?"

"It's almost midnight now. Do you have any demonstrations for us to watch to see how the infection affects a computer?"

"Yes, at the back of the room there are several computers set up for just that purpose. Each one is a high speed Pentium® machine and they are running the popular Nascar 3D game. If you hurry, you will be able to see exactly what happens to the performance of the game at the precise stroke of midnight."

The audience crowded around the machines and watched as the cars whizzed around the track. It was exactly five minutes before midnight. At the moment the clock began to chime, one by one the games on the computers slowed down to a crawl. The cars jerked along the track and the colors were blurred. The sound coming from the speakers was squeaky and sounded like so much gibberish.

"Now, watch as my assistant installs the antidote disks," Kong said.

With the games still operating, the assistant inserted one of the antidote disks into the A-drive on each computer and pressed "enter." Within a few seconds, the computer screens returned to the normal speed being displayed before the clock struck midnight. The audience was very impressed and they began to chat amongst themselves.

"Could we all return to our tables now?" Keung asked. "Ladies and gentlemen, I want to thank you all for attending tonight's affair. I hope you will read carefully the material we have given you and will officially sign up to be one of our authorized distributors for the antidote product. If you have any more questions, please stay and talk with either Kong or Shing. I must take my leave now, for I'm an old man and should not be up past my bedtime."

The audience clapped and praised Keung as he left the banquet hall. He was indeed a very shrewd businessman, and they were now very happy that Hong Kong had been taken over by China.

Chapter Forty-Three

New Year's Day, 1 January 1998, was a Thursday, so most companies had scheduled a four-day holiday for their employees. More than fifty million personal computers were in homes around the world, so as families woke up to enjoy their holiday, sooner or later a family member would turn on the computer to play some game or surf the Internet. Then, sooner or later that family member would discover the computer was not at all behaving well. In fact, Steven's infection spread so well over the Internet that more than ninety-eight percent of personal computers in homes were infected.

By evening, neighbors were talking with neighbors, comparing notes, and they all discovered they had the same problem. Their high-speed computers were all operating dismally.

"My games are almost useless today. How are yours?"

"Mine are also defunct. My wife even complained when she tried to write a letter to her parents. The computer was fast enough for her word processor to work, but when she pressed the print button, it took almost ten minutes to print one page. She threatened to use our typewriter, for she was tired of waiting."

"My new Power PC™ machine seems to be just fine," said one neighbor. "I always told you guys Pentium® machines suck," he laughed.

In Hong Kong, Steven's father was watching the evening CNN newscast. The newscaster announced he had a late-breaking story. "This is Rick Smitherton in the CNN news center in Atlanta. We are receiving numerous reports from viewers indicating that their home personal computers have slowed down to a crawl. We have set up a special CNN hotline for you to call if your computer is experiencing such behavior. We have Sue Ricardo, Microsoft's communications manager, on the phone, and she wants to make a comment."

"This is Sue Ricardo in Redmond, Washington. I want your viewers to know that a team of Microsoft engineers has been spending all day trying to analyze what is going on. It seems that the computer's CPU is only reacting to every hundredth instruction, and yet the computer produces correct answers to arithmetic problems. Our engineers must admit they have never seen anything like this. On Monday, Microsoft plans to organize a task force, jointly with Intel, to investigate the cause of this phenomenon."

"Sue, could something like this be caused by some form of a virus?"

"Our engineers scanned their hard disk and memory, using Microsoft's latest virus scan software, and they were not able to detect anything. They examined the amount of empty space left on their hard disk and it seemed to be normal. A lot of complex viruses take up extra room on the hard disk, but there did not appear to be any such virus present. At least none that we know about."

"Sue, some of our listeners told us they own late-model Apple computers, and they are not experiencing any problems. Do you think that offers a clue to this mystery?"

"We heard that from some of our neighbors. We plan to investigate that as well."

"Thanks for your comments. We all hope your task force can find out the cause of this. Is it fair to say that computers in the workplace will behave the same way?"

"Yes. All of the machines we checked in our offices seem to be similarly affected."

"That's about all we have at this time. Again, if you are experiencing a computer slow-down, call the number on your screen."

"I wish Steven was here to hear this. I'm sure he could shed some light on what could cause computers to slow down," Steven's father said.

"Yes, dear. Steven is brilliant. He should volunteer to be on the Microsoft task force."

By Friday morning, the entire world was aware that some insidious infection or virus was plaguing home computers, and MIS managers dreaded what they would find when they went back to work on

Monday. Some company executives went to their offices on Saturday, where they discovered the same slow-down phenomenon.

In Haikou, CT and Miu watched the same news report, and they were ecstatic.

"It's obvious all of those home computers were infected from the Internet. The Hong Kong web site worked fantastically," Miu said.

"That's right. Wait until people return to work on Monday. They will find the same problems. Miu, I need to leave now and go to the plant. I want to personally supervise the shipment of antidote disks to the distributors. Do you realize we have firm orders now for more than a hundred thousand of them? This is just the beginning of a fantastic business for China. We never had such large orders for CD records."

★ ★ ★

In Beijing, Steven sat quietly in the cafeteria of the government compound, eating his meager meal. He wanted to return to Hong Kong so he could be with May, but Tsi informed him the chairman wanted to award him personally for all of his good work.

"Why doesn't he award me now and let me return right away?" Steven asked.

"The chairman is a conservative man. He wants to be sure your infection has spread throughout the world before he gives you such a coveted medal."

"Can I at least call May on the phone and wish her a Happy New Year?"

"I'm sure I can arrange that. Come to my office and use my phone."

In Hong Kong, May Chou was lonely. She had hoped Steven would return in time to enjoy a New Year's Eve Party with her. She was required to attend the party given every year by the embassy, and was supposed to enjoy herself, but in her heart she longed for Steven.

"Can I have this dance, my little turtledove?" a fat politician asked her.

"I suppose so," May said, not wanting to offend the man, for he was an important man in the Chinese government hierarchy.

"And afterwards, can I take you to your apartment, where we will not be disturbed?" he asked.

"No. I'm supposed to meet someone there. It would not do if I came home with you." The politician frowned, stopped dancing with her, and stormed off the dance floor.

"Something is wrong with May," he said to himself. "Last year she obliged my advances without even a whimper."

Steven's call did little to cheer her up, for he also sounded so despondent. He asked her why she thought the chairman wanted him to hang around for a few more weeks, and she couldn't understand why either.

May decided to call Shing on Monday morning to see if he knew when Steven would be returning. She would have to make up some excuse for calling, because as far as Shing was concerned, he had done her a favor by not requiring her to spy on Steven anymore.

On Monday morning, corporations around the world found themselves literally shut down. MIS directors were being called into emergency meetings, for their computer centers were operating at a fraction of their normal speed. Individuals attempting to send e-mail messages found it was quicker to leave their offices and walk down the hall and speak directly to the recipient.

Secretaries initially were not harmed by the slow-down, but they soon found the print queues were enormous, for the networks had been designed to share workloads from fast machines.

When corporate executives read the *Wall Street Journal*, they noticed the full-page color ad with the smiling face of the chairman of China displayed prominently in the center.

"What do you make of this?" one executive asked his MIS director.

"I was about to tell you, sir. Our computers are all operating at a snail's pace today. If what this ad says is true, these bastards have known about a virus that would cause such a phenomenon, and they have kept it to themselves long enough for them to develop an antidote."

"Do you think the commies are behind this thing?"

"It sure looks like it. How else could they magically come up with an antidote at just the right time when it is needed?"

"How much do they want for the antidote disk?"

"The ad doesn't say, but they list one of the Hong Kong distributors we often deal with. I think I'll give them a jingle and find out how much they want for it."

All across the world, the ad was being read with similar reactions. Everyone assumed immediately the Chinese caused the infection, for no one believed they had the technical skill to develop an antidote for a virus that eluded detection using state-of-the-art virus scanners.

At Microsoft, a team of skilled software diagnostics engineers, working with a team of CPU designers from Intel, began their arduous task of analyzing why computers were slowing down. Their mission was to find out what caused it and to suggest an antidote. Marketing people from both firms were beginning to worry, for as long as the personal computer world was in such an uproar, it was quite probable that sales for new software and new computers would come to a screeching halt.

In the board room of Apple Computer, the CEO and his marketing staff held a special meeting. "Do you mean to tell me all of the world's personal computers are running slow this morning, with the exception of Apple computers?"

"That's right, sir. Even the Pentium® machines in our lab are all running slow, but the Power PC™ machines sitting next to them are running just fine. Our engineers are trying to figure out why that is."

"It sounds like we have an opportunity to really blow our horn here, if we could only find a reason why our machines are clean," one marketing executive stated.

"That's correct, but we sure don't want the world to think we caused this mess. We are not to make any official comments to anyone. Do you understand? At least not until our engineers give us a solid answer."

In the lab, Alan Smith, VP of engineering, was meeting with his engineers. As the group formed around the conference table, Alan could not help but remember his last meeting with Steven, where they joked about slowing down all of the IBM-compatible personal computers in order to give the Apple machines a performance edge.

"Could this somehow be Steven's work?" Alan asked himself. "But how in the world could he have spread his software over such a wide geographic area?"

The Year of The Tiger

At the Las Alamos, New Mexico, government research facility, a staff of researchers sat in a conference room waiting for their director to join them.

"Good morning, gentlemen," Dr. Schilling said as he entered the room. "What's this I hear about some kind of slow-down virus? Do you mean to tell me our new 200-Mhz Pentium® machines are acting up as well?"

"'Acting up' is a poor phrase. They are performing like the old 486 machines we used five years ago. We get the correct answers when we feed the computers our scientific problems, but we have to take a coffee break each time we do so, for the calculation times are incredibly long."

"What do you suppose is causing this problem?"

"Have you seen the ad in the *New York Times*? Here, take a look at it."

Dr. Schilling scanned the ad and turned to his fellow colleagues. "It sounds to me like the Chinese may have caused this so they could capitalize on having antidotes for sale immediately. What do you guys think?"

"We agree. We decided to buy one of their antidote disks to see if it really works. My secretary called up one of the distributors listed in the ad, and we are having one shipped to us. It should be here this afternoon."

"Let me know if it works. By the way, what did it cost?"

"A hundred dollars. The distributor gave us some kind of crap that we had better not try to copy it, for if we did, he claimed it would self-destruct!"

"That sounds like a good story. Anyway, let me know how it works."

The disk arrived at 3:30 P.M. in its little plastic case with a one-page instruction sheet. The engineers all gathered around the technician as he placed it in the drive slot of his computer.

"Why don't we make a dozen copies before we try to use it?" one man asked.

"Good idea. John, can you try and copy it?"

When the copy command was enabled, the screen message said emphatically if the disk was copied, it would fail to perform the antidote function properly. "Do you think we should believe this message?"

"I guess we should, at least for now. Once we apply the antidote to see if it works, then we should try again to copy it."

The technician loaded the disk in the computer and ran the program. When the technician ran a bench-mark test, the computer was fast again! "Let me try it in my computer," another engineer said.

The technician loaded the disk, the drive whirred, but this time a message appeared, saying each antidote disk was only good for disinfecting one machine. The message included instructions for purchasing a second disk.

"Damn, that really sucks. Let's try copying it."

When the technician clicked on the copy command, a message appeared that said it was illegal to copy, and since the disk had been used, it was no longer any good. Instructions for purchasing a new disk were again provided.

In laboratories all across the world, purchasers of antidote disks were experiencing the same results. MIS directors, who normally were against making illegal copies of software, figured that copying antidote disks was fair game, since an illegal virus caused them to be required. However, when they tried to copy the disk, the message they received on their screen really pissed them off.

"We're going to have to buy one antidote disk for each and every computer in our facility," one MIS director stated. "Damn, that's more than a thousand disks, which will cost us a hundred thousand dollars. That is absolute blackmail! And how do we know the virus won't emerge again next week or next month?"

The Microsoft/Intel task force ordered a couple of the disks and found the same results. They found if they ran a directory tree, just to see what was contained on the antidote disk, the disk would also not perform properly as an antidote.

"This is the most insidiously clever piece of software I've ever seen," one engineer told the team leader. "I'm afraid we have a real serious problem here, for sales are going to drop if we don't find a way to calm the waters soon."

"Let's see if our software is somehow contaminated," the team leader told his engineers. "First, set up a number of new computer systems that do not have any software loaded. Then load an early version of Windows 95™ to see if they run okay. In a second group of machines, load our most recent version and see if they still run okay. After that, load an early version of our office suite and repeat with our latest version of the office suite."

"Sounds good. We should have those tests completed by lunch time."

"If it turns out some of our software contains the virus, I'll have to recommend to the management that we purge our entire worldwide inventory, even though that will cost the company tens of millions of dollars."

On Monday morning, May Chow went to work as usual at the Chinese embassy in Hong Kong. The charge d'affaires greeted her and laughingly told her that her computer would be very slow this morning. He gave her an antidote disk to use, which he said would correct the problem.

"May, do you realize how many computers have slowed down this morning?"

"I suppose many millions of them. Is this disk the product Steven developed for China to sell?"

"Yes, and according to some of the Hong Kong distributors, their phones are ringing off the hooks this morning. They have never experienced such a demand for any product."

"And all I need to do is insert this disk in my drive and press 'enter'?"

"That's right. Just like giving your computer the equivalent of a flu shot," he smiled.

"Wing, I need to catch up on some of my paperwork, so if you don't have anything for me now, I think I'll shut my door and concentrate on getting some reports written this morning."

"That's fine. I have to go to a meeting downtown as well. I'll see you this afternoon."

May closed her door and picked up the red phone on her desk. She then dialed a number she only used on special occasions. "Hello, this is Shing Ling. What can I do for you?"

"Ah, Shing, this is May Chow. I wanted to wish you a happy new year."

"Yes, May, it is good to hear from you again."

"I wondered how the program is progressing. I found my computer to be running slow this morning, along with many millions of others."

"That's right, May. Our program is very successful. Our distributors have sold more than a hundred thousand disks so far, and this is only the first day since people are back in their offices. I've ordered CT to increase his production, because it looks like we will sell even more than we initially believed we would."

"I'm very glad. I suppose Steven is very happy about this success, as well."

"Yes, he certainly is."

"Speaking of Steven, will he be returning soon? If he is, I will need to rearrange my social schedule."

There was a long pause on the phone as Shing decided what to tell her. Finally, he answered, "May, you will not need to be concerned any more with Steven. I'll be sending you your next assignment in a few days. In the meantime, why don't you take a few days off and enjoy Hong Kong's nightclubs, or take some scenic trips around the country?"

"Do you mean he will not be returning to Hong Kong?"

"Like I told you, you will no longer need to concern yourself with Steven," Shing said, sounding a bit irritated.

"I understand," May said. "Good-bye."

Chapter Forty-Four

By the end of the first week of January, computer stocks dipped by more than forty percent, which caused the stock market as a whole to drop to a five-year low. Apple Computer shares actually rose to a five-year high, even though there was no public statement from Apple regarding why none of their machines were contaminated. MIS directors in major corporations were begrudgingly conceding they must purchase antidote disks for each and every machine in their company. If they didn't, their internal computer users were going to buy them anyway, for they wanted their machines to return to the performance they had grown accustomed to. After all, a hundred dollars didn't seem like a lot of money to pay to put things back the way they were before.

Major software firms were in a panic, because sales for their bread-and-butter products dropped to almost zero. Microsoft's task force was no closer to an understanding of what caused the slowdowns, let alone how to produce an antidote. Each time they tried to diagnose what was on the antidote disk, they kept getting the horrid little messages telling them they had done something evil by trying to copy the disk.

"We found where the virus is coming from," one of the task force members stated one afternoon, after running exhaustive tests on the array of personal computers in the lab. "When we load the latest revision of Windows95™ in a new computer, the computer immediately slows down, whereas when we load the original revision, the computer is not harmed. If we remove the latest version from a contaminated machine, and install an earlier version, the infection remains."

"Does this mean every computer in the world that uses our latest version of Windows95™ software became infected because our software was infected?"

"It looks that way. Of course we have only sampled a dozen or so copies produced over the past year, but each one we tested contaminated our test computers."

"If you say the contamination remains, you must be running out of computers to use for more testing."

"That's for sure. We have reformatted the hard drives, and still the contamination remains, even if we load old Windows™ version 3.1. I've never seen anything like it."

"There is one silver lining in this otherwise doomsday cloud," one of the engineers said to the team leader. "Once you apply an antidote disk to a given computer, the infection goes away. But more important, when I reload such a machine with what I know to be infected software, the infection does not stick. It's like the antidote provides protection against future sickness."

"That's reassuring to hear. You should get the word out on all of the bulletin boards and see if others are finding that same result."

On 15 January 1998, John Toliver attended a high-level meeting at the office of the Advanced Research Projects Administration in Washington, D.C. CEOs from the major computer software and hardware firms were in attendance, besides the usual government officials.

"Gentlemen, we have a world crisis on our hands," the head of ARPA said as he stood at the end of the conference table, puffing on his pipe. "The information we have indicates that virtually every personal computer in the world has picked up the infection that causes their speed to drop by inordinate amounts. To date, none of our research or engineering labs have come up with any solution, other than for all of us to pay the bloody Chinese their hundred dollars for an antidote that is eluding all of our great minds.

"I've invited Mr. Toliver to come to this meeting, since he has recent experience dealing with the Chinese on technology matters. John, would you please address this group and tell them what you know about this matter?"

John stood up, opened his notebook, and began to speak. "Gentlemen, about two years ago, my organization was responsible for breaking up what we called the Chinese CD record piracy activity.

The Year of The Tiger

Although we never proved it, we believed then, and we still believe now, that the Chinese government was directly responsible for funding the development of, and sanctioning the production of, illegal CD records that flooded the market.

"During our investigation, I visited a plant in Haikou that is used to produce CD-Rs, which are blank CDs that software companies such as yours use to record software programs on for sale to manufacturers and users of personal computers. We always suspected the plant in Haikou produced CD records as well, but were never able to get the goods on them. We do know for a fact that they did produce CD-Rs, and I believe all of the firms represented here have purchased them for some time. Is that right?"

The CEOs of the software firms all nodded their heads. One of them stood up and asked, "Are you trying to tell us the Chinese may have contaminated the CD-Rs they sold us?"

"That's certainly possible," John said. "Is there any way your engineers can analyze the blank CD-Rs to see if they contain any funny code sequences that are not supposed to be present?"

"We do that at incoming inspection," another CEO said. "But maybe we need to look more closely. My God, if that's what's been happening, the Chinese bastards have been feeding us this infection for a couple of years, waiting for just this moment to hold us hostage with their damned little red hundred-dollar floppies. But where would they have gotten the technology to infect computers in such a sophisticated way, let alone develop such a clever antidote code?"

"Let me try and answer that," a tall man in the back of the room said, as he stood up and walked toward the podium. "My name is Alan Smith, and I'm VP of engineering at Apple Computer. I came to this meeting without a formal invitation, for I believe I know the root cause for this disaster. As many of you know, this virus is not affecting Apple computers. As a consequence, we at Apple have been trying to understand the reason for that. I came today to tell you what we have found to date, which I believe will shed some light on this subject.

"I believe I know who originated this insidious virus. If I'm right, we may be able to clean up this mess in short order." Alan proceeded to tell the audience about the Microsoft/Apple copyright case and, in particular, the role that Steven Lee, an employee of Apple at the time, played in the matter.

"Steven was a very bright and clever software engineer," Alan said. "In order for Apple to analyze whether Microsoft copied any code from Apple to make their Windows™ software work, Steven designed a set of test-sequence utilities that slowed down IBM-compatible personal computers by as much as a thousand times, so he could watch execution sequences in slow motion. The symptoms that all PCs have today appear to be identical to the symptoms that PCs would demonstrate whenever Steven would load his test sequences onto their hard drive. They would run incredibly slow, but would not skip a beat, meaning the computer would continue to work reliably, only very slow.

"In addition, Steven was very clever about how he loaded his test sequences into the computer he was testing. He would give his code sequences the same names as the executable files in the Windows™ operating system software. Then, by loading his files as hidden files, it was impossible for anyone to see that they are on the hard disk. That would explain the difficulty the Microsoft/Intel task force is having, don't you think?

"In summary, gentlemen, I believe Steven is somehow involved in this matter, for he possesses the ability to produce what we are all struggling with now. My belief is that somehow Steven convinced the Chinese to spread his code sequences around the world, and I'm sure he developed the antidote for them. If he hadn't included the little wrinkle that Apple computers not be infected, I would probably have never thought about him. I guess he thought he was doing Apple a big favor by excluding them from his hit list. However, we at Apple Computer have made a corporate decision not to exploit this matter."

Alan continued to tell the audience about how Steven had taken it to heart when Apple lost the case, and how he threatened to get back somehow or other at the system. The audience sat in stunned silence, when Alan finished and sat down.

"Gentlemen, if Mr. Smith is correct, we may have our most important lead so far. I'm going to ask you, sir, to come with me to the Justice Department after this meeting and tell them your story. Mr. Toliver, I would like to ask you to come with us as well, for I believe what you have to say on this matter is of vital importance. Meanwhile, would the rest of you, who are normally at each other's throats in the marketplace, please remain here and work out a program for careful analysis of the CD-Rs you have been receiving from China. I'll just bet they are full of all sorts of little red bugs or something."

★ ★ ★

"Hello May. This is Steven."

"Steven, I've been thinking about you all day and wondering how I could contact you. Where are you calling from?"

"I slipped out of the government compound and found a phone booth in a local pharmacy. The Chinese seem to want me to stay here quite a bit longer. It has to do with something about awarding me with a special merit of honor. Hell, I've been awarded enough with the money they placed in my bank account. I told them I wanted to return, but they keep giving me the runaround. Do you have any idea why they would treat me like this?"

"Steven, your life may be in danger," May blurted out, realizing she had just broken every rule in her communist spy manual.

"What do you mean?"

"You have to trust me on this," May said. "I have information that indicates the Chinese plan to take your life. They believe you will become greedy and try to sell the antidote code to other countries. They were pissed when you asked for such a high commission rate from the sale of the antidotes."

"How do you know all of this?" Steven said, not wanting to believe what he was hearing.

"You will have to trust me on this," May said. "Steven, can you tell me the street address where you are staying?" Steven told her as best he could. He told her each morning he went jogging in a local park near the compound before eating breakfast.

"Does anyone look after you when you go jogging?"

"Presumably not, but the past few times I've gone, I've seen the same couple of guys pushing their bicycles on the trail beside the jogging path. I wonder if they are there to be sure I don't take off somewhere."

"I'm sure they are. Listen, Steven, you must believe me. The same guys who gave you the great deal and all of the cash in Switzerland are about to place a contract on your head. I'm going to have to help get you out of the country."

"How are you going to be able to do that?"

"Steven, don't ask so many questions."

May outlined a plan in which she would request a short vacation to fly to Beijing, ostensibly to visit her aging aunt. She would arrive in Beijing the next morning. She told Steven he should forego his daily jogging in the morning, and instead he should plan to jog just before dinner. She would rent a red sports car and would pick him up at the end of the trail at five o'clock sharp.

"What do we do then?" Steven asked.

"I'll work on those details from this end. You should return now so you won't arouse any suspicion. Remember that you must go jogging at the specified time tomorrow evening, and you must bring your visa and passport with you. Leave your other personal belongings, since you don't want anyone to know you plan to split. I love you, Steven. I can't wait to see you again. Good-bye for now."

Steven hung up, visibly shaken. He hurried back into the compound and went directly to his room, where he plopped down on the bed. How was it that May knew so much? Could he trust her? Could he trust anyone? He stayed in his room all day, not daring to leave, not even to go to the cafeteria to eat his daily ration of tasteless Chinese food.

"There's a man named Chi on the phone for you," Keung's secretary told him over the office intercom.

"Thank you. I'll take the call in my office."

"Yes, Chi, I've been waiting for your call. The matter we have been talking about is now ready for implementation. I would suggest it be done tomorrow evening, after he has retired. I'll see to it the usual receptionists and guards at the compound have the night off. It should then be easy for you to gain entrance and kidnap him. Please be swift and painless. I never want to hear from you again on this matter."

"Of course not. Will the funds be at the usual place?"

"Yes. Your usual fee is there; in addition, a nice bonus will be sent to you if you accomplish your mission without any embarrassing questions being asked by the Beijing police."

"Good-bye. It will be done."

Byron Westmoreland of the United States Justice Department had just been briefed. He stood up and paced the floor behind his large mahogany desk. "Mr. Smith, you believe this man Steven Lee is capable of producing a code that would slow down all of the computers. You also believe he may have a couple of screws loose when it comes to the matter of the Apple/Microsoft copyright litigation."

"Yes, he certainly seemed to want to get even. I've talked with several of the engineers who attended his going-away dinner, and he clearly wanted to get back at the system in a big way."

"Do you know what happened to him after he left Apple?"

"I believe he first went to Hong Kong to visit his parents. Then I believe he returned to the States to work for a company called ASV, which is in Fremont, California. Some of my engineers told me he got canned there shortly after he joined. They lost touch with him after that."

"John, I'm going to ask your boss if you can work with one of my operatives on this matter. It could well be that this man Steven is the culprit. If we can connect him with the Chinese, we can blow the whistle on this whole deal. It really pisses me off that the Chinese have so blatantly claimed their superior R&D personnel have been the only ones able to develop an antidote for this virus. If we can prove these bastards were the cause of the virus, I'll bet the court of world opinion will blast them right off of the map."

"I'll be glad to participate," John said. "And, by the way, I recall on one of my trips to Hong Kong I sat beside a young fellow who also called himself Steven Lee. He was going to visit his parents. I wonder if he could be the same person who worked at Apple? I'll bet he's the same guy!"

Chapter Forty-Five

May Chow boarded Chinese Airlines flight 135, which was scheduled to arrive in Beijing at noon. She had no difficulty getting time off, for Shing had already informed the charge d'affaires he wanted her to rest up in preparation for her next assignment.

She brought two lightweight suitcases with her; one containing her personal belongings and the second one containing some clothes she purchased for Steven. Since she worked for the Chinese government, she did not need to have her luggage inspected upon arrival.

Within an hour after landing, she was able to drive from the airport in a rental car to a small back-street hotel near the government compound where Steven was staying. She checked into the hotel under an assumed name and went to her room to wait until it was time to make her move.

May was a realist. She knew once she was spotted picking up Steven, she would be on the most-wanted list by the Chinese People's Government, and her papers would no longer carry any weight. Therefore, before leaving Hong Kong, she paid a man she knew a lot of money to draw up some false papers for both her and Steven. She would need to change her identity as well, so while she waited in her room, she bleached her hair and cut it very short and close to her face.

"There, now even Steven will not know who I am," she thought.

Her plan was for them to drive all night long, heading toward the coast. One of her friends owned a dock on the Gulf of Chihli, and he could be persuaded to provide them with boat passage to the west side of South Korea. From there, they would make their way to Seoul and from there to freedom.

At 4:45 in the afternoon, May checked out of the hotel and loaded her bags in her rented car. She drove by the government compound building and past the park where the jogging trail was located. She was a bit early, but she wanted to do a quick dry run to see how best to leave the area, once Steven was in her car.

After a couple of trips around the block, she started to watch the trail for any sign of him. As she passed the compound, she saw him emerging from the side door. He was wearing his familiar jogging outfit, and as usual he started running immediately once he was outside. She noticed two other men leave shortly afterwards and they were clearly following him. They were pushing their bicycles and they proceeded to the riding trail that was to the left of the jogging trail. May sized up the situation and decided to intercept Steven at the very end of his trail, because the bicyclists would be several yards away from him by then.

"Do you want a ride?" she yelled at him, as he came into view over the crest of the trail.

"I sure do," Steven said, jumping into her car.

May sped off, watching the two cyclists turn and run toward a phone booth on the side of the park. "Did you know you were being followed?" she asked.

"I saw my buddies, as usual. I don't know how they knew I changed my schedule today, but they certainly found out somehow."

May leaned over and kissed Steven on the cheek. "We have a lot to talk about, but first we have to get the hell out of town and fast. How do you like my hairdo? Is it true blondes have more fun?"

John Toliver and Derek Thorpe from the Justice Department arrived in Hong Kong the same night Steven and May were leaving Beijing. They checked into the Hong Kong Hilton and met in the lobby to discuss what their itinerary would be the next day.

Before coming to Hong Kong, John and Derek had met with the management of ASV to find out why Steven had been fired. At that meeting, they were told about the investigation Lamont's detective agency had undertaken, so they met with Lamont the same afternoon. He revealed to them all he knew, and said he assumed Steven was still in Hong Kong fooling around with the Chinese spy, May Chow.

"According to the gum shoe, Lamont, Steven is tied in with the Chinese government, at least through this gal, May. We need to go see her first thing tomorrow morning, before we visit Steven's parents," Derek said.

"That makes sense. It's even possible Steven is shacked up with her, and if so, we can nail him and find out what's going on."

"I think we should also interrogate the charge d'affaires at the embassy," Derek said. "He introduced me once to his secretary, whose name was May Chow. I wonder if she's the same person?"

"Okay, let's get some dinner and hit the hay. The jet lag will get us if we don't get some rest."

At 12:00 P.M., Chi and two of his buddies arrived at the government compound. They were dressed in black pants with black leather jackets, and they wore stocking caps so they would be indistinguishable in the night. They found the lobby deserted as expected, as they made their way quickly down the hall to the room where Steven was staying. As they approached the door, they pulled out handkerchiefs that were doused with chloroform. When they pulled open the door, they rushed into the room, expecting to have to hold Steven down. Instead, they found the room empty, except for some of his personal belongings in the closet.

"Where in hell is he?" Chi said under his breath. "I was told he retires early each night. Now what are we supposed to do?"

Outside the compound, Chi placed a call, using the phone booth near the park. The person he called was not at all pleased, and Chi had to keep telling him it was not his fault. Steven simply had vanished.

May and Steven drove to the outskirts of Beijing, and they parked their car in a parking garage near a hotel complex. Across the street was another car rental agency, so May went in and rented an old Russian car, using her new identity papers. In a few moments they were again on their way, feeling a lot less conspicuous.

May asked Steven to drive so she would be able to fill him in on everything. They had a long drive ahead of them to the coast, but they both felt it would be better if they did not try to stay at some roadside

The Year of The Tiger

hotel. By morning, the authorities would certainly be looking for them. May explained everything to Steven, including the fact that initially she had been assigned to be his watchdog. She repeated over and over again that she was in love with him, and she wanted to run off with him to wherever they decided, once they could get out of the country.

"Do you really believe Shing or Kong want me dead?" Steven kept asking her.

"I'm absolutely certain."

"If that is the case, we need to do two things," Steven said. "We need to get out of the country and into Switzerland, where my money is, and I need to blow the whistle on China regarding the mess the world's computers are in."

"How can you do that?"

"Once we find a safe, secure place to live, I can get on the Internet and provide the world with my antidote for free. In addition, I'll tell the whole world the truth about how China has duped them."

"One thing at a time, Steven," May said. "Let's first get out of the country in one piece."

"That's a great idea."

In Hong Kong, Derek and John had breakfast with Jules, who was Lamont's local man. Jules told them Steven lived in a high-rise near the wharf, but he hadn't seen him since he had been taken off the case. He said May Chow was indeed a Chinese spy who functioned using the cover of the secretary to the charge d'affaires in the embassy.

John and Derek arrived at May's apartment and were told by the manager she left for a two-week vacation to visit her aunt in Beijing. "Sounds like another spy mission to me," John said.

From there they went to the high-rise building where Steven lived, and were told by the manager that Steven was on an extended trip and had been gone for more than three months. "How does he make payments for his rent while he is gone?"

"Each month a check arrives by registered mail from Switzerland. I believe he does his banking there."

"I guess we should go visit his parents now," Derek said.

Betty Lou answered the bell when it rang. "Who is it?" she said.

"We are representing the U.S. Justice Department, ma'am. We have some questions for you, if you could spare us a few minutes."

Betty Lou let them in and offered them some tea. Ming was not yet home from work, so Betty Lou felt a bit threatened by these two men. But their papers seemed to be in order.

"Mrs. Lee, when was the last time you saw your son, Steven?"

"I guess about four months ago. He is so busy he often takes off and doesn't stop in and see us for months at a time. Why do you ask?"

"We have reason to believe he is somehow involved in the personal computer fiasco that is going on in the world today. I'm sure you must know what I'm talking about."

"Do you mean the infection that seems to slow everything down? Do you think my Steven is somehow responsible for that?"

"We aren't sure. We just want to question him. Do you know where he went on his recent business trip?"

"No. He only told us he would be gone for two or three months."

"Does he still see a woman named May Chow?"

"Yes he does. She's such a lovely thing. Say, why don't you ask her if she knows where he is? They seem to be very close these days. My husband and I hope Steven will settle down and marry her. She is so very nice and gentle."

"Ma'am, are we speaking about the same person? The May Chow we are referring to is a notorious Chinese spy who works in the Chinese embassy."

"Oh my. That can't possibly be the same person."

"Did Steven meet her in the Chinese embassy?"

"Why, yes, I believe so, but it just can't be the same person."

"Ma'am, we are going to leave you these cards in case you need to contact us. Again, we only want to talk to Steven about certain things. We are not accusing him of doing anything wrong. We just want to talk to him. We would appreciate knowing if he contacts you."

When they left, Betty Lou was visibly shaking. She knew Steven was working for the Chinese government. Why did these men want to speak with him? Was it possible Steven was somehow mixed up in this computer mess?

"I wish Ming would come home," she said to herself. She poured herself another cup of tea and sat on the sofa with tears forming in her eyes.

Chapter Forty-Six

Keung was livid. Steven had somehow escaped and was nowhere to be found. He left his belongings, so it was clearly a prearranged escape. Someone must have tipped him off, for he was picked up and whisked away before Chi and his gang arrived to take care of him.

"Shing, I have bad news for you," Keung said. "Our friend, Steven, has somehow slipped from our grasp, and his whereabouts are not known. I must ask you again, do you think it possible he has made a deal with some other foreign government?"

"I don't see how that could be possible. As you know, my operative in Hong Kong, May Chow, has been keeping watch over him for many months before he came to Beijing to help out the Marketing Department, and he certainly has not had the opportunity to make such a deal while living here with us."

"Would you please contact May and see what she knows."

"Of course. I'll do so immediately."

Shing picked up the red phone and dialed the embassy. He was answered by Ming, who informed him May had taken a week off to visit her aunt in Beijing.

"You fool, May has no such aunt," Shing screamed in the phone. "She is a war orphan and does not even know who her parents are, let alone who her aunt is."

"Why would she tell me such a story?" Ming asked.

"I have no idea, but if she calls in, you had better try and find out."

Shing called the airport and confirmed the flight number May had taken. He then contacted the car rental agency in Beijing and found she rented a car matching the description of the car Steven had climbed into.

"Damn, she has defected with Steven," Shing said out loud. "Keung is going to have my head for trusting her. The young fool must have fallen in love with Steven, and I was the one who told her she would never see Steven again. Keung will really have my head when he finds out about that."

★ ★ ★

Steven and May reached their destination at four in the morning. The drive had been uneventful, for there were few cars on the road. They drove well under the speed limit to avoid being stopped by the police.

"You said we are going to visit your uncle?" Steven asked.

"He is not my real uncle. He is a man who befriended me when I was in an orphanage many years ago, and I've always referred to him as my uncle. His wife, whom I've always called my aunt, died a few years ago. Since then, he lives alone near the seashore."

"Uncle Ming, can you hear me? It is May Chow, whom you have not seen in many years. I'm sorry to awaken you so early."

The door opened a crack, and then opened wide when Ming recognized her. "When did you become a blonde?" he asked. "At first I did not recognize you. And who is this with you?"

"His name is Steven," May said. "We are both very tired and need a place to stay for a day or two. Tomorrow I'll tell you what this is all about."

Uncle Ming told them to sleep in the loft, where he had an old bed with a real goose-down mattress. As a consequence, when the two of them fell asleep, they rolled toward each other and slept in each other's arms all night. They did not wake until noon the next day, and were famished when they came down from the loft to have breakfast.

When Keung heard the story about how May Chow defected, he was all over Shing about it. "When are you going to learn never to trust a pretty face? Why did you have to tell her anything regarding his return? Damn you, Shing. Do you realize if Steven escapes, he will try to get back at us? He will surely sell the antidote to others out of spite."

"Let me regain my honor by being in charge of the manhunt to find them," Shing pleaded.

"Okay, but I don't want to see your face again until he is in our custody."

In Hong Kong, John and Derek returned to the townhouse to question Steven's parents again. "You should understand we want to question Steven about the computer fiasco, for we have reason to believe he has played some part in it. It seems he may be working for the Chinese government, since he took a flight to Beijing almost four months ago and there is no record of him ever returning. What kind of work is he doing for the Chinese?"

Ming and Betty Lou spent long hours discussing what they would do or say if they were interrogated again. They decided they should tell all they knew. "Steven only told us he sold the Chinese some kind of a software product that would make China become the world's leader in software for personal computers."

John and Derek looked at each other. Steven was behind the computer deal after all! "Can you sketch for us the times and places he has visited since he began to work for the Chinese?"

Ming told them all he knew, including the two trips Steven made to Haikou. John was now absolutely sure the plant there was somehow responsible for producing the virus and distributing it. After a few more routine questions, John and Derek left.

"We have our man. Now if we can only catch him when he returns."

★ ★ ★

May and Steven smelled the food cooking. They jumped up and quickly dressed and climbed down from their loft. Uncle Ming was cooking eggs with noodles and chicken dumplings.

"When did you learn how to cook?" asked May, as she cleaned her plate.

"I've always liked to cook. When my wife was still alive, she let me work in the kitchen whenever I wanted to."

"That was certainly the best food I've had in a long time," Steven said, thinking about the bland diet he received in the government compound.

"Now, what are you two up to?" Ming asked.

May told Uncle Ming most of the story, leaving out certain key elements she felt he shouldn't know, in case authorities were to question him in the future.

"We need to book passage on a steamer heading for South Korea," May said. "Do you still have any connections down on the wharf?"

"I'll see what I can do. Meanwhile, why don't you two relax here and mind the chickens and pigs for me. I should be back in about an hour."

In town, Ming went to the headquarters of the shipping company he used to work for, and strolled into the office of the man responsible for scheduling foreign shipments.

"When is the next ship leaving for South Korea?" Ming asked.

"Tomorrow morning at 9:00 A.M. Do you want a lift?" the man asked, laughing. He and Ming had worked together for twenty years and they were always joshing about this or that.

"Not me, but I have a niece and her friend who need to bum a ride. Is that possible?"

"Anything is possible. Are they on the lam, or are they just seeking a cheap trip?"

"No comment. For your information, they are in need of cheap transportation."

Ming and his friend had always promised each other that whenever their dealings were the least bit shady, they would just wink and proceed.

John and Derek faxed their respective bosses the news that they were sure Steven was behind the computer fiasco. They said they would hang around Hong Kong a bit longer looking for May Chow, to see if she could corroborate their beliefs.

Meanwhile, in the U.S., sales of the antidote disks were booming. Even Manny Chang, the head of Electro-Mart records, got into the act. He became an approved distributor of the antidote disk, which he sold bundled with computer game disks, a new product line for him.

The task force established between Microsoft and Intel had drawn a complete blank. Microsoft pulled all of its tainted software off store shelves and took a one-time financial charge of three hundred million dollars. Other software firms were forced to take similar financial hits.

The analysis of CD-Rs made in Haikou did not produce any meaningful results, for Steven's files were well hidden below the surface of the disk.

At Apple Computer, Alan Smith set in motion a small task force to examine the code Steven gave to Alan the day of his last meeting. However, the more they dug into it, the more confused they became.

"I'll bet he has encrypted this code somehow," one of Alan's engineers commented. "It just does not make any sense to me. And, if you recall, we were never able to get it to work in the lab like he said it should."

Steven and May were safely aboard the SS Shanghai, bound for the western coast of South Korea. Uncle Ming's friend provided them with papers that afforded them the right to enter Korea legally. The passage, which was over very rough waters, would take three days.

"If you two get seasick, just stick your head over the side. I don't want to have you make a mess on the deck," the skipper said, smiling. "Meanwhile, if you get hungry, we have some smoked fish and chicken for you in the galley."

Steven and May spent most of the trip leaning over the railing, so by the time they arrived, they were both pale and not feeling well.

"Last stop," the skipper shouted down the hall to them. "Everyone must be on the deck so the customs man can check your papers."

The papers worked fine, so in an hour, May and Steven stepped off the vessel onto dry land. "I feel better already," May said.

"Me too. Now let's see about getting a bus to Seoul."

The trip to Seoul was an experience in itself, because the only bus running was an old renovated school bus full of people of all ages, many of whom were carrying chickens and holding pigs. The stench was awful, and May and Steven found themselves hanging their heads on the side again.

They decided to spend a day in a motel room near the airport so they could shower and catch their breath. They planned to leave the following day for Japan, and from there on to Switzerland. After their shower, they both fell asleep and did not awaken until noon the next day. They had to hurry to get to the airport in time, but finally were able to relax when they boarded Korean Airlines flight 222 bound for Tokyo.

"CT, our friend has flown the coop. Does Miu have full knowledge of the infection and antidote software, in the event you need to modify them for any reason?"

"Yes, but is it possible Steven will sell out to some other country?"

"I hope not. We are still tracking him down. Yesterday he was seen with his girlfriend boarding a freighter bound for Korea. Our people in Korea are following their every movement. They checked into a motel near the airport and were last seen boarding a flight for Tokyo."

"What should I do about this?"

"Just be aware of it. Meanwhile, how many antidote disks have you sold?"

"It has been only one month since we announced the product and we have sold in excess of one million disks. Our distributors expect to see their orders double each week from now on. We are making a lot of money."

On flight 222, a man got up from his seat in first class and walked back to the seats where Steven and May were sitting. He handed Steven a note and walked back to his seat. The note said: "When we land in Tokyo, you will be under arrest. Our agents at the airport have already informed the authorities you are to be our prisoners for return to China. The Japanese do not want to have an international incident, so they will not help you in any way. We do not want to harm you, but nevertheless we will not return without you and your girlfriend.

"When the plane lands and taxis down the runway, you are to stay in your seats until every other passenger has left the plane. Then you will follow me to the rear of the plane, where the door will be opened. We will depart into a waiting car. Do you understand what you are to do? If you refuse to follow these instructions, I'm authorized to take you both by force, and my orders are to shoot to kill, if necessary."

Steven read the note and nudged May, who was dozing. She read the note and asked Steven to point out the man who gave it to him. When she saw who it was, she froze.

"He is a professional killer named Chi," she said. "He was probably the one who would have killed you in Beijing, if I hadn't interceded. He cannot be trusted, for his only purpose is to kill you. If we follow him out the back door, he will kill both of us. If we do nothing, he will try to kill us as well. So, we need to spend the next four hours deciding what we can do to thwart his actions."

"Do you think the Japanese authorities will just stand by and let him have his way?"

"Probably not, but you never know who he might have paid off."

"What a mess I've gotten you into," Steven said. "Maybe I should give up, in exchange for you being set free."

"Don't kid yourself. I'm wanted now just as much as you are. I'll bet Shing wants me just as dead as you, because I double-crossed him."

During the flight, the two of them took out a piece of paper and scribbled down various scenarios to follow. It appeared Chi was with only one other person, so they at least were not outnumbered. With only one hour left to go, May got a brilliant idea. She reached over and whispered into Steven's ear.

He smiled and said, "That just might work."

She pulled the call button and the rear galley steward walked over to see what she wanted.

"Do you see that man in the third row seat in first class? He is wearing a blue suit and is seated next to the shorter gray-haired man in a tan suit."

The steward acknowledged he saw both men.

"Do you know who they are?"

"No, I don't. Who are they?"

"They are the agents for the famous Chinese rap star, Chow Moy. They are going to Tokyo to arrange for Moy's next concert series."

"Hey, that's really neat."

"Yes, and I noticed a contingent of high school students sitting right behind them. I'll bet they would like to get posters with Moy's autograph."

"I'm sure they would. What are the names of the agents?"

"They call themselves Chi and Tsi. I noticed when they boarded they were carrying a box full of posters. Why don't you make an announcement when we land to the effect that Chi and Tsi would welcome anyone who wishes to obtain an autographed poster of Chow Moy?"

"I'll do that. What else can I do for you two?"

"Do we deplane from the front or from the rear of this plane when we reach our gate?"

"From the rear, for it is easier for passengers in coach to do so."

"Thank you. Now don't forget to make the announcement."

The plane landed on time at the Nikita Airport in Tokyo. The steward made an announcement on the intercom as the plane came to a halt at its assigned gate.

"Ladies and gentlemen, we have a special treat for you today. I find we have two distinguished Chinese gentlemen on board who are the agents for the famous rap star, Chow Moy. They are visiting Tokyo to arrange for Moy's next concert series. I'm told they are quite willing to give each of you an autographed copy of Moy's poster as you deplane. So let me introduce Chi and Tsi, who are seated in the first-class section, in rows 4F and 4E."

Immediately, passengers seated near Chi and Tsi stood up and thrust out their hands to greet them. Chi and Tsi didn't know what hit them, for the crowd formed around them completely blocking the aisle.

In the confusion, Steven and May got up calmly and left by the rear door. Once on the tarmac, they hurriedly went inside the terminal and went directly to the gate where a flight bound for Switzerland was already announcing its final call. They decided not to wait for their luggage, but told the ticket agent to forward it to their hotel in Zurich. Once on board, they watched out of their windows as the crowd left the Korean Airliner. As they taxied down the runway, they saw Chi and Tsi running down the back stairs, looking in all directions for them. Steven felt like giving Chi the finger, but thought better of it.

Chapter Forty-Seven

Steven and May toasted their newfound freedom and wealth. It was 15 February 1998, and they felt secure in the villa they rented in the Chinese sector of downtown Zurich. When their plane from Tokyo arrived two weeks ago, Steven immediately phoned his parents to assure them he was safe and sound. They, of course, told him about the two men from the U.S Justice Department. who wanted to question him. He told them they should not worry, for he would soon exonerate himself from all of his deeds.

"Is May with you?" Steven's mother asked.

"Yes she is, and we plan to marry. I wish I could invite you to the wedding, but it is best we remain anonymous for now."

Steven and May signed a long-term lease for the villa using assumed names, and they applied for Swiss passports using the assumed names as well. For all intents and purposes, Shou Lee and May Chow ceased to exist.

Before changing his name, Steven transferred his funds to another account. Because of the investment plans he defined with the bank, his wealth had increased to more than HK$2 million, so he and May were set for life.

"It's now time for me to strike a final blow against China," Steven said one morning. "I've arranged with a friend to let me log onto the Internet and tell my entire story. I'll provide the world with a free copy of my antidote, and once I've done that, the sales of antidote disks from China will immediately drop to zero."

★ ★ ★

In China, Keung's phone was ringing off the hook. "Keung, have you heard the news? Steven has gone public on the Internet with a full confession of his wrongdoings in the computer-infection matter, and he is implicating us as well."

"So, he seeks revenge. But what harm can that do to our business? I understand from our distributors that sales are up to five million disks this month alone. Do you realize that quantity amounts to half a billion dollars in just one month?"

"Yes, but Keung, you don't understand. Steven has provided a download button on his web page. If the person connected to the network presses the button, he will receive a free copy of the antidote software. He has ruined us. I just called the distributors, and their orders have dropped to zero in the past hour. Also many recent customers are demanding their money back."

"Call Shing. He's the reason Steven is still free. I want to disgrace him in front of his staff by stripping him of all rank and authority. I'll then send him and his family to Manchuria to spend the rest of their days."

The news spread quickly about Steven's download button on the web page. All across the world, orders for antidote disks were being canceled. MIS directors were downloading Steven's code and within a few days all computers in the world were operating normally again.

In Washington, John Toliver and Derek Thorpe addressed a special session of the United Nations. Within twenty-four hours, a strongly worded letter was sent to Keung Fu Huang from the UN Secretary General, asking for a full return of all of the monies China had bilked from customers around the world during the previous two months. The letter stated if China were to refuse to make full payment, the World Trade Commission would slap sanctions on all goods sold to the peoples of China for the next twenty years.

In Beijing, Keung Fu Huang sat quietly in his office, staring at the small bottle on the table. He finally reached for it and drank it quickly. He jerked only once and fell to the floor, his hand still grasping the pen he used to prepare his last remarks for his press agent to publish the next day.

In Haikou, CT and Miu sat quietly in their apartment, not fully comprehending what had happened. The plant in Haikou would be shut down again, and CT and Miu would have to find other work on the mainland. He did not even have Shing to counsel him, for Shing had simply vanished.

"This has been quite a day, hasn't it?" May asked her new husband.

"Yes, it has. I got married in the morning and went public on the Internet in the afternoon. According to the Internet provider, my free downloaded antidote software has set all records for free software being pulled off the net in a twenty-four-hour period. Maybe I'll get some kind of award for that," he laughed.

"Why don't we go to our favorite restaurant tonight and go dancing after that? When we come home, let's not stop making love until the sun rises tomorrow morning. This has been a memorable day, and one I don't want to ever forget."

Epilogue

The invention of the microprocessor has had a profound effect on how business is conducted in the world. Computers, which were initially relegated solely to the domain of MIS departments, have found their way onto every desk and in every nook and cranny of every business, whether large or small. Secretaries, who for years painstakingly typed reports with multiple carbon copies, now routinely bang out hundreds of pages of error-free text, thanks to personal computers loaded with advanced word-processor programs. Accountants, who used to wait their turn until the MIS department had time to process their requests, can now prepare multiple financial investment scenarios at their desks, using feature-rich spreadsheet programs. Even database management, which was always relegated to the main-frame crowd, has become easy and effective to use at the workgroup or individual user level, thanks to recent developments in personal computer software.

Although this book is pure fiction, the story line does raise a number of real social and economic concerns. One concern has to do with how quickly users of personal computers become totally dependent on faster and faster machines in their work environment. Users take the blazing speed of modern personal computers totally for granted, and when even faster machines become available, they quickly convince themselves they must have such machines in order to do their work more effectively.

This vicious cycle has been going on now for more than ten years, and there doesn't seem to be any end in sight. Similarly, solid-state memory chips become denser and faster each year, allowing personal

The Year of The Tiger

computer software to be more powerful and feature-rich than ever before. As a consequence, just as occurred in this book, most users of personal computers would absolutely rebel if they were told on Monday morning that they would find on their desk the "old relics" they were quite happy using only three or four short years ago.

Another concern raised in this book is just how fragile our economy is, in the event such a catastrophe were to befall us. Our national economy, and for that matter, the world economy, is held together by the number of financial transactions companies are able to make per day or per minute, as they compete for the almighty buck. A transient thrown into that picture, such as having all computers slow down dramatically, can have a profound impact on our society, let alone on the computer business infrastructure. As businesses find themselves depending more and more on the speed of the "Information Super Highway," they will be unable to compete effectively if the speed limit on that highway were to suddenly be reduced by several orders of magnitude.

We can all be thankful there has not yet been a virus developed that can dramatically slow down personal computers. And yet your author has witnessed software used in the laboratory to reduce the effective clock rate of personal computers to facilitate the analysis of new computer architectures, much the same way Steven used the programs he developed to analyze whether Microsoft had incorporated any of Apple's operating system code in their Windows™ products.

Let's hope in the future that greedy persons or nations do not decide to implement such virus programs for their own personal gain, for it is theoretically possible for them to do so. Meanwhile, let's all enjoy our fast PCs while we can, for who knows what we may find on our desks in the future?

Your Author